"Hot chocolate?" she asked, her voice sounding hollow.

Ryder attempted a cocky grin even though his skin was an alarming shade of white.

"Or something stronger?" Annabeth asked, nodding at the test on the bathroom sink. There was no mistaking the bright blue plus mark in the test window. "Definitely something stronger."

He was staring at her, his blue eyes so piercing it was hard not to cringe away. But she didn't. She met his gaze, refusing to buckle or fall apart. When he pulled her into his arms, she couldn't decide whether to brush him off or melt into him.

"It's late." Ryder's voice was soft, his arms slipping from her. "You... I... I should let you get some sleep." He glanced at the test. "I better go."

Keep it together, Annabeth. This is best. At least she knew what to expect. The biggest surprise was how devastated she felt when he pulled the front door closed behind him, leaving her with two steaming mugs of cocoa and one bright blue pregnancy test.

Two for the Texan

USA TODAY BESTSELLING AUTHOR

SASHA SUMMERS

&

TRISH MILBURN

2 Heartfelt Stories

Twins for the Rebel Cowboy
and *Twins for the Rancher*

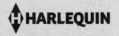

ISBN-13: 978-1-335-47332-5

Two for the Texan

Copyright © 2022 by Harlequin Enterprises ULC

Twins for the Rebel Cowboy
First published in 2016. This edition published in 2022.
Copyright © 2016 by Sasha Best

Twins for the Rancher
First published in 2018. This edition published in 2022.
Copyright © 2018 by Trish Milburn

Recycling programs for this product may not exist in your area.

For questions and comments about the quality of this book, please contact us at CustomerService@Harlequin.com.

Harlequin Enterprises ULC
22 Adelaide St. West, 41st Floor
Toronto, Ontario M5H 4E3, Canada
www.Harlequin.com

Printed in U.S.A.

CONTENTS

Sasha Summers grew up surrounded by books. Her passions have always been storytelling, romance and travel—passions she's used to write more than twenty romance novels and novellas. Now a bestselling and award-winning author, Sasha continues to fall a little in love with each hero she writes. From easy-on-the-eyes cowboys, sexy alpha-male werewolves, to heroes of truly mythic proportions, she believes that everyone should have their happily-ever-after—in fiction and real life.

Sasha lives in the suburbs of the Texas Hill Country with her amazing family. She looks forward to hearing from fans and hopes you'll visit her online: on Facebook at sashasummersauthor, on Twitter, @sashawrites, or email her at sashasummersauthor@gmail.com.

Books by Sasha Summers

Harlequin Special Edition

Texas Cowboys & K-9s

The Rancher's Forever Family
Their Rancher Protector

Harlequin Heartwarming

The Cowboys of Garrison, Texas

The Rebel Cowboy's Baby
The Wrong Cowboy

Visit the Author Profile page at
Harlequin.com for more titles.

Twins for the Rebel Cowboy

SASHA SUMMERS

To the lovers of bad boys and
those hoping to reform them.

Writing is hard work. But I have an amazing team!
I am so thankful for my brainstorming (and "focus")
team: Allison, Marilyn, Patricia, Joni, Storm and
Jolene. To the best agent, Pam Hopkins, and my
wonderful editor, Johanna Raisanen, who make my
books better. To cowboys, for your infinite
hero inspiration. And for the love and support
of my wonderful, funny and inspiring kids!

Chapter 1

If she'd been told she'd be spending the evening stranded in a honky-tonk bar, karaoke-ing her heart out to a roomful of truckers, Annabeth Upton would have laughed. She didn't go to bars and she'd never been a fan of karaoke. But today had been tough. Tough as in her job was on the line, the phone creditors were getting nasty and her car slid across an icy road into a ditch. *Tough* might be an understatement.

In the past three hours, she'd played a few rounds of dominoes and won a game of pool while waiting for news on her car. And since she had no way home and the storm outside was still pelting the tin roof with hail and sleet, the only options left were karaoke or getting drunk. She wasn't a big fan of hard liquor, so she'd start with karaoke. After that, and her day from hell, she might need a drink.

Thankfully, her audience wasn't too picky. People started calling out requests when she finished the first song. Four songs later, she was ready to pass the microphone. But since Etta James's "At Last" was one of her all-time favorite songs, she wasn't about to say no to the old guy who requested it. "Last one, for you," she said.

She cleared her throat, spun the microphone in her hand and waited for the music to play.

She could worry about the car and the repair bill later. *And* the courtesy call from the school board informing her that the job she was temporarily filling was opening for interviews. Hopefully she'd proved herself during her emergency appointment. Hopefully the whole interview and vetting process was a formality, not something to give her ulcers. She'd wanted to be principal of Stonewall Crossing Elementary since she was a little girl and she couldn't imagine giving it up. Or how they'd make it if she had to go back to a teacher's salary. Not that there was a thing she could do about that right this second.

Grandma Flo would tell her worrying would get her wrinkles, a bad taste in her mouth and not much else. She took a deep breath.

"At last—" her voice rasped out, steady and on-key. So far so good. She closed her eyes and let the music carry her.

She kept singing, her nerves easing. She should be grateful. Her accident hadn't been too bad, and Cody was safe with her in-laws instead of with her. If he'd been in the car when she'd slid into the ditch… Nope, not going there. He was safe and sound and, other than the car, she'd walked away with only a bump on the head.

Her voice grew raw and thick as she continued.

Someone whistled, making her smile.

She fumbled the words as the door opened, blowing in cold air and sheets of ice before it slammed shut. A few people yelled, irritated by her singing or the interruption, she didn't know which.

She sucked in a deep breath, hoping for a big finish. She held the last note, soaking up the applause from the inhabitants of Ol' Ned's BBQ & Bar. She held her long crushed-velvet skirt in her hands, crossed her boot-clad ankles and curtseyed. Then she headed straight for the bar.

Ol' Ned was a mountain of a man, covered in a mask of long, thick facial hair. Other than his full lips—which were curved into a smile—he was fairly indistinguishable. He slid a shot glass across the bar to her. "That one's from Mikey here." Ned nodded at the older man sitting to her left.

She stared at the amber-colored liquid. Why not? She winced, swallowing the liquid before she could second-guess herself. It burned all the way down her throat. "Thank you," she croaked to Mikey.

Mikey laughed.

"And the other's on the house," Ned rumbled, sliding another shot her way. "Voice like an angel."

"Ain't that the truth?" Mikey agreed.

She smiled, flattered in spite of herself. Her all-state choir days were long behind her, but she still loved to sing.

"Looks like one, too," Mikey added.

Ned spoke up. "She's too young and too pretty for you, Mikey."

"Ah, Ned, come on now." Mikey laughed. "A man's never too old to appreciate a fine-looking woman. Besides, the missus would skin me alive if I tried to trade her in for a younger model."

Annabeth's smile grew. "I'll try to remember you're spoken for." She saluted them both with her second shot and emptied the little glass, welcoming its warmth.

Mikey winked at her.

"Well, hell, darlin', I'm not spoken for." Another new voice had her spinning her stool around. This guy hadn't been here earlier, because she would have noticed him. For one thing, he was under fifty. For another, he was easy on the eyes. But he was staring at her as if she was a prize elk and he was a big-game hunter. "Play?" He held a pool cue out to her.

Yes, she could play. But this cocky guy hadn't been here earlier to know that. Greg had taught her to play. She was good—good enough to win a little money when she was in college. And right now, with two shots warming her belly, she was beginning to feel a little cocky herself. "Sure." She took the cue, ready to wipe the confidence off Mr. Ego's face.

"How about a bet?" he asked, stepping closer. "I'm feeling…lucky."

You need *a breath mint.* She glanced at the floor, trying not to giggle. She was going to teach this joker a lesson, and enjoy it. "That's nice." She arched an eyebrow. "You'll need it."

Mr. Ego laughed, invading her personal space. "And the bet?"

She put her hand on her hip, thinking. "I win, you sing a song." She winked at Ned, her tequila-infused courage goading her on.

"What do I get if I win?" he asked, looking at her boobs.

She poked his chest with her pool cue. "Eyes up here, buddy."

"Troy," he said. "I'm guessing your name is Angel?"

Oh, please. "No. Well, Troy, what were you hoping to get? And we'll go from there."

Troy winked. "Your number."

She bit her lip to keep from laughing. Apparently tequila made her giggly. He was not getting her number. She glanced at Ned and Mikey. Ned's arms were crossed, his eyebrows dipped so low she couldn't make out any evidence of his eyes. Mikey was leaning back against the bar, sizing Troy up. So they weren't Troy fans, either.

"Try again." She smiled sweetly at Troy.

Troy shook his head. "A drink?"

That seemed harmless enough. After all, Ned and Mikey were keeping an eye on things. She was going to beat him, anyway. "Sure."

He held out his hand, his smile a little unnerving. "Shake on it."

She put her hand in his, a flick of unease racing down her spine.

"Annabeth?" That was a voice she recognized.

Ryder Boone, all intense and broody, was making his way to her side. She sighed, relieved to have someone familiar show up. But Ryder was staring at Troy, eyes narrowed and assessing. Ryder stepped between her and Troy, putting her eye level with his wall of a chest, and cupped her face in his rough hands. She frowned at Ryder, startled by his touch. Was something wrong? "Ryder, what are you—?"

And then he kissed her. Ryder was kissing her. Ryder Boone was kissing her?

Not just any nice-to-see-you peck, either. His lips always looked full, soft and inviting. Now she knew they felt that way, too. They were like heaven, nipping at her lower lip until she was gasping. She swayed into him, the steel of his arms catching her and pulling her closer. Her head was spinning, too mixed-up to process what she was feeling… Only one thing was absolutely certain—Ryder Boone could kiss. It might have been almost six years since a man's kiss had every inch of her aching with want, but Ryder had her aching and wanting, desperately. Now.

His lips parted hers, the tip of his tongue touching hers. Her fingers dug into his leather jacket, clinging. His mouth lifted from hers, the rough pad of his thumb brushing across her lower lip.

Ryder. She was all hot and bothered. Over Ryder.

"Ready to go, Princess?" Ryder's voice was gruff.

She shook her head, trying to shake the fog of desire from her brain. Why wasn't he kissing her anymore? Wait. What the hell was happening?

"Princess?" he repeated.

Right, he was asking her something. "'Go'?" she managed, staring up at Ryder. Was he serious? And if he was, did he mean what she thought he meant? They may have flirted for years, years and years, but he'd never touched her. Besides, it would have been weird, since he was Greg's best friend.

"She's not going anywhere." Troy spoke up. "We just made a bet, didn't we, Annabeth?" Troy might be grinning, but he wasn't happy. The change in his stance was subtle but clear. Troy was bracing for a fight.

And Ryder was ready. His sky-blue gaze fixed on

Troy, the slightest tick in his jaw muscle revealing his agitation. She shivered, stepping closer to Ryder warily.

Ryder's hands rubbed her arms, his attention returning to her. He arched an eyebrow, smiling his I'm-going-to-rock-your-world-tonight smile at her. She'd seen it in action, many times. Not that she'd ever been on the receiving end of it…before. Was he serious? Or was she having a reaction to the tequila?

"What's it gonna be, Princess?" His lips brushed her brow while his fingers threaded through hers. "You want to finish your game? Or you ready to go?"

His scent filled her nostrils, further clouding her mind. She blinked, the slightest tremble running down her spine. "Now?"

He bounced his eyebrows playfully, his gaze focused on her mouth. "Now."

And then he kissed her again. It wasn't a soft, slow sort of kiss, either. He twisted her hair through his fingers, tugging her head back as his mouth devoured hers. She went from light-headed to holding on for dear life. His breath, his tongue, his soft little growl as he deepened the kiss. She was drowning and she loved it.

He broke off slowly, breathing hard. He seemed just as stunned as she was. Could he want her the way she was wanting him? "Ready?" His voice was gruff.

She managed a nod. She was ready. Until this second, she hadn't realized just how ready she was. And never in a million years had she expected to do *this* with Ryder. But now, yes please, she was ready.

"Night, boys." Ryder touched the brim of his cowboy hat in mock salute, threw some cash on the bar, slid his arm around her waist and led her to the door.

It was frigid outside, but all she felt was the slow

burn in her belly and the startling heat of Ryder's palm against her side. By the time he'd loaded her into his truck and climbed up beside her, Annabeth was buzzing with anticipation. She didn't think about why he'd decided tonight was the night or what might happen tomorrow. Nope, she climbed into his lap, knocked his black felt hat into the backseat, cradled his face between her hands and kissed him. It had been so long... so damn long. And she was lonely.

Ryder was Ryder. She'd never thought about having a hot one-night stand but, if she was going to, Ryder was probably the best candidate. He knew what he was doing, according to his conquests, and he didn't want complications.

"Princess," he growled.

"Shh," she answered, sliding her hands under his shirt to feel the rock-hard abs beneath. She shivered, frantically sliding his belt free and unbuttoning his pants. "I need this, Ryder. I need you."

Ryder had to stop this.

Seeing Annabeth with Troy Clark, knowing the way Clark operated, had goaded him into action. He was running on a couple hours of sleep, so he wasn't in the best condition for a fight. Kissing Annabeth seemed... easier. Clark was an ass, but he'd back off if he thought Annabeth was with Ryder. Ryder never guessed she'd react this way—that *he'd* react this way.

This was Annabeth. The Annabeth who'd defended him from bullies in first grade. The Annabeth who'd helped him with hours of English homework. The Annabeth he'd taught to drive stick. The Annabeth who'd married his best friend. She was Greg's widow—off-limits, the "princess." She was a good girl, too good for him—and always would be. He had no right to touch her.

But she said she needed this, needed him.

And, damn him, he'd always wanted her.

Her hands slipped into his hair, tugging frantically. He groaned, pressing her to him, savoring the feel of her. One hand slipped beneath her sweater, greedily cupping her full breast. The weight of it in his palm made him moan. She shook, a broken little sob spilling into the cold air. It was his kiss she craved, grasping the back of his neck and pulling him closer. And his touch that made her breathing hitch and her entire body tremble. He watched, letting her move against him. She was lost, pulling his hair, eyes closed, her long neck arched back as she came apart on his lap.

His heart was pounding. She was the most beautiful thing he'd ever seen. Hair a mess, lips swollen. His fingers traced the seam of her mouth as she sighed, her arms wrapping around his neck. He couldn't wait. His hands were relentless—stroking, touching, pushing her long skirt past her thighs to her waist. With one tug, her underwear ripped free. Nothing separated them. And he couldn't wait. She was warm, encasing him deep inside her. Her ragged whisper of "Oh Ryder" drove him on.

His hands slid up her back, the silk of her skin and the brush of her soft curves inflaming him. He smoothed her hair back, his hands exploring her body, her curves, her softness. His nose brushed along the length of her neck, inhaling her scent. His lips latched on to her earlobe, making her gasp. Her hands moved up his chest, sliding along his shoulders to cradle his head. She arched against him, groaning hoarsely as they fit more deeply together. It was her groan that struck some sort of primal chord inside him. All at once, she was everywhere, holding him, overwhelming his senses. He gritted his teeth, fighting for control as she lost herself in the passion. Her body bowed, every inch of her tightening around him.

Her release sent him over the edge. His climax hit hard, rocking him from his boots to every hair on his head. He couldn't breathe, couldn't think… All he could do was hold on. He gripped her hips, desperate to keep her tight against him. Even when it was over, he couldn't ease his hold on her, couldn't let her go—he didn't want to. He wanted to etch the feel of her, the smell of her, into his mind before she slipped away. His hands tangled in her hair as he kissed her. He'd do whatever he could to hold on to this intimacy before the reality of what had happened sank in.

Annabeth ended the kiss, shaking her head. "Ryder…" she gasped, her voice unsteady.

How could he make this better? He smoothed her hair, but couldn't look at her. He didn't know what to do. But he knew he needed to do something.

"Ryder?" There was already regret in her voice, he heard it.

"Annabeth—" But that was all he managed to whisper. What could he say? He was banging his dead best friend's wife in the cab of his truck. His head fell back against the seat. He'd ruined everything—like he always did. "Shit," he murmured, still gasping for breath. As soon as the word slipped out, he knew he'd sent the situation from bad to worse.

She tried to climb off his lap but wavered, her skirts pinned beneath him. He caught her, cradling her close and breathing in her scent. He wasn't used to feeling uncertainty, or panic. But something about her pushing away from him, almost as if she couldn't bear his touch, filled him with bone-deep loss. He pulled her skirts free and let her go, watching her smooth her clothing into place. She sat stiffly at the end of the bench seat, looking just as dazed and confused as he felt.

He started the truck, adjusting his clothes as discreetly as possible. His mind worked overtime, looking for something to say to break the silence filling the cab of his truck.

"Why...were you here?" she asked, running her fingers through her long golden hair.

"Jasper called."

She glanced at him. "Who?"

"The mechanic here. One that towed your car in? He told me what kind of car had slid off the highway and I knew it had to be you...your car. Figured you'd need help...or be stranded." Greg's car. No one else drove a midnight-blue 1967 Impala in this part of Texas. Which meant Annabeth, maybe Cody, was involved. Greg's wife. Greg's family. He swallowed, clearing his throat. She didn't need to know the phone call had scared the shit out of him. He'd left all his lights on, and the door to his apartment was probably open. "I'll have to order parts for Lady Blue." Best thing about Greg's car, it was all metal. He didn't want to think about what might have happened to Annabeth if she'd been driving anything else. "Glad you're okay."

"Thank you." She was using her principal voice now, never a good sign.

"On your way to get Cody?" he asked. She didn't say anything, so he risked a glance her way. She was staring out the window, nodding. So she wasn't going to talk to him. Fine. Why should he expect her to? He'd just taken advantage of her. In his truck cab. He shook his head, his hold tightening on the steering wheel.

What the hell was he thinking? Hadn't he screwed up enough relationships in his life? Annabeth wasn't just another woman, she was his friend. And he didn't have many of those.

He glanced at her, wishing he had the words to fix this. Instead, he got caught up in how damn pretty she was. Pretty and smart and funny. Good and innocent and sweet. He stared straight ahead, turning the windshield wipers up.

Annabeth Upton was the marrying type, not the one-night-stand type. He called her Princess to remind him of that. *Didn't work tonight.* He'd broken his promise to Greg and jeopardized one of the only friendships that mattered to him.

He hit ice several times, but he kicked his truck into 4x4 mode with no problems. It took twice as long to get back to Stonewall Crossing. By the time they turned into Annabeth's neighborhood, the ice had turned to snow.

He pulled into her driveway, leaving the truck running and the lights on. "Let me check the power." He held his hand out for her keys. All it took was a hard rain and half of the small town lost power. An ice storm could be downright crippling.

She put the keys in his hand, barely looking at him.

He slammed the truck door behind him and hurried up the first two steps of the porch, slipped and landed, hard, on his butt.

"You okay?" Her voice was laced with unmistakable laughter.

"Yeah, yeah," he answered, sliding as he managed to stand. "Laugh it up, Princess." But, sore butt and all, he'd rather she was laughing than giving him the silent treatment.

He made sure the tiny house had electricity and the faucets were working before heading back to the front door.

Annabeth stood just inside. She looked at him, blushed and then hung her coat on one of the pegs behind the door. "Sorry you had to go out in that."

"Nothing else to do," he shrugged. Which was a piss-poor thing to say. He'd gone because it was her—period.

She rolled her eyes. She'd been rolling her eyes since he could remember. It always made him smile.

"Good damn thing, too, or you'd have ended up alone at Ned's place." His shoved his hands into his pockets. "Troy Clark is bad news, Annabeth."

She crossed her arms over her chest. "Really?"

"Yes, really," he snapped. "You don't know what kinda guy he is."

"Maybe. But I didn't end up with my skirts around my ears in his truck tonight, did I?" She flopped into a chair, covering her face in her hands. "I can't believe…" She shook her head. "I… I…"

He stared at her then, murmuring, "I'm sorry." It wasn't enough. His good intentions didn't matter. He hadn't stopped things from getting carried away. Instead, he'd held on to her for dear life, wanting her so bad it hurt. What was worse, he knew he'd do it again if he could. Only this time he'd love her the way she should be loved, take his time, in bed, and worship every inch of her.

"Ryder?" She looked up at him. Her huge hazel eyes sparkled with unshed tears.

If she cried, he'd be useless. He knew what needed to happen next. "It was sex, Annabeth, that's all." Damn fine sex, in his mind. "Best if we pretend tonight didn't happen." No matter how hard that might be for him.

She sniffed, nodding.

But then an awful realization occurred to him. "You're on the pill, right?"

Annabeth went completely white, then red, her hands fisting in her lap. "No. No, I'm not. Because I'm a widow. A widow with a five-year-old. I haven't… since Greg died. So no."

It was Ryder's turn to sink into a chair. "Shit."

"You already said that once." She stood, paced into the kitchen, then back. "Why didn't you use something? I mean, you're *you*."

He shook his head. "I didn't think… I never thought we'd…" He broke off, words failing him. "It's *you*."

"What does that mean, it's me?" Her hands were on her hips. "You were all over me."

"I was trying to get you out of there—"

"For sex."

He shook his head.

"But…but you kissed me," she argued, a range of emotions crossing her face. She stopped pacing, to glare at him. "Wait, back up. You came to get me because Jasper called. Then you saw me with Troy and went all caveman? Is that what you're saying? You didn't want Troy to have me, but you didn't want me—" She broke off, red-faced and trembling.

He didn't say a thing. She was right. *Initially*, that was what had happened. He opened his mouth, took one look at her, and closed it again.

"So, I was this pathetic—" Her voice broke. "You were trying to stop some sleazy hook-up guy and I—I *forced* myself on you?"

"You didn't force anything." But now wasn't the time to tell her he'd always wanted her. "Annabeth—"

She held her hand up. "I really appreciate the ride home, Ryder, but I need you to go."

"Wait." He gripped her shoulders. "What if you are preg—"

"Do not finish that sentence." Annabeth glared up at him. "It's just…sex, right? Tonight didn't happen. You picked me up and brought me home. The end."

"Now, Annabeth—"

"That's it," she cut him off.

"Wait."

"No!" she yelled.

He stared at her, gritting his teeth. God, she was stubborn. And beautiful. And soft…and warm. His stomach tightened.

"Just go." Her voice was shaking. She was shaking. Leaving didn't feel right.

"Please," she added. "Go."

"I'll go," he murmured, forcing himself to release her.

She nodded, watching him.

He pulled his coat closed, opened the door and stepped out.

A gust of cold air blasted him, carrying a faint cry of distress to him. He froze, turning in the direction of the sound and slipped. He landed flat on his back. "Shit!"

he yelled, half on Annabeth's icy walkway and half in the icy-wet grass. He sighed, staring up at the sky.

He heard the noise again, a long, pitiful sound.

Annabeth's voice rang out, "Oh my God! Are you okay?"

"I'm fine. Stay there."

"Ryder—" She burst out laughing.

He heard the sound again, a long, pitiful wail. He pushed himself up into a sitting position. "You hear that?"

But she was laughing too hard to hear him.

He shook his head, pushing himself onto his feet. He stood, listening. The sound started again, then another. From the house behind Annabeth's. "That house still vacant?"

"The Czinkovic place? Sadly, yes." She wrapped her arms around her shoulders. "Why?"

"You don't hear that?" he asked. "Now that you're done laughing?"

She grinned, but didn't say anything. They stood still, listening to the roar and whistle of the wind, and the faint cry coming from the empty house. "What is it?" she asked, stepping carefully onto the front porch.

"I'll find out," he said.

Chapter 2

Annabeth watched her sweet little boy's eyes go round as her grandmother chattered away.

"And then I found my teeth in my underwear drawer." Grandma Florence patted Cody on the head.

Cody put the escaping gray kitten—the kitten making such a terrible racket the night of the storm—back on Grandma Florence's lap. "Oh."

Annabeth shook her head, stirring the onions in the skillet. "Grandma, I can get you another case for your dentures." At least her grandmother only lost the storage containers and not the dentures themselves. That would get expensive real quick.

"It won't do any good." Her grandmother leaned forward, her whisper low and conspiratorial. "Because they're not *lost*. Someone's taking them. I think it's that

Franklyn. He's always in my things, digging around. And he has that look."

Annabeth knew the medical assistants at Grandma Florence's home didn't get much pay or much thanks, but poor Franklyn didn't have a thieving bone in his body. What he did have was the patience of a saint. "What look?" Annabeth glanced at the older woman.

"You know…that look." Florence screwed up her face in horror. "Like he's watching me. Plotting things. Up to no good."

Cody burst out laughing at his great-grandmother's expression, making it impossible for Annabeth not to laugh, too.

The tiny prick of needlelike claws drew Annabeth's attention down to her calves. Tom was hanging from her jeans, his little white-tipped tail sticking straight up. He mewed, his pink tongue on full display.

"You're adorable," Annabeth said to the kitten. "But it's a good thing I don't have a spatula in my hands or—"

"Ma," Cody reprimanded her, kneeling at her feet to gently detach Tom from her pant leg. "Be good." Cody lifted the kitten in his arms, carefully cradling the animal as he carried it across the room to the box he'd made for its bed.

"Cats in the kitchen." Grandma Florence clicked her tongue. "Never heard of such a thing. Cats are barn critters. 'Course one time we had a cat that got too close to the—"

"Grandma Flo." Annabeth was quick to interrupt. Her grandmother was rarely lucid enough to have a real conversation, but the old woman had a never-ending stream of stories to share. And not all of them had child-friendly endings. "How's work?"

Florence sighed. "I've never met such a lazy group of people in my life, Hannah."

Annabeth turned back to the cooking with a smile. Grandma Florence had dementia. On good days, Florence would call her Annabeth. But sometimes Annabeth was Hannah, Florence's daughter and Annabeth's mom, or Glenna, Florence's sister.

"You do the best you can," Annabeth encouraged her.

"I do." Her grandmother nodded. "I do. Someone's got to run a tight ship."

Grandma Florence ran the assisted-living community where she lived. At least that's what Grandma Florence thought. And the staff cooperated, within reason, to keep the feisty old woman under control. So far, it was the only facility Grandma Florence hadn't successfully escaped. Annabeth hoped it would stay that way, or they'd have to move her again—and the next facility was two towns over.

Cody giggled, making Annabeth glance his way. He lay with the kitten on his chest. Tom seemed just as delighted, nuzzling and licking Cody's nose.

The sheer joy in his laughter warmed her heart. God knew she didn't want or need something or someone else to look after. Managing Cody, work and her grandmother didn't leave her time for herself—let alone a stray fur ball. But Ryder had worked for a half hour to free the little guy from the abandoned house next door, and she couldn't turn it out into the freezing cold.

Cody's giggle jerked her back to the present. He pulled a colorful string of yarn across the floor, and Tom scampered after it, all ears and tail and gray fluff.

Her sweet boy never asked for anything, so how could she tell him no when he'd asked to keep Tom? She didn't. And now Cody and Tom were inseparable— unless Tom was climbing up her pants, panty hose, the curtains or the tablecloth.

There was a knock on the door. "Anyone home?" Ryder called out.

Ryder... She'd spent four weeks refusing to think about that night. Or Ryder. Or how mortified she was. She never acted without thinking things through. She could blame either the two shots or Ryder's kiss for her outrageous behavior. She hoped, for everyone's sake, it was the shots.

She took a deep breath before calling out her standard "Nope." Sure, he hadn't dropped by for dinner since *it* happened, but he used to. All the time. If she was being completely honest with herself, she—and Cody—had missed him. And there was no point in getting weird about things, either. Ryder was a part of her life. She liked having him around.

She'd just have to try harder to forget every touch, scent and sound from that night...or the way she ached when she thought about his hands on her. So she just wouldn't think about it.

"You sure?" Ryder called out.

"R-r-ryder," Cody laughed. "Mom's m-making 'sgetti."

"With meatballs? Smells good," Ryder said. Annabeth turned as he walked into her small yellow kitchen, heading straight for Florence. "Well, if it isn't the prettiest gal I know."

Florence waved him to her wheelchair. "Get yourself on over here and give me a kiss."

"Try to stop me," Ryder said, hugging the older woman's frail body tightly and kissing her cheek.

"I was wondering when you were coming home, Michael. It's not good to spend so much time at the office. Especially when you've got a pretty little wife like Hannah, here, waiting at home." She patted Ryder's hand. "You're a lucky man. You need to treat her right."

Ryder looked at Annabeth. "Don't I know it."

Annabeth rolled her eyes, wishing his teasing didn't sting. He might have chosen to be alone, but she hadn't. Life was work, work she'd always thought she'd share with someone. She wanted to treasure the same memories, the same people, with someone who knew and loved her soul. But Greg was gone. Dating wasn't on her detailed master plan for the next five years or so.

"Cody," she spoke to her son. "Wash up and come to the table, please."

"Yes, Ma." Cody put the kitten in its padded box bed. "Stay put," he whispered, rubbing its little head before he hurried down the hall to the bathroom.

"Cats in the kitchen," Grandma Florence said. "Never heard of such a thing." Ryder steered her wheelchair to the table.

"You staying for dinner?" Annabeth asked him as she set another place. At this distance it was hard to miss the bandage around his wrist and the dark, greenish-yellow smudge on his brow. "What happened?" She didn't know which was worse: fighting or bull riding. She wasn't a fan of either, but Ryder was Ryder.

"Bull wanted me to get better acquainted with the wall of the arena. So I obliged and flew straight into the pipes." He held up his wrist. "Just a sprain. Almost healed up now." Ryder cocked an eyebrow, his crooked smile doing a number on her. "Don't you worry your pretty little head over me."

She sighed, loudly. He laughed.

"Did it h-hurt?" Cody asked, staring at his wrist.

"Nah." Ryder shook his head. "After breaking my collarbone, this was nothing."

She remembered visiting him in the hospital then. "You were in so much pain."

"Your lemon bars helped," he answered, with a wink.

"I imagine the pain meds did, too." She shook her head.

"Ma's l-lem-mon bars are great," Cody agreed.

"Totally." Ryder nodded, sitting at the table. "And, since you're asking so nicely, I'd love to stay for dinner."

"Ma," Cody sat. "Can I take T-T-Tom for show-and-tell?"

"Tom, huh?" Ryder asked, serving Florence some spaghetti.

Cody nodded, watching Ryder.

"Good name." Ryder nodded at the boy.

And, just like that, her son was grinning from ear to ear. She loved to see him smile like that, as if he was a carefree five-year-old. "We can't take animals to school, baby." She grinned at him, cutting up Grandma Florence's spaghetti. "But you can take in a few pictures if you want."

Cody nodded. "'Kay."

"Lady Blue's ready. Parts came earlier this week," Ryder said around a mouthful of spaghetti. "She's purring like a kitten—" He winked at Cody. "Good as new."

"Great." She poked at the pasta on her plate. If Lady Blue was ready, then so was the bill. She still had almost twenty thousand to pay off on Grandma Florence's last hospital stay. But she'd figure something out. She always did. "Guess it's a little harder to work with an injured hand?"

"Not really. I'm good with both my hands." His words made her warm all over.

"How's Mags, Teddy?" Grandma Florence asked Ryder. Teddy was Ryder's father, Mags his mom.

"She's fine, Flo." Ryder didn't miss a beat.

"You tell her I'm still waiting on her chicken pie recipe. That recipe…" Florence sighed and shook her head.

Dinner conversation flowed. Ryder had funny stories from his latest rodeo stint, how his cowboy hat had a hole "clean through it" after getting hooked by a bull. Somehow he managed to make his almost serious injury into a comedy. Cody could hardly wait to show Ryder the model car he was building. And Grandma Florence told them that there was a flasher running around the retirement home.

Sunday nights were her favorite. She didn't let herself think about the next day, the stress she was feeling—she tried not to.

She'd spent the past year being the principal Stonewall Crossing needed, and hopefully that was enough for the school board. But try as she might, she couldn't ignore that her assistant principal Ken Branson knew the right people, had money, *and* a wife and kids. He was the total package. And serious competition for the job—if he applied.

She realized Ryder was watching her and shrugged off her worries. Her worries would keep until the company was gone and Cody was in bed.

She stood, clearing the table while the others chattered on. When that was done, she pulled out the apple pie she and Cody had made earlier that day. The scent of cinnamon and sugar filled the air and soothed her nerves. She loved baking. She loved cooking. There was something about preparing a meal and feeding friends and family that made her happy.

She cut two decent pieces for Cody and Grandma Florence and a larger piece for Ryder.

He nodded at her when she put the plate in front of him, his blue eyes lingering on her face a little longer than normal.

"You got your momma's gift in the kitchen, Annabeth." Florence reached for Annabeth's hand.

Annabeth took it, kneeling by her chair to savor her grandmother's moments of clarity. "She said she learned everything from you."

Tears filled Florence's eyes. "'Course she did. It's a momma's job to train her daughter in the kitchen. What sort of a wife and mother would she be if she couldn't take care of her menfolk?" She winked at Ryder and smiled at Cody. "She'd be so proud of the woman you've become. Your daddy, too."

"I'm trying." Annabeth smiled.

"I know, Annabeth." Grandma Florence shook her head. "You work too hard sometimes."

"I do what needs to be done." Annabeth kissed her cheek.

Grandma Florence shook her head. "Who takes care of you?"

Annabeth couldn't answer that.

"Me," Cody piped up, kissing her on the cheek. "Right, Ma?"

Annabeth nodded, hugging him to her. "Yep."

"Lemme see that kitty o' yours, Cody." Grandma

Florence patted Annabeth's hand. "Thank you for dinner, Annabeth. You never forget our Sunday dinner."

"It's something I look forward to every week, you know that." Annabeth held her grandmother's hand in both of hers. This woman had been the one to teach Annabeth what it was to be strong while keeping a sense of humor. There wasn't a day that went by that she didn't hear one of Grandma Flo's bits of wisdom in her head, guiding her.

"Here he is, Grandma," Cody announced. Tom was squirming in his arms but settled down once he was placed on Grandma Flo's lap.

"Well, he's a fine tomcat." Grandma Florence held the cat up, turning the mewling animal this way and that. "He'll have long legs. A good mouser."

"He will be fast." Cody babbled on, his stutter barely tripping him up he was so excited. And Grandma Florence, bless her, didn't say a thing.

Now if Annabeth could get the boys at school to stop teasing him, Cody might not be so quiet all the time.

Ryder pulled the dish towel off the hook by the sink. He smiled as he fingered the row of lemons stitched along the trim of the towel. No doubt Annabeth had stitched each one herself. Lemons were Annabeth's thing. She had a yellow kitchen with lemon-print curtains and lemon-print towels. Hell, she even smelled fresh and sweet like the fruit itself. He swallowed, her scent tickling his nostrils as she leaned closer to place a dish on the rack.

"You don't have to," Annabeth murmured. "Rest your wrist."

He didn't say anything, just dried off the plates she'd stacked in the dish rack.

What would she say if he told her the injury was her fault? After he'd left the kitten in her hands, he'd spent the rest of the night drinking. He hadn't had more than a couple of hours' sleep when his riding and drinking buddy DB picked him up and took him to the rodeo. If he'd been thinking clearly, not torn up with guilt yet wanting her, it wouldn't have happened. He'd have been thinking about the ride, not her. Not that she'd see it that way. No, she'd argue with him, tell him he was a grown man capable of making his own decisions…

She sighed as he dried another dish. He smiled.

It was the least he could do after inviting himself to dinner. Annabeth always made something special for Florence's Sunday-night dinner. Annabeth always made him feel welcome. Florence and Cody made him feel wanted. Two things he never felt at his father's table. He'd stayed away the past few weeks and he'd missed it. But tonight, he had news he had to share.

All of his hard work, endless tinkering and attention to detail might just pay off. He was a master mechanic; engines just talked to him. And his bodywork was a work of art. Apparently, the owner of a big custom garage in Dallas agreed. According to his boss, John, Jerry Johannsson, known as JJ, had seen some of Ryder's bodywork and was impressed enough to track down Ryder's whereabouts. JJ had badgered John, who wasn't much of a talker, with all sorts of questions. Whatever John had said convinced JJ that Ryder should come for a visit. John wasn't happy about Ryder's interest, but he kept his opinions to himself. Maybe now

Ryder would finally get out of Stonewall Crossing and away from his past.

As soon as John had told him, Ryder had headed to Annabeth's house to share the good news over dinner. If there was one person who would support him, it would be Annabeth.

But something was wrong, he could tell. Tension seemed to weigh Annabeth down, and he didn't like it. Whatever it was, his news could wait until he could fix whatever was wrong.

She tucked a long strand of her golden hair behind her ear, drawing his attention to her. To her ear…her neck. He spent plenty of time thinking about her— them—even though he knew better. Best thing he could do was find some sweet thing and wear himself out. Hell, the pretty medic that wrapped his wrist had offered to take him home for a more "thorough assessment." He'd been curious. Her cherry-kissed lips and fiery red hair were tempting. But in the end he'd gone home alone. Just like he had every night since the night he'd shared with Annabeth. And it scared the crap out of him.

"Dishwasher broken?" he asked.

She nodded. "I still remember how to operate a sponge, so we're good."

He grinned at her. "Bet I can fix it."

She shook her head.

"You don't believe me?" he teased, nudging her with his elbow.

She looked up at him, her hazel eyes so big he paused. "I know you can, Ryder. It's just…" She shook her head, plunging her hands back into the soapy water. "It's fine."

"Sure, if you like washing all your dishes by hand, maybe." He set the dish in the drying rack and waited.

She couldn't hold back her laugh, a free and easy sound. "Maybe I do."

"I know better, Princess." He took the plate she offered.

"Stop calling me that." She sighed. "You don't need to fix it. Okay? It's not a big deal."

"Right." He frowned. "It's a dishwasher."

She glanced at him, a tell-tale flush on her cheeks.

He sucked in a deep breath. "What?"

She shook her head, turning back to the dishes.

"What's eating you, Princess?" he murmured, willing her to look back at him.

"R-Ryder," Cody held up the kitten. "Tom saw Doc F-F-Fisher. Says Tom is a good cat."

"My brother would know. Fisher's all about cats and dogs." Ryder smiled at the boy and took the kitten, holding it up so they were eye to eye. The kitten swatted at Ryder's nose. "Plenty of energy." He laughed.

Cody nodded.

"That's an understatement," Annabeth added.

Ryder turned the kitten so it was nose to nose with her. The kitten started purring, his little paws kneading the air. She shook her head, but took the kitten and held it under her chin. "Yeah, yeah, you're adorable."

Ryder winked at Cody, who winked back. It was then that he noticed Grandma Florence snoring softly in her wheelchair.

"Naptime?" Ryder asked softly.

"She d-does that." Cody grinned. "Any new cars?" Cody loved talking about cars—he was a lot like Greg that way. Every now and then, he'd take Cody to John's garage with him. The boy had an endless fascination with the way things worked. He loved to tinker, putting things together, taking them apart. And Ryder respected that. A man should know how to work with his hands, to take care of things around the house and in the garage.

"Wh-what about the Cadillac?" Cody asked.

Ryder grinned. "Finished."

"Can I see it?" Cody asked.

Ryder looked at Annabeth in question.

"Not tonight," she hedged, not meeting his eyes. She handed Tom back to Cody, but Ryder saw the quick kiss she planted on the kitten's head. "I've got to get Grandma home and finish the laundry before bed. Then I have a little work to do."

He heard the exhaustion in her voice. "What can I do?" Ryder glanced at the clock.

She scowled. "Cody, go get your clothes picked out for tomorrow while I get Grandma's things together."

Ryder waited, knowing once Cody was out of the room he was going to get an earful.

"Ryder, you can't keep doing this." She pointed around the room. "People will talk."

"People? Like who?" he asked, resting his hip against the kitchen counter while she wiped down the stove top.

"People," she grumbled. "Like Lola Worley."

"Yeah, sure, Lola Worley probably is talking." He shrugged. Lola was one of three sweet blue-haired ladies who owned the only beauty shop on Main Street. She was courting the owner of the only bakery on Main Street, ensuring she'd hear all the gossip Stonewall Crossing had to offer. Lola had big ears and an even bigger mouth. But, according to some, she had an equally big heart. "What are they talking about?"

"Us," she snapped, clearly exasperated. "You. Being here *all* the time. Taking care of things."

"*All* the time?" He scratched his head. He hadn't been here in a long time. Too long. She was worried about him being here? She'd never given a hoot before.

"Things are…different now." She swallowed.

He stiffened. Damn it all. "Why?" But he knew why.

"Because *this* is a big deal." She took the towel from him and hung it up.

His attention wandered to her mouth. So she had been thinking about what had happened between them? He wasn't the only one losing sleep over that night—

"The interim appointment is up in two months. The school board has already opened the principal position to applicants." Disappointment hit him hard, but he shoved it aside to listen to her. That was news to him. It explained the tension. She worked hard, harder than anyone he knew. She turned away, pacing the floor. "They have to, I know that, but I need this job." She sighed. "I'm sure Ken Branson will apply, and he knows everyone."

"Branson is a tool." Ryder snorted, trying to ease her mind. He'd never seen her this worked up. He placed his hands on her shoulders, aching to pull her close. "Annabeth, you'll get it." He smiled. "I've never known anyone as stubborn and persuasive as you, Princess. And that says a lot, coming from the family I do."

She smiled, relaxing a little.

"It's just, you're single and I'm single…" She shrugged.

"Good thing Grandma Flo's here to chaperone us," he teased, but knew there was more. "What else is going on?"

She shook her head, but her gaze wandered down the hallway to Cody's room.

"Cody?" he encouraged.

Her lips tightened, as though she was reining in her temper.

"He okay?" he spoke softly.

"The boys, at school," she whispered. "They're giving him a hard time about his stutter."

His anger was hot and fast, but he suspected she didn't need that right now. "Kids are mean, Princess, you know that. And Cody is tougher than you think." His hands tightened on her shoulders. "Who is it?"

She shook her head. "Nope." Her smile warmed him through.

He grinned. She knew him. "What?"

"The last thing I need is you threatening some schoolkids." She rolled her eyes.

"Kids, no." He shook his head. "Parents, maybe."

She giggled. And he loved the sparkle in her eyes as her gaze connected with his. "Ryder—"

"Joking, Princess." He laughed. "Not that it's not tempting."

She nodded. "Yes. Very." Her expression shifted then, from amused to intense. Her gaze fixed on his, carefully searching. "You don't owe us anything, you know?"

His hands fisted. "Don't start that again, Annabeth—"

"Stop, Ryder." Her smile grew tight. "Greg wouldn't expect you to babysit Cody and me. Stop doing what you think he wants you to do."

Yes, he'd promised Greg he'd look out for them, but… How could he explain that he did it because he needed to? Taking care of them made him feel better, too, as though he was important to someone. "That's not why I do it."

Her forehead creased slightly. "It's not?"

"Time for checkers before I go." Grandma Florence sat up, her sudden declaration sending the kitten scurrying across the kitchen and into his box.

He smiled as Cody's squeal of delight came from his bedroom. "Think Cody heard you, Flo."

Two seconds later Cody came barreling into the kitchen with his checkers box. "Ryder, you can play the w-w-winner," Cody said.

"Deal," he agreed, squatting in front of the dishwasher. "Gives me time to see what we need to fix this thing."

"Ryder," Annabeth started to argue.

He opened the dishwasher and peered inside. "Got a flashlight, Princess?"

"Ryder," she tried again, her tone sharper.

He smiled. "It's a little dark in here." He held his hand out.

"Here." Cody gave him a flashlight.

"Thanks, champ." Ryder clicked on the flashlight, inspecting the motor in the base of the near-ancient dishwasher. "It's the least I can do to pay you back for dinner." He heard her little grunt of frustration and grinned. "Why don't you go put your feet up for a second, relax." He could be just as stubborn as she was. And if she wouldn't tell him what was eating her, he'd take care of what he could.

Chapter 3

"You don't seem to understand how important this is." Winnie Michaels dabbed at the mascara running down her cheeks. "They're fifth graders, for Pete's sake. And it's one lil' bitty ol' point, Annabeth."

Annabeth kept her I'm-listening expression firmly in place. The principal before her, Davis Hamburg, had told her it was important to convey sincere empathy while never losing control of the situation. She'd been repeating this over and over for the past thirty minutes, but Annabeth and Winnie had been in the same class growing up and they hadn't exactly been pals. Annabeth had been one of the lucky recipients of Winnie Michaels's especially effective public shaming techniques. Winnie used to call her Annabeth Banana-breath and encouraged more than a few of her posse to chant along during gym class or recess. She received more than her fair share of banana bread, banana muffins, banana skins and browning bananas throughout her school years. It was ironic that the one thing Annabeth had craved when she was pregnant was bananas.

"That's just it, Ms. Michaels. Kevin was two points from passing. He'd have to get his grade up to audition for a solo in the spring concert," Mrs. Schulze, the music teacher, calmly explained.

But Annabeth didn't say a thing. Kevin Michaels was a pain in her rear on a daily basis. He lied, cheated and picked on the younger kids—Cody among them. But when push came to shove, none of the kids would turn him in. Out of fear, she suspected, and there was nothing she could do about it. Kevin was just like his mom.

Winnie stared at her.

Annabeth stared back.

"I never thought you were the spiteful type," Winnie spoke softly. "That you'd punish my son for our childhood rivalry."

Mrs. Schulze looked acutely uncomfortable, glancing back and forth between the two of them expectantly.

Annabeth's eye twitched. "Once Kevin gets his grade up—"

"He'll be in middle school." Winnie shook her head, opening her cavernous purse and digging around inside it. "This is his last concert here." She pulled out a pair of gloves, three tubes of lipstick, a scarf, two phone chargers and a bag of what appeared to be pulverized goldfish crackers.

"He'll still perform in the chorus, Ms. Michaels," Mrs. Schulze tried again.

"With all the *little* kids." Winnie sighed. "It's *embarrassing*."

"There are only four solo parts, Winnie," Annabeth spoke calmly. "Over thirty kids signed up to audition for the solos." She glanced at Mrs. Schulze, who nodded. "All of the other students will be in the chorus, that's most of fourth and fifth grade. Even if Kevin's grades were passing, there would be no guarantee he'd get a solo."

Winnie pulled out a wadded-up handkerchief and blew her nose. "Well, I think this is unfair, that's all there is to it."

"I'm sorry you feel that way," Annabeth continued. "Did Kevin turn in the extra-credit assignments Mr. Glenn gave him?"

Winnie shrugged, shoving her things back into her purse. "You tell me, Annabeth. Since you know everything."

Annabeth resisted the urge to bury her head in her hands.

"This was a waste of my time, plain and simple. You don't like Kevin so you're singling him out. I don't know why we had this *meeting*," Winnie sighed.

Because Winnie had called and called and been so rude to the school secretary that Annabeth had given in. She knew it was useless. Parents signed a grade contract at the beginning of every year, they knew that only passing students were allowed to participate in extra-curricular activities—from field trips to school performances. Why Winnie thought Kevin was different was a mystery. But she'd keep her mouth shut and her *concerned* expression in place until she was alone in her office.

"I know people on the school board—" Winnie started in.

"I encourage you to bring your concerns to them, Winnie," Annabeth interrupted, stealing the other woman's threat. "If you feel the grade contract is unfair, the school board should review the policy."

Winnie pushed herself to her feet, scowling at Annabeth, then Mrs. Schulze. "I will. I will tell them my *concerns*. About you. And the way you're running this school." And with that Winnie Michaels stormed from her office.

"Can I get you anything, Ms. Upton?" Mrs. Schulze asked. "You look a little green around the gills."

Annabeth smiled. "I'm not a fan of confrontation."

"Well, you handled it like a pro. I'm sorry Kevin isn't up for a solo—" Mrs. Schulze broke off, crossing her arms over her chest. "Actually, I'm not. I'm not the least bit torn up about it."

Annabeth allowed herself a small grin. "It sounds like you have plenty of kids to audition. I'm sure you'll pick the best for the parts."

Mrs. Schulze nodded. "You go on home and get some rest. Don't let this hiring nonsense get to you. Everyone at the school knows you're the one for the job."

"Thank you, that means a lot." Annabeth shrugged. "Let's hope the school board agrees."

Mrs. Schulze paused in the doorway. "Cody does really well singing. Not one stutter. And he has a lovely voice. Just like his mama."

Annabeth grinned after the retreating teacher. She was lucky to have such a supportive staff.

"Sorry." Ken poked his head in. "Did I miss the meeting?"

"Yes." She stood, putting away two of the student files she'd pulled earlier in the day.

"How did Winnie take it?" he asked, leaning against the door.

Annabeth rested her hip against the desk. "She wasn't pleased." Which was why he'd missed the meeting. No one wanted to get on Winnie's bad side. But that was part of the job, following the protocol and enforcing the procedures in place—even if it meant an unhappy parent now and then. "But that's the necessity of the grade contract. Mr. Glenn tried to accommodate Kevin but he didn't do the extra credit."

Ken nodded.

She went back to straightening her desk, more than ready to leave for the weekend. "Anything else we need to talk about?" she asked nonchalantly.

"I'm interviewing for the position next week," he offered. "I know things could get awkward, but it's business, after all."

She looked at him, hoping she looked enthusiastic rather than nauseous. "Of course, Ken. I appreciate the heads-up. Good luck. I'm sure it will go well." She wished she could mean it, she really did. But it was the right thing to say.

He cocked an eyebrow at her. "I'm not a big believer in luck, Annabeth. It's all about working hard and fighting for what you want. And, to be frank, I want this position. But I hear I'm not the only one they're interviewing." He was watching her closely. "Besides you, it's me and two others. One from San Antonio and one from Illinois, with years of experience from what I hear." His laugh was forced. "Since that's something neither of us have, looks like a tough race is ahead."

Perfect. Just what she wanted to hear. Her phone rang.

"I'll let you get that." He pushed off the door frame.

"Enjoy your weekend. Get some rest, you're looking worn-out."

"Night, Ken. You, too," she said before answering the phone. "Annabeth Upton," she snapped.

"Um… Hey, stranger," came Josie Boone's voice. "I was hoping to take you out to dinner tomorrow night. Sounds like you could use it."

"God, yes." Annabeth collapsed into her desk chair. "Just promise there will be wine."

"Tough week?" Josie asked.

"You could say that." She yawned. "I'm not sure I can get a sitter—"

"Bring him over to my dad's. He and Lola can play checkers or make cookies," Josie cut her off. "I just want to make sure you're okay."

"Why wouldn't I be?" She sighed, knowing she sounded defensive.

Josie laughed. "Well, you sound pretty wound up."

"Sorry," she groaned. "Guess I am." She powered down her computer. "I'll try to shake off the attitude before then, I promise. I'm picking up some fried chicken and watching a superhero movie with Cody tonight."

"A superhero movie, huh? Will there be a shirtless scene?"

"If I'm very lucky." She grinned. "Not all of us get to go home to a hunky husband."

"I am one lucky woman," Josie agreed. "So, tomorrow?"

"Sounds good. I'll call Lola first and make sure it's okay with her."

"Okay. Text me later. And enjoy your date with Cody."

Five minutes later she was collecting Cody from the gym. "Sorry I was a few minutes late, Cody."

"It's fine, Ma. Look." Cody started dribbling the basketball.

"Wow." She put her hands on her hips. "Look who's a dribbling pro."

"Coach taught me." Cody was still all smiles.

"Principal Upton?" A very fit, very handsome man approached. "Coach Goebel, just started. I'm subbing for Coach Hernandez while he's recovering from his back surgery."

She shook his hand. "Nice to meet you." Ken was in charge of all the substitutes, so meeting Coach Goebel was a surprise. Even more so because none of the teachers had mentioned him. Well, they might have. She'd been a little preoccupied with her upset stomach—and Winnie. But still, she could only imagine what the reaction to Coach Goebel had been. It wasn't every day a new, good-looking man came to town—married or not.

"You, too." He nodded. "Cody's a natural with a basketball."

She ruffled Cody's hair. "His dad was, too."

"Does he still play?" Coach Goebel asked, watching Cody dribble in a wide circle.

"Who? Cody's dad?" Annabeth drew in a deep breath. "No, Greg was killed in Afghanistan about six years ago." It was getting easier to say. The ache was there, but the pain didn't bring her to her knees anymore.

"I'm sorry." He shook his head. "I lost a lot of buddies. Nice to be back and part of the world again. Don't miss it over there."

"You were military?" she asked.

"Army." He nodded. "Now, I'm a substitute coach. Single, carefree and loving every minute of it."

She heard the way he stressed *single* and looked at him. "Guess it's a pretty big change of pace?"

He smiled, the corners of his eyes crinkling nicely. "No complaints."

"Well, thanks for keeping Cody occupied while I closed up shop."

"It was fun." He shook his head. "Principal Upton—"

"Call me Annabeth."

"Bryan." He swallowed, clearly interested. "It was really nice talking to you, Annabeth."

Bryan Goebel was the last thing she needed. Besides the distraction he was likely to cause amongst her single and desperate staffers, he was a threat. All it would take was one look, one misconstrued conversation, and her already precarious employment situation would become ten times worse. God, Ken would have a field day... Her thoughts came to a screeching halt. "How did you hear about the position? Stonewall Crossing's a little off the beaten path."

"Ken." Bryan Goebel grinned. "We go way back. I was thinking about a change of scenery. And he can be very persuasive."

Annabeth forced a smile. *I'll bet.* "Ken's always thinking." He was such an ass. "You ready, Cody?"

Cody nodded, dribbling the ball to the storage closet, and then running back to her side.

"You have a good weekend," Coach Goebel called after her.

"You, too, Coach," Cody answered.

Annabeth nodded in return, but her smile was forced. She'd like to think Ken was just helping out a former serviceman and friend. But she *knew* Ken. After all, he'd just said he'd fight for the job. And using a hot, single guy would definitely cause talk, if not serious problems, for her.

Right now, she had bigger things to worry about. She couldn't ignore it anymore, she had to get answers. She only hoped the answers were the ones she wanted.

Ryder kicked the blankets off and sat up. His phone was ringing. His pulse was racing ninety-to-nothing, his heart in his throat.

"Yeah?" he grumbled.

"Ryder?" It was Annabeth.

"What's wrong?" He rubbed a hand over his face, glancing at the alarm clock. It was midnight. "Everything okay?" Which was a stupid question. She wouldn't be calling if it was.

"No." She sounded strange, tense.

He froze, waiting for more information. "Annabeth?"

"Can you come over?" Her voice broke. "Now, please?"

He stood, pulling on his jeans. "On my way."

"Thanks," she murmured before hanging up.

He tucked the phone in his pocket, hurriedly tugging on a black T-shirt and leather jacket, and hopping into his boots as he headed out the door. He forced himself to take a few deep breaths, clearing his mind, before starting his motorcycle and heading toward Annabeth's place.

He wasn't a worrier by nature—he'd always sort of rolled with what life gave him. But the panic in Annabeth's voice had triggered an immediate response. She didn't scare easy. Or get rattled. Annabeth was solid, grounded...

She was home, not at the hospital—which meant she, Cody and Flo weren't injured or sick. Which was good. Still, she *had* called him, so there was something seriously wrong. He parked in her driveway. Her living room and kitchen windows were illuminated.

The door opened before he had time to knock. Annabeth stood just inside, pale, with red-rimmed eyes. He stepped inside, pushing the door closed behind him. "Hi."

She nodded, sniffing. "Can you...can you sit down? I need to talk...we need to talk."

"Everyone's okay?" he asked, adrenaline and anxiety coursing through his veins.

She had a hard time meeting his gaze. "Cody and Flo are fine." Her hazel eyes finally met his. "I'm sorry I woke you. And called you over..."

"It's fine." He rubbed her arms, his eyes searching hers. "All good."

She nodded, waiting for him to sit before she took a deep breath. "I know it's late... Actually I didn't realize how late it was." She frowned. "My mind wouldn't shut off. And I knew it couldn't wait. I mean, it could, but it couldn't—you know?"

No, he didn't know.

"Let me start by saying, I know you. I have no intention of attempting to change who you are." She was fidgeting, twisting her hands in front of her. "But what sort of person would I be if I didn't tell you?"

Ryder leaned forward, resting his elbows on his knees. What the hell was she talking about? "Annabeth—"

"I have two charts," she said, holding up one finger before hurrying into her small kitchen. She returned with two poster boards. Each had some sort of graph, with different color tabs and her clean script in the margins. "Option A or Option B. I've mapped out how much time we have, how we can handle this, who needs to be involved… I'm thinking the fewer the better."

Ryder glanced at the two boards, but it didn't clear anything up. "Annabeth—"

"Hold your questions," she interrupted. "Or I'll never get it all out."

He ran a hand over his face, sighed and sat back in the chair. Sure, why not? Not like he had someplace to be—like bed. Sleeping. "Shoot."

"Okay." She nodded, smiling tightly. "Okay. So, we're six weeks or so in. There's another couple of months before it goes public." She held up the two posters. "Option A is with you temporarily, Option B is without." She shrugged. "John mentioned something about a Dallas job when I picked up Lady Blue? Is that happening?"

He nodded, slowly answering, "It's a done deal."

"Well, congratulations." She scanned her posters, putting the Option A poster behind the couch. "I guess that's the question then. I'm sure you're excited to get out of Stonewall Crossing. I can do this on my own. No need to mess things up for you." She sat opposite him, gripping her poster.

"Princess," he murmured, smiling at her scowl. "I have no idea what you're talking about."

"Oh." She blinked, placing the poster facedown on her cluttered coffee table. "Ryder I… We are…" She sucked in a deep breath and shook her head.

He heard that strange nervous tension in her voice and moved to crouch in front of her. "Don't fall apart on me now."

"I won't." She sniffed. "I'm stronger than that."

"Don't I know it." He didn't resist the urge to smooth a strand of her long hair. The way she was looking at him…as if her world was falling apart and she needed rescuing… She wanted him here, but she still hadn't said why. This from a woman who was never short on words or opinions.

But she didn't say a thing. She just sat there, tense, quiet and pale.

He'd never wanted to hold someone as much as he wanted to hold her, right now. He said the first thing that came to mind. "Like the pajamas."

She ran her hands over her knees—clad in pale blue flannel pajamas, covered in rainbows and butterflies. "Cody got them for me last Christmas. Greg's folks took him shopping. They're my movie night pj's."

"What did you watch?" he asked, looking at the half-eaten bowl of popcorn and the empty juice box containers.

"*Superman.*" Her eyes were huge, boring into him with an intensity he felt deep in his bones. He ran his thumb along her temple, tucking a long strand of golden hair behind her ear. Touching her seemed to ground him, to ease the growing anxiety in his chest.

He smiled at her, earning a small smile in return. Ever since she'd tripped Tyler Gladwell on the playground and offered Ryder her hand, he'd known Annabeth was the kind of girl a fellow should hold on to forever. But Greg had beat him to it.

She blew out a shaky breath, her gaze slipping from his. It was easier for him to breathe then. Where had this pull come from? All he wanted was to touch her. Which was the last thing he should do. The last thing he had the right to do.

"So…" She stood, putting space between them.

"Why don't we start over?" he said, standing beside her. "I'm guessing you had a rough day?"

"Yes." She glanced at him, then swallowed.

"I can't fix it if I don't know what's wrong, Princess." He took her hands in his, squeezing gently.

She nodded. "I've been cranky and tired and frustrated. I have every reason, you know? Grandma's bills aren't going to pay themselves. Greg's settlement covered the first two strokes and the resulting complications and therapy, but there's nothing left, and bills keep coming in. And Cody... Ryder, I know growing up is hard, but his stutter makes it that much harder. Ms. Chavez is amazing, our new speech teacher, but it's not like his stutter is going to go away overnight. Stress can complicate it, too." She spoke quickly, her words pouring out of her. "And the job. I need this job, you know? So I assumed all of this was why I was feeling so out of sorts. But that's just not me, you know?"

He nodded.

"But there were other things...well, actually two things. I thought it was stomach flu. And then I was late. And I've never been late. Except when I found out I was expecting Cody. I wanted to pretend this wasn't happening but I'm not a coward. I had to know." Her eyes met his. "You need to know."

He couldn't breathe. He tried, but it felt like a horse had kicked him square in the chest. He knew what she was saying. Damn it.

"Ryder..." She paused. "I'm pregnant. I'm fine doing it on my own. I know now's your time to get out of Stonewall Crossing. I understand. I won't stop you. I just thought you should know—so there's some sort of plan."

"Plan?" he repeated, his mind racing. She was pregnant. He got her pregnant.

She nodded.

He stood, needing space. Her words seemed to echo in his ears. She was pregnant but didn't expect his help. That was good...wasn't it? Shit. No matter how hard he tried, he couldn't breathe. The walls were closing in, making him hot and uncomfortable. "Be right back." He hurried into the bathroom to splash some cold water on his face.

Annabeth watched him go. She should have waited. She should have waited until morning, after a good night's sleep. As if she'd get any sleep.

As soon as she'd come home from work, she'd closed the bathroom door, ripped open the pregnancy test box and read the directions. Then she'd read the Spanish version of the directions, then the English version again. She'd opened the foil package holding the test and put the innocent white plastic stick on the edge of the sink. The "Results in 3 Minutes" outlined in bold was almost a threat. And three minutes later, her world changed forever.

She'd had a few hours to process it. *Superman* was a long movie. Considering what she'd told him, Ryder was handling it pretty well.

The question was simple: Would he want to be a father? But with his dream job and the promise of a new life outside Stonewall Crossing, she had her answer. And she didn't blame him—not really.

She wrinkled her nose, willing the tears back. It didn't matter. She'd been managing on her own just fine so far. She didn't, wouldn't, need him.

"I need some hot chocolate," she called out to Ryder as she headed into the kitchen. "Want some?"

He didn't answer.

She pulled the milk from her refrigerator, needing something to do while Ryder was doing whatever it was he was doing. With a few clicks, the old gas burner flamed to life. She turned it down low and poured two cups of milk into the saucepan. She opened the cabinet, moving cans and boxes until she found the hot chocolate packets.

She glanced down the hall. No Ryder. He needed time, and she'd give it to him.

The first bubbles in the milk appeared. She couldn't leave it, the milk would scorch. She stirred the milk with a wooden spoon, feeling colder with each passing second. Once the milk reached a nice rolling boil, she sprinkled in the cocoa and turned down the burner. She poured the cocoa into two mugs and carried them to the bathroom.

Ryder was bent over, his hands on his thighs. He was breathing hard, as though he'd been running for miles and couldn't catch his breath.

"Hot chocolate?" she asked, her voice sounding hollow.

He straightened, attempting his normal careless stance and cocky grin even though his skin was an alarming shade of white.

"Or something stronger?" Annabeth asked, nodding at the test on the bathroom sink. There was no mistaking the bright blue plus mark on the test window. "Definitely something stronger."

He was staring at her, his pale blue eyes so piercing it was hard not to cringe. But she didn't. She met his gaze, refusing to buckle or fall apart. The longer he stared at her, the more nervous she became. She jumped when he took the mugs from her, placing them on the bathroom counter. When he pulled her into his arms, she couldn't decide whether to brush him off or melt into him. Then he made the choice easy for her, pressing her head against his shoulder and running his fingers through her long hair. She could hear his heart, racing like crazy, under her ear. His breath was unsteady, too. But he stood straight, holding her so close his heat warmed her. It would be easier if he didn't feel so damn good, if he didn't feel so right…

"It's late." Ryder's voice was soft, his arms slipping from her. "You… I… I should let you get some sleep."

She stepped back, grappling with his words and what they might mean. "Okay."

"Give me time…to think." He kept looking at her, his gaze wandering over her face, her stomach, before he glanced back at the test. She saw the muscle in his jaw harden, the leap of his pulse along the thick column of his tan neck. "I'll go," he added.

She stepped back, out of his way. If he wanted to leave, she wasn't going to stop him. But the look on his face, the shame and self-loathing, made her wonder if she'd ever see Ryder again.

Keep it together, Annabeth. This is best. At least she knew what to expect. The biggest surprise was how devastated she felt when he pulled the front door closed behind him, leaving her with two steaming mugs of cocoa and one bright blue pregnancy test.

Ryder sat on his bike, staring at the closed door of Annabeth's house.

He couldn't breathe.

He couldn't think.

A baby.

He stared up, sucking in lungfuls of bitter cold night air. A shooting star caught his eye, giving him a point of focus. He had to get his head on straight, had to think about what this…a baby…meant.

Being a parent? A father? He didn't know how to do that.

With a quick kick, his bike roared to life. He headed straight to the gas station on the edge of town and picked up two longneck beers. After they were tucked into his saddlebag, he headed out of town.

The city had built a fence around the Stonewall Crossing cemetery after a few headstones were shot up with a pellet gun. Kids probably. His family donated the stone and wood for the decorated, and highly effective, fence that now surrounded the cemetery. It didn't stop anyone who *really* wanted in, but most kids looked for an easier target.

Ryder parked his bike, shoved the beers into the pockets of his leather jacket and jumped onto one of the four-foot-tall decorative stone posts of the fence. He gripped the top of the fence, shoved his boot into the chain link and swung himself over. The drop was a little farther than he expected, making him wince when he hit the dirt.

He paused then, his nerves unexpected.

With another deep breath, he headed across the fields. He knew where he was going, even if he hadn't been there in five years. He'd never planned on coming back. Greg sure as hell wouldn't expect him to stop by. But, damn, right now he needed his best friend.

He stood staring at the white marble headstone. He read the inscription four times before he got the nerve to step closer. *Gregory Cody Upton. Loving Husband and Father.* He'd never had a better friend—except maybe Annabeth.

Annabeth. He looked up, staring blindly at the star-laden sky.

"Hey." He cleared his throat. "Brought you something." He pulled one beer out, using his pocket knife to pop the cap off. "Figured you were going to need a drink."

He set the beer on the headstone and opened the other beer for himself, taking a healthy swig before he spoke again. He couldn't say it, not yet, so he said, "Cody's getting big. Good kid, smart as a whip. He can look at something and see the way it fits together, how it works. Bet he'll be an engineer or something. He's got Annabeth's smarts—he's gonna be a man you'd be proud of." He stooped to remove the dried leaves that piled around the base of the headstone.

When the stone was clean he sat, leaning against it as he turned his gaze back to the sky. "I need you to hear this from me." He swallowed down some beer, easing the tightening of his throat. "Annabeth—" He broke off and took another sip. "I had no right to… I… She's going to have a baby." He cleared his throat again, the press of guilt and self-loathing all but choking him. "My baby…and I'll do right by her."

He paused, closing his eyes. "You know. You know how I felt about her." He turned the bottle in his hands. "I'm not you, never will be. Cody's always gonna know who you are and what kind of man you were." He took another sip. "I'm hoping you'll be okay with them being my family now." He stared up, letting the howl of the wind fill the night.

"I'll take care of them," he promised softly. He meant it, wanted it, but had no idea where to start.

He sat there, ignoring the bitter cold, and finished his beer with his best friend.

Chapter 4

"You're sick?" Josie asked.

"Yep," Annabeth lied, pulling everything from the last kitchen cabinet. She'd been cleaning since four this morning. Her brain wouldn't turn off and she couldn't sit still. As silly as it was, she'd hoped she and Ryder would be figuring this out together. Instead, she was grappling with what to do—on her own. Her neatly color-coded poster hadn't offered much comfort this morning.

Instead of succumbing to a full-blown sob-fest, she'd busied herself. How many times had Grandma Flo told her a real lady never let her emotions run amuck? *Best use that pent-up energy to* do *something*. So all morning, she'd been *doing*. Specifically, cleaning. The tiny bathroom had been scrubbed, sterilized and organized. Her bright yellow kitchen smelled fresh, but she wouldn't be done until each and every cabinet and shelf were orderly.

"Does this have anything to do with my wayward brother-in-law's late-night visit?" Josie asked.

Annabeth dropped the can of peaches she'd been holding. "What… How…"

"Lola heard him—er, his bike."

Ryder and that damn bike. "Dammit—"

"She promised me she wouldn't tell anyone else," Josie interrupted.

"You believe her?" Annabeth knew Lola Worley far better than Josie did. While Josie was off exploring the world, Annabeth had stayed put and knew all about Lola's favorite pastime: gossip. Lola was Josie's soon-to-be stepmother, so Annabeth wasn't sure Josie could see the older woman objectively. To be fair, Lola *was* a lot less inclined to poke her nose into other peoples' business now that she had a sweetie, but…

"I do. She likes you, Annabeth. Last night's visit might be newsworthy but she'd never cause you trouble." Josie paused, then said, "I'm coming over."

"No," Annabeth pleaded. If she had a supportive shoulder to cry on, she might actually cry.

Josie argued, "It's not like you to get all hermit-like. Whatever is going on, we'll figure it out. And, if you're getting thoroughly laid, I promise not to be horrified or judgmental, okay?"

Annabeth laughed then. She couldn't help it. "Oh, Josie, I wish."

"Hmm. Okay, well, I'm coming. And I'm bringing wine." And she hung up.

"Ma?" Cody was coloring at the table. "Can I build a tree house?"

"I don't think we have a tree big enough for one, sweetie."

"'Kay," he said, the brown crayon in his hand never slowing. Tom was curled up on the table in front of Cody, his long white-tipped tail swaying back and forth with a slow, undulating rhythm.

"You want a tree house?" she asked.

"Yeah." He stopped coloring. "What about that tree?" He pointed out the small window above the kitchen sink.

"That *would* be the perfect tree for a tree house. Only problem is, it's not ours." Her gaze lingered on the empty house she'd loved since she'd come to live with Florence as a little girl. The Czinkovic house was like a dollhouse. Wraparound porches on both stories, picture windows, detailed trim-work and a massive yard with fruit and pecan trees. It was the kind of house a little girl imagined living in, with her perfect family at her side.

She glanced down at her son. All he wanted was a tree house. She wished she could give him what he wanted. After all, a tree house wasn't all that much to ask for. "If it was our house, I'd help you build one." Her gaze lingered on the house. "After we were done building your tree house, you could help me paint the big house. Maybe a dusky pink or purple—"

Cody wrinkled up his nose. "Ma! I c-can't live in a pink or p-p-purple house!"

She sat beside him, slipping an arm around him and pulling him close. "Okay, little man, what color then?"

Cody cocked his head, staring at the grand old house for a second. "Not sure," he said, dumping his box of colors onto the table. "This?" He picked up a yellow. "Your f-favor-ite."

She shrugged. "Maybe."

Cody sat it down, moving colors around until he found a pretty lilac blue. "This?"

Annabeth held it up to the window, looking at the color, then the house. "I like it, Cody. A lot."

He smiled up at her. "Is J-Josie c-coming over?"

She nodded.

"Eli, too?" he asked, smiling when Tom stirred long enough to roll onto his back.

"I don't know." Eli was Josie's stepson. He was a little older than Cody and a great kid. "How'd you like to go make cookies with Ms. Lola and Carl over at the bakery tonight?" she asked.

"Do I get to eat 'em?" he asked, grinning.

"Some of them," she relented.

"Sure." He nodded, picking up a green.

She stared at the picture her son was creating. It was a tree house, a wonderful, whimsical tree house with a ladder that wrapped around the wide trunk of the tree. "Is that an elevator?" she asked, pointing to a rope with something tied to it.

"For Tom."

She smiled, ruffling Cody's hair. She reached forward, stroking the kitten's head and ears until the purrs reverberated off the kitchen walls.

"He's h-h-happy." Cody giggled. There wasn't a sweeter sound in her world.

"What's not to be happy about? He's got you and me, kiddo. He's one lucky kitten."

Tom mewed faintly, making them both smile.

"Think that means he agrees?" she asked Cody.

"Yep." Cody nodded.

She pressed a kiss to his head, breathing in his sweet

scent, his soft hair tickling her nose. Cody was her boy, the reason she worked so hard each and every day. He was thoughtful and considerate, funny and kind. She was proud of him.

"Here." Cody handed her a green crayon and pointed at the base of the tree. "Some grass?"

She started to color, a companionable silence filling the small kitchen. She loved these quiet times, just the two of them. Tom mewed, making her smile. *Fine, three of us…* But starting over again terrified her.

Cody was made from solid love. When she'd found out she was expecting Cody, she'd thought Greg would be there to help out. Greg had been so excited about a baby, even more so when he found out they were having a son. There'd been the promise of a family, happy and whole.

Cody's smile was Greg's. So were the kinks in his little toes. She couldn't help but think of Greg each and every time she saw Cody barefoot. It used to tear her up inside, but now it made her smile. Greg was a good man, a good husband. Even though he never met his son, Annabeth knew he'd left the best parts of himself here in Cody.

This baby… Ryder's baby. She drew in a deep breath. Poor little thing was made in a truck, clumsy and hurried and, honestly, a mistake. It wasn't the beginning she would have imagined for her child, if she'd imagined having another child—which she hadn't.

She'd had a hard time imagining sex, let alone the possible consequences. Greg was the only man she'd slept with. So sex, without Greg, was a foreign concept. It hadn't always been perfect, but they'd had the time to learn each other's bodies, to give each other real pleasure. The exact opposite of what happened with Ryder. They'd had no time, no experience and no hesitation. And yet somehow it had been one of the most intense experiences of her life.

"Nice," Cody said, smiling up at her. "You can make some f-flowers if you want."

She should be enjoying time with Cody, not thinking about her love life. Or, more accurately, her lack of a love life. This baby was coming. There was no way to make this okay, but there had to be a way to make it less of a mess than it was.

There was a knock on the door. "Hello?" Josie called out.

"Come in," Annabeth answered.

Eli, Josie and Hunter all spilled into her small kitchen. Seeing Hunter, the eldest Boone sibling, made her think about Ryder and the mess she was in.

"Hey." Annabeth stood, tugging her giant sweatshirt past her hips. She hadn't bothered to put herself together today. Now she was acutely aware of her oversize sweats and sloppy ponytail. Not that she had time to worry about it too much. Hunter had the boys bundled up and out the door, "to a livestock auction for some man time," before she'd said more than a dozen words. It was only when she and Josie were left alone in the kitchen that she noticed the way Josie was looking at her.

"What?" Annabeth asked.

"What's up?" Josie asked, opening the cabinets and taking in the morning cleaning spree.

"Nothing—"

"Don't tell me nothing." Josie smiled at her. "I know about the job. And I know Flo's hospital bills still exist.

And I know Cody's getting grief at school, but this is something else."

Annabeth started packing up Cody's crayons. "Why does there have to be something else?"

"Because Annabeth Upton gets dressed every day. She puts on her makeup, does her hair and believes you fake it 'til you make it. Your mantra is 'make lemonade out of the lemons life gives you' so…yes, there has to be something else." Josie put her hands on her hips. "Don't get me wrong, I think you're crazy for always being so together, but this—" she pointed at Annabeth "—isn't you."

Annabeth slid into the kitchen chair, watching Tom bat one of the crayons across the table and onto the floor.

"*Is* it Ryder?" Josie rifled through the cabinets until she found two empty glass Mason jars. "You're one of the only people he talks to, you know that? When he comes out to the ranch, he's still so distant."

"He still blames himself," Annabeth spoke softly.

"For?"

"His mother's death." She'd never forget how devastated he was.

Sophomore year Ryder was already a hell-raiser. His mom had gone to pick him up after he'd snuck out and drunk too much to drive home. She'd swerved to avoid a deer and the car had landed upside down in a ditch. Ryder had cut through her seat belt to get her out, but he couldn't resuscitate her. His father shut down for almost a year, leaving Hunter to pick up the pieces. Ryder took the blame—and more risks than ever. Starting fights, run-ins with the law—and nothing she or Greg said had helped. But whether it was the guilt and anger eating him or the need for his father's attention that drove him to such measures, Annabeth wasn't sure.

"It wasn't his fault." Josie frowned.

"I think everyone knows that except Ryder. And, maybe, his father."

Josie's frown grew. "Teddy blames him?"

She shrugged. "Ryder thinks he does. And Ryder does. And that's all that matters."

"That's what I'm talking about. You're the only one that knows that." Josie shook her head. "That thing—that connection—you two have."

"What?" Annabeth looked up. "What thing?"

"Oh, please." Josie opened the bottle of wine she'd carried in and filled both glasses halfway.

"Seriously," Annabeth pushed. "What thing?"

Josie sat across from her, a confused look on her face. "I always got the impression you two were hot for each other. Even in high school, there was that—zing." She paused. "Not that either of you acted on it. Greg was there."

Annabeth stared at the wine in the Mason jar, wishing she could drink it but knowing she wouldn't. "Well, we did."

Josie almost snorted her wine.

"And I'm pregnant."

Josie started coughing.

"And I don't think he's interested in being a father." Annabeth stood, getting a glass of water for Josie.

Josie took a long sip, stared at Annabeth then took a long sip of her wine.

"Exactly." Annabeth nodded.

Josie sat her glass down, collecting her thoughts. "What's the plan?" Josie finally asked.

She thought of the poster in her room. "I'm not sure," she admitted. "I have… I have a chart—" She broke off.

Josie took Annabeth's hands in hers. "Oh, sweetie, we'll figure it out."

Annabeth nodded, refusing to give in and cry.

"Flo said to tell you she's in a meeting," the nurse said, a tolerant smile on her face. "I'm sure she'll be done soon. She likes to exert a little power now and then."

Ryder nodded, tucking the box of chocolates under his arm. "Who doesn't? I'll let her finish up." He winked at the pretty nurse, watching her flush in response. Yesterday, he'd have asked for her number. But yesterday was another life. Now, this life, was all about being responsible. He was going to do what he should do—for Annabeth, Cody and his baby. The first step was getting permission from Annabeth's family—Flo.

"You can send him in, Nancy," Flo called loudly from her room.

Ryder touched the rim of his hat at Nancy and entered the bedroom where Florence Chenault lived. Every inch of wall space was dotted with newspaper clippings, drawings and framed photos. A tall wooden dresser filled one corner of the room, standing out amongst the other institutional-grade furniture. The single bed was covered in quilts and a chenille sweater. Flo sat in her wheelchair, wearing a green velvet robe and her hair in a fancy updo.

"You're a fine sight," Ryder said, offering her the box of chocolates.

Flo grinned. "And you, Ryder Boone, are a scamp."

"Guilty." He hugged her, dropping a kiss on her cheek.

She opened the box of chocolates and offered it to him. "Go on."

"I got it for you," he argued.

"Uh-huh." She placed the box in her lap, popping a candy into her mouth before adding, "And when a scamp shows up with gifts, it means he's after something."

"Known a lot of scamps?"

She smiled sweetly. "I have, young man, I have indeed. Your father was one of them." She patted the corner of her bed. "You sit a spell and tell me what you're after."

Ryder sat, placing his hat on the bed beside him. "Annabeth—"

"It's about time," Flo cut in, her eyes fixed on his face. "You going to make an honest woman out of her?"

Ryder swallowed. "If she'll have me."

She nodded. "Open that top drawer." She pointed at the dresser in the corner. "In the little blue box in the back corner. Careful, it's breakable."

Ryder did as he was told, lifting the blue porcelain box and carrying it to Flo.

"Open it." Flo waved her hand at him. "My hands get so shaky sometimes."

Ryder's hands weren't all that steady either, but he opened the box.

"Those belonged to Annabeth's parents," Flo said.

Ryder stared at the three rings inside. One was a bridal set, slim and delicate, with a large round diamond. The other was a wide gold band, the word *Forever* etched on the inside of both bands.

"Hannah wanted Annabeth to have these, but Greg didn't want 'em. You don't have to use them, either."

Flo paused. "Seems like maybe they'd bring you two luck, since Michael and Hannah loved each other so." She pointed to the rings. "Not that you two are going to need any luck, Ryder. You two are the only ones that don't see how you fit together."

"You think so?" He wanted to believe her.

She nodded, reaching forward to pat his hand. "She loves you, Ryder Boone. Whether that silly, stubborn girl sees it or not."

"She is stubborn." That much he agreed on.

"A real man never speaks ill of his woman, remember that." Flo frowned. "You better treat her right, you hear me? If you don't, I will come back from the grave and drive you crazy with haunting."

"Does this mean I have your blessing?" he asked.

"I'm a mite disappointed you've waited so long, I'll be honest." She sat back in her chair, narrowing her eyes a bit. "First, you tell me why you want to marry my girl, why you deserve her, and we'll see."

He swallowed, knowing the truth wasn't the right way to go. "She's Annabeth, Flo. Guess I've come to realize what a...an amazing woman she is."

"Mmm-hmm." Flo's eyebrows went up.

"If you're looking for poems and pretty words, I'm going to disappoint you." He chuckled. "I might be good at charming the pants off a woman, but courting's another thing."

Flo popped another chocolate into her mouth. "Try."

He shook his head, staring out the window. He knew Flo wasn't trying to irritate him. She had every right to make sure he was worthy of Annabeth. Problem was, he knew he wasn't. His words were rushed. "You want me to tell you she's smart and sassy? That she's so damn pretty sometimes it hurts to look at her? Or making her smile makes a shi— A bad day good?" His throat felt tight, his palms sweaty... "I don't deserve her. But I'll try to. Every damn day." Tripping over his words was nothing new. He could only hope he'd manage the right ones when he was on his knee in front of Annabeth. He looked at Flo, staring at the box of chocolates in her lap. "Flo?"

"You'll do just fine." Her smile wavered, her gaze wandering out the large window in her room. "But marry my girl soon. Hannah wouldn't be much good without you, Michael."

Ryder nodded, sad that Flo was gone.

"Now that you have a baby on the way, you need to be more careful," Flo added. This was news to Ryder. Had Annabeth's parents been in the same position he and Annabeth were in? Flo continued, "You drive too fast. Man wasn't meant to zoom around going eighty miles an hour in big metal cans. Slow down, son, take time to stop and smell the roses. Make some memories to treasure. Life goes by too quick, I promise you. It's your memories that will keep you company long after everyone else is gone."

Ryder nodded again, wondering if Flo had said as much to Michael. Annabeth's parents died in a car crash. "I promise." And he meant it. She might be talking to Michael, but he'd take her advice to heart. "I'll take good care of her."

Flo nodded. "She's my only baby, my joy. See that you do."

He didn't know the little person growing inside of Annabeth, but he knew the baby was his. And, in the past twelve hours, he'd come to terms with that.

It twisted his heart to think of the loss Flo had lived through. Hannah had been her only child, Annabeth her only grandchild.

"Mrs. Chenault?" Nancy came in, small white cup in hand. "We have your vitamins."

"Oh, goodie." Flo's voice dripped with sarcasm. "They keep telling me these are vitamins, like I don't know better?" She rolled her eyes—just like Annabeth.

Ryder smiled.

"Then we have our backgammon tournament," Nancy continued.

"Is that today?" Flo perked up. "We'll have to wrap this up, Michael."

"Yes, ma'am." He stood, tucking the rings into his jeans pocket and putting on his hat. "I'll go take care of my business, you go kick some backgammon butt."

"Oh, I will." She giggled, waving a quick goodbye before Nancy wheeled her in the direction of the activity center.

He couldn't go to Annabeth's house, not yet. His talk with Flo had put things in perspective. He couldn't just drop by and ask her, straight out. If he was going to do it right, he needed to go home, clean up and think about what he was going to say. There was no doubt some arguing and rationalizing would be involved—Annabeth was good at that. So he had to be ready for whatever roadblock she might throw up and somehow manage to make it special.

But he didn't stop at his small apartment over Hardy's Garage. He kept driving, past the garage, past the school and Annabeth's street, down Main Street. It was only as he turned his truck under the stone-and-wrought-iron entrance that he realized he was heading home to Boone Ranch.

He parked his truck in front of the Lodge, the bed-and-breakfast his father had operated and lived in for the past few years. Why he'd ended up here was a mystery. The last thing he wanted was one of his father's disappointed looks or loaded silences. His father spoke volumes with a simple shake of his head. So why had he come here? He could go. No one knew he was here. But he knew.

He opened the truck door and climbed the steps, nodding at the group of visitors assembling for the night's stargazing tour. It was one of the diversions his father had dreamed up for his guests. Bird-watching, nature photography and trail riding were others. Between Hunter's efforts to work with the state on white-tailed and exotic deer population studies and Archer's neighboring animal refuge, guests were treated to an almost safari-like experience. And people loved it, flocking from all over the country to visit Texas and stay on a working ranch. A ranch with every amenity and world-class cooking.

He stepped inside, dodging his nephew, Eli, as he ran by. Cody followed, laughing. The tantalizing scent of freshly baked cookies reached him.

"Eight, nine, ten," his sister Renata's voice echoed. "Ten more, boys."

He checked his boots for mud, rested his hat on the hat tree and his coat on the peg beneath before heading into the great room. His father sat before the fire, his reading glasses perched on the end of his nose as he read over some ranching magazine. Seeing his father never failed to stir up years of self-doubt best left ignored. Or to remind him of his part in his mother's death. He swallowed, speaking gruffly. "Dad."

His father's brows dipped as he set aside his magazine. "Ryder." He stood, tucking his glasses into his pocket. "Good to see you, son."

Ryder nodded.

Renata ran into the great room. "Ready or not, here I come... Hey, baby brother." She hugged him, pressing a kiss to his cheek. "Off to find some rug rats."

"Have fun." He smiled.

"Don't eat all the cookies," she chastised before heading out.

"I'll try," he answered, aware his father was watching him. His unannounced arrival was suspect. He didn't *drop by*. Hell, he had no idea *why* he was here. But he was.

"Hunter here?" Ryder asked.

"Looking for him?" his father countered.

"Not really, why?"

His father shook his head, waving him into the kitchen. "Lola and Carl dropped the boys off earlier, after feeding 'em a bag of sugar each from the looks of it. But there might be some cookies left over in here, if you want."

Ryder nodded, following his father into the kitchen. Hunter was washing dishes, a towel thrown over his shoulder.

"She found 'em yet?" Hunter asked.

"No, but I found something," his father said.

Hunter turned, smiling. "Hey."

"Look how domestic you are," Ryder teased. "And it's only been, what, two months?"

Hunter shook his head. "Jealous?"

Ryder arched an eyebrow at his brother and stuffed a cookie into his mouth.

"How's John? Anything new at the garage?" Hunter asked.

Ryder shrugged. "Been pretty steady since the storm. Mostly weatherizing though."

"Nothing to sink your chops into?" His father smiled.

Ryder shrugged.

"Heard you were on the circuit for a bit, how you took a nasty spill. Glad to see you're no worse for wear." His father had always hated Ryder's rodeoing. Teddy Boone believed in hard work, responsibility and family. Sometimes Ryder wondered, if he hadn't torn their family apart, would he see respect in his father's eyes instead of wariness and disappointment? He'd never know.

He watched his father move around the kitchen, spry and agile. "Ride times good?" His father offered him a large glass of milk.

Ryder nodded.

"How'd you do?" Hunter asked.

Ryder shrugged.

Hunter laughed, shaking his head.

A squeal from the other room made all three of them jump.

"Found you, Eli!" Renata laughed. "You can come out, Cody. Eli's it."

A small stampede of footsteps announced their return.

"Hey, R-Ryder." Cody smiled. "Good?" he asked as Ryder shoved another cookie in his mouth.

"Snickerdoodles are his favorite." Renata nudged him in the side.

"Mine, too," Cody said, grinning.

"Smart kid." Ryder winked at him.

Cody's ear-to-ear smile looked so much like Greg's it took his breath away. There were days he missed Greg, his no-nonsense take on life, and their easy camaraderie. It was bittersweet, to see his best friend so clearly in this little boy. A little boy who'd never know his father. The little boy who, if he could convince Annabeth they could make it work, would be his stepson. Cody would be a great big brother to the baby...a son he'd be proud of. He ruffled the boy's hair, resisting the sudden urge to hug him. "Having a good time?" he asked.

Cody nodded.

"Annabeth was under the weather, so Josie went over to cheer her up," Hunter offered. "We figured Cody'd have more fun here."

Ryder frowned. Annabeth wasn't feeling well? He should know this, should be taking care of her. "She okay?" he asked before he could stop himself. He didn't miss the slight narrowing of Hunter's eyes.

Cody shrugged. "She said she was tired."

"You ready to hide?" Eli asked Cody.

"Last time," Hunter said, though his attention never wandered from Ryder. "We'll take Cody on home and pick up Jo before it gets too late."

Renata and Cody ran off while Eli started counting in the great room.

Hunter cast a quick glance at their father before adding, "You ready to tell us why you're here?"

Ryder cocked an eyebrow. "Why does there have to be a reason?"

"You gonna stop using questions as your answers?" his father interjected.

Ryder and Hunter laughed then. Ever since Ryder was a boy, he'd answer questions with questions to muddy the waters—hoping to avoid trouble or consequences. It had irritated their father to no end.

"You in trouble?" his father asked.

Ryder opened his mouth, ready to answer with some smart-ass comeback. Assuming Ryder was in trouble would be the first conclusion his father would jump to. And, even though his father was right, he couldn't dismiss the anger his father's question stirred up.

"Ryder?" his father repeated.

"No, sir," he answered. "On my way to Fisher's for my steel-toe boots," he lied.

His father frowned while Hunter crossed his arms over his chest, waiting.

"I can't just stop by?" Ryder felt his cheeks burn, the words damn near choking him.

His father stared at him, long and hard. "'Course you can, Ryder. This is your home."

"Might stop by more often for these," he murmured, holding up a snickerdoodle cookie.

There was a loud thump, sending their father out of the kitchen with a smile, and leaving Ryder alone with his big brother.

"'Fess up." Hunter's voice was low, neutral.

Ryder placed his half-eaten cookie back on the plate.

"I'm thinking it's the same girl that's had you wrapped around her pinkie since grade school."

Ryder couldn't help grinning.

Hunter sighed. "Jo thinks something's going on between you and Annabeth."

Ryder met his brother's stare.

"Then you're one lucky son of a bitch." Hunter stared

at him, long and hard. "But she and Cody have been through a lot. She comes with a kid, a big job, her grandmother... Makes things harder, when so many people are involved, if things don't work out. A lot of people can get hurt. Like me and Amy—a lot of hurt there." Hunter shook his head. "I was damn lucky to get a second chance with Jo."

"Guess I was hoping not to talk about the end of something that hasn't started yet." Ryder felt his temper rising. His brother's mess of a first marriage and nasty divorce was nothing like what he and Annabeth were facing. Yes, he'd messed up more times than not, but—just once—it'd be nice not to get a lecture from his family.

Hunter nodded. "Just don't screw things up."

"I don't plan on it." Ryder sighed, his chest heavy. "But it'd be a hell of a lot easier if I knew what to do next."

"Start with telling her how you feel. Then show her what she means to you." Hunter grinned. "Then do it again, every day."

Hearing his brother say it out loud made it sound easy. He suspected it wasn't, but at least now he had a place to start. It was something he'd make damn sure he stayed on top of. Ryder picked up the cookie and popped it into his mouth.

Chapter 5

Annabeth parked her car and rested her head on the steering wheel. This had been one of her all-time longest days—wrapping up one of the longest weeks of her life. She'd been so busy she'd lost track of time. Once Greg's parents had picked up Cody from school, she'd had team meetings, campus improvement council and a mountain of certificates to review and sign before the academic awards ceremony next week.

This weekend she planned on sleeping, if she wasn't too nauseous. She'd never once thrown up when she was expecting Cody, but she'd been fighting to keep every bite down for the past few days. She'd gone through an entire box of crackers and a few bottles of ginger ale, but neither had done much good.

She turned off Lady Blue and climbed out of the car, tugging her briefcase and laptop bag out with her. It was only as she opened the door that she realized the front porch light was on. And the kitchen light was on. And music was playing.

"Hello?" she called out, too exhausted to be scared. It was Stonewall Crossing, after all—folks looked out for each other. If she had something to worry about, one of her neighbors would have let her know.

Ryder walked out of the kitchen, all smiles. Her lime-green-and-lemon-yellow-pattern apron looked downright sexy over his skintight black T-shirt and jeans. "You work long hours, Princess."

She stood frozen, surprised, as he took her bags and helped her out of her coat. His thumb brushed the base of her neck, sending a shiver down her spine and jolting her into action. "Cody's spending the weekend with Greg's folks, so I wanted to wrap up all the loose ends before I left." She followed him, unable to resist the view of his perfect butt encased in snug, work-worn jeans. "A little surprised to see you here—" Her stomach roiled as the mingling scents of garlic, rosemary, and…freesia filled her nostrils. She pressed her hand over her mouth and swallowed.

"You okay?" His smile dimmed as he looked at her. "You look a little green."

She shook her head, swallowing repeatedly, as she stared around the kitchen. The small table was covered in her best tablecloth and set with her mother's china. Candles flickered invitingly beside a massive bouquet of flowers. And a bottle of sparkling grape juice sat beside two wineglasses on the counter. "What's this?" she murmured.

"Dinner." He pulled a chair back for her.

She cocked an eyebrow at him, too bewildered—and

tired—to argue. She sat, her mind racing. She should be mad at him. She should be yelling at him for running for the hills. She should kick him out and crawl into bed. But she was too tired. All she managed was "Why are you cooking me dinner?"

"To apologize." The uncertainty in his voice drew her full attention. She'd never seen him look so…nervous. Her stomach tightened, apprehension filling her.

"For?" She forced the words out.

"Acting like a dick." He knelt in front of her, taking both her hands in his. "You deserve better, we both know that."

She was speechless.

"It's not like we're strangers."

She opened her mouth, but nothing came out.

"You and Cody are important to me. You always have been." He cleared his throat. "Let me take care of you?"

Important to him. She knew that. She knew he would be there if she needed him. "Ryder…" Her voice was husky. She pulled one of her hands from his to take a sip of water. "What are you saying?" Her head was spinning. "Exactly?"

"Marry me." His gaze traveled over her face. "Will you marry me?"

Marry him? "What?" she croaked. Emotion and nausea had her stomach churning.

He smiled. "You heard me."

"I did, but…" She shook her head, then nodded. "Why? You don't want this—"

"I might have not have known it a week ago, but yeah, I do want this." His hand cupped her cheek, his voice warm and sincere. "We'll be good together, Princess. You might have to—" The stove timer beeped and Ryder jumped up, opening the oven to pull out whatever was cooking. The scent of garlic quadrupled, and her stomach clenched violently as Ryder placed a pan of lasagna on the plate trivet in front of her.

"Oh, God." She covered her mouth. She was not going to toss her cookies in the middle of Ryder's proposal. She stood, ready to run for the bathroom.

"Annabeth…" The anguish in his voice made her pause.

Here was this gorgeous man, wearing her apron and mismatched oven mitts, cooking a romantic dinner for them…asking her to marry him. And her stomach was going to rebel any second.

"I need a minute." She held up a finger.

"I know I ran out on you, but I won't ever do it again." He threw the oven mitts over his shoulders, crossed the room in two big steps and gripped her shoulders. "I don't mind spending all night convincing you how right we are," he murmured, drawing her close as he bent his head.

Oh no. "Ryder, stop!" She pushed against his wall of a chest right before she threw up all over the kitchen floor.

Ryder knew now was not the time to laugh. But, damn, it took everything he had not to. One look at her horrified expression and he couldn't resist a slight chuckle. "Is it me?" he teased.

She scowled at him. "You could say that." She pointed to her stomach.

For some reason, that made him laugh. "Already causing trouble."

She sighed, stepping away from the mess on the floor. "I'll get the mop."

"You lie down. I'll clean this up."

She stared at him, so tired and frail looking his heart hurt. "I can do it, Ryder."

"You can." He sighed, stepping over the mess. "But you don't have to. I've got this."

She frowned at him but didn't fight as he led her to her bedroom. She sat on the edge of the bed, too pale for his liking. He knelt to remove her boots. His fingers stroked along her calf before pulling her foot free. He smiled as she stretched and wiggled her toes. It was impossible not to stroke the arch of her left foot, to resist touching her. He looked up, swallowing at the sight that greeted him.

Annabeth's eyes were closed, her toes arching as he massaged her foot. She looked sexy as hell, her fingers gripping the quilt, the slight part of her lips, and hiss of her breathing. He could imagine laying her back on the big, empty bed and worshipping every inch of her. He drew in a deep breath. Now wasn't the time. Instead, he pulled off her other boot and kneaded her foot until she groaned.

"I'm not tired," she murmured.

He released her foot and stood, freeing her golden hair from its long braid. She could barely keep her eyes open. "Sure you're not."

Her hazel eyes met his. "I need to take a shower first."

He forced himself to walk the few steps from her small bedroom to the tiny bathroom. After he'd cleared an army of bath toys from the tub, he filled it with warm water and lemon-scented bubbles. Annabeth-scented bubbles.

He poked his head into her bedroom to find her sitting in exactly the same place. She was staring at the floor, looking deflated. "Bubble bath's ready."

Her surprise was evident, but her delighted smile was huge. "Thank you."

He winked at her, wishing there was more he could do. How was he going to convince her he'd take some of the weight off her shoulders? He had no idea.

Once she'd closed the bathroom door behind her, he cleaned up the kitchen floor and sealed the lasagna and garlic bread in a Tupperware container. When that was done, he paced the length of the house. This wasn't exactly the way he'd pictured tonight. But she hadn't turned him down, not yet.

"You're going to wear a hole through the wood floor," Annabeth called from the bathroom.

"I can fix that," he called back.

Her laugh made him smile.

A few minutes later, he heard the whirring of an electric toothbrush, then the bathroom door opened. She stood, hair twisted up in a towel on her head, in her rainbow pajamas.

"I'm thinking you're not hungry?" he asked.

She shook her head.

He took her hand and led her to her room. When she was sitting on the edge of her bed, he started drying her hair with the towel. "Brush?" he asked.

She rolled her eyes but pointed at the dresser.

He grabbed her brush, gently working any snarls or tangles from her long hair. "Feeling better?"

"Ugh."

He grinned, setting the brush aside. "Need anything?"

"Sleep," she said, breaking into a yawn.

He wasn't about to let her go to sleep just yet. His plans of seduction might be out the window, but he'd convinced the justice of the peace to marry them tomorrow morning. Now all he had to do was convince the bride.

He knelt in front of Annabeth, pulling the rings from his pocket.

Her eyes went round. "Where did you get these?"

"Flo." He smiled. "Wouldn't be right without her blessing."

She shook her head, the unmistakable sheen of tears in her eyes.

"Don't you cry on me, Princess." He took her left hand and slid the engagement ring on. "Just say you'll marry me. And then I'll let you get some sleep."

She stared at the ring, blinking furiously. When she looked at him, he wasn't prepared for the raw emotion lining her face. He didn't like seeing her vulnerable or afraid. He didn't like her fragile. She was the strongest person he knew.

"And if I say no?" It was a whisper.

"You can't." He hadn't expected the sharp stab of pain. "How hard have you fought for this job? You deserve to keep it. Marrying me makes this baby a good thing instead of a liability."

He saw her bite her lip before she asked, "So you're doing this for me?"

"I'm doing this for us." He sighed. "Marry me. Tomorrow."

"Tomorrow?" Her eyes went round.

"I figured the sooner, the better. Unless you want a big wedding?"

She shook her head. "God no, but we can't do this willy-nilly—"

"Did you just say 'willy-nilly'?" He laughed.

"We need a plan, Ryder," she continued.

"Fine. *After* the ceremony. The JP owes me a favor." He waited, watching the shift of emotions on her face. "No fuss, no stress, just you and me."

Her eyes locked with his as a long stretch of silence filled the room. He wanted to pull her into his arms, to reassure her that everything was going to be okay. He wanted to kiss her. Damn, he wanted her. But more than anything, he wanted to hear her say yes.

She nodded.

"Yes?" He hadn't realized he'd been holding his breath.

"Yes." She stared down at their joined hands. "I... I know you're making sure there's no *scandal* for me and Cody and the...baby to deal with. I won't ask you to give up your life because we...were careless." She pulled her hand from his and scooted back on her bed to lie down. She didn't look at him, even though he was staring at her. Anxiety coiled in his stomach as she continued, "Before things get too complicated, we'll come up with a solid plan—so things go smoothly until we... Until it's time to divorce."

"Annabeth," he murmured, lying down on his side to face her. His chest hurt, a pain he'd never felt before. "I'm not asking for anything half-assed." And he sure as hell didn't like how willing she was to let go of what he was offering.

She smoothed the hair from his forehead, a slight

smile on her lips. Her touch left him breathless. "How many times have you said it, Ryder Boone? You're not the forever type." Her voice trailed off and her eyes closed. "But you are a good man. And a real friend."

He was an idiot. Hearing his careless words from her lips only confirmed that. Amazing how much a week could change a man's perspective on life. Forever had never included Annabeth before. He wanted Annabeth to rely on him, to count on him. He wanted to be there for her, Cody and their baby. It would take time to convince her he was in this for the long haul, but he had time. Sure, this might put his plans with JJ on hold, but his child came first.

One look at her told him how exhausted she was. She'd said yes—it was a start. She had every right to doubt him. Actions spoke louder than words. Hunter's words replayed through his head. He'd find a way to show Annabeth he was serious about this.

She sighed, her hand falling to rest on her stomach as she rolled onto her back. He stared at her hand, then covered it with his own. A baby. His baby. He had all the motivation he needed right here. The baby. Cody. Annabeth… A family. His family. Was he scared? Hell, yes. For the first time in his life, he had something to lose. He'd let her make her plan, but his wasn't going to change. He was in this, for real, for life.

Chapter 6

"Congratulations, Mr. and Mrs. Boone." Mack McCoy smiled at her.

Annabeth Boone. She was Annabeth Boone.

"You're a lucky man, Ryder." Mack shook his hand.

Right now, that's exactly how she was feeling. *She* was lucky. If Ryder hadn't proposed, what would she have done? Would she have asked for his help, like Josie suggested? Or would she have tucked tail and run to her in-laws' place? Would they take her in? It's not like this baby had anything to do with them. But, thanks to Ryder, nothing had to change…for now.

"I am." Ryder pulled her close, planting a soft kiss on her mouth before she could respond. Her body, on the other hand, was definitely reacting to his touch. Being close to him seemed to light an instant fire inside her. Waking up next to him, wrapped in his scent and warmth and arms, felt too good. So good, she'd lain there until he'd woken up. Even then, she'd have happily stayed cocooned against him. But he'd hustled her from the bed and to the justice of the peace.

Now she stood, wearing a cream sweater and jeans, married to the *rebel* Boone.

Mr. McCoy laughed, handing her the wedding certificate in its faux-leather holder. "Not to rush you two, but the missus has a honey-do list a mile long waiting for me at home." He winked. "I imagine the two of you have your own plans for the day."

She focused on the certificate she held, not the mix of emotions Mack McCoy's teasing caused. Ryder had made it clear he wasn't attracted to her from the beginning. If it hadn't been for Mr. Ego at the bar, he wouldn't have pretended he was, and she wouldn't have jumped him... For all she knew, their time together hadn't been anything special for him. Considering he'd all but bolted out of the bed when he woke up this morning, she didn't think his interest level had changed.

The smart thing to do, the thing she was best at, was focusing on the positive. And, right now, she had a lot to be positive about.

"Appreciate you coming in on your day off." Ryder nodded.

"Yes, thank you," she agreed.

"You can name one of your kids after me and we'll call it even." Mack McCoy smiled. "Middle name is Joshua, just in case you don't like Mack."

She smiled, trying to find something to say. She'd been a little tongue-tied all morning, ever since she'd woken up with her cheek on Ryder's bare chest, wrapped in his rock-hard arms.

"Morning, Mack." Renata Boone's singsong voice startled them all. "Saw your truck was out front so I thought I'd drop off those new tourism department brochures."

They hadn't really talked about how they were sharing their news with everyone. They hadn't really talked about a *lot* of things. And now Ryder's sister was here, staring at them in total confusion. "What's happening?" Renata asked.

"Give your brother a hug, Renata. It's not every day a man gets hitched." Mack clapped Ryder on the shoulder.

"What?" Renata's blue eyes went round. "Married?"

Annabeth waited, smiling what she hoped was a suitably excited smile.

Renata squealed, tossed the fliers she was holding onto the entry desk and hugged her brother. "It's about time. I thought you'd never get the nerve up to ask her."

Annabeth shot Ryder a look. He shrugged, hugging his sister. "You can't rush these things."

"Then why are you marrying her at the justice of the peace?" Renata let go of her brother and pulled Annabeth into a strong hug. "I'll have to apologize for my brother, Annabeth. He's not exactly a pro when it comes to romance."

"No." Annabeth smiled. "I liked the idea. Getting married here."

"You did?" Renata asked.

"I've done the whole wedding thing," Annabeth answered honestly. Even without the rush to the altar, she wouldn't have wanted another big wedding. "I'm more interested in being married." Married, to a partner, a friend, someone to rely on. She looked at Ryder, unnerved by the intensity in his pale blue eyes.

"When you put it that way, it makes perfect sense." Renata smiled.

Annabeth didn't resist leaning into Ryder when he slipped his arm around her waist. If anything, she wanted his support.

"You tell Dad?" Renata asked.

Ryder laughed. "It just happened."

"Normally the family knows before it *happens*," Renata argued. "You two might be fine without all the ceremony, but this town isn't going to let that happen."

Ryder shook his head. "Renata."

"Come on, Ryder." Renata frowned. "Annabeth's the principal of the elementary school. You're a Boone, your family built this town. There has to be a celebration. People will think it's weird if we don't."

She has a point. "I don't see the harm in a little get-together," Annabeth agreed, shooting for enthusiasm. "Then we can tell everyone at once." She smiled up at Ryder.

Ryder wasn't sold on the idea. "You sure?" he asked. She nodded.

"Nothing too big, I promise," Renata went on. "I'll take care of everything, don't you worry. We'll just open up the Lodge, invite…everyone."

"Everyone?" Ryder asked.

Annabeth's stomach rumbled, sudden nausea rising up.

"Didn't you feed her before you came?" Renata asked. "Ryder Boone, you've spent too many years being doe-eyed over Annabeth. Now that you've got her, you better take care of her. You two go on and I'll call you later, once everything's set." She paused, winking. "Maybe I'll wait and call you tomorrow."

Ryder Boone had *never* been doe-eyed, ever. But An-nabeth was surprised by the pleasure Renata's words gave her. She only had a few seconds to glance at Ryder—before being engulfed in another of Renata's hugs—but there was no missing the color on his cheeks. Or the tightness in his jaw. Either he was irritated by his sis-ter's teasing or... No, he had not and would never be sweet on her. They were—and always had been—just friends. She thanked Mack McCoy and let Ryder lead her out of the small building.

"I can tell Renata to cancel the party, if you want?" Ryder offered.

Annabeth glanced at him. "If you don't want to—"

"Didn't mean that." He smiled. "I can see that brain of yours working. Guess there's a lot we need to talk about, huh?"

"The list keeps getting longer," she agreed.

"Think you can stomach some pancakes or some-thing first?"

Pancakes sounded good. "I'll try."

He took her hand in his and led her down the brick sidewalk toward Pop's Bakery. "Might as well let Lola and Carl know, too. Between them and my sister, Stone-wall Crossing will know you're my wife before we're done eating."

Wife. "Ryder," she murmured, pulling against him.

"What's wrong, Princess?" His pale blue eyes bore into hers.

"It's a lot," she murmured, trying not to get distracted by the heat in his gaze...or the memory of the way he looked tousled and shirtless in her bed. "All of it."

"I know." His attention lingered on the ring on his left hand. "Let's eat and go home."

They hadn't discussed that, either. "Home as in my place? Or home as in your apartment? Or, are you… If you don't want…" She cleared her throat. "You don't have to stay with me—"

He frowned. "The apartment won't hold you, Cody and the baby."

She looked around them, panicked that someone might hear him.

"Seems pretty pointless to get hitched if we're not sleeping under the same roof."

He shoved his hands in his pockets and stared down the street. "So I'll be staying with you. Even if you'd rather I slept on the couch."

He was right. In a town the size of Stonewall Crossing, there was no such thing as privacy or personal business. If their lightning-fast wedding didn't cause a wave a gossip, the two of them living apart immediately after the wedding surely would.

"You're right," she murmured, confused and anxious.

Ryder's pale blue eyes swept over her, the muscle in his jaw clenching briefly. "Still hungry?" His gaze was intense, further rattling her.

The knots in her stomach tightened. The last thing she meant to do was make him angry. But she'd gotten good at being on her own. Relying on him meant opening herself up, being vulnerable. She tried to explain. "Like I said, it's a lot. I've been on my own for almost six years now—"

"You're not alone anymore, got it?" he argued, his gaze falling to the sidewalk at their feet.

Maybe not right now. She wasn't the only one whose world had been turned upside down overnight. He'd done everything he could to help, and she was holding him at arm's length. "Got it." He was frustrated and angry—and he looked adorable. There was no way she could stop the smile from spreading across her face. "I'm sorry." She stepped forward, forcing him to look at her.

His gaze met hers as he let out a deep breath. The corner of his baby blues crinkled as he smiled. He shook his head at her, tugged her coat closed, and took her hand in his.

"You're kinda cute when you're angry, Ryder Boone," she admitted.

He looked at her, one eyebrow cocked. "Hell, I'm cute all the time, Princess."

She laughed, letting him lead her down Main Street to Pop's Bakery.

Ryder's phone was ringing before they reached the bakery. It was Hunter. And Hunter was the only one he didn't want to talk to right now. He loved his big brother, but he'd be less likely to get all warm and fuzzy over his unexpected marriage than his sister.

"Need to get that?" Annabeth asked.

He shook his head. "Nope." He silenced his phone and tucked it into his pocket.

"Ryder." She tugged on his hand. "I'm not trying to tell you what to do, but maybe you should call your family?"

She was so pretty, she always looked so damn pretty. He studied her, enjoying the sight of his *wife*. He smiled, brushing a lock of her long golden hair from her shoulder. "Probably." The tip of her nose was red from the cold air. "But it'll take too long." He pulled his phone from his pocket, typed a short text and sent it.

"Ryder." She was clearly disappointed in him. Arms crossed, deep frown, hell, she was even tapping her foot.

He grinned. "Come on, Princess, let's eat." He held the door open for her.

"Morning, you two," Carl Stephens called out. "What's got you out and about on such a chilly morning?"

Ryder looked at Annabeth. She was blushing and he liked it. "Food," Ryder answered.

"What'll it be?" Carl asked. "The griddle's still going if you want some pancakes? Or French toast?"

"Pancakes, please." Annabeth nodded.

Ryder nodded, helping Annabeth shrug out of her coat. "Any chance of eggs and bacon or sausage, too?" He hung her coat over the back of her chair, then pulled the chair out for her.

"You bet. Help yourself to the coffee and all the trimmings. Lola's got all those flavor things and sweeteners, in case you're interested in making your coffee all fancy." Carl was hovering, watching every move he made.

Ryder's phone started vibrating again, bouncing off the metal button of his leather jacket. He saw Annabeth glance at him, her disapproving frown making him smile all the more. Something about his smile made her roll her eyes, and then he was laughing. And Carl, joined by Lola, looked back and forth between the two of them.

"Well, I'll be," Lola said, her eyes wide with excitement. "If that isn't a ring I see on your finger, Ryder Boone."

Carl bent forward, peering through the lower part of his glasses. "Is it?"

"Which means…" Lola turned to Annabeth, her hands clasped together and pressed to her chest.

Ryder watched the women, amused. His wife might not know it, but the flush on her cheeks told Lola the answer. He grinned as Annabeth held out her hand for the older woman's inspection.

Lola clapped her hands together. "I knew it! I just knew it. Your momma would be proud, damn proud to see who you married."

Ryder swallowed down the lump in his throat. He hoped so. He accepted Carl's enthusiastic handshake and Lola's hug before the rest of Pop's Bakery learned the news and jumped up to join in. Annabeth stood at his side, pink-cheeked and gracious and beautiful. Not as beautiful as she'd looked this morning, sleepy-eyed and smiling against the pillows. Memory gripped him, the silken skin of her cheek against his chest, the whisper of her breath. He'd woken up and bolted from the bed straight into a cold shower. And if he didn't think about something else real quick, everyone in Stonewall Crossing would know how much he wanted his wife.

"This is a surprise." Winnie Michaels was all wide-eyed assessment. "I never pegged you as the marrying sort, Ryder." Winnie smiled up at him. "Especially to someone as goody-goody as our Annabeth. Not your normal type—from what I hear anyway."

Ryder heard the edge in Winnie's voice. So did everyone else in the bakery. He knew some folks were going to give them a hard time—he expected it. But the slight tensing of Annabeth's shoulders, the way her smile dimmed, made him fiercely protective of her. "I'm lucky she'd have me." He took Annabeth's hand in his. It was ice-cold to the touch. He slid his arm around her shoulders, pulling her against his side.

Winnie's eyes narrowed. "Well, the timing is great. I mean, I'm sure she appreciates having someone to help out and support her while this whole job thing is going on." She smiled. "And, with you being a Boone and all, I guess that helps, too..." She looked back and forth between the two of them. "When are you two leaving for the honeymoon?"

Annabeth was ramrod stiff in his arms, her lips pressed flat. He needed to get her out of here, quick, before she let Winnie Michaels have a piece of her mind. While he would pay money to see his Annabeth put Winnie in her place, he suspected his wife would regret it. She worked too hard to be a model citizen in their small community. And having a catfight with one of her student's parents, however warranted, was not the sort of attention Annabeth needed right now. "Not for a while." Annabeth sounded cool and calm. He was impressed as hell.

"Lola, you think we could have that breakfast to go?" he asked.

"No honeymoon?" Winnie asked. "Isn't that bad luck? To not have a honeymoon?"

"We might not be going anywhere yet, but that doesn't mean there won't be a honeymoon." Ryder winked at Lola, but he made sure everyone heard him. There were more than a few snickers.

"You best hurry with their breakfast, Carl," Lola yelled toward the kitchen, still giggling. "Don't want to keep these lovebirds waiting." She might be a gossip, but she had a good heart. She must know what he was up to, helping Annabeth into her coat, chattering away—and preventing Winnie from getting a word in edgewise.

"I imagine your family's tickled pink," Carl said, as he handed a large brown paper bag to Ryder.

"They don't think I deserve her." Ryder nodded, pulling his wallet from his back pocket.

"Nope." Carl waved his hand at him. "Consider it a little wedding present."

"Wonder how Greg's folks feel about it?" Winnie asked.

He drew in a deep breath. That was a question. A good question. He'd no interest in hurting Annabeth's relationship with the Uptons…but he might have already done that by getting her pregnant.

Annabeth's arm slid around his waist. "Judy and the Major love Ryder. He was the closest thing Greg had to a brother."

"You and Greg were two peas in a pod," Lola said with a nod.

"That's nice, then, keeping it in the family." Winnie smiled that mean, tight smile some women wear so well.

To his surprise, Annabeth laughed. "Oh, Winnie."

He had to give it to her, she knew how to make lemonade out of the bitterest of lemons. Even now, with Winnie prodding the grief-filled places in Annabeth's heart, she managed to laugh it off. What else could she do? He'd never been prouder.

He pulled her close, pressing a kiss to her forehead. "You ready to go, Mrs. Boone?"

Her huge hazel eyes turned on him, so full of warmth he could feel it. "I'm ready, Mr. Boone." Her smile grew. "And I'm starving."

She was talking about food, he knew it. Other than the night in his truck, she hadn't shown the slightest interest in him. But something about the look in her eyes and the husk in her voice sent his blood to boiling. He'd like nothing more than to take her home, feed her pancakes and spend the rest of the day—and maybe the night, too—in bed.

Chapter 7

"What did you ever do to Winnie Michaels?" Ryder asked her as soon as they climbed into his truck.

She almost dropped the to-go cartons containing their breakfast. "What did *I* do?" She stared at him, ready to launch into all the things Winnie had done to her, when he started laughing. He knew about the teasing, the Annabeth Banana-breath. He'd been there.

"Teasing you." He was grinning ear to ear.

She sighed, sitting back in the seat, staring at his profile. A man shouldn't be that good-looking. His body was compact, lean and muscular—good for riding bulls. Her gaze drifted along his jean-encased thigh to his chest. She swallowed, remembering the feel of him all too well. Her inspection continued upward, his neck, his angled jaw. Full lips. Long, dark, lashes. Dirty-blond hair, cropped short. Chiseled bone structure and piercing pale blue eyes…that were looking at her right now. Her cheeks grew hot.

"Winnie's always been a…*charmer*," he said with a shake of his head.

"I wish I *had* done something. Then I could try to make amends." It was true. She didn't have many memories of Winnie that weren't "charming" in some way or the other. "How do people get that way?"

"What way?" He pulled the truck onto Main Street, waving a greeting as they passed two locals sitting on a bench in front of the old courthouse.

"Twisted inside." She glanced at him. "Mean. She is. She's just…*mean*."

Ryder's gaze settled on her before he started laughing again.

"What?" she asked. His laugh was contagious. "Why are you laughing?"

Ryder rolled to stop at the stop sign and looked at her. "Because she was, without throwing a punch, picking a fight. And all you do is say she's *mean*?" He checked the street for traffic and headed to her house. "I can think of a long list of words to describe that woman. And mean is the mildest one of them."

She was laughing now, too.

"You're *amazing*, Annabeth," he murmured, cutting off her laugh immediately.

She glanced at him, curious. "Me?"

"Yeah, you. It might sound stupid, but I'm proud of you."

"You are?" she choked out.

"You didn't take the bait, even when it was being shoved down your throat." He glanced at her, looking a little uncomfortable. His next words were accompanied by a smile. "And… I like looking at you."

She rolled her eyes. "I can't decide if you're making fun of me or flattering me."

"I was trying to give you a compliment." He was smiling, but there was no trace of the usual teasing on his face.

"Well…thank you. I guess I could return the favor, but I'm sure you've had plenty of women go on about all of your praiseworthy assets. I wouldn't want to inflate your already healthy ego."

"*All*, huh?" He was grinning as he pulled his truck into her driveway next to Lady Blue.

"Exactly." She was laughing as she pushed open the car door.

And that's when the smell hit her. Nothing else smelled quite like it. Skunk.

"Don't see anything on the road." Ryder came around the front of the truck. "But it's somewhere close."

She nodded, her stomach instantly reacting to the fumes. "There goes my appetite." She shoved the bag with their breakfast into his hands and covered her nose, running to the porch steps.

And there, curled in a ball, was Tom. He was shivering, his pathetic mews instantly plucking at her heartstrings.

"How did you get out?" she said to the terrified kitten, stooping down to scoop the little fur ball into her arms. But the smell was so strong her eyes began to sting. That's when she noticed how matted and wet Tom's fur was. "Oh, no…"

"Up to no good, Tom?" Ryder was behind her. "I'll get him."

"I won't argue with you." She took a step back, her stomach roiling, nostrils burning and eyes watering fiercely. "I've got some tomato juice. And some tomato sauce, too, I think."

Ryder handed her back the bag containing their breakfast. "We'll need it—don't let him in the house. I'll get my gloves." Ryder made his way to his truck and popped open the lid of the large metal toolbox. "If you can squeeze by him, you might want to prep the bathroom."

Considering their strange beginnings, giving a kitten a tomato bath on her wedding day didn't seem all that out of place. She took a step toward the door and Tom leaped forward.

"Here's the thing," she said to the cat. "That mean old skunk is gone, so you're safe now. But I can't let you in the house smelling like that, Tom, sorry. The worst part's over."

Ryder returned, wearing a worn yellow raincoat and some well-used leather gloves. "He might disagree with you once the tomato juice bath starts." Ryder picked up the kitten, wrinkling his nose. "Whew-y. We'll wait here. You might want to change, too. Things are going to get loud and messy."

"What every bride wants to hear on her wedding day," she said, squeezing into the house.

Ryder's laughter followed her into the bedroom. She changed into a threadbare pale blue tank top and some yoga pants covered in paint splatters. Twisting her hair into a knot, she headed into the bathroom and removed all the linens and throw rugs. Less to get splattered with stink and tomato sauce. In the kitchen, she found four large cans of tomato juice—she could never resist a sale. She eyed a large jug of imported tomato sauce a student had given her for the holidays and grabbed it, too. Hopefully that would be enough. Tom was just a kitten, after all. A kitten with a lion-size stink.

She carried it all back to the bathroom, calling out, "Ready."

Tom was curled up against Ryder's chest, the power of the kitten's purrs surprising.

"Try making friends with a squirrel or a rabbit next time, will ya?" Ryder said, staring down into the adoring yellow eyes of the kitten he held. "They don't spray."

Annabeth's voice was muffled as she said, "Ready."

Tom's ears perked up and he turned toward the door, mewing once.

Ryder grinned. "You only think you wanna go in there." He pushed through the front door and headed straight into the bathroom.

Annabeth was there, practically naked in her skin-tight get up. He almost dropped the cat.

"Close the door." She waved him over, covering her nose with one hand. "Anything to contain the scent from the rest of the house."

He kicked the door shut behind him, sealing himself into the small room with a reeking cat and the most beautiful woman he'd ever met. And she did look beautiful, with her hair piled up in a messy knot and her huge hazel eyes peering over her hand. How could he be holding a skunk-coated cat and still want to kiss her? Hell, all he wanted to do was pull her against him and tug her hair free...

He had it bad. He needed to find a way to blow off some steam—and soon. "I got this," he growled.

Annabeth rolled her eyes, making the urge to kiss

her that much stronger. "You can't hold him and wash him." She bent over the tub to pick up one of the cans of tomato juice. The sight of her rear made him groan. She popped up, holding a can. "Where do you want me?"

He stared at the ceiling, biting back a half dozen inappropriate suggestions before he bit out, "Bathtub."

She climbed in, scooting to the back of the tub, a can of tomato juice at the ready.

Ryder knelt on the floor beside the tub, holding Tom away from him. "You behave," he warned the cat.

"It's going to be okay, Tom." Annabeth's soothing tones caught the kitten's attention—and his. She smiled at the kitten then looked at Ryder. "You ready?"

He nodded, holding the kitten away from his body. He gripped Tom by the scruff of the neck, the other hand supporting the kitten's back legs.

Annabeth filled her hand with tomato juice and rubbed it into Tom's back.

And the kitten went crazy. Yowling, flying claws, growls, the little thing was in full panic.

Ryder kept a firm grip while Annabeth attempted to coat every inch of Tom. She rubbed juice in as thoroughly as the flailing limbs and claws would allow. Ryder watched, impressed with how unflinchingly she worked. Tomato juice spattered the front of her blue tank top and forehead, but she kept at it. She ignored the claw that scratched her forearm, working until every inch of Tom dripped tomato juice.

"You look like something from a horror movie." He laughed. "Both of you." It was true. Her shirt and pants and face had multiple tomato spatters—but it could almost be blood. Tom looked drowned and acted possessed.

Annabeth glared. "You should talk."

"Looks like we're all going to need a shower." He winked at her. "Wanna take one together?"

"Are you seriously hitting on me?" She kept rubbing tomato juice on Tom, and Tom kept yowling. "Now? While the cat is screaming bloody murder?"

He shrugged. "Bad timing?"

She laughed then, so surprised she slipped back, spilling tomato juice all over her shirt and pants. "Damn it!" She was still laughing.

"You okay?" Ryder shifted the kitten, making sure not to let go.

"Fine." She sat up, taking a deep breath and covering her nose with the back of her now dripping hand. "Yuck." She stared down at the pool of tomato juice in her lap.

"Time for a rinse?" he asked, turning on the warm water. He pulled the detachable showerhead free and offered it to her. "Ready?"

He pushed the pin in on the faucet and water sprayed from the handheld shower nozzle.

"Ryder," she squeaked. "I *wasn't* ready."

She was dripping wet, so was the ceiling. And the cat, and the small mirror over the sink.

"Ready now?" he asked, trying hard not to laugh.

She glared at him, shaking her hands at him and spattering him with tomato juice and water. "Yes," she hissed, aiming the nozzle at him.

"Hey, hey." He shook his head, holding the still-wailing Tom in front of him. "Aim for him."

"You've got a little something right there." She pointed at his chin.

"Let's get him taken care of first." He used his pickup

voice, all low and coaxing. "Poor little guy could get a chill."

Annabeth rolled her eyes again, but immediately began rinsing Tom. A little baby shampoo and the cat was clean. He placed the kitten on the bathroom counter and started rubbing the squirming kitten brusquely with the one towel she'd left in the bathroom. "Hope you haven't lost your appetite?" he asked, looking back at her.

She stood, rinsing herself off with the showerhead. Her pale blue tank top was plastered to her, giving him a good view of her breasts. He'd imagined her, plenty of times, remembering the full weight of her curves beneath his hurried hands. But seeing her, knowing his fantasy didn't come close to the woman who was now his wife, did something to his insides.

"Well, hello there," Annabeth said to Tom, who was straddling the side of the tub, swatting at water drops. "You survived." The kitten mewed as she picked him up and sniffed him. Her nose wrinkled. "Better than it was, but…"

She was staring at him. He was standing there, gripping the damn towel, staring right back. In a yellow raincoat. What the hell was the matter with him? "Need a towel?"

"Sure," she murmured, her cheeks turning red as she crossed her arms over her chest. "Thanks."

He opened the bathroom door and Tom skittered out. "You go on and shower," he murmured, pulling two towels from the built-in cabinet outside the bathroom and placing them on the counter. "I'll finish getting Tom dry and warm up our breakfast." He pulled the door shut and stood there, staring at the door.

Chapter 8

Annabeth wiped the steam off the small bathroom mirror and looked at herself. Her breathing was uneven and her stomach twisted. Not because the lingering scent of skunk still hung in the air, but because of the look in Ryder's eyes. She didn't know what to think. Was she seeing what she wanted to see? Or was Ryder attracted to her? Could he actually see her, want her, as a woman?

She combed through her wet hair, tucked the towel tightly around her chest and opened the bathroom door. Tom was sitting right outside, his fur sticking up every which way.

He mewed at her, weaving his way between her ankles.

"Glad you don't hold a grudge," she spoke softly, smiling down at the kitten.

"Starting a load of laundry," Ryder called from the kitchen. "Wanna hand me your clothes and the towel?"

She peered around the corner to find Ryder pulling off his shirt and throwing it into the washing machine. The muscles in his back shifted and the waistband of his pants slipped low. His body was amazing, strong and capable and completely mind-blowing.

Swallowing, she hurried back into the bathroom, snatching her clothes and towels. Why was the sight of a shirtless Ryder getting her all flustered? She shot a look at her reflection. She'd been without a man for five years. No dating. No flirting. Nothing. Now she had someone who looked as though he'd stepped out of a muscle magazine stripping in her kitchen. Add in her raging pregnancy hormones and it made sense that she was a little disconcerted.

She strode back into the kitchen and shoved everything into the washing machine. But when she spun around, Ryder was staring at her.

She met his gaze. "Your turn." It shouldn't matter that she was wearing only a towel; she didn't have anything to put on after her shower. And she looked like a drowned rat.

The muscle in his jaw bulged. "My turn?"

"Shower." She swallowed. "It's all yours."

His attention wandered to her mouth. "You want to wash my back?" He reached for her, the pad of his thumb running along the curve of her neck.

She froze, fighting the slight shiver that ran along her spine. She would not press herself against the expansive wall of muscle that was his chest.

He took a step closer, one hand resting along her shoulder, the other cupped her cheek.

Her lungs emptied and her heart kicked into overdrive. They were half-naked in the kitchen. And she wanted him to kiss her more than anything.

But that couldn't happen. She couldn't let it happen. Kissing Ryder would only add to the confusion. They needed to talk—to come up with a plan. Now. A clear-headed plan without this newfound attraction muddying up the water. It was hard to push her longing aside, hard to resist the pull between them. But she had to. "I'm hungry," she blurted out.

He grinned. "In the microwave."

She turned, putting some much-needed space between them. "Thanks for starting the laundry."

"Got some clean clothes on the bike." He pointed toward the door. "Be back." He was out the front door before she could stop him. Out the front door, with his shirt off. If Mrs. Lavender saw him like that, everyone in Stonewall Crossing would hear about it. Then again, they were married now. It really shouldn't matter if he sat on the front porch in his boxers...

Married.

She was Ryder's wife.

She had to tell Cody.

She had to tell the Major and Judy, Greg's parents. She wanted to tell them in person—a phone call wouldn't do. They were the only parents she'd had since Flo's battle with dementia set in. Without them, she wouldn't be able to work the hours the principal position required. They looked forward to their weekend visits with their only grandson and loved it when she called for their help. She knew they needed Cody to keep Greg close to them. And, whether or not Ryder was in the picture, she had every intention of keeping that bond strong.

Ryder came back into the kitchen, pausing at the sight of her. Still wrapped in a towel standing in the kitchen. "Rethinking washing my back?" His pale blue eyes sparkled.

"No." She rolled her eyes. "I was thinking about Cody. And the Major and Judy."

Ryder's grin dimmed. "How are we going to tell them?"

"We?" His instant assumption that he'd be part of the conversation was a pleasant surprise.

He leaned against the door frame, his leather saddle-bag gripped in one hand. It was impossible not to notice the play of muscles in his arm. "We."

"I was thinking about asking them for dinner tomorrow night? When they drop off Cody?" she suggested. "With Flo?"

He nodded. "Sounds good. You gonna eat?"

"I should probably get dressed first." She glanced down. "I don't know what's gotten into me."

"Cut yourself a break, Princess. You can't expect to come out of skunk duty looking dolled up."

She shook her head, suddenly exhausted. She yawned.

"I like the outfit." He pushed off the door frame, dropping a kiss on her temple before heading into the bathroom. "I just need to figure out how to get you out of it."

She shivered. He was teasing, she could hear it in his voice. "You're incredible."

"I've heard that before. Eat your pancakes. Then we'll take a nap."

A nap sounded too good to resist. "Then we talk."

He winked at her, pulling the door closed behind him.

She pressed the reheat button on the microwave and went to her bedroom, then slipped into a long cotton nightie and fuzzy socks. As she walked back into the kitchen, she heard Ryder humming in the shower. She was smiling as she sat down to her pancakes.

Ryder stared down at Annabeth. She was sound asleep, her long lashes resting against her cheeks. She'd kicked the quilts down to her knees and her thin nightgown did little to hide her stomach. His baby was in there.

After his shower and his late breakfast, he'd climbed into bed with her. He'd been working himself to death to wear himself out. He needed a nap as much as she did…and he couldn't pass up the chance to hold her. She'd been stiff, refusing to relax against him until she fell asleep. Once she'd drifted off, she had no problem wrapping herself around him. He closed his eyes, enjoying every second. The feel of her hand on his bare stomach. The whisper of her breath on his chest. The silk of her hair against his neck. Her scent, her little sounds and movements—she was driving him crazy.

He'd slipped from the bed and wandered through the kitchen. He folded the laundry, pulled on his clean clothes and poured himself a glass of orange juice. On the refrigerator door hung a brightly colored picture of a tree house. He smiled at Cody's creation. He knew the tree. It was a perfect tree house tree.

And he knew the house. The crudely drawn lilac-blue house in the picture was the perfect family house—a storybook house. Annabeth had always loved the Czinkovic place. When they were kids riding their bikes around town, she'd stop there. She'd had a plan, pointing out each window and explaining what each room would be if it was her house. Greg would nod, listening intently to every word she said. But Ryder hadn't understood her fascination with the place. Now he did. She'd wanted the family that lived there, not just the walls they lived in. She'd wanted everything he'd had and wanted to get away from.

He slipped out the back door of the house, careful not to disturb her. There was no fence, so he wasn't sure where Annabeth's yard ended and the Czinkovic house property line began. But a row of red-tipped petunias, two magnolia trees and several fruit trees made a sort of natural fence line. Cody's massive oak tree sat in the middle of the house's backyard. He stared up, seeing Cody's design in the sprawling limbs of the old tree.

He turned, assessing the house. It seemed to be in good shape, but he suspected it would need a thorough inspection. Some updates would be needed—wiring and plumbing. No signs of foundation concerns, but it would need lots of TLC.

He walked the property, sizing it up. Taking notes...

They would need a place to grow. Chances were his dad would offer him property on the ranch to build, like he had with his brothers. But he'd always liked his space. Being in town, near Annabeth's work and Cody's school, made the most sense. Staying in Annabeth's teeny-tiny house didn't.

Once he'd written down the Realtor's name and number, he headed back to Annabeth's house. The yard needed raking, so he pulled open the shed and set to work. Most of her tools were in terrible shape. From the look of the lawn mower, he'd have to put more than elbow grease into it to get it running. He dug through the small shed until he found an old metal rake. Its handle was splintered and rough, but Annabeth had put a few layers of duct tape over the worst spots to keep using it. It made him smile, to see how resourceful she was. She knew how to take care of herself, without all the fancy bells and whistles. Not Annabeth. No, she made do with what she had—with a smile on her face. They may not have planned any of this, but he'd never had anything feel so right, so fast. He pulled on his work gloves and set to raking the leaves from the front yard.

Time and again, his gaze wandered to the empty house, imagining Cody sitting in the window, watching the birds. If he could give his family—something he never thought he'd have—a nice home, then he would.

Growing up, he'd never felt as though he fit anywhere, even at home. He wasn't as smart as his brothers. He'd struggled in school and had taken a lot of teasing for it. The more teasing he'd got, the angrier he'd become. The angrier he'd been, the more trouble he'd got into—striking out and earning a reputation that had made his father shake his head and his brothers lecture him whenever they'd had the chance. His mother had been his only defender. And then she'd died in a car accident coming to help him. And all he'd felt was anger.

When he was young, the rodeo had fit. Riding bulls had eased his restlessness. He'd loved the freedom, the fight, it gave him. It had kept him out of trouble, mostly. It didn't call to him the way it used to, but he still rode for the fun of it now and then.

But it was the vintage Packard his father had inherited from some long-lost aunt that had introduced Ryder to the real love of his life—cars. He could fix cars, build them from nothing or return them to their glory. He was a mechanic, working nine to five, and he was damn proud of that. Sure, he had a substantial share of the Boone fortune, but he'd never touched it. He'd wanted to make his own way—he'd needed to. Now he needed to take care of his family. He had a plan, one he was excited about.

When the yard was done and three large black bags were full of leaves, he crept back into the house. Staring down at her, at his baby, made him smile. "Annabeth?" he whispered.

Tom had been curled up against her side. The yellow-eyed glare he sent Ryder made him chuckle. Annabeth stirred a little, rolling onto her side and curling into a ball. The kitten climbed over her and curled up by her stomach.

"Princess?" he whispered again. "You're going to sleep the day away."

She rolled onto her back, blinking several times. "What time is it?"

"Almost five."

"Five?" She sat up, then grabbed her stomach and flopped back. "Remind me not to do that." Tom mewed, jostled by her sudden movements. "Sorry," she murmured to the kitten, scratching the little gray head.

He sat beside her on the bed. "Good nap?"

She nodded, yawning. "I feel great." He watched her stretch, reaching over her head with her arms and extending her long legs with a satisfied squeal.

"Looks like it." He grinned, resisting the urge to touch her. Tom climbed into Ryder's lap, a vibrating ball of fur.

"What have you been up to?" She smiled a sleepy-smile at him.

Her smile made his heart thump. "A little yard work."

She frowned. "Ryder—"

His phone rang, interrupting what looked like another tirade about him helping out. He didn't even look at the phone as he answered. "Yeah?"

"We going to get something to eat before tonight?" DB's scratchy voice startled him.

"Tonight?" Ryder glanced at Annabeth, relaxed, propped up on the pillows, staring out the window.

"Rodeo? Tonight?" DB laughed. "You serious? You forgot?"

Ryder laughed. "Kinda had other things on my mind." Annabeth looked at him, her hazel eyes full of something he didn't understand. "I'm not gonna make it."

"What?" she asked, sitting up. "Don't change your plans."

"Call you back," Ryder said, hanging up the phone without waiting for a response from DB. "It's nothing, Princess."

"Tell me, then." She swung her legs over the side of the bed, putting her right beside him. She smelled like heaven. "If you committed to something, you need to follow through." He agreed, especially when it came to their marriage. If going tonight would help prove he was a man of his word, he would.

"Rodeo, in Smithville, tonight." He shrugged, smoothing a length of her long golden hair from her forehead. "It's nothing."

She covered his hand with hers. "I haven't been to

the rodeo in…a long time. Sounds like fun. We can have our talk tomorrow."

He laughed, turning his hand under hers and twining their fingers together. "Not exactly how I pictured tonight."

She stared at him. "You… How did you picture tonight?"

He swallowed. "You. Me. Here." He looked at the bed. "Right here."

Her cheeks turned an adorable red. "Ryder…stop." She blew out a long breath. "You…you don't…" She tried to pull her hand away but he wouldn't let go. "I think the rodeo is a much better idea—"

"I'm not so sure about that," he cut her off.

She rolled her eyes. "Well, I am." She tugged at her hand, sighing in frustration.

"Ouch," he murmured, reluctantly letting her hand slide from his.

"So, I'll find something to wear. And you can call whoever—" Annabeth stopped, staring at the phone. She closed her eyes, shaking her head. "Oh… Or would you rather I didn't go?"

"I'm only going 'cause you're making me, remember?" He stood, staring down at her. "So what's that about?"

She had a hard time holding his gaze. "I… I don't know much about your rodeo world…or if there's someone special. You know—a buckle bunny you've got a soft spot for?"

"Annabeth Boone." His voice was low. "After we go to the rodeo, would you go dancing with me? If memory serves, you loved to dance."

She hesitated, barely suppressing her excitement. "Are you sure?"

His hand slid through her hair, silk against his work-roughened fingers. "I'm sure. You're my wife and I'm fine with everyone knowing it." More than that, he wanted people to know it. He couldn't think of anything else he'd rather do—other than keeping her in bed all night.

"Then I'll get dressed," she said, pushing him out her bedroom door. "You could use another shower, cowboy."

"The bulls don't care," he argued.

"Well, I do," she sassed, her brows arching.

He knew that. And respected it. "Then I'll head to the apartment to get ready." He paused. "And I'll pack a bag?"

She blushed again, nodding, and so pretty he couldn't help himself. He leaned in, kissing her before she could argue. It was a soft kiss, a quick kiss, and not nearly enough to satisfy him.

Chapter 9

Sitting in the stands, bundled in Ryder's thick Carhartt jacket, was easy. Watching Ryder flail around on the back of a bull that looked like evil with horns was not. She knew he rode bulls, and she'd seen him do it before. But they'd been young and death hadn't devastated her world. Now that it had, those eight seconds were the longest of her life. Reassuring herself over and over that Ryder was the most physically fit and capable man she'd ever known helped. At the same time, she knew he had no real control over the bull. All he could do was hold on.

When he jumped free, he dusted his brown Stetson on his thigh and sauntered to the gate. Annabeth jumped up, petrified. Apparently he didn't notice the thousand-pound bull circling the arena. But she did. It was only after he was safe behind the metal gate that she could swallow the lump of terror in her throat.

"You okay?" the woman beside her asked, bouncing her sleeping baby on her knee.

Annabeth realized she was standing up, making a spectacle out of herself. "Fine. Guess I got a little carried away." She started making her way from the stands. "Sorry," she murmured, careful not to step on anyone's purse, drink, or child.

When she was standing on the platform, the reality of the day hit her. She was here, watching her husband, the father of the baby she carried, ride a bull. A bull. She was angry and relieved and so confused she could hardly see straight. Not that she had any right to be so mad—she'd been the one who'd forced him to ride. What was wrong with her? Why was she such a mess? Why did watching him tonight terrify her so? He was fine. Now she could relax. And when Ryder made his way onto the platform, making his way through handshakes and claps on the back, she couldn't decide whether to kiss him or leave.

His blue eyes found her and time seemed to stop. His cheeks were tinged with a ruddy flush. He moved with a sense of confidence. And the look on his face, the pure satisfaction, unlocked something deep inside her. He was so damn handsome, demanding her attention, her body's response, it worried her. Ryder would never be controlled—he wasn't built that way. It would be better if she kept him at a distance, smarter. But she didn't want to.

His expression shifted. His gaze swept her from her boot-clad feet to the headband she'd slipped on before they left. By the time he stood before her, the look in his eyes had her heart pounding a mile a minute. He stopped inches from her, the muscles of his jaw taut.

She wanted to wrap her arms around him, but said instead, "That was some ride."

He grinned, but the slightest furrow marred his brow. "You okay?"

"I'm a little wound up, I guess." That was putting it mildly. Never in her adult life had she fantasized about being kissed, passionately and publicly. But that's what she was thinking about. She wanted him to kiss her, to reassure her he was here, alive and well.

"Wound up?" he asked, leaning close. "You cold?"

She shook her head, then nodded. His arms slowly slid around her waist, triggering a shudder so strong she swayed into him. She stared at the pressed and starched blue shirt beneath her fingers, comforted by the feel of his heartbeat beneath her palm.

"Annabeth?" His voice was low and rough, drawing her gaze to his. "What's wrong?"

She couldn't put it into words. It had been so long since she'd felt like a woman, since she'd been aware of a man the way she was aware of him. It was exhilarating—and absolutely terrifying. "I guess I got scared." She tried to smile. "Been a while since I've seen you risking life and limb, you know?"

The furrow on his brow deepened. "Worried about me?"

She swallowed, the knot in her throat preventing her from answering. So she shrugged, staring at his chest again.

"Hey." He tipped her head back.

She hadn't meant to stare at his mouth, but she did. And her imagination went crazy.

"You keep that up and I'll kiss you." His whisper was husky, making her shudder again.

Her gaze met his, locking with those baby blues.

"You're beautiful." His gaze traveled over her face. "And, after some dancing, there will be some kissing."

She stepped away from him then, tugging the coat closed. "Then let's go dancing."

The look of surprise on his face had her laughing.

The rest of the night was like a dream. He took her to the only bar in Stonewall Crossing the locals frequented. She'd been there a handful of times, but had quickly learned that socializing with her students' parents could have negative side effects. Those times, she'd tended to hang by the pool tables, not the large retrofitted barn dance hall in the back. She loved dancing but since Greg died, she hadn't danced.

Ryder was the perfect gentleman, all charm and sass. He proudly introduced her to people she didn't know and reintroduced her as Mrs. Boone to those she did. After the initial shock, the response was pretty positive. And the shock was to be expected. He was who he was, with the reputation he had. To say settling down with the elementary school principal was a little out of character was a huge understatement.

"If he was going to settle down, there was no doubting who it'd be with." John Hardy, Ryder's boss at the garage, was all smiles.

Annabeth smiled back at him. "Are you saying he's been sweet on me?" She had to ask.

John laughed. "Oh, honey, that's an understatement."

Ryder's arm rested along the back of her chair, his fingers playing absently with her hair. He was talking to another man, Mario Rodriguez, one of the vet techs at the teaching hospital, totally unaware of their conversation.

"I never knew." Annabeth had a hard time believing Ryder cared about her in a romantic way.

"'Course not." John took a sip from his longneck. He leaned forward, lowering his voice. "Ryder took it hard when Greg died, real hard. Some days I could smell the liquor from the night before in his sweat. He didn't know which way was up. Then you called."

Annabeth leaned forward too, curious. "I called?"

He nodded. "You invited him to dinner."

She'd invited him to dinner several times...

"You lit into him for missing Cody's birthday." John shook his head.

Annabeth remembered then. Two years ago. "Cody was disappointed," she murmured. But that wasn't the whole truth. She'd been disappointed. Not seeing him there, among their friends and family, had felt wrong. If she dared admit it to herself, she'd been relying on Ryder even then.

When she looked at John, he was watching her. "He needed to know you missed him. That was all the permission he needed, I think."

"Permission?" she asked.

"To love you." John smiled.

To love her? Her heart twisted sharply. He loved her and Cody, she didn't doubt that. They were his family. But he didn't *love* love her. If he was dropping hints about getting her into bed—well, he was a man. And men rarely passed on the opportunity to jump into bed with a woman, according to every single female she knew. She was there. He was there. They were married. Why not hop into bed and make the most of the opportunity?

She looked at Ryder. How many nights had she

woken up hot and bothered and tangled in twisted sheets? But could she live out those incredible dreams without falling in love with him? Because, if she gave in, she worried this time her heart would never recover.

The music changed, dropping into an easy rhythm, and Ryder took her hand. "Dancing time."

She clung to his hand and followed him onto the dance floor, a bundle of nerves. "Go easy on me. It's been a long time."

He spun her into him, sliding one arm around her waist. He dropped a soft kiss onto her lips. "Like riding a bike." His words tickled her ear. She was mind-numbingly aware of his hand on her lower back, of the intensity in his pale blue eyes. He pulled her closer, leaving no space between them. "Just hold on to me." And he started moving.

She couldn't think. She should be concentrating on not breaking his toes, but she couldn't break the hold of his gaze. Melting into him was her only option, so she did. He led, guiding her around the room with ease, as if there was no one else on the hardwood floor.

When the music ended, his hold didn't loosen.

She smiled, her nerves over dancing replaced by something entirely different.

The fiddler started again, the notes fast and short. Ryder grinned. "I've always wanted to do this with you." He took her hand and stepped away from her.

Always wanted?

It was the last thought she had before the steps demanded her attention. It took a while for them to get their speed up, but they figured it out. He pulled her in, turned them around then spun her up and under his arm before drawing her back into his chest. Faster and faster, they spun around the floor. The faster the music, the faster Ryder moved. Annabeth was downright breathless by the time the final note played.

"Damn, Princess." Ryder laughed, breathing hard.

"Not so bad yourself," she answered, laughing in turn.

"This next one is for Stonewall Crossing's own newlyweds, Annabeth and Ryder Boone," the band leader announced. "I, for one, am plum tickled to hear about this match."

The bright lights dimmed and the music slowed.

She stepped into Ryder, slipping her arm tight around his waist. From the look on his face, he seemed to approve. He kissed her forehead, took her hand in his and tucked her head against his chin. She rested her head on his chest, wrapped in his scent, the thundering of his heart and overwhelming happiness.

He was in love. He always had been—always would be. She was his wife, his Princess.

Holding her close, breathing her in, he knew he was where he needed to be. More important, he was where he wanted to be. He could only wish someday she'd feel the same.

His fingers slid through her long hair, stroking the fine strands between thumb and forefinger. If he angled his head just right, he could bury his nose in her hair and savor the citrus warmth of her scent. So he did, pressing her against him until her heartbeat echoed his.

The last call came two hours later, but they were still wrapped up on the dance floor. Spinning her like crazy, moving slow and holding her close, whatever it took to keep her in his arms. Maybe it was because everyone knew they were newlyweds, or it was clear he wasn't in the mood to share her, but no one tried to cut in.

"We just wanna thank y'all for a fantastic Saturday night. We'll be back the end of the month. Hope to see some of you then." The singer of the band tipped his hat back and took a bow.

"We'll have to come back," Annabeth said, clapping. "We could bring Cody. There's enough kids his age…" But her words cut short and her smile faded away. "Maybe." He watched her eyes sweep the room, no doubt evaluating the other kids that were there. Were they the kind of kids who would tease Cody? Or would he spend the night running around, having fun, smiling and laughing?

"Bet he'd enjoy it." Ryder took her hand as he led her off the dance floor. "We could bring Eli with us. The two of them seem to get along real well."

Annabeth's hazel gaze found his. "That might work."

Ryder held her white wool coat out. "I'm not just a pretty face, Princess."

She rolled her eyes, a bubble of laughter spilling from her full red lips. "Ryder—"

He slid her coat on and pressed a kiss to her cheek. "How are you feeling?"

"Exhausted." She turned, smiling up at him. "Thank you. I haven't had this much fun in years."

He shook his head. "That's a crime, Mrs. Boone."

She blushed, turning a very pretty color of pink. "It's just the way it is—"

"Was." He tugged on his leather jacket. "You ready?"

He didn't know why he felt nervous. Tonight had changed things. It wasn't about getting Annabeth into bed—not anymore. Maybe it was because he knew how he felt about her. He'd slept with plenty of women, but he'd never been in love with them. No, now it was about getting Annabeth—and keeping her. But he had no idea where to start—

"Penny for your thoughts?" Annabeth's question broke the silence on the short drive home.

"Nothing worth sharing." He was still coming to terms with the fact that he was in love with her.

"Work? Rodeo? Family?" she probed.

He glanced at her. "You light up when you dance. Must have missed it."

"After Greg died, it wasn't…a priority." She paused. "I don't know. Cody was a baby and Grandma Flo was just starting to get sick. And I was a single working parent." She started to laugh. "Dancing seemed…frivolous."

He looked at her then, a wave of admiration washing over him. She'd done so much on her own. "You're quite a woman."

She rolled her eyes. "I know, a real *Princess*."

He pulled into the driveway, put the truck in Park and looked at her. "You're stronger than most men I know."

The cab was dimly lit, but he knew her cheeks were tinged with color. She didn't know what to do with his compliments or how to respond.

"I'm waiting," she murmured, her fingers absentmindedly picking at the stitches on her wool coat.

"For?" But he knew. Normally he'd tack on some smart-ass comeback. Teasing had always been his way of keeping things from getting too serious. Now, serious was what he wanted.

She frowned.

"I mean it." He wanted to say something more, to tell her how special she was. But the words wouldn't come.

A furrow formed between her brows, but she didn't say anything. Instead, she turned her full attention to the bit of thread she'd worked loose on her coat. "We still haven't worked through what we're doing…how we're doing it."

"It?" he asked.

"The whole being-temporarily-married thing." She stumbled over the words.

Temporary. His lungs emptied, hard and fast. She wanted to make temporary plans. He wanted to make a real family. Now he needed to convince her of that.

"I imagine you have a few ideas." He leaned against his door. He stared out the front windshield of the truck, feeling like an idiot. Getting a woman into bed was a hell of a lot easier than getting into her heart. "Inside? Before all the heat's gone."

She nodded, sliding out of the truck without a word. He followed, fighting back his frustration and defeat.

Tom greeted them inside the door, mewing pathetically and winding between their legs.

"Guess he got lonely," Ryder said.

"Tom!" Annabeth froze in the kitchen door.

Ryder peeked over her shoulder. "He got lonely all right." Shredded bits of paper towel were spread all over the kitchen. Even the now-empty cardboard rolls were gnawed and tattered. "Come on, Mom, he got bored."

Annabeth glared at him. "Couldn't he read a book or something?"

"Bet he'd get a kick out of that." Ryder laughed, his mood lightening. "Rip it to pieces."

Annabeth shook her head, stooping to pick up the

kitten that all but trembled from the power of his purring. "You are naughty." She held him close, her nose wrinkling up. "And you still stink." She giggled as he reached out with kneading paws. "Yes, yes, you're adorable." But she kept him at arm's length, her lips pressed tight.

Tom's purr echoed in the room.

"Tom, you be nice. She still loves you, but your... cologne might not agree with her delicate condition."

Annabeth sighed with exasperation—but she was smiling.

"The little guy can't help it, Princess. Cats are curious, it's in their nature." He took the kitten. "And he's a boy, so there's bound to be some mischief."

"Because mischief is part of the male's DNA?" she asked.

He nodded.

"You're making me rethink the need for a cat." She pulled the broom off the hook on the wall.

"Ah, come on now." Ryder put the squirming kitten down. "He's cute." He pushed off the door frame. "I'll clean up this time."

"Since this mess is your fault," she murmured.

He laughed.

"If you're sure you've got it under control, I'll get the chart." It was a question; he heard it.

"Discussing Option A?" He drew in a deep breath. "I think I can handle this."

She paused, her hazel eyes lingering on his face. "Thanks again—for tonight." She smiled. "I had a really nice time."

He didn't understand the look on her face, the way her gaze searched his. Now would be a good time to say something…sweet. But all the words he wanted to say lodged in his throat, making it impossible to say a thing. He cleared his throat, nodded and watched her walk away.

He dispensed with the paper towel while she busied herself in the living room. Once he was finished, he joined her there. Option A sucked. Living arrangements, time periods, divorce deadlines and custody arrangements… Not exactly what he was hoping for. Sure, she might have tried to show him that night, but he'd been too busy freaking out over getting her pregnant to think straight. Now… His stomach hurt as he read over it once, then again, before looking at her. "This is your plan?" he asked.

She nodded. "I don't want you to have to postpone the new job." She pointed at the chart but he didn't look away from her. "I figure the less time we live together, the easier it will be for Cody."

"I told you I wasn't going anywhere," he argued.

"And I told you I wasn't going to ruin this opportunity for you." She crossed her arms. "I won't do it. You've wanted to leave for…forever. Cody and I have a life here. I want to raise him here. I'll never keep the baby from you, ever. If you prefer, we'll work out set custody terms—alternating holidays and weekends." She shook her head. "It's just, this is home. And your family will want to be a part of this, too…"

"So they get to be a part of his future, but I get holidays and weekends?"

"If you want—"

"You think it's that easy? That no one's going to care that I up and left you while you were pregnant?" he interrupted, his frustration mounting.

She frowned. "Then why did you marry me?"

He sighed, his hands on his hips. "I told you why."
Stubborn woman.

"To do the right thing? So that's it? You're going to
settle? Life in a town you hate. Working at a place that
will always be your second choice. Married to a woman
you don't love. And saddled with a baby you never
wanted? Every day will be consumed with regret and
resentment. That's no way to live—"

"And you married me because—?" he countered.

"I thought... I don't know. I panicked." She stumbled over her words. "It was temporary. A way for us
both to *survive*."

He stared at the poster. *She still doesn't trust me.* "So
we live together, but apart." He flicked the sticky note
that read No Sexual Relations. "Until May tenth?" He
looked at her. "Why May tenth?"

"It's after the school board meeting. And it's a school
holiday, a long weekend. I can send Cody to the Uptons and you can go to Dallas, if they'll let you wait?"
she asked. "It'll be easier for you to move out..." She
grabbed his arm. "*I'm* going to take the fall for this. I
will make this okay."

"No one will believe it, Princess." He smiled, covering her hand with his. He tried to keep the sneer off
his face. "I'm good at being the bad guy."

She shook her head. "I'll tell everyone I still love
Greg. No one can argue with that." She paused. "We're
friends, Ryder, good friends. And, together, we'll be
good parents."

Her words cut like a knife. "If this is what you want,
I'll try." But not for Option A. No, he'd try his hardest
to win her heart.

He stared at the chart again, drawing in a deep breath. The sooner Option A was on a burn pile or shredded in the trash, the happier he'd be. Nothing got in his way when he set his mind to it. And he'd set his mind on keeping his wife.

Chapter 10

"Mom!" Cody climbed out of her father-in-law's car and came barreling across the yard to her waiting arms.

Annabeth swallowed the butterflies and caught Cody in a big hug. "Missed you."

"I missed you, too. How is Tom?" he asked. "Hey, R-Ryder," he added, grinning at Ryder.

"Tom's a little smelly," she said, wrinkling her nose. "Ryder and I really tried to clean him up, but I think skunk spray must have some glue in it."

"Skunk?" Cody frowned. "How'd he get o-o-outside?"

"He must have slipped out." Annabeth shrugged. "I think it turned out for the best, though. He doesn't want out anymore."

"You should have seen your mom, Cody. She was covered in tomato juice, from head to toe." Ryder laughed.

"Get p-pictures?" Cody asked.

"No." Annabeth sighed. "He acted like a true gentle-man—until he mentioned it now."

"I would've liked to see that myself." Her father-in-law laughed. "I've rarely seen her with a hair out of place."

"Good to see you, Major." Annabeth kissed the older man on the cheek. "Good weekend?"

"With Cody around? Of course." He grinned at his grandson. "Nice to see you, Ryder. You're looking fit." He shook Ryder's hand.

Annabeth watched, nervous over the Major and Judy's reaction to her marriage. They'd always loved Ryder. And, after last night, she was truly worried about making him the villain when she knew he was the hero.

Ryder nodded. "You, too, sir."

"It's been a long time." Judy hugged her, then Ryder. She looked back and forth between the two of them, smiling. "Seeing you together... I almost expect Greg to walk out that door...any minute." Her voice trembled a little, the smile on her face dimming.

The Major was surprisingly demonstrative with his wife, something Annabeth had always loved about him. So it was no surprise to see him wrap a supporting arm around his wife's waist.

"We all miss him," Ryder said.

She looked at him, taking in the very real grief on his face. Of course he missed Greg. He'd been his best friend, his brother, his sounding board about life. They had that in common, missing Greg. She smiled at Ryder, clasping her hands so she wouldn't be tempted to reach for him.

It was unexpected, how easy it was to fall into a routine with this man. He'd tried to sleep in Cody's bed last night, but it was too small. And the couch was hard as rocks. So, for the second night in a row, she'd slept wrapped in his arms. And she'd actually slept, without dreams or interruption, just deep, invigorating, peaceful sleep. Waking up was another matter. She'd never woken up so responsive—and hungry—for another's touch.

Not that she needed to be thinking about it now, face-to-face with Greg's parents.

"Come meet Tom!" Cody waved his grandparents into the house excitedly.

"Can't wait to meet him. I feel like I know him already." Judy smiled at her as she followed Cody down the hall to his bedroom.

"Want a drink?" Annabeth asked her father-in-law.

"Thank you, Annabeth." The Major sat. "What have you been up to, Ryder? Judy and I saw you last season when you came through at the Marble Falls rodeo. She about came unglued when you got carried out of the arena after that bull turned his head into your shoulder." The Major shook his head. "Damn physical work."

"Lucky nothing broke that time," Ryder admitted, glancing quickly at her. "Been spending a lot more time working at John Hardy's garage, less time on a bull."

"That's good to hear." The Major sounded genuinely relieved.

Ryder smiled. "A fella's luck can only last so long."

She didn't want to think about that. "Day jobs aren't too bad," she interrupted. "As long as you like what you do." She loved her job—headaches and all.

"How's the school?" The Major accepted the glass of ice tea she offered him. "Thank you."

She wrinkled her nose. "I'm looking forward to summer."

"Cody was telling us you're worrying over your job?"

She blinked. "He was?" So much for trying to shield Cody from stress. She frowned, quickly explaining things. "There's no point in worrying over it, I know that. Grandma Flo would tell me to keep my chin up and my big-girl britches on."

Major and Ryder laughed.

"Good advice, I suppose," the Major said with a chuckle.

"You'll keep the job." Ryder was so confident.

She shrugged, unable to ignore the pleasure his words stirred. His belief in her meant more than it should. "We'll see."

Judy joined them then, a strange look on her face. "I know this is none of my business…" Judy glanced over her shoulder then whispered, "Is there a man in your life, Annabeth?"

"Why on earth would you ask her that, Judy?" The Major looked stunned.

"There's a man's shirt on her bed," Judy said. "And a pair of boots peeking out from under her bed. Not that I was snooping… The door was open…"

All eyes were on her. And, from the heat in her face, she knew she was turning very red. The Major scowled, Judy tried for a smile and Ryder looked ready to laugh.

"Do we know him?" the Major asked.

She opened her mouth, but Judy interrupted. "How does Cody feel about him?"

She took Judy's hand in hers, knowing her mother-in-law worried about anything that would threaten the bond she had with her only grandchild. "Cody loves him, very much." Which was absolutely true.

Judy nodded, visibly relieved. "Well, then, I like him already."

"What's his full name?" the Major asked. "And his birthday."

"Major, you are not going to run a background check on him," Judy chastised.

Ryder chuckled then, earning the full weight of the Major's scowl and a disapproving shake of Judy's head. He held up his hands in surrender. "No need." He took a deep breath. "I'm the no-good man in her life. We got married this weekend."

The kitchen was absolutely silent.

Ryder glanced back and forth between Judy and the Major, all teasing gone. "I promise you both, I'll do right by her, by Cody, and Greg, too."

Pressure squeezed her chest, momentarily knocking the breath out of her. Whether it was the look on Ryder's face or the weight of his words, she couldn't be sure. When he reached out to her, she took his hand and let him draw her into his side.

Judy burst into tears. "I'm so happy." She sniffed, taking the handkerchief her husband offered her. "I prayed, you have no idea how hard I prayed."

The Major took Ryder's hand, pumping it heartily. "Guess I can't say I'm completely surprised, but it would've been nice to have been at the wedding."

"We just went to the justice of the peace. I didn't want anything fancy this time around. But Renata is planning quite a party, and I hope you'll come," she said to soothe the Major. "It would mean a lot…if you're free."

"Of course we'll come." Judy was still dabbing at her tears. "Cody will be over the moon."

Annabeth nodded.

"'Bout what?" Cody carried Tom into the room.

"Your mom has some big news," the Major spoke. "Your Grandma and I are going to head out. But we'll see you later this week?"

Annabeth frowned. "You're not staying for dinner?"

"Not tonight." The Major shook his head. "You have a nice dinner, just your little family—this time."

"Once we know what Renata's planned, we'll let you know," Ryder agreed.

After another ten minutes of goodbye hugs and happy tears, Annabeth flopped onto the couch and patted the cushion next to her.

Cody sat, looking up at her with round eyes. "What's wrong?"

"Nothing," she reassured, taking his hands in hers. "Nothing at all. I have to tell you something and it just occurred to me you might be mad about it."

"Why?" Cody asked.

Annabeth glanced at Ryder, who shrugged. "Well, I probably should have talked to you about it—"

"I should have asked you first," Ryder jumped in, sitting beside Cody.

"Asked?"

"If I could marry your mom." Ryder's words were so calm it took a minute for Annabeth to realize what he'd said.

"M-marry Mom?" Cody looked back and forth between the two of them. "You want *me* to say if it's o-okay?"

Ryder nodded.

Cody stood up and faced them. He crossed his little arms over his chest, tapping his left pointer finger on his chin. Annabeth couldn't help but smile, glancing Ryder's way to gauge his reaction. Ryder wasn't smiling. If anything, he looked worried.

"Will you help her?" Cody asked. "So she d-doesn't have to w-worry 'bout money?"

She leaned forward, resting her elbows on her knees. "Cody—"

"Yes." Ryder nodded.

"She works so hard because she *has* to." Cody glanced at her, almost apologetically. "So she can take care of me and G-Grandma Flo. But you can h-help with all that."

"I will." Ryder nodded. "But I'll tell you, Cody, I've never known your mom to do something she didn't want to do."

She sat back, listening to them. Apparently her son knew everything. Relying on Ryder to "fix it" didn't sit well with her, though. She couldn't afford to trust anyone else. It was a risk, relying on him, for her or her children's future.

"I guess." Cody shrugged.

"Are you two done? Not that either of you asked, but I love my job." She sighed. "I feel important—and I like being able to provide for you." She stood, ruffling Cody's hair as she headed into the kitchen. "Anyone want some lemonade?"

"No, th-thank you," Cody answered.

She glanced back, waiting for Ryder's response. But that's when she saw it. Ryder loved Cody. There was no denying the tenderness on his face, the look of a father. It took her breath away.

Ryder's pale blue eyes settled on her. "I'm good."

She nodded, hurrying into the kitchen. Her heart was pounding. Just when she thought she knew how to handle Ryder Boone, he threw her a curveball. It was one thing to be a gentleman, to step up when he should. It was another thing altogether to let another man's child into his heart—to love unconditionally.

She took a sip of lemonade and her stomach growled. She glanced down, placing both hands over the slight swell of her belly. She should eat something.

"Ma?" Cody asked, standing in the doorway with Ryder. "You o-okay?" Her son was looking at her, but Ryder was staring at her stomach. Ryder's hand rested on Cody's shoulder.

"I'm good." She smoothed her shirt. "What did you two decide?"

"Yes. Of c-course." Cody looked up at Ryder. "I'm glad he's g-gonna be my dad."

Ryder nodded, squeezing his shoulder.

Her heart ached at her son's easy declaration. She looked at Ryder, then Cody, and blew out a slow breath. Maybe her plan was a huge mistake. One that would hurt everyone. Not that there was anything she could do about it now. She nodded, forcing herself to smile. "Now that that's decided, how about you tell me what we're making for dinner with Grandma Flo," she said, opening the refrigerator and looking inside. There wasn't much to choose from. Grocery shopping hadn't been a priority this weekend.

"Waffles?" Cody asked, staring into the fridge.

She smiled down at him. How many nights had she fed him waffles recently? For the evenings when she was too tired to cook a real meal, waffles had become a staple. Not that Cody complained. He didn't complain about anything.

"Waffles sound good," Ryder agreed. "You're in luck. I can actually cook waffles." He moved the milk jug. "And bacon. And eggs."

"You think Grandma Flo will approve?" she asked.

"She wants to be with us, Ma." Cody smiled. "I don't think she cares 'bout the food."

That was one long sentence. A long sentence without a single stutter. She glanced at Ryder, saw the smile he was wearing and knew he'd caught it, too.

"What time do we need to get her?" Ryder asked.

Annabeth glanced at the clock. It was four thirty. On a Sunday. The weekend had gone too fast. "Now."

"Cody and I'll go," Ryder offered. "In case there's something you need to do to get ready for the week."

"Yeah, Ma, you chill," Cody piped up.

"Chill?" She burst out laughing.

Cody nodded, grinning.

"I'll get some laundry going and then I'll chill." She ruffled his hair.

Cody stood on tiptoe, kissing her cheek. Ryder leaned forward, adding his kiss to her cheek. Cody's grin grew bigger.

She rolled her eyes, making Ryder wiggle his eyebrows at her. "We'll be back shortly, Mrs. Boone."

Cody giggled, all but bouncing out the front door.

Ryder was exhausted and it was only Tuesday. The past few weeks had been some of the best of his life. He had a family, one he was proud of. There were lots of smiles around the dinner table, easy conversation and active interest in each other.

Last night had been…different and frustrating. A lot of his frustration was his own fault. He knew he should sleep on her lumpy couch at night, but he couldn't do it. Lying next to Annabeth, feeling her against him, was something he looked forward to all day. But last night she'd been restless. She'd whispered Greg's name in her sleep, almost a plea. Guilt consumed him, followed by anger. Not at her, or Greg, but himself. Even now, she'd pick Greg over him. Because she could rely on Greg— something she still couldn't do with him. As misplaced as it was, he was jealous. Of Greg. His dead best friend. What was wrong with him?

He'd stared up at the ceiling, frustration coursing through him. He'd been ready to slip out of bed and the house when she whimpered.

He'd rolled onto his side. Moonlight had spilled through her lace curtains, making it easy to see her erratic breathing, the rapid-fire shift of emotions on her face. Whatever she'd been dreaming about, it wasn't good. He'd pulled her close—to soothe her. And, maybe, himself.

Then her hands had slid down his chest, edging toward the waist of his boxers and making him ache. When he'd tried to disentangle her, she'd kissed him. It had taken every ounce of control not to respond. He'd wanted to—he'd been about to burst. But she'd been asleep. Instead, he'd wrapped her in his arms and tucked her against his chest.

She'd sighed, turning her face into his chest.

He might have controlled his body, but his mind had had other ideas. Every time he would doze off, Annabeth would be there—wanting him as much as he wanted her. He'd wake with a start, on edge and breathing hard. Over and over, all night long. He hadn't gotten much sleep.

He drove by the house, but there was no one there so he headed to the elementary school. Lady Blue was one of the only cars in the parking lot.

He parked and headed inside.

She didn't see him, lost in the pile of files stacked high on her desk. Her cheek rested on one fisted hand. The other tapped a pen against whatever she was reading. She seemed just as tense and edgy as he was.

But then she dropped the pen and leaned back in her chair, covering her stomach with her hands.

"You okay?" he asked.

She almost jumped out of her chair. "You scared me to death."

"Sorry." He came into the office, sitting on the corner of her desk. "Wondering if you were done for the day. If not, I could take Cody home."

She glanced at her computer screen. "Dammit."

He laughed.

"Is it really six o'clock?" she grumbled, standing and stretching.

"Long day?" he asked, noting the circles under her eyes.

"You could say that." She looked at him, frowning.

"What'd I do now?" he asked, longing to pull her against him for a nice long hug.

"This." Her voice was pinched—he'd never heard her sound like that. He took the narrow coil of paper she handed him but stared at her. Something was wrong. Very wrong. "You okay?"

"Look." She all but snapped the word at him.

So he did. The images in the small squares were

black-and-white, too grainy to tell what they were of. "Am I supposed to know what this is?" He stared at the images. Her sigh was so exasperated that he forgot all about the paper he was holding. "What's wrong, Annabeth? Talk to me."

"That's... Those are the babies." Her voice was tight and high-pitched.

He inspected the paper again. "Where?"

She shook her head, leaning against him to point out a white dot. "There...and there." Her finger tapped another dot.

He froze. "Two?"

"Yes, two." There was that strange, squeaky voice again. "Two."

He dropped the paper on the desk and wrapped both arms around her. He pulled her close, offering her comfort he knew she needed. "Hey now," he spoke softly. "It's going to be okay, Annabeth."

She was rigid in his arms.

"Are you okay?" He kept his tone low, soothing. "What did the doctor say?" Why hadn't he known she had a doctor's appointment? He'd have gone with her. He wanted to be a part of this. But, from the way she was acting, now wasn't the time to have that conversation.

"I'm fine. Too skinny, but fine." Her words were mumbled.

She felt just right to him. "We can fix that." His hands kept a steady rhythm, rubbing up and down her back. "Anything else?"

"Besides the fact that there's two of them?" She wasn't squeaking anymore, but she was a long way from relaxed.

He pulled back. "Annabeth."

She looked at him, her hazel eyes sparkling with unshed tears.

He swallowed, fighting the need to run far away from the depths of emotion he saw there. This was Annabeth and she needed him. Right now. He wasn't going anywhere. "Let's go get something to eat, get Cody in bed and I'll give you a foot rub."

Her chin quivered. She took a deep breath and pressed her lips together.

"Everything's going to be okay," he repeated, for both of them. He tilted her head back, pressing a soft kiss to her lips.

She melted against him then, twining her arms around his neck and burying her face against his neck. "And a bubble bath?" she murmured softly.

"Whatever you want, Princess," he promised.

He didn't move, enjoying how they fit together.

"Anything?" she asked.

He swallowed, wishing the memory of his dream didn't immediately spring to mind. He nodded.

"Even if it's ice cream?"

He smiled. "For dinner?"

"Dessert?" She looked up at him, the first glimpse of a smile on her face.

"Definitely." He kissed her again, unable to resist.

And she kissed him back. Soft, sweet, clinging just enough to force his pulse into a rapid beat.

"I like kissing you, Mrs. Boone," he murmured against her lips. "Even if it's not part of Option A."

Her expression changed, uncertain and flustered. Her gaze traveled over his face, that small crease forming between her brows. He reached up, smoothing the crease before cupping her cheek in his palm. Her skin was satin in his rough palm.

"I like ice cream." Her voice wavered.

He shook his head, taking her hand in his. "Let's get out of here then go get my kids and my woman some food."

She paled, tugging free of his hold to turn off her computer. "Give me five minutes?"

"Sure." He shoved his hands into his pockets. "Where's Cody?"

"In the gym. Now that he's figured out how to dribble, he can't get enough of it." She didn't look at him as she tidied the stacks on her desk.

"I'll go get him." Women were emotional when they were expecting, or so he'd heard. If she was all over the place right now, he needed to be as calm as possible. Even though he wasn't.

Twins. One baby was challenging. But twins? He grinned.

He headed for the gym, remembering all of the concerts and events he'd attended for Hunter's son, Eli. It only now occurred to him that he was going to be spending a lot of time here. Between Annabeth, Cody and the babies… Well, he might as well get comfortable with the place.

Chapter 11

"You're the luckiest woman on the planet." Janet Garza pulled her copies off the copy machine. "Seriously, you have no idea how jealous Abigail, Lori and Maricella are. When he came up here to pick up Cody... The things they're saying about what they want to do to your husband." She fanned herself with a bundle of papers. "I guess it's okay, as long as none of the kids overhear. We'd be corrupting minors." She laughed.

Annabeth smiled, pulling the ink refill cartridge from the supply cabinet before locking it. "I don't think I want to know."

"Probably not. Not that I'd peg you as the jealous overprotective type, but I wouldn't want you to harbor any negative thoughts about coworkers." Janet winked.

She didn't think she was normally very jealous or overprotective, but that's exactly the way she was feeling. "Which is why you're telling me this?" Annabeth shook her head. She and Janet had taught the fourth grade together for three years. Annabeth respected her as a teacher and liked her as a person, but Janet was fond of telling a good tale.

Janet shrugged. "I didn't say anything. Not really." She pressed some more buttons, then turned. "Oh, but I didn't get to tell you about Winnie."

Annabeth held up her hand. The last thing she wanted was information on Winnie Michaels—unless she was moving. "I'll take a pass on that one, Janet." She glanced at the clock. "The decorating committee's in the gym to set up for the spring concert tomorrow." She waved at Janet, dropped off the ink cartridge in her office and headed to the gym—also their cafeteria. It was lunchtime, so the noise level was a low roar. The old-fashioned street sign in the corner reminded the students to keep their chatter at yellow or below. It was yellow but, to Annabeth's ears, it was nearing the red light.

A few moms and one father stood on the small stage, several boxes stacked in front of them. Annabeth knew them all by name—they were the go-to parents for every event throughout the year.

"Good to see you, Holly, Jim, Irene and Carol." She shook each of their hands. "What's the plan for tomorrow night?"

"Well, hello, Mrs. *Boone*." Carol nudged her with her elbow. "How have you been? Anything exciting happen recently?"

"Oh, that's right, I think I heard something?" Holly joined in.

Jim just shook his head, chuckling.

"I'm sure it's just gossip," Irene added, grinning. "Right, Mrs. *Boone*?"

Annabeth resisted the urge to roll her eyes. "You mean me getting married?" she asked. "Yes, it's true."

"Nothing wrong with marrying your best friend," Jim mumbled. "Solid start."

Annabeth nodded. It was a good reason for getting married. And a much better reason than Ryder getting her knocked up. With twins. *Twins*. She swallowed, still digesting yesterday's news. "Thank you, Jim."

She laughed through the chorus of congratulations and hugs, wanting to talk about anything but her marriage. Her constant state of frustration, her irritability—she didn't know why she couldn't shake it. All she wanted was some time to herself, to have a long cry… or to take her husband to bed and do all the things she'd been dreaming about. She couldn't take any more surprises—she needed continuity and reliability. Things she knew Ryder couldn't offer her.

Carol was talking. "…and Holly found a bunch of flower garlands and lantern lights on clearance last year—"

"Couldn't get the box in my car but I'll bring it up after school," Holly offered.

"Besides the ladder, what will you need?" Annabeth asked.

"Able bodies," Jim interjected. "Maybe you can ask that new husband of yours to come lend a hand."

"I'll ask him," she agreed reluctantly. She didn't want Ryder to become a fixture here, too. It was bad enough that he'd slipped so easily into her life. He was everywhere, a reminder of everything she wanted but was destined to lose again. The sound of his voice eased her.

His scent both calmed and excited her. She couldn't wait for bedtime so his arms would cradle her against him all night long. It was ridiculous. She was *acting* ridiculous.

And then there was Cody. He was crazy about Ryder and he had no problem showing it. Ryder seemed just as enamored with his stepson, holding his hand, answering the million questions Cody would ask about cars and the rodeo at the dinner table. But what would happen when Ryder left? Cody would be crushed.

And it would be her fault. Since he'd been born, she'd invested so much time and energy into making sure Cody was taken care of. Now one stupid mistake could break his little heart.

"Can we send out this reminder note?" Irene asked, holding out a paper to her.

Annabeth scanned the note, nodding. "Sure. It'll go home this afternoon."

"I think that's everything." Holly shrugged. "I'll bring the box up after school."

"And I'll try to get some extra hands to help out," Annabeth assured them, her attention wandering around the cafeteria. Kindergarten and first grade were eating now, requiring all hands on deck.

"Two big nights in one week," Irene spoke up. "Hope you don't have to work too late this week, or you'll be wiped out before your party this weekend."

This weekend. The wedding party. Right.

Renata had been as good as her word. It seemed like all of Stonewall Crossing was coming to the Lodge on the Boone Ranch Friday night for her and Ryder's wedding party. It was Wednesday and she was already dreading it. As if her pregnancy nausea wasn't bad enough, now her stress was getting out of control.

"Isn't the school board meeting this week?" Jim asked.

"No," Annabeth assured him. "Not yet." She smiled. She had a few more weeks to worry over a job she couldn't afford to lose—especially not with twins on the way. Annabeth turned right as a piece of fruit cocktail flew across the cafeteria. "That's my call."

"Go get 'em," Carol called after her.

Annabeth made her way to the kindergarten table. She arched her discipline eyebrow and waited. At this age, all it took was a stern face before the culprit came clean. Sure enough, Hugh burst into apologetic tears.

"He didn't mean to, Ms. Upton," another classmate, Franz, sounded off. "It…slipped."

Annabeth refused to smile. "It slipped?"

Hugh, still crying, looked at Franz in sheer confusion. But Franz refused to budge. "Off his spoon."

Annabeth narrowed her eyes. "Will any more fruit be slipping off your spoon?"

Every head at the table shook simultaneously, making it even harder to maintain her disciplinarian stance. "I hope not."

She walked around the cafeteria, trying to ignore the way her stomach rebelled. She couldn't throw up; there was nothing left in her stomach. And she didn't want to go back to her office. Sitting only made it worse. Being up and walking around made her stomach bearable—most of the time.

"My turn," Ken Branson said as he approached her.

"It's fine." She smiled.

"No, really, I'll take it from here," he assured, patting her shoulder.

"Okay." She headed back to the main office, confused by Ken's willingness to stay in the cafeteria. He hated cafeteria duty. He hated pretty much anything to do with actual kid interaction at this point. Once she walked into the main office, his attitude made sense. Kevin Michaels sat, his arms crossed, scowling. When he was angry, there was no doubting he was Winnie's son.

"Is Kevin here to see me, Ms. Barnes?" Annabeth asked the school secretary.

"Yes, ma'am." Mrs. Barnes nodded, looking apologetic.

"Do you have a teacher's referral for me?" she asked Kevin.

He thrust the paper at her but wouldn't look at her.

Annabeth scanned over the notes the teacher had made. "Looks like we need to have a talk in my office."

Kevin looked at her then, so angry his jaw was tight. "Gonna call my mom?"

Annabeth read over the referral again. *Maybe not.* "I'd like to hear your side of things first."

Apparently that wasn't the answer he was expecting. His eyebrows rose and his jaw relaxed a little. He stood, leading the way to her office. Once he was seated in one of the two chairs facing her desk, she sat in the other.

"Why did you threaten to punch Billy in the face?" she asked.

Kevin frowned, crossing his arms over his chest.

"You and Billy are friends," she prodded gently.

Kevin glanced at her, then at the picture of Cody on her desk. He frowned. "He said something."

Annabeth's stomach chose that moment to make a sci-fi movie sound.

Kevin laughed, too surprised not to. "You okay,

Ms. Upton?" He looked at Cody's picture again. "Mrs. Boone."

"Haven't had time for lunch." She tried to redirect him. "What did Billy say? *Exactly?*"

Kevin sighed. "He was talking about my mom."

Annabeth didn't say a word. Kevin Michaels might be a pain in her rear, but he loved his mother. "Can you tell me what he said?" Her stomach clenched, so she shifted in her chair.

Kevin shook his head.

"How about you write it down." She shifted again, trying to find a comfortable position.

Kevin didn't react.

Annabeth stood, rifling through her drawer for a packet of crackers. "I can call Billy in," she offered.

Kevin shook his head fiercely.

"Kevin, if you're not willing to tell me what happened, then I don't have a choice." She broke off a tiny piece of cracker and chewed it slowly. She was out of ginger ale, so this would have to do. "This is your chance."

"He said my mom was a piece of trash and nobody likes her." Kevin's voice hitched. "And he called me a liar."

Annabeth's heart sank. Nobody liked to hear someone talk about their family that way. "What happened before that?"

Kevin leaned forward, his face turning red. "You mean did I do something?" he yelled.

"I need the whole picture, Kevin." Annabeth stayed calm. "Billy had no right to say those things, but it will help me decide how to handle it if I know everything."

Kevin sat back, crossing his arms over his chest again.

She sat at her desk, turning her attention to the paperwork spread out across her desk. If he wasn't ready to talk, she'd give him some time to think things through. Kevin was very good at pressing buttons. Something more had happened to make Billy fight back.

"I said Ryder Boone had asked my mom to marry him and she turned him down." Kevin's words were thick, as though he was having to work to get them out.

Once they were, Annabeth wasn't sure what to do about it. Billy's parents worked on the Boone Ranch—his mother was a cook at the Lodge and his father a gamekeeper. So Billy, like so many in Stonewall Crossing, were protective of the Boone family.

"Is that true?" Annabeth asked. She knew it wasn't.

Kevin scowled at her.

"Kevin—"

"Why wouldn't it be?" Kevin snapped. "My mom's way prettier than you are." Kevin's voice rose as he kept talking. "And I don't talk funny like Cody does. He could love us, if he wanted to. Why wouldn't he want us instead of you?" He sniffed, on the verge of tears. "Why not?"

He broke her heart. She couldn't be mad at him, even if the words were hard to hear. Every boy wanted a father, someone to love their mother. By defending the Boones, Billy had hit on Kevin's biggest weakness.

Movement in the doorway caught her eye. Bryan Goebel stood there, hovering just outside, probably concerned over Kevin's noise level. She gave the slightest shake of her head. He stepped back, but his shadow lingered on her office floor.

"People can't choose who they love, Kevin." She spoke softly. "It's hard, isn't it, living without a dad?"

"You don't know." Kevin frowned at her. "Your life is perfect."

She folded her hands on her desk, swallowing down the laughter his words stirred. "My parents died when I was in first grade. In a car crash."

Kevin's eyes went round.

"I moved here to live with my grandmother." She shrugged. "She took good care of me, but it wasn't the same."

"My dad left when I was in second grade."

Annabeth knew the story. Most of Stonewall Crossing did. While Winnie Michaels had a questionable and very public relationship with a married man, Winnie's husband got involved with that man's wife. They left town together—leaving Kevin behind. As far as Annabeth knew, the only good thing about Kevin's father was the reliability of his child support.

"It's hard. And it hurts." She nodded, searching for the right words. She didn't know what to do for Kevin. But she wished he was involved in something, some outlet that would keep him out of his toxic home environment and let off some steam for a few hours each day.

Kevin stared at his hands. "I get angry sometimes."

"We all do." She nodded. "How we deal with the anger is what matters."

"*You* get angry?" From the look on his face, he didn't believe her.

She smiled, nodding. "Yes, I do."

"Doubt it." He shrugged, then asked, "So what's my punishment?"

"What do you think it should be?" she asked.

He looked at her, thinking hard. Finally, he shrugged again.

"I have an idea." She sat forward. "Coach Goebel, are you out there?"

Bryan popped his head in.

"Didn't you say you needed some help after school? Inflating balls, checking gym equipment and scraping the marks off the court?" she asked, hoping he'd take the not-so-subtle hint she was sending him.

"Yes, ma'am." He nodded, walking into her office.

Kevin looked up at him, surprised. "After school?"

"Yep." Coach Goebel nodded.

"For at least the rest of the week," Annabeth added. "I'll have to tell your mom, Kevin."

"Okay." He nodded, looking back and forth between the two adults.

"You can go back to class now," Annabeth said. "But ask your teacher to send Billy to me."

Kevin frowned. "Can't I just apologize to him? He never would have said that if I…if I hadn't made that stuff up about my mom and Mr. Boone."

Annabeth's stomach made another disturbingly loud noise, drawing Bryan's and Kevin's eyes her way. "I think apologizing would be the right thing to do. But I still need to talk to Billy about choosing his words more carefully." She might not be a Winnie Michaels fan, but calling the woman trash wasn't okay. "Please think about what I said though, Kevin. We can't pick who we love—that applies to our friends, too."

Kevin nodded, then hurried out of her office.

She really wanted to rest her head on her desk. And she really wanted to throw up the small amount of cracker she'd just eaten into her trash can. But Coach Goebel was still there, watching her. As ridiculous as it sounded, there was still the chance Bryan Goebel was

Ken Branson's ally. And, even though she felt like quitting this very minute, she would not give up this job.

"I didn't mean to interrupt, but I heard him yelling and thought you might need backup." Bryan grinned. "You did a great job with him."

She smiled. "Thank you."

"He can hang out with me and Cody for the rest of the week." He nodded. "Easier to play basketball when there's more players."

Cody. She bit back her groan. She'd just forced her son to give up basketball for the week. Or to spend time with the boy who bullied him the most.

Ryder balanced on the top step of the ladder.

"You know you're not supposed to stand on that, right?" Annabeth said.

"How would you know? Unless you've done the same thing," he replied, draping the strand of lights over the hook he'd hung.

"Ryder." Her exasperated sigh made him chuckle.

He climbed down the ladder, his smile fading. "Annabeth, I got this. Why don't you take Cody home?" She seemed to be getting thinner each day. He knew she was having a hard time keeping her food down, but there had to be something they could do.

"I'm fine." She waved him away, turning to the last box.

"More lights," Irene said. "The last of them."

"Good." Ryder smiled at the parent volunteers, appreciating the work they were doing for their kids. And he didn't mind pitching in—he wanted to be an involved parent. But Annabeth had done enough. She'd already been here twelve hours.

"I can get the last of it." Annabeth opened the box and tilted it onto its side. A huge rat jumped out and skittered across the table where the box rested, leapt to the stage and ran straight for the cover of the curtains. Annabeth jumped back, pinwheeling her arms to steady herself. Ryder was there, his big hands catching her about her waist and steadying her. "Rat! Big big rat."

"Oh, my God," Holly moaned. "I brought that into the school."

Ryder shook his head. "Now we just need to get him out again." His eyes swept over Annabeth. "You okay?"

She nodded. "What do you need?"

"A broom, a trash can, and something large enough to slide under the trash can." He was already looking around the gym.

Annabeth pulled a ring of keys off her hip. "Broom's in the janitor's closet, over there." She pointed in the direction the rat had run.

"Great." He chuckled. "Anyone else wearing boots?" he asked.

"Me," Jim volunteered. "Anyone not wearing boots might as well climb on the tables or get out of the gym. Those bastards bite, and they carry all sorts of bacteria and disease."

Ryder approved of Jim's no-nonsense approach. He took Annabeth's keys and retrieved a broom while Jim found a trash can.

"If we prop open the side door, maybe it'll run out?" Carol said.

The chances of that happening were slim, but he agreed. "Sure." Ryder propped open the side door. As luck would have it, there was a trash can right outside.

After a few minutes' search, he located a piece of wood that should work. And that's when the screaming began.

Ryder ran inside to find the rat running around the room, searching for a way out. Maybe they'd get lucky and the damn thing would run outside.

But just as Irene's screaming stopped, Cody, another boy and the coach ran into the room and directly into the path of the rat. Ryder ran faster than he'd ever run, swinging that broom with all the strength he had. He hit the rodent, sending it across the room from Cody. But now the damn thing was mad. Jim approached it, holding the trash can at the ready, but the rat stood on its hind legs and charged the man. Jim backed up, startled, but the rat kept coming.

Ryder kicked into gear. "Coach?" He nodded in the direction of the board.

Thankfully the man was sharp. The coach grabbed the board, approaching Jim and the rat from the right while Ryder took the left.

"You ready?" Ryder asked, hoping Jim realized he was holding the trash can.

Jim snapped out of it then, glaring at the aggressive little rodent before nodding.

"On three?" the coach asked.

It worked. The rat was under the trash can and everyone breathed easier.

"How're we going to get it outside?" the coach asked.

"With this." Ryder took the wood from the coach. "You hold it? Don't lift it or let it shift, I don't care if we do pinch its toes."

The rat was outside and running across the field in two minutes.

"Should've killed it," the coach muttered under his breath.

"At least it's not in the building." Ryder nodded. "Ryder Boone." He held his hand out.

"Bryan Goebel." The man shook his hand. "Nice to meet you."

"Quick on your feet."

"Wouldn't be much of a coach if I wasn't." The man laughed.

"You okay out here?" Annabeth hurried outside.

"Taken care of," Bryan said.

"Thank you." Annabeth's relief was obvious. "Ryder, I think I will take Cody home now."

Ryder nodded, thankful. She needed to be avoiding stress, resting when she could. He'd spent a lot of time researching pregnancy the past few days and, according to everything he'd read, the first trimester was a fairly risky time. "See you in a bit. I'll cook something when I get there."

She waved, then disappeared inside the building.

"She okay?" Bryan asked.

"She's fine." Ryder glanced at the other man, recognizing the look on Bryan Goebel's face. The longing, the tenderness… Bryan Goebel was sweet on his wife.

Chapter 12

Annabeth smoothed the wispy blond hair from Cody's sleeping face. She was still wound up from the evening's events. Yes, she was overreacting, but she was pregnant. Otherwise, seeing that horrible rat running at Cody wouldn't have shaken her up so badly. It was silly. Ryder wouldn't have let anything happen. Deep inside her, she knew that. He hadn't let anything happen. Everyone was safe, because of him.

Ryder...

He'd reacted quickly, without thought. If he'd been rattled or uncertain, she hadn't seen it. He'd had everything in control. Moving with a confidence, and speed, that ratcheted up the already raging attraction she had for her husband.

What really worried her was she knew it was more.

She wasn't ready to face what *more* meant. But she was afraid her heart had become intensely involved.

She turned off the hall light and walked into the kitchen, the telltale rumble of thunder outside reminding her of the various leaks in the roof. Lightning flashed in the small window over the kitchen sink. The sink, where Ryder stood. He didn't seem bothered by the coming storm. He was elbows deep in a sink of soapy dishes, humming to whatever country tune was coming from the radio. It looked as though he was content, maybe even a little happy. How she wished that was true.

If she was smart, she'd go to bed. Standing here admiring how his tight gray T-shirt clung to each and every muscle was a bad idea. Her attention lingered on his mighty fine rear. She swallowed, aching with desperate want. If she went over there and wrapped her arms around him, what would happen?

She hesitated for a moment, then did exactly that.

He froze. But not for long. He wiped his hands on a dish towel, then covered hers with his. His hands were hot and damp—encompassing her. She kissed his shoulder, pressing her nose against his back and breathing deep. His head-to-toe shiver surprised her.

Ryder kept her arms in place, even as he turned to face her. He stared down at her, the heat in his gaze challenging the very real warning inside her head. She wanted him and, for whatever reason, right now he wanted her.

His hands cupped her cheeks, tilting her head. The touch of his thumb along her lower lip startled her lips apart. His kiss was fierce. Lips parted, breaths merged, and tongues stoking deep. She melted into him, welcoming the heat that inflamed her. He pressed soft kisses to the corner of her mouth, her cheek, the hollow at the base of her neck. The slight scratch of stubble along her skin plus the sudden tenderness of his kisses had her aching for more. She slipped her hands beneath the hem of his shirt, pressing her palms against his skin.

He pulled his shirt off and let it fall on the floor at their feet.

Her hands traced over his chest, dragging her fingers over each ridge and indentation. Muscles. Golden skin. Raw strength. He was mesmerizing.

"Mrs. Boone," he murmured against her neck. "Option A. We're breaking the rules."

Option A. She blinked. Option A. The plan with no sex and a temporary marriage. The plan she'd dreamed up to keep things under control. To protect them both. She stared at the wall of muscle that was his stomach and chest, a soft sound of pure frustration escaping her lips.

"Annabeth?" His voice was a low growl.

She wanted him—too much. "I'm sorry," she murmured. "After today... I just... You..." She shook her head. "I crossed a line—" It was hard to meet his gaze.

He was staring down at her, shirtless, gorgeous and barely controlled. "Hell, Princess, cross it." His words were colored with unfiltered hunger.

She sucked in a deep breath, her lungs shuddering at the force of it. The look in his eyes, the heat of his hands and strength of his arms around her. She wanted this. She wanted him. She stepped forward, slipping her hand to the base of his neck and pulling his head down to her.

As their lips met, he lifted her in his arms and carried her to the bedroom. With the heel of his boot, he nudged the door shut. He didn't lay her on the bed, but set her on her feet instead. He knelt in front of her, unbuttoning each of the buttons along her pajama top. When it hung open, he kissed her stomach, along her ribs, under the swell of her breast…leaving a spark of fire in his wake. His hair brushed along her skin, heightening each sensation. And his big hands held her up, solid against her back. His mouth brushed over her nipple, stealing whatever breath she had left.

She shrugged out of her top. It wasn't enough. She needed all of him.

His broken groan shook her where she stood. He wasn't touching her. He didn't have to—his desire was all the encouragement she needed. She started to kneel with him, desperate to feel him against her. But he tugged her pajama bottoms down and stood, the brush of his chest against her own heightening her senses even more.

His hands tangled in her hair as his mouth sealed hers. The touch and slide of his tongue was too much. Her hands fumbled with his belt buckle and jeans. Somehow he managed to get out of them.

They fell back onto the bed, but he rolled them, bringing her on top of him.

She stared down at him, at the beauty of his body, the angles and planes and rugged masculinity. His hands stroked up her arms, his gaze devouring every inch of her. He was just as hungry as she was. His fingers brushed along her neck, wrapping in her long hair to pull her face to his.

His kiss was deep, leaving her lungs empty and her body writhing. He rolled them again, holding her tightly against him. When she dared to look at his face, she was stunned by his expression. Possessiveness—he looked at her as if she was his.

She wanted that…wanted to be his.

He rested on one forearm, his hand cradling her face as he moved slowly into her. She closed her eyes, too overwhelmed by the raw friction, the exquisite pressure. He grew still, his gasping breath cooling her heated skin. She looked at him, at the control he fought for. She kissed his neck, wrapping her legs around his waist. "Make love to me, Ryder."

He was a good lover. He could take his time, drive a woman mad. But something about Annabeth made him lose that, something about her drove *him* mad. She held him tightly, arms and legs and hands. Her body sheathed him so tightly he worried he'd be done before they got started.

He heard her words and looked down at her. Her hands cradled his face as she arched her back, joining them more deeply in the process. She moaned, her breath hitched, but she never looked away. And he happily drowned in her hazel eyes.

Damn, she was beautiful. Her body and her heart. He loved her. He would love her the way she deserved to be loved.

He moved, soaking up every reaction. Sweet sighs, the roll of her hips, the flush on her skin and the small shudders his touch caused. Watching her was magic, giving him the desire to make it last—to give her what she craved. Her hands tightened on his back, gripping his sides fitfully, dragging a moan from his throat. She was so close. He nuzzled her breast, drawing first one nipple into his mouth, then the next. She whimpered, her nails raking the skin on his back. His mouth on her skin made her crazy. He held her, watching, as every inch of her contracted. Her eyes closed as her neck arched off the pillow. She cried out, threatening Ryder's control. This was about her.

I love you, Annabeth. He pressed kisses along her neck as her cries began to ease. *I love you.*

He let go, finally, moving frantically against her. He held her against him, the feel of her pulling him under. Her hands slid down his chest, gripping his hips in encouragement. The power of his release startled him, rocking him to the core. Her arms held him close until he calmed. But whatever calm his body might be feeling, the throbbing beat of his heart was anything but. He rolled onto his back, careful of her. She turned into his arms, sighing as he pulled her close against him. His heart was still thundering as he pressed a kiss to her temple.

A full-on storm raged outside, a hard rain was falling. But he didn't mind. He was right where he wanted to be, happier than he'd ever been.

"Schools are closed," Annabeth announced, so pleased she wanted to jump up and down like a little girl.

Ryder, sleepy-eyed and barely awake, grinned. He rearranged his pillow, the quilts sliding low to his waist in the process. "You look torn up about it, Princess."

She shook her head. "Not one bit." She slid back into bed beside him, pulling the quilts over them. She frowned then. "You still have to go to the garage?"

He quirked an eyebrow at her. "You suggesting I call in sick?"

She slipped out of the pajama top she'd put on to answer the phone. "I am." She slid on top of him, kissing the tip of his nose.

His hands landed on her rear, sending all sorts of amazing tingles down her back. "Think that can be arranged." His voice was rough and sexy.

She kissed him, loving the way one of Ryder's big hands slid along her back to cradle her head. His lips tugged on her lower lip, and she melted against him hungrily. She moved, gripping his head to tug him close. There was something freeing, knowing they had hours before Cody woke up, hours before they had to face the day.

Ryder groaned softly, pulling her under him.

Her bedroom door creaked as it opened, giving Annabeth just enough time to nudge Ryder off.

"Ma?" Cody's voice was a croak. "M-my bed's wet. W-water coming in."

"Oh, Cody, I'm sorry." She couldn't exactly get up—she was naked.

Ryder slid to the side of the bed. "I'll check it out." Ryder shivered. "Brr. Why don't you climb in the bed there and warm up."

Annabeth tucked the sheets around her before wrapping Cody with quilts. Tom appeared, leaping up to sleep on Cody's chest. It took less than five minutes for Cody to fall asleep, then she slipped into her pajamas.

The house was cold, so she tapped the thermostat and turned the heat up. The unit clicked several times before a gust of warm air came through the floor vents.

Ryder stood on a chair, lightly pressing on the ceiling. A huge patch was clearly soaked through.

"It's bad, isn't it?" She shook her head.

Ryder nodded. "It's bad. Not just in here." He jumped down, took her hand and led her into the small living area. The patch extended for almost half of the room. There were several puddles on the wooden floors, the rhythmic *tap-tap* of water muffled by the water already accumulated.

"How bad?" she asked, refusing to let this ruin the sense of peace she'd woken to.

"New roof bad. New heater, too, probably. And then there's the wiring..." Ryder pushed the hair from her shoulder, enfolding her in his arms. "We should move out to the ranch for a while."

Annabeth stared up at him. "We...we can't inconvenience your dad that way."

"It's no inconvenience, Princess." He kissed her forehead, then her nose. "We can't stay here, it's not safe. This is gonna be a major cleanup, too." He looked at the roof. "Be a good idea to put most of this in storage, for now."

"All I wanted was a morning in bed with you." She frowned. "Talk about a mood-killer."

"There are beds there. Big, comfy beds." The muscle in his jaw was working. "Morning, afternoon, night, I'm there." He kissed her, leaving no doubt that he meant it.

She burrowed into his arms, ignoring the leak and the puddles and the cold for a minute longer.

"I'll call my dad." Ryder's voice was muffled in her hair.

"It's barely six," she argued.

"He's up, I guarantee it." He smiled, his hold easing.

"I guess I'll get dressed and see about finding packing materials." Her brain was already making lists of things she'd need to do. "What a mess."

"Nothing that can't be fixed." He tilted her head back. "How's your stomach?"

She smiled. "Hungry."

"Good." He headed for the kitchen and pulled out a skillet and eggs. "Breakfast will be ready in a bit."

She watched him, smiling at his outfit. Boxer shorts, boots and his thick work coat. And he still managed to look hot. "You want your pants?" She laughed.

He smiled at her. "Am I distracting you?"

She cocked her head. Did he know that she wanted to drag him back to bed? She sighed. The bed where Cody was now soundly sleeping. "Yes, you are," she admitted.

His jaw was working again, and she liked it. "The couch isn't wet," he suggested, an egg in his hand.

She rolled her eyes, but her breath was unsteady. "What am I going to do with you, Ryder Boone?"

He grinned, his signature I'm-going-to-rock-your-world grin. "I have some suggestions—"

She held up her hand, heading from the kitchen. "Stop." But she was giggling.

Chapter 13

Ryder stood watching his wife mingle with the people of Stonewall Crossing. He knew she was exhausted. Neither one of them had been getting a lot of sleep recently. Between the storm, the damage to the house and moving into the Lodge, he and Annabeth hadn't had much time alone. But he felt confident he was making headway with his plan—destroy Option A.

Sure, living under the same roof as his father took some getting used to. But Annabeth was one of those people who kept the peace, without even trying. And Cody was settling in. His father had given them the only suite in the Lodge, so he had his own room—even if he'd spent last night sleeping between them. Overall, life was damn good.

"I think she gets prettier every time I see her." John Hardy clapped him on the back.

Ryder nodded. "No one prettier."

John chuckled.

Ryder shook his head. "I'm whipped."

"That's all right." John laughed. "A man would be downright foolish not to be with a woman like that."

Ryder watched Annabeth laugh. He couldn't agree more.

"I need to talk to you, if you have a minute?" John asked.

"Yes, sir," he agreed, leading John into one of the smaller rooms off the great room.

"My kids have all up and moved, you know that. None of them are interested in my line of work, anyway. You are." John paused. "Now, with Annabeth and your family, I figure you might be willing to take on the garage."

Ryder stared at him. John Hardy had always believed in him, giving him a job and a roof over his head since he was eighteen. He was a good man, someone Ryder was proud to know. It hadn't been easy to say no to JJ, and JJ wasn't ready to give up yet, but Ryder knew he was where he belonged. And now this.

John held up his hand. "I know you're sore about staying put, not getting to work with JJ, but hear me out. If the garage was yours, you could do the body-work and custom jobs you've always wanted to. Stonewall Crossing might be a little off the main road, but they'd come—for your work."

His own garage. With an established clientele. Here, not starting over. He was getting everything he always wanted.

"Just think about it. Seems like you're settling down all right, putting down those roots you've never wanted to plant before. This might help with that." John nodded, clapping Ryder on the shoulder again. "I'll let you stew awhile while I hunt down some more of that honey lemonade Fisher made."

Ryder nodded, wishing he was better with words. "You're a generous man, John."

John smiled. "And you're a good man who loves an engine almost as much as I do." He nodded once then headed off in search of Fisher's lemonade.

"Hiding?" Hunter asked, coming in as John left. "Renata really did invite everyone, didn't she?"

"The entire damn town."

Hunter grinned. "Your wife's looking for you."

His wife. The woman he took every opportunity to touch, to kiss and hold.

He smiled, heading back to the great room. There was no shortage of activity. The ice storm had delayed the party a week. And now, with the cold and ice hanging on, the party couldn't spill out onto the series of decks that ran down the hill behind the Lodge, the way Renata had originally planned. Add in the endlessly revolving servers coming to and from the kitchen, and it was a little too close for comfort. His brother Fisher sat with Cody and Eli and a few other kids, making paper airplanes out of Renata's fancy wedding announcements. His father and a few of his cronies were seated along the back wall, their chairs grouped around the massive fireplace. His other brother, Archer, had been cornered by two women with single daughters. To marry a Boone in Stonewall Crossing was pretty damn close to becoming Hill Country royalty.

"Hey." Annabeth smiled as soon as she saw him. It warmed him through, seeing her look at him like that.

"How're you holding up?" He took her hand in his and stared at her. She was, without a doubt, the most beautiful woman he'd ever seen. And when she smiled up at him like that, she made him feel like the only man in the world. A man who wanted to kiss her more than anything. His fingers laced through hers.

"Ryder," she chastised him. "You shouldn't look at me like that."

Ryder laughed. "Like what?"

She turned to face him, flushed. "Like *that*..." Her voice was unsteady.

He grinned. "I don't know what you think I'm thinking. I was thinking about me." He kissed the back of her hand. "And you—"

"Exactly." She nodded, wiggling her fingers.

"And Cody going fishing when it warms up," he added, watching her cheeks turn a deep scarlet. "What did you think I was thinking?" he teased.

"Nothing." She shook her head. "Nice to know I'm in your thoughts."

He slid an arm around her waist. When was she not in his thoughts? Every decision he'd made had been with her in mind. He stroked her side, getting accustomed to the way his heart reacted to her. "You are, Princess," he whispered.

She smiled up at him.

"Ma." Cody tugged on Annabeth's denim skirt. "Can I take Eli to my room? To play with Tom? Or watch a m-movie?"

"'Course you can," Ryder replied.

Cody looked at Ryder, then Annabeth. She nodded, ruffling his hair. "'Kay, thanks." The two ran out of the room.

"Can I go with them?" Ryder asked.

"Nope." She shook her head. "You're not leaving me." Her smile faded into a frown.

He didn't have time to ask what was wrong—his father was headed their way. Once he saw the people his father had in tow, he realized what Teddy Boone was up to. He and his father might not see eye to eye on some things, but they both wanted to help Annabeth any way they could.

"Annabeth, you remember Mack?"

Mack enveloped Annabeth in a hug. "Good to see marriage is agreeing with you, Mrs. Boone."

"Well, thank you for marrying us," she said, smiling.

His father grinned. "Don't know if you know Don and Haddie Miles?"

"In passing, I think." Annabeth was all warm smiles and handshakes. "It's a pleasure."

Pleasure might be pushing it, but Ryder just smiled. Haddie Miles was one of the few women who used to rub his mother the wrong way. Hell, she was an older version of Winnie Michaels.

"Look at you, Ryder," Haddie said. "What a fine man you've turned into. Either Annabeth doesn't know what a rascal you are, or she's decided to try to redeem you."

Ryder didn't flinch. "She knows all about my past, ma'am. And she's shown me the error of my ways." Haddie smirked, but the men present turned a universally appreciative gaze upon his wife.

"And this old pain in the rear is Charles Sharp." Teddy stepped back so the gnarled older gentleman could shake Annabeth's hand.

"Call me Cutter," the old man said as he waved Teddy back. "My eyesight's not so good," he grumbled, coming to stand inches from Annabeth. His milky eyes widened. "Hell's bells, boy, you married well." Cutter shook his head. "And she's the principal, too, Teddy? The one there's all the fuss over?"

"Cutter—" Haddie shushed the older man.

Ryder felt Annabeth stiffen and took her hand in his.

"I see why now." Cutter laughed. "Ol' prune face Branson can't stand to be put in his place by any woman. One that looks like this? Hooey, gotta chap his hide."

It took everything Ryder had to swallow his laugh.

"I don't think you're supposed to talk about school board business here, Cutter," Mack said, trying to rein the older man in.

Cutter made a rude sound. "Like to see 'em try to fire me." His eyes narrowed as he assessed Annabeth again. "Why do you think you're the best one for the job, Annabeth Boone?"

"Now, Cutter…" Don placed a hand on the other man's arm.

"I'll leave her be." Cutter shrugged out from under the other man's touch. "After she answers the question."

Ryder saw the look of panic on Annabeth's face. He knew, deep down, she was tempted to use this opportunity to sell herself. She wanted the job and she'd worked hard to get it. And, as she reminded him time and again, the job helped her make ends meet. Not that she needed to worry about that now.

"Mr. Sharp, I can't, in good faith, answer that question. Not here. I know I'm not the only candidate." She glanced at each of them while leaning in to him. His arm slipped around her waist, offering her the support she was looking for. "I'd feel wrong, unethical, trying to get ahead like that."

Cutter made another rude sound. "You can bet your sweet ass Branson wouldn't have said that." He laughed.

"I expect you'll be taking your honeymoon this summer?" Mack asked.

Ryder smiled. A honeymoon? Sounded like a good idea. Everyone would expect it. And it would give him the time he needed with Annabeth. "The sooner the better," he agreed.

"Where are you thinking about going? My daughter, June, and her husband went to Paris. They said it was awful. The people were rude and everything cost too much. One time—" Haddie was off. She was a talker, he remembered that much.

Annabeth shifted from one foot to the other, her hand pressing his tightly. She did it again, harder. He glanced at her, noting how pale she looked. He steadied her with his arm, taking her hand in his. Her fingers were icy cold. He scanned the room, looking for help. He caught the eye of Josie, chatting happily with Lola and Flo. He tilted his head slightly, hoping Josie would get the message. He saw her frown, glance at Annabeth and head their way.

"Annabeth?" Josie interrupted. "I'm so sorry. I need to steal you."

"Oh? Of course." Annabeth smiled warmly at the group. "We'll make sure not to go to Paris, Mrs. Miles. Thank you for sharing that with me. It was lovely to see you all."

He wanted to go with her, but he knew better. Josie would take care of her.

"What are your plans, Ryder?" Mr. Miles asked. "Now you've got a wife and son, I imagine you're looking into bigger and better career opportunities."

"Ryder's a damn fine mechanic," his father interrupted. "John Hardy's always singing his praises. And he should. Works hard, for John and when he's helping out here." His father nodded at him. Ryder tried not to stare back, stunned by his father's words. "When he's not riding bulls that is," his father added reluctantly.

"I've seen him ride," Mack joined in. "Had me on my feet counting down. Damn impressive."

"Lucky bastard," Cutter growled. "Love your job, love your wife—that's a damn good life."

"Amen." Teddy nodded.

"Ain't that the truth," Mack added.

Ryder couldn't have said it better himself.

"Did you eat this morning?" Josie asked her. "You look so pale."

"I ate, I just didn't keep much of it down. But I did eat." Annabeth smiled. "I'm fine. Just got a little overheated I think."

"It's awfully stuffy," Josie agreed. "Still, you should probably try to eat something." She pressed against the kitchen counter as one of the servers rushed past, carrying a large tray. "None of this looks good?"

Annabeth eyed the chilled shrimp, the canapés and mini éclairs, and tiny cornbread thimbles full of chili. She shook her head. "The smells are enough."

"How about some chicken noodle soup?" Josie had the refrigerator open.

Annabeth thought about it. "Sure."

"You go wait in Teddy's office so you have a moment's peace," Josie told her. "Go the back way, down this hall. I'll warm some up and bring it to you."

"Thank you, Josie." She hugged her friend.

"Your husband was worried about you." Josie held her by the shoulders. "I know things aren't settled between you," she whispered, "but I know he loves you."

Annabeth swallowed the lump in her throat.

"Go on." Josie shooed her in the direction of the hall.

Annabeth went, flopping into the overstuffed leather chair with a sigh. She peered out the window, appreciating the view. From here, Teddy could see land. No houses or roads or fences, just his property. Property that had been in the Boone family for generations. It must be a humbling thing, to be the caretaker of such a vast property. But he had his sons to help. All of them. She hoped, in time, Ryder would find a way to make peace with his family. There'd always been tension whenever the Boones were together. Now, not so much...but they were a long way from the united family they could be. The sort of family she wanted.

She stood, pacing the floor. She was an idiot. She wanted a home and family. She wanted a husband, someone she could build a life with. She wanted to believe Ryder could be that man, but she couldn't shake the feeling that she was headed toward another heartbreak.

Ryder was Ryder. There were times she wondered if he'd changed—if she and Cody were what he wanted. That's what she wanted to believe. But when the twins were teething, Cody was sick and she had to work a twelve-hour day, would he still be here? Was he ready for that?

Now was not the time to give up being practical.

He'd always been motivated by his loyalty to Greg, not his feelings for her. She needed to remember that. Her heart needed to accept that.

Her stomach clenched and she pressed both her hands against it, stifling a groan. She was not a fan of morning sickness or throwing up. She couldn't wait for this first trimester to be over. Almost there—

"Annabeth?" Hunter stood just inside the door. "Are you okay?"

She straightened, smoothing the white linen tunic over her stomach nervously. "Fine. Just a little overheated."

Hunter stood there. "You need anything?"

"No." She shook her head.

"Do you want me to get Ryder?" he asked, the intensity of his expression unnerving her.

"I'm fine."

He smiled. "Dad's friends can be a lot to handle."

She laughed. "That's an understatement. I hope I didn't disappoint your father."

"I wouldn't worry about that, Annabeth. We're all happy you're part of the family."

Josie arrived, carrying soup and crackers. "Here. Maybe this will agree with your stomach."

"I thought you were overheated?" Hunter asked, cocking an eyebrow.

Josie shot Hunter a look, placed the soup on the table by the window and handed Annabeth the linen napkin she carried.

Annabeth watched the silent exchange between the husband and wife.

"I didn't ask because I didn't want you to have to lie," Hunter said.

"I wouldn't have lied, if you'd asked." Josie crossed the room, sliding her arms around Hunter's neck.

He sighed, rubbing his nose against Josie's.

"I'm guessing I'm going to be an uncle?" Hunter asked, never looking away from his wife.

Annabeth stared into her soup, too nauseated to eat. "Yes."

Hunter looked at her. "I can't say I'm surprised."

"He wants to do the right thing," she said, wanting to defend Ryder.

Hunter smiled. "Annabeth, Ryder's my little brother. I've watched him grow up, I know him—whether he likes it or not."

She crossed her arms, frowning. "He's a good man—"

"With you, yes," Hunter agreed. "You bring out the best in him, always have."

She blinked back the tears that stung her eyes. Even if Ryder loved her, did it matter? Loving her wouldn't change who he was. She wanted to believe it.

"You're worried?" Hunter asked.

"Can you blame her?" Josie asked. "Even when people are congratulating her, it's like they're also warning her about him."

Annabeth smiled, nodding.

"What do you think?" Hunter asked her.

She chewed on her lip, willing the tears away. "He's been trying to take care of me and Cody, for Greg. Now, this… He's trapped." Her hands brushed over her stomach. "I know him, too, Hunter. He's a restless spirit. One I won't keep for long."

Ryder came through the door, his face lined with worry. "You okay?" He crossed to her, wrapping his arms around her. "Feeling all right?"

"I'm fine," she murmured, turning her face into his shirt.

"I thought she might want some peace and quiet," Josie spoke.

Ryder turned, but his hold on her didn't ease. "Thanks, Josie. Hunter." She felt Ryder's hands tighten on her arms. "Guess you know?"

"That Josie and I are going to have a niece or nephew?" Hunter's voice was calm. "Yep. Congratulations. I'm happy for you both."

Ryder's grip eased on her. She knew Hunter's opinion was important to Ryder, no matter how much he tried to pretend otherwise.

Her stomach gurgled loudly. "Sorry. My stomach isn't cooperating," she moaned.

He looked down at her. "Did you try eating?"

She pointed at the soup. "Josie just made that for me."

He let her go, nodding at the bowl.

"You're so bossy," she teased, sitting. She lifted the bowl, grimacing at the smell of celery and chicken broth.

"At least try." Josie sat on the footstool.

"I can't eat with all of you watching me." Annabeth laughed.

"Come on, Ryder, let's head back. It won't look good if you're both missing," Hunter said. "You need anything else?"

Annabeth shook her head, trying not to laugh at her frowning husband. "I'm fine."

"Renata has some slide show she put together," Hunter added. "About the two of you. When you're ready."

"She does?" Annabeth stirred the bowl, swallowing a spoonful. It was surprisingly good. She managed to have some more, the mild flavors soothing her sour stomach. She waved them off, enjoying half of her bowl before deciding she was done. Josie tried to feed her some crackers, but she didn't want to push it. She felt much better when she headed back to the party.

Annabeth helped move chairs around in the great room, but there wasn't enough room for everyone to sit.

"Come on, Flo, right up front." Ryder parked Flo's wheelchair front and center.

"Best seat in the house," Flo exclaimed. "You're spoiling me."

"Part of my job," Ryder teased.

Annabeth watched, touched by his thoughtfulness.

"Annabeth, you give this boy extra kisses for taking care of me." Flo shook her finger at her.

Annabeth laughed as Ryder pulled her into his lap, in a chair beside Flo.

"Extra kisses sound good," he whispered in her ear. With one look, he made her feel beautiful…and teary eyed.

Renata lowered the large screen the Lodge used for business retreats or movie nights. As the lights dimmed, Cody and Eli scampered in to sit on the floor and lean back against Ryder's chair.

Music started and the title sprang up: "Annabeth and Ryder's Love Story."

Everyone oohed over their baby pictures. Ryder was adorable, there was no denying it. She'd never seen images of a young Teddy and Mags Boone. He was handsome and she was amazingly beautiful. A quick glance at Teddy gave her pause. It was clear the old man still loved and missed his wife.

The montage of their growing-up years was bittersweet. While Annabeth's parents were absent, pictures of Greg were everywhere.

"Is that Dad?" Cody asked after one hilarious picture of the three of them covered in mud, holding a puppy high.

Annabeth nodded. "That was his dog."

"What h-happened?" Cody asked.

"The dog slid down the riverbank, and the water started to rise. The dog couldn't get back up—"

"Your mom climbed down before we could stop her," Ryder interrupted.

"But it got them down there with me," Annabeth added. "And the dog was safe."

"Safe. But all four of 'em were covered in mud," Flo interjected.

Cody laughed, shaking his head.

Annabeth ruffled his hair, smiling at the top of his head. She needed to tell more stories about Greg, so he'd know his father.

"Oh, look at that." The amusement in Lola's voice drew Annabeth's attention back to the screen. She was at one of the town festivals, manning a kissing booth. She was kissing Ryder. She didn't remember that. She glanced at Ryder, who was grinning.

By the time the pictures entered the high school years, it was clear that Annabeth was wild about Greg. But Ryder was there, too. At graduation, he was smiling at her. At one of the vacations to the beach, she'd fallen asleep on his shoulder while Greg was fishing. When Cody was born, Ryder was in the hospital. He was cradling Cody, looking at him with such awe and adoration it was hard to believe Cody wasn't his. It was a good thing Ryder had been living in Las Vegas when she'd gotten pregnant, or people would undoubtedly talk.

There were more. Cody working on his toy car while Ryder worked on the real ones. Ryder taking Cody fishing with his brothers. And Ryder staring at her when she was talking to Grandma Flo. It was from a few years back, and Grandma Flo wasn't in her wheelchair yet.

The look on his face took her breath away.

"I was quite a looker." Flo's announcement made everyone laugh.

So many occasions and events, whether he was standing alongside her or somewhere in the background—Ryder was there.

A blank slide popped up, the words "Congratulations, Annabeth and Ryder! Wishing you a life of love and laughter!" scrolling slowly by.

Her heart was racing by the time the last picture popped up. It was a picture of them dancing.

"I took that one," John Hardy called out.

Cody hopped up, hugging Ryder, then hugging her. "Love you."

She hugged him tightly. "I love you, too."

"Picture!" Lola was up, holding her phone out. "Since there aren't any wedding pictures, we should take some here."

"Great idea," Renata agreed.

Before she knew what was happening, the chairs were cleared away and she and Ryder were standing in front of the fireplace.

They took so many pictures her cheeks hurt from smiling. But she understood how important it was, to have something tangible from this day. When she'd lost Greg and his memory seemed to be slipping away, she'd pulled out the old albums for comfort. She had no right to deprive Teddy or the Boones. As she and Ryder and Cody gathered around Flo's chair, she was happy, too.

"So happy for you precious dears." Flo kissed them each on the cheek. "Now get to work on more grand-babies. Right, Teddy?"

Teddy blushed furiously. "Well, now, Flo, when they're ready…" he trailed off.

"We'll get on it." Ryder smiled.

"I want a brother." Cody nodded, all wide-eyed excitement.

Annabeth laughed; she couldn't help it.

Ryder winked at Cody. "We'll see what we can do."

"One more, just the happy couple." Renata waved everyone else aside, waiting for Fisher to wheel Grandma Flo back to Lola.

"You may kiss the bride," Mack called out from the back of the room.

Ryder faced her, smoothing her hair from her face to give her a quick kiss.

"Ryder Boone, you can do better than that," Flo chastised, making everyone laugh.

Annabeth giggled, nervous. Partly because of the people watching and partly because of the way he was looking at her. He kissed her softly, sweetly, his hands coming up to cup her face. She covered his hands with hers and the kiss lingered. It was all too easy to get lost in the heat between them. She wanted to give in, to get lost in him…until the whistles and catcalls started up.

Ryder broke away, pressing a kiss to her forehead and sliding his arm around her shoulders. Annabeth could tell he wasn't thrilled over all the attention, but he was trying. It didn't help that half the people congratulating them insisted on bringing up Ryder's history with women. Even Flo got in on the act. She couldn't stop her growing irritation. But Ryder kept smiling, shaking hands long after she was done.

"You feeling okay?" he asked.

"I'm feeling fine." She hadn't meant to snap.

"What's wrong?"

She looked into his pale blue eyes. "I'm frustrated."

"I'm getting that." He nodded. "About?"

She stared at her feet. "I'm tired of hearing about… your past." She shook her head. "Everyone has a past, but some are more *colorful* than others." She smiled at him. "But I don't see anyone else getting so much grief. Doesn't it bother you?"

"Sure." His gaze traveled over her face. "Only thing I can do is prove I've changed."

Had he changed? She hoped so. She couldn't think of anything she wanted more. Her heart hurt.

"Actions speak louder than words, Mrs. Boone." He caressed the side of her face. "Seems like the only thing I can do is love you until no one in Stonewall Crossing can doubt it." He smiled at her, shaking his head. "No one. Not even you, Princess."

Chapter 14

Ryder stood under the shower, letting the steaming water pour over him. He was tired. The past week he'd had a complete transmission overhaul on a two-day turnaround. And in the evenings, he and Hunter had been riding the fence line to replace any posts the storms had damaged. Times like this reminded him just how big the ranch was.

DB had called him about a rodeo, but he'd turned him down without a second thought.

Annabeth came into the bathroom. "There's a phone call for you." She tapped on the shower door. "The whales said the water level is getting a little low and asked that you wrap up your marathon shower."

Ryder laughed, turning off the water. "Damn whales."

He heard Annabeth giggle.

He pushed open the glass door and wrapped a towel around his waist. Annabeth was brushing her teeth, in an oversize tank top. He stood, enjoying the view. He needed to spend more time feeding her. She was beautiful, no doubt about it, but she could use more meat on her bones.

"Want a kiss?" she asked, turning toward him with a toothpaste-sudsy mouth.

He didn't hesitate, closing the gap between them in three steps and pulling her against him.

"Ryder, no!" she squealed, laughing. "Joke."

He bent his head, dropping a kiss on her nose, then let her go. He stared down at her baby bump. His baby bump. She was starting to show. And he loved it. His hands covered her stomach, smoothing along the sides of her rounded belly to support the underside. Something about the sight lodged a knot in his throat.

"Give me a sec?" Annabeth asked, slipping from his hold long enough to rinse the toothpaste from her mouth. She took his hands and placed them back on her stomach.

"Doctor appointment is next week?" he asked, stroking her stomach. According to the baby book, she had a lot going on inside of her right now.

She nodded. "Tuesday at four thirty."

"I'll be there." He smiled. "I'm going to kiss you now." He pressed a soft kiss to her mouth, her breath hitching. He wanted to believe she wanted him, that their incredible night together was the first of many incredible nights together. But he still had to work at getting kisses. Or holding hands. Or sleeping with her head on his shoulder every night. He kissed the tip of her nose. "If we're going to get to the meeting on time, that's all you're getting, Princess."

She sighed.

"Nervous?" he asked. She might be cool as a cucumber, but he was tied in knots about the school board meeting. She wanted this job. And that meant he wanted her to have it.

She shrugged, pulling a compact from the lemon-print bag with all her toiletries. "No point being nervous." She met his gaze in the mirror. "They've already made their decision." But she was staring at his chest, distracted and dazed and…aroused?

He stepped behind and slid his arms around her, holding her. "Guess so." He dropped a kiss on her shoulder. She smelled good, but she tasted better. He threw caution to the wind and slid her bra strap aside, kissing the skin beneath. He groaned and stepped back, amazed at how quickly his body responded to her. He risked looking at her in the mirror and groaned again.

Her eyes were round, her breathing harsh and unsteady. The flush of desire on her cheeks made him ache.

"What was that?" Her voice was rough and sexy as hell.

"Princess." He ran his fingers down her back, loving the way she shivered. So she wanted him. But did she love him? Could she love him? He cleared his throat. "Sometimes I forget about Option A. Or I think we should burn it or let Cody feed it into the shredder in your office and never talk about it again…"

Her brow creased, her hazel gaze boring into his. She nodded. "I need clothes." She laughed, an unsteady breathy sound, and hurried out of the bathroom. "Think a lot of people will turn out?"

He followed her into their bedroom and pulled out a pair of pressed slacks and a button-down oxford. "With the announcement and all, I imagine parents will be curious to see what's decided."

In true Texas-weather fashion, the temperature had climbed from the thirties to the eighties in a matter of days. She looked like spring in the yellow polka-dot sundress and white sweater she pulled on.

"Things are starting to get tight." She turned, pushing the sleeves of her sweater up. "Is it... Am I obvious?"

Too him, she was perfection. Still a little too thin, maybe. But he suspected her stomach was only obvious to him because he knew she was carrying his babies. "Nope. You look beautiful."

She rolled her eyes, sat on the edge of the bed and buckled her heels. "Are you sure your dad doesn't mind watching Cody tonight—"

"Annabeth," Ryder interrupted, tucking his shirt into his slacks. "Dad's tickled pink he's got a boy around that's interested in model cars again." He tugged on his boots. "They probably won't even know we're gone."

Annabeth stood, smoothing down her skirt. "I don't like imposing—"

"You're not imposing." He gripped her shoulders. "You're family."

She nodded, though the smile on her face wasn't convincing.

"Ready?" he asked, surprised at how edgy he felt. "You're meeting with the board privately, before the community meeting?"

She nodded, but her smile cooled, as if she was bracing for something.

"Hey." He took her hand. "Everything's going to be okay." He squeezed her hand. "Right?"

There was something in her huge hazel eyes he didn't understand—and it scared him. He didn't like fear, wasn't accustomed to it. If something scared him, he faced it head-on and fought it. What was there to fight? How could he win her?

Tonight he'd know if she needed him or not. If she got the job, she could take care of things on her own and she'd expect him to go. If she didn't get the job… well, she'd be devastated. Either way, he couldn't win. And there wasn't a damn thing he could do about it.

"Right." She headed out of the bedroom, tense and rigid.

He followed, his stomach full of lead and his heart heavy. No matter what happened tonight, he wouldn't give up. No matter what happened tonight, Annabeth was his wife. He'd figure out a way to fight—to hold on to her and their family. He had to.

Annabeth snuck into the dim high school auditorium and scanned the crowd. The meeting had already started and there seemed to be some discussion about team sports. She saw Ryder instantly—and felt the air leaving her lungs.

She got the job. She would stay the principal. After their brief meeting, she'd gone to the bathroom to pull herself together.

Option A said he'd move to Dallas and take his dream job. Option A. The one she didn't want.

She made her way to where he sat, his words replaying in her mind. *Everything's going to be okay*... How was anything going to be okay? She was beyond excited about the job, but there was so much more at stake.

"Hey," he whispered when he saw her.

She smiled at him, biting her bottom lip to stop the quiver. She saw the slight furrow of his brow and willed herself to really smile. It would have been easier if he wasn't looking at her, waiting to hear. She stared right back, memorizing the chiseled brow and strong jaw. She was in love with him—but she'd have to let him go.

He winked.

Her heart stuttered a little, but she rolled her eyes as if it was no big deal.

"You good?" he whispered.

She wrinkled her nose, smoothing her hands over her stomach. But, for the first time in weeks, her nausea had nothing to do with the babies inside.

His expression went from playful to intense. "Need to go?"

She shook her head.

He nodded, but didn't look convinced. "So?" he prodded.

"As you all know, we've been interviewing candidates for the principal position at Stonewall Crossing Elementary School. This has been quite a process." Haddie Miles's voice rang out. "And we truly appreciate the quality of excellence each of our candidates had to offer our fair town."

Cutter grumbled something, clearly impatient with Haddie's speech.

"That being said, we felt that one candidate's experience, familiarity with our community and references were the perfect fit for our fine school." Haddie turned to the gentlemen of the school board, who all seemed content to let Haddie do the talking. "We would like to thank Mr. Ken Branson of Stonewall Crossing, Mrs. Olivia Sanchez of Glendale, Illinois, Mr. William Marshall of San Antonio and Mrs. Annabeth Boone of Stonewall Crossing for your time and patience throughout our deliberation."

Ryder's hand captured hers. His fingers threaded with hers, warm and soothing... She glanced at their entwined fingers. If not getting the job meant she kept Ryder, she didn't want it. If she could keep him... But that wasn't true, either. She wanted him to stay because he wanted to, not because he had to.

She looked at Ryder again.

It was too late, the damage was done. She'd been so naive. Marrying her had been the easy part. Divorcing her would cost him...everything. No one would ever forgive him, no matter what she said. And it would be her fault. She swallowed down the bile that nearly choked her.

She never wanted to hurt him.

So many hearts would be hurt. Their families'. Cody. Hers...

Why had she ever agreed to this?

"We are pleased to offer the position of principal to Mrs. Annabeth Boone." Haddie Miles paused. "Where are you, Mrs. Boone?" She shielded her eyes and peered into the auditorium.

Annabeth stood, waving.

A smattering of applause broke out in the auditorium, making her look around for the first time. Quite a turnout, especially for Stonewall Crossing. The loyal volunteers were there. Most of the elementary staff sat on the far side of the dimly lit auditorium. No wonder she hadn't noticed them when she came in. Ken Branson wasn't pleased, but he was wearing his plastic smile.

"Mrs. Boone, the board has your contract for you to review. And, of course, you'll have two weeks to decide if you still want to be principal." Haddie laughed and Annabeth sat down.

The audience laughed, as well.

Annabeth wanted to cry, but forced herself to smile.

"As that concludes the board's official business, we'll open the floor to questions and concerns. Please remember to follow the rules…" Haddie carried on.

She stared straight ahead, smiling at the wall in front of her. She had to keep smiling, even though she wanted to cry.

"Told you so," Ryder whispered, kissing her cheek softly. "Congratulations."

"You did." She glanced at him, more nervous now than she'd been all night. It was real, she had the job. She'd be okay. She could take care of Grandma Flo and Cody. And the twins. He could go now. The sting in her eyes caught her off guard.

"Meeting adjourned." Haddie Miles whacked a gavel on the table with a surprising amount of force.

"Congratulations," Janet said as she slipped into the row behind them.

"Yay!" Janet was there, and Lori and Abigail.

"So glad it's you," Lori added. "You'll take care of us."

Grandma Flo's words went through her head. *Sometimes hiding your feelings is better than showing them.* This was definitely one of those times. "Thank you," she tried to gush. "I'm so relieved." She let go of Ryder's hand, turning in her seat to smile at them all.

"Congrats." Bryan Goebel sat behind Ryder. "Haven't been here long, but it's plain to see you're the right choice." He laughed. "Just don't tell Ken I said that."

"Thanks, Bryan." She paused. "Has Ken mentioned the opening? Coach Hernandez decided it was time to retire after all."

Bryan nodded. "Good to know."

She spent the next few minutes accepting congratulations, all the while wishing she was home in bed. And not at the Lodge, but in her own tiny house. She wanted to cry it out, pull herself together and attack tomorrow with purpose. The sooner she and Cody were back in their tiny house, back in their routine, the sooner things would start to feel normal again. Normal—without Ryder.

For now, she kept up the small talk, aware of Ryder's strong hand on the small of her back. What would she do without his strength?

"Mrs. Boone?" Haddie called her.

"I'll be back." She glanced at Ryder.

"I'll wait." He was watching her, a mix of concern and pride on his face. "Ice cream?"

She nodded, smiling.

He smiled back, a heart-thumping, knee-weakening smile.

"I'll hurry." She made her way to the stage, hoping she carried herself with some sense of confidence.

"Annabeth—" Ken caught her before she reached the steps. "Congratulations. Can't say I'm not a little disappointed, but there's no one I'd rather lose to."

She smiled, taking the hand he offered her. "Thank you, Ken, that means a lot."

He nodded, shaking her hand before joining his wife.

"Here's the paperwork." Cutter pushed a manila envelope across the table. "Too much money if you ask me, but no one did."

"Congratulations again, Mrs. Boone." Haddie shook her hand. "Meant to give this to you earlier but *Cutter* forgot it in his truck."

"Thank you, Mrs. Miles," she replied, shaking the woman's hand.

"First a wedding, now the job." Mack shook her hand. "I'd have to say you're having a good year."

And babies. She nodded.

The conversation was short. Review the offer and let them know in two weeks. The board did have some thoughts on some building additions they'd like to discuss with her, but that could wait until all the paperwork was signed. And they wanted to determine next year's calendar, discuss a new track surface and options for teacher training. None of which seemed to matter right now. By the time she climbed into Ryder's truck, she was on the verge of tears. She closed her eyes and rested her head on the back of the seat.

Ryder climbed in and turned on the heat, but didn't move. "You going to take the job?"

She opened her eyes, staring up at the lining of the truck cab. "Of course."

"You don't seem happy." His tone was neutral.

"I am. Besides, life isn't always about doing what you want to," she argued. "It's about doing what you need to do."

"Okay." He paused, driving two blocks before asking, "Why do you need this job?"

She looked at him, swallowing hard.

"I was watching you tonight, Princess. You were

happy until the meeting. Tired, yes. Stressed, sure. But once they said your name, you looked like Tom when Cody goes to school. Like you're losing something?"

"I don't know what you're talking about." She frowned at him. *I am losing you.* "I've been managing. I can do this."

He moved across the bench seat and took her hands in his. "Damn right, you can." His brow furrowed. "But you don't have to if you don't want to."

She looked at their hands. "Ryder."

"Talk to me," he said, his voice low.

She shook her head.

"You don't have to pretend with me." His words twisted her heart.

She glanced at him, but it was too hard. "I have the weight of the world on my shoulders. Medical bills that are sky-high—"

"I didn't know—"

"A house that would probably be better off flattened than repaired—"

"Annabeth," he tried again.

"A son, a sweet precious boy, who needs building up—and someone to look up to. This job pays significantly more than my teacher's salary. I don't know what the offer is exactly—" she tapped the manila envelope in her lap "—but it will take care of the things I *must* take care of." She shook her head. "Yes, this job is long hours and crazy parents and rats in the cafeteria...but it also provides the one thing my children need. Stability. With the twins coming..." She drew in a shuddering breath. "I need stability. We need it." She pressed her hand to her stomach. "If something falls apart, I can take care of it. *I* have to take care of *my* family."

The quiet grew, filling the truck cab until Annabeth couldn't take it.

Ryder slid back into his seat and turned on the truck. He pulled through the soda shop on the way home, buying her a double dip of her favorite—butter pecan. But he didn't say a word all the way home.

The top scoop of ice cream had all but melted by the time she went inside. Cody was so excited she gave the remainder to him, making him promise not to get too sticky since it was still a while until bath time. Ryder took Cody into the kitchen to prevent splattering the wooden floors with ice cream drips.

"How did it go?" Teddy asked.

Something about Teddy Boone's question broke the dam. Maybe it was the glimmer of pride she saw on his face. Or the fact that she'd never had a father to look at her that way. Or that she was overwhelmed and exhausted.

Whatever it was, she burst into tears, her legs giving out beneath her. She flopped onto one of the leather sofas and pressed her hands over her mouth so Cody wouldn't hear her, but she couldn't stop the sobs.

Teddy sat beside her, hugging her against his barrel chest. "It's all right, Annabeth. It's all right. It's just a job. If those idiots don't see the gem you are, good riddance."

"I—I got the j-j-job."

Teddy kept patting her back, rocking her back and forth. "Oh. Well, then. You don't want it?"

She shook her head. "I do. I *do* want it."

"You don't have to take it, Annabeth. You're a Boone now." He kept on rocking. "You can do anything you want. Hell, you could help me out here, at the Lodge. That'd be a real treat."

Her sobs kept coming.

"Aw, honey, you're breaking my heart." Teddy's voice was rough. "Been a long time since I comforted a woman. I'm afraid I'm not much good at it."

She shook her head as she pulled out of his arms. "You're the sweetest man, Teddy. I'm just an…emotional mess right now." She sniffed. "I'll take a shower."

"Ryder and I will get Cody to bed," Teddy offered.

"You don't have to—"

"Wouldn't have offered if I didn't want to." Teddy's voice was firm. "You go on, take a shower, read a book, whatever you need, you hear?"

Annabeth nodded, carrying the manila envelope into the bedroom with her. She closed the door, opened the envelope and scanned the information. They were giving her a raise—a big raise. No wonder Cutter was worked up. A big bump in medical benefits and retirement matching, as well. There was no way she could turn this down. She tossed the papers onto the bed, stripped and turned on the shower.

She rested her head against the tiles, willing the throb of her headache aside. She shampooed her hair, shaved her legs and stood under the jet until her skin was wrinkled. By the time she stepped out she was overheated and shaking. She didn't bother with her pajamas, or brushing her hair. She slipped into bed and stared up at the ceiling, her mind racing.

Her phone rang. It was Josie. "Hi."

"Annabeth? Do you have a cold?" Josie paused. "I'm so sorry I missed the meeting tonight. Eli had his Agriculture Club meeting and Hunter got called into the vet hospital for an emergency, so I was trying to be a good stepmom."

"Eli's meeting was probably more fun."

"Well?" Josie asked. "Are you still the principal of Stonewall Crossing?"

"I am." Annabeth tried for enthusiasm and ended up bursting into tears all over again.

"Annabeth?"

"I'm fine," she blubbered. "Just…so…emotional."

"I'm on my way."

"No, no," Annabeth pleaded. "I'm already in bed."

"It's seven forty-five." Josie sighed. "Please let me come over. I'll bring Eli. We can watch a chick flick and cry on your bed?"

She couldn't stop crying. "I'm already crying."

"Good." Josie laughed. "I'm on my way." She hung up before Annabeth could answer.

Annabeth tossed back the blankets, staring at her rounded stomach. Soon there would be no way to hide it. She wrapped her arms around the bump. "We're going to be okay," she whispered. "Your mom's got this single-mom thing down." Her own words set her off again. "I'll take care of you, I promise."

"Annabeth—" The anguish in Ryder's voice startled her.

She opened her mouth, but nothing came out. Why was he looking at her like that? Like he was hurting? She sniffed and wiped the tears from her face. "I'm tired." She bent to pull a nightie from the bedside drawer when her stomach clenched tightly. She covered her mouth and ran for the toilet, fighting her way into the nightie as she went.

Her stomach rejected the three licks of ice cream, half a sandwich and handful of crackers she'd eaten that day—as well as the extra-large protein smoothie she'd had for breakfast. She had nothing left, but her stomach kept heaving.

"This can't be normal." Ryder placed a cool washcloth against her forehead.

She shook her head, horrified that he was there. It was bad enough that she was an emotional wreck, but he was here, in the room, at her side, while she dry-heaved into the toilet. She held her hand up, croaking, "You don't have to be in here…"

He squatted beside her, rubbing the cool washcloth across her forehead again. "I need to be here," he argued. "I need to take care of you." His hand cradled her cheek, but she refused to meet his gaze. She was mortified. "Think you're done?" he asked.

She nodded slowly.

His strong hands clasped hers, pulling her up. Dizziness had her swaying where she stood, so Ryder swung her up into his arms. She didn't argue. She liked being in his arms, his big, warm, strong arms. She felt better there.

"You're skin and bones," he murmured.

"And babies," she added.

She could feel him smiling at her even though she refused to look at him as he placed her on the bed.

"Josie's coming over," Annabeth blurted out. "She heard me crying—"

"Why were you crying?" The anguish was back, forcing her to look at him.

He was so beautiful it hurt. "I… I'm pregnant."

He sat beside her on the bed, gently towel-drying her hair. His fingers brushed the nape of her neck. He set the towel down, sliding his fingers through the long locks of her hair. "Why are you so determined to keep me out?" His fingers kept moving, working gently through a snarl.

"I'm… I just…" Her mind raced. She'd made him a promise. She couldn't exactly say, *I love you and I want you to want to stay married to me even though I promised to divorce you once we knew about the job.* Could she?

She took a deep breath and forced herself to look at him. His brow was creased, his frown tense. As soon as he saw her gaze on him, he cocked an eyebrow at her. She touched the spot between his eyebrows, rubbing out the furrow there. He smiled, a lop-sided grin that had her heart pounding. His hand caught hers.

Maybe she should just spit it out there?

"Hey, guys." Josie arrived, carrying a bag. "I brought three tearjerkers, and two romantic comedies so we wouldn't get too maudlin."

Annabeth jumped up, then groaned.

"Come on, Princess." Ryder stood, leading her to the overstuffed chair in the corner. "You sit. I think Josie and I can get things set up."

"I don't think I ever want to get pregnant." Josie grimaced as she helped Ryder spread up the bed. "But I definitely want kids."

Ryder's expression was so comical, Annabeth had no choice but to laugh.

Ryder's pale blue eyes settled on her face and she was wrapped in the comfort of his smile. It would have been better if she'd never known how good it could be. If nothing else, her time with Ryder had reminded her that love was more than responsibilities and work—it was about joy and having fun. If he left tomorrow, she'd hold on to the memories they'd made together.

Chapter 15

Ryder nudged his horse forward with a light squeeze of his knees. His father rode along the other side, clicking occasionally at the massive draft horse he preferred riding. Ryder smiled, enjoying the quiet companionability that had settled over them as they worked. He knew his father and knew he was up to something. He rarely rode fence lines anymore, but he'd volunteered to take Hunter's place that evening.

"Go ahead, Dad," Ryder prompted him.

Teddy tipped his beige hat back on his head and rested his hands on the horn of his saddle. "With what?"

Ryder sighed. "Speak your mind."

Teddy nodded. "Time was you'd have avoided riding out with me when you knew I had something to say."

Ryder couldn't argue. "Times change."

His words startled his father, but he nodded before

saying, "You're working hard. And I appreciate it. Around here, with the ranch. At Annabeth's house— your house." His father turned all of his attention on him. "Is she expecting?"

"Yes, sir," Ryder said.

"Is that why you married her?"

Ryder nodded once.

"A lot of marriages start that way. Seen a few end because of it, too. I don't want that for you, son. I don't want that for any of you." Teddy shook his head. "She's a mighty stubborn little thing."

Which was an understatement. In the two weeks since the school board meeting, she'd spent every waking minute acting like he was a parent at her school. She was all professional charm, but she avoided any time alone with him—or eye contact. That didn't mean there was no hope. It just meant he had to try harder. Ryder laughed. "Yes, sir."

"But you love her. I can see it." Teddy clicked his tongue, keeping the horses moving along the barbed-wire fence as they talked. "Always have, if Renata's pictures are right." He looked at his son again. "She acts like you're leaving."

Ryder nodded.

"Is that the plan?" Ryder heard the tightness in his father's voice. "Are you leaving?"

"No, sir," he answered quickly. "But she seems to think so."

His father laughed. "Women are hard to work out. But your wife, well, I think I see where she's coming from. She was expecting when Greg passed on. She's expecting now and—with your history—I imagine she's waiting for you to go, too. Not die, but leave her alone." His father grinned. "It's what she knows, relying on herself."

Ryder stared at his father.

"Flo might have helped me figure some of this out," his father admitted. "I went to see her a few nights past and found her in her right mind. Not many women like Florence Chenault."

Ryder nodded, reeling from his father's newest revelation.

"Back in the day, we were close." His father laughed. "I figured she'd tell me what was going on, since you wouldn't."

His father's words stung.

"Not that you and I have ever been good at talking." His father held up a hand, adding, "That's my fault, not yours. But there comes a time when there's no way to avoid talking, so…"

Ryder cocked an eyebrow at his father. "So?"

"Start talkin'." His father glared at him. "How are you gonna keep Annabeth and Cody in the family?"

Ryder sat back in his saddle, looking up as the thin white clouds moved steadily across the sky. He wished he knew. "Guess I need to try harder." He'd sent flowers to her office, made ice cream runs, helped with the school field trip to the veterinary hospital and passed up two plum riding opportunities in case she needed anything. But all that seemed to do was irritate her even more.

"Have you tried talking?" his father asked.

Ryder grimaced. "We just said I'm no good at it."

"Who said that? I said we—" he pointed back and forth between the two of them "—weren't good at it. With other people? I'm not so sure."

"She's more likely to argue than listen," Ryder grumbled.

This time his father laughed. "Well, son, that's good news."

Ryder shot him a look. "How's that?"

"Arguing. Looks like that baby isn't the only thing you have in common."

Ryder shook his head. "Babies."

His father slapped his hand against his thigh. "I'll be." His father was all smiles for the rest of the ride.

But Ryder thought, maybe, his dad had a point. And, at this point, talking was the only thing he hadn't tried. He could only hope he'd find the right words.

Annabeth stared at the flowers on her desk. Ryder had sent her yellow roses. Why? Because she loved yellow. He'd also sent her lemon soda. Why? Because she liked lemons. It was like he was trying to lessen the blow that was coming. And it was coming, she knew it was. He'd been home late for the past few weeks, sneaking in when she was supposed to be sleeping. Even though all she'd done was lie there and worry. She had a hard time believing there were that many fences to mend or that there was a rodeo every night... Not that it mattered. It was good he was putting distance between them.

So all the little gifts were to ease his guilt. Did he think he could buy her off? That sneaking off to do whatever he was doing was okay? She'd hoped he'd behave until after they were divorced. And they hadn't even begun to talk about divorce proceedings.

Her attention wandered to the beautiful framed picture of her, Cody and Ryder at their wedding party.

And another one, just the two of them. He was looking at her the way she was looking at him—as if there was love there.

She sighed, filing away the papers from this afternoon's parent-teacher conference and scrolling through her emails. She had a few parent complaints and a meeting request from the school board, but nothing too pressing. It could wait until tomorrow.

Right now, there was nothing she wanted more than to cook dinner with Cody and to try to hunt down her husband for a long-overdue talk. She loved him and she wanted him to know that. She didn't know if they could make it work, if he could find a way to love her forever, instead of for the time being.

She stopped by the gym for Cody, thanked Bryan for letting him hang out and drove Lady Blue to the Lodge.

"When's the h-house going to be fixed?" Cody asked.

"Ryder said there was so much work to be done that it was going to be a while. Tired of the Lodge?"

Cody laughed. "No way."

Annabeth shook her head. "Oh really?"

Cody nodded. She knew how close Teddy and Cody were getting, their love of model cars acting as a sturdy glue. But that's what worried her. Cody was getting too comfortable in the Boone family—they both were. Maybe the babies would ensure they were always family no matter what happened between her and Ryder. But how would she cope with that? Seeing what she wanted, what she had and what she lost.

She drew in a deep breath. No more speculating until she'd worked things out with Ryder.

"How about spaghetti and meatballs tonight?" she

asked, turning at the impressive wrought-iron-and-stone gate that announced they'd reached Boone Ranch.

She saw Cody press his nose to the glass, hoping for a sighting of Uncle Hunter's whitetail or axis deer. Or maybe even some of the exotic game he'd started working with. Cody thought the animals were fascinating. Not as fascinating as cars, but a solid second. It probably helped that Eli was really into animals. He was older, the kind of kid someone Cody's age would look up to. The fact that he was a good kid, kind to Cody, respectful to his family, and funny, was a huge relief for Annabeth.

Teddy looked up from the check-in counter at the Lodge. "You're home early."

"I thought I'd make dinner for you tonight," she offered. "Spaghetti and meatballs? I know that's Ryder's favorite."

Teddy frowned. "He said something about working late tonight."

She nodded, trying not to be disappointed. "It'll keep."

Teddy's smile was strained. "I'm sure he'll be starved when he gets home."

"How was y-your day?" Cody asked Teddy, climbing up onto the stool beside the older man.

"Well, let's see. We have a couple here all the way from Minnesota. And a few businessmen thinking about renting the place out for a retreat or something. Other than that, it's been pretty quiet."

Cody nodded. "Had a s-spelling test."

Teddy nodded. "How'd it go?"

Cody shrugged. "D-dunno yet."

Annabeth smiled at the exchange. "Cody, why don't

you go spend some time with Tom while I get started on dinner."

Cody nodded, hopping down and scurrying to his bedroom.

"You don't have to cook, Annabeth." Teddy was watching her. "There's stew and corn bread or chicken-fried steak in the dining room."

"For guests," she countered. "I appreciate it, Teddy, I do. But I have to do something to feel like I'm pulling my weight around here."

Teddy scratched his chin, then nodded. "I'm pretty partial to spaghetti and meatballs myself."

Annabeth smiled. "Good." In her room, she changed into some black leggings, one of the few things that didn't feel tight on her stomach. She tried on several T-shirts, but all of them hugged her bump in a way that left no doubt as to her condition. She gave up, pulling on one of Ryder's long flannel button-up shirts. She put her hair into a ponytail, slid on some slipper socks and headed back into the kitchen.

She was humming to the radio, rolling up meatballs, when she heard Ryder say hello to his father. She spun around as he entered the kitchen—looking dirty and tired and so handsome—it took everything she had not to welcome him home properly.

"You're not barefoot." His voice was low and gruff, a broad grin on his way-too-handsome face.

"It's a little too cold to be barefoot. And unsanitary—" Then she got it. Barefoot, pregnant and in the kitchen. She scowled at him. "Oh. I thought you were working late."

His smile faded. "Dad told me you were here."

She stopped, an uncooked meatball in her hand. "So you came home?"

"Nice shirt." He sat his tool belt on the bench and crossed the room. "We need to talk, Princess."

Her heart sank. "We do."

"I know what you're going to say." Ryder shoved his hands into his pockets. "So I want you to let me go first. Please."

"Okay." She forced the word out.

His frown deepened as his gaze traveled over every inch of her face. "I'm sorry I waited so long to do this." He sighed, opening then closing his mouth. His attention wandered to the meatball in her hand. "But I don't want to do this while I'm covered in dirt and sweat. Let me clean up first?"

She nodded, unable to speak. He was sorry. He was sorry he'd waited so long to end it? What was he sorry about? She turned back to her cooking, slapping the meatballs onto the tray and ignoring his exit from the room.

Cooking relaxed her. The meatballs went into the oven, and she started chopping onions, oregano, basil and mushrooms—stirring it into a hearty tomato sauce with a splash of red wine. She buttered the bread with her homemade garlic mixture and toasted it until it was crisp and light.

Cody helped her set the table. On the other side of the family kitchen, connected through the large pantry, was the industrial kitchen for the Lodge guests and special events. Annabeth had popped in there to borrow spices, overwhelmed by the fancy gadgets and high-end equipment the kitchen staff used. She made do with her four-burner gas cooktop and her oven just fine.

"Go tell Grandpa Teddy and Ryder dinner's ready." She dropped a kiss on Cody's head.

The phone rang but Annabeth ignored it, that's what Teddy had told her to do. The staff would pick it up, eventually. But it kept ringing, so she pulled a tablet and pen from the drawer and answered. "Boone Ranch, how can I help you?"

"Evening, this is Jerry Johannssen calling for Ryder Boone. He available?"

Annabeth didn't know the name. "He should be in for dinner any minute."

"Good, good—" Annabeth could hear another phone ringing on the other end of the line. "Hold on a sec." Jerry's voice was muffled. "I gotta take this call. Can you get a message to him for me?"

"Of course." She clicked the pen and waited.

"Just remind him I'm waiting for his phone call. I know he's got things to take care of there, but this is a once in a lifetime opportunity. Now I've got a pretty little 1969 Mustang just waiting for his touch. He can start tomorrow— all he needs to do is call me." He paused. "And that one-bedroom apartment is his, too."

She felt cold. "Apartment?" she murmured.

"Can't exactly commute to Dallas daily." Jerry laughed. "Just have him call me, will you?"

Annabeth stared at the words she'd written. *Ryder— Job in Dallas—One bedroom apartment—leaving tomorrow? Call Jerry Johannssen ASAP.* The black words were stark against the white page. "Yes. This job, this is a permanent position?"

"I sure as hell hope so." Jerry laughed. "Thank you kindly." And the phone went dead.

Annabeth set the phone on the marble counter. *We need to talk*. She was an idiot. A complete idiot. Of course he was making plans—she'd told him to. She'd let him know, every chance possible, that he was free to do whatever he wanted because she didn't need him.

She sat on the bench, her heart and stomach and head racing and churning and aching.

The way he looked at her tonight…it was goodbye.

Cody came bouncing back into the kitchen. "You o-okay?"

She pasted on a smile. "Great. Hungry."

"Me, too." Cody wrapped his arms around her neck and pressed a few kisses against her cheek. She hugged him to her, burying her face in his hair and taking comfort in his sweet scent.

"Something smells good." Renata swept into the kitchen.

"There's plenty." Annabeth put the heaping bowl of spaghetti down on top of the table. "How was your day?"

Renata shook her hand, dismissing it. "It's hard being a young person in an older community."

Teddy entered at that point. "Who's old?"

Renata smiled. "Not you, Dad, you get it. You understand you have to embrace new things, like technology, to advertise and draw new tourists."

"I'm hip," Teddy said, making everyone laugh.

"What did I miss?" Ryder asked, all wet hair and dashing smiles.

"Grandpa T-Teddy's f-funny," Cody said.

Annabeth placed the salad on the table and sat, trying not to react when Ryder sat beside her.

"Smells amazing," he said, serving himself a heaping helping.

"And it's your f-favorite," Cody added, nudging Annabeth with a smile.

She felt the heat in her cheeks, but refused to look at anything but the salad on her plate.

"Annabeth, that's not near enough food for you now," Teddy scolded. "Cody, get your ma a big glass of milk, too."

Cody hopped up.

Annabeth glanced at Ryder.

"Dad—" Ryder sighed.

"What? She needs to be eating more—a lot more." Teddy frowned, then went wide-eyed. "Oops."

Annabeth smiled. She couldn't help it.

Renata was staring at her, eyebrows arched and waiting.

Cody, oblivious, placed a huge glass of milk on the table. "Here you go."

Annabeth eyed the glass of milk. "That should do it."

"So?" Renata asked.

"Cody…" Annabeth took her son's hand. "I'm pregnant."

Renata jumped up, squealing, as she dropped a kiss on Ryder's cheek, then Annabeth's, then hugged Cody.

"What's that?" Cody asked.

"Your mom's giving you a brother or sister," Renata explained.

"Or one of each," Ryder added.

Annabeth didn't want to look at him. Not now. She wanted to enjoy this, to feel nothing but love and contentment. Instead, a hole was forming in her heart. And seeing the smile on Ryder's face was like salt to the world's worst paper cut. She tore her gaze from his and focused on Cody. This was big news for him and she didn't want him to be worried or upset.

"Twins?" Renata was squealing again, lifting Cody in her arms and spinning him around. "Two babies, Cody. What do you think of that?"

Cody giggled, wobbling on his feet when Renata sat him down.

"I'd say this deserves some celebrating." Teddy grabbed the phone. "I'm calling your brothers over for dinner."

"I'm not sure I made enough." Annabeth eyed the mountain of spaghetti.

But Teddy was heading out of the kitchen, talking to someone on the phone.

"There's enough for at least two weeks' worth of leftover lunches," Ryder said. He knew how frugal she was. He'd teased her about the stockpile of single-serving meals in her freezer. But she couldn't stand seeing anything go to waste.

"So, no leftovers," Renata agreed. "But plenty for the family." She pulled Annabeth to her feet and stood back to look at her. "Can I?"

Annabeth saw Renata's hand hovering over her stomach and nodded. "Sure. Nothing to feel yet—"

"Anytime now," Ryder interrupted.

He'd know. He spent more time reading the baby book than she did. Even though he knew the babies would be moving soon—that they were coming. Was he really planning on leaving?

Renata's hands pressed against her stomach, the soft fabric of Ryder's shirt rubbing against her skin. "That's quite a bump." It was easy to see Renata was figuring out when things had happened. When she stood up, she looked back and forth between Ryder and Annabeth curiously.

Cody came forward, pulling up her shirt to stare at her stomach. "Hi," he said. "And hi."

Annabeth felt the sting of tears in her eyes and ruffled her son's fine blond hair.

Ryder's hand was warm against the skin on her back. "I'm sure they're saying hi right back, Cody." He knelt beside the boy.

Cody was staring intently at the swell of her stomach. "Does it hurt?"

Annabeth laughed, watching her son. "No."

"Be sweet to Mom," Cody spoke softly. "She's the best. Don't worry about n-nothing. R-Ryder and I can p-protect you. And Tom will, too."

Ryder was looking at her, she could tell. She shouldn't look at him, but she did. She could spend hours lost in those eyes, pretending he loved her the way she craved. It would be easy to reach out and slide her fingers through the short dark blond hair, stroke the side of his face. Her hand itched to do it. She flexed her fingers, fighting the instinct.

Ryder captured her hand and pressed a kiss to her palm. It was impossible to resist touching him then. Her fingers rested along his cheek, absorbing his warmth.

Chapter 16

It took less than fifteen minutes for all the Boones to converge. More chairs were added, making it close quarters. She was almost in Ryder's lap when everyone was seated, but she tried not to think about it. Instead, she watched the dynamics of the family around her.

The brothers were fascinating, every conversation lined with a competitive yet playful edge. Other than Teddy, Hunter seemed the most content. The love he and Josie shared was evident in every glance and touch. She'd never know Eli was Josie's stepson, the bond there was so strong and real. A lot like watching Ryder and Cody... Her chest ached.

Archer was the most aloof, observing everyone without any obvious reaction. He didn't smile often or have much to say about anything but work. But when he caught her eye, he raised his glass in a quick salute. She smiled, nodding in return.

Fisher kept people laughing. He knew how to make everyone welcome and entertained. Especially the boys. Eli and Cody were in stitches as Fisher shared a story about one of the fourth-years at the veterinary hospital and a very affectionate Great Dane.

She was smiling, too, caught up in the boys' laughter, when Ryder shifted. His hand rested on her thigh. And, try as she might, she was instantly aware of his breath on her shoulder, the low rumble of his laughter.

She all but jumped up to clear the table when the food was gone.

"That was delicious." Fisher smiled down at her. "Thanks for the eats, sis," he added, winking.

"Glad you enjoyed it."

"You headed over later?" Fisher asked Ryder so softly she wasn't sure she'd heard correctly.

But Ryder led him out of the room and she was left with Renata and Josie and cleanup duty.

"You should sit and actually eat something." Renata shook her head. "You didn't eat anything except a carrot stick. And you didn't touch the milk Cody got you."

She smiled, scrubbing the garlic from the pan. "I'm fine."

"I bet there's some Italian crème cake left in the other kitchen," Renata kept going. "No one can say no to Bitty's cake."

"I'm fine—"

"Renata's gone." Josie laughed. "She's right, Annabeth. You're eating for three. Three." Josie paused, eyeing Annabeth's stomach. "Eat some cake and don't feel guilty about it."

Renata carried a cake plate back into the kitchen as

they finished the dishes. "Y'all sit, and I'll get plates. How's the new book going, Josie?"

Josie was a children's author and illustrator. Her books were about a little country town a lot like Stonewall Crossing. And, to Annabeth, her friend's illustrations were worthy of framing.

"Things are good. Nothing like finding your rhythm." Josie took a bite of cake and closed her eyes. "This is too good."

Annabeth shrugged and took a bite. Good was a huge understatement.

Renata chattered on about her work at the tourism department for the county. Annabeth listened. She had to get through tonight, finalize everything with Ryder, before she could deal with anything else. Would she still be welcome for cake and chit-chat once she was the former Mrs. Ryder Boone? Her stomach clenched and she dropped her fork.

"You okay?" Renata asked.

"Fine." She tried to smile, but the clenching didn't ease.

"Annabeth, you look really pale." Josie took her hand. "You sure you're okay?"

"I'm fine." Annabeth stood. "I'm going to check on Cody." She hoped being on her feet, stretching, might ease the cramps. Cody and Eli lay on the floor of the great room, a game of checkers underway. She waved and decided a walk and fresh air would do her some good. She slipped out the back door and onto the wide wraparound porch. She moved slowly, resting against the support beams now and then, and thinking calm thoughts. She had to relax—all this stress wasn't good for the babies.

She walked all the way around the house and found Ryder on the front porch, talking on the phone.

"I already told you I can't make it tonight." Ryder laughed. "Maybe tomorrow."

She leaned against the railing.

"I have a few things to work out here…" He laughed again. "She doesn't know. Not yet."

Doesn't know what? Was he talking to Mr. Johannssen? Was this about his new job? His new life? She was sitting with his family, eating cake, talking about their babies and the future, and he was…already moving on. Talking to her was the only thing holding him back. Maybe she should approach the situation like a Band-Aid. It would hurt less ripping it off quickly.

"Ryder?"

He turned, his smile disappearing. "Gotta go."

"We can't keep putting off our talk." She wrapped her arms around herself. "I know you said you wanted to go first, but I can't wait."

He frowned, looking around them. He stepped closer to her, but she stopped him.

"I need you to know how much I appreciate everything you've done for me and Cody. Because I do. But it's time for me and Cody to go home." She refused to look at him, it hurt too much. "Our home."

"Annabeth…" His hands settled on her shoulders. "Come on—"

She shook her head. "I'm done. I can't do this anymore. I know I'm emotional and pregnant, but I'm not the only one that's involved here. We're going to hurt so many people. Cody?" She shook her head. "It's not fair to him, don't you see? I have the job, there's no reason for you to stay with us." Her voice was shaking.

"No reason?" he hissed, his hold tightening.

She stared at him, her words so thick they almost choked her. "They will always be your children. I'll never keep them from you. But I can't keep pretending that you want anything else from me, Ryder. That you want me when this was never about you and me. My heart can't take it anymore, don't you understand that? This won't last. We both know it. I've got to get over you so I can learn to be on my own again. We've made such a horrible mistake, don't you see that?" She shrugged out of his hold. "So, please, please, just go."

He stood there, staring at her.

"I know you have other plans…that you're moving on. There's a one bedroom-apartment and a job waiting for you in Dallas right now. It's time to live your life—the life you *want*." She shook her head. "If we could leave the Lodge, we would, but Cody and I are stuck right now. Please." She swallowed. "It would be best for me… Please, stay in your apartment."

His eyes bore into hers, intense and searching. "This is really what you want? Me…gone?"

No. She wanted him to argue, to tell her he loved her. "It's what I need," she murmured.

She didn't watch him walk down the steps of the porch or drive his truck away. She sat, blindly, in one of the rocking chairs on the porch of the Lodge. By the time the sun disappeared on the horizon, Annabeth knew something was wrong.

Ryder slammed his sledgehammer into the cracking plaster, gratified when the whole wall came free and collapsed.

Annabeth's words spun in his head until it ached. She needed him to leave. She needed him to leave her alone.

He made short work of the wall, venting his frustration on the warped wood and rusted nails.

He knew he hadn't done enough, but he'd held on to hope that she'd see what they could be. That she'd find a way to believe in him. To see what he wanted to be. He'd hoped that would be enough.

His phone rang.

"Drinkin' tonight?" DB asked.

Ryder was breathing hard, dripping sweat and exhausted.

"Or you still too tangled up in her skirts to think for yourself?" DB prodded.

"No," he bit out. No matter how much he wanted to be tangled up in those skirts.

"I'll come get you," DB offered.

Ryder wiped his face on a towel, then hung it back on one of the newly framed walls. "I'll meet you there." He hung up, staring at the phone in his hand. He didn't have to ask where they were going, it was always the same place. Same drinks, different women.

He drew in a deep breath, but it didn't help the pain in his chest.

My heart can't take it anymore...

All he wanted to do was take care of her heart, body—all of her. He didn't want to hurt her. And it killed him that she didn't see that.

His phone rang again. He groaned when he saw his brother's number. "Leave me alone," he ground out.

"No, I sure as hell won't," Hunter bit back. "Where are you?"

"I don't need your shit right now, Hunter—"

Hunter cut him off. "Annabeth's in the hospital, Ryder."

Ryder was running out the door before he knew where

he was going. His heart was racing, pure unfiltered terror clawing his insides. He jumped into the truck, started the engine and peeled out, stomping on the gas and flying down the street to the highway.

He left the truck in the emergency driveway and ran inside, fear driving him. His father was there. So were Josie and Hunter.

Josie pointed. "She's in the back."

Ryder headed in that direction, ignoring his brother's scowl and his father's concern. Right now, they didn't matter. He just needed to know she was okay.

"Sir," a nurse was calling out to him, but he ignored her, peeking behind curtains as he went. "Sir!"

He froze, turning to glare at her. "My wife. Annabeth Boone?"

The woman glared right back. "Follow me."

He wanted to scream at her to tell him where Annabeth was so he could get there faster. She was alone—

"In here," the woman said. "Calm. You hear me? She doesn't need any excitement."

He brushed past the woman into the dimly lit room. Annabeth lay on her left side, her hands resting on her stomach. She had a belt around her belly and the room was filled with a strange alternating, static-sounding beat. She looked so still, thin and fragile. As though he could break her by touching her.

He crossed the room and bent low, pressing kisses along her brow. "Annabeth?"

She turned, her eyes fluttering open. "Ryder?" Her chin crumpled.

"I'm here, Princess." He sat on the bed, resting his forehead against hers. "Just let me stay."

Tears spilled from her beautiful hazel eyes and down her cheeks.

"I love you, Annabeth. I love you." His hands tangled in her hair. "Don't ask me to leave you, because I can't. Whether or not you think you need me, I know I need you. I can't lose you."

She was crying, hard sobs racking her body.

"Shh." He held her close, his eyes burning. "What do you need? Tell me, whatever it is—let me do something."

She slipped her arms around his neck. "Stay."

He relaxed, melting against her. He was on the verge of tears, but he had to be strong. Together, they could handle whatever was happening. As long as he had her, it would be okay. He kissed her, cupping her cheeks, rubbing her tears away. "What did the doctor say? What happened?"

"I stood up—" she sniffed "—and got so dizzy. I guess I fainted."

He frowned, kissing her forehead, then her cheeks. He didn't want to think about her lying on the ground. "Why'd you do something like that?" he tried to tease.

She laughed, stroking his face with her hand. He covered her hand with his, pressing a kiss to her palm.

"I wasn't there to catch you," he murmured, his voice gruff.

"I'm sorry, Ryder—"

"Shh, we'll figure this out." He kissed her again. "You know why I call you Princess, Annabeth?" She shook her head. "That's how I see you. Like a princess from a bedtime story. Sweet, giving, smart and funny. A good woman. Beautiful in every way." He smoothed her hair back again. "Better than anything I'll ever deserve. But everything I've always wanted. Calling you Princess helps

me remember how special you are. And how damn lucky
I am."

She was staring at him with round, damp eyes.

"It's going to be okay. Doc Meyer will know what's
wrong—"

"Probably looking at pre-eclampsia," a voice from
behind them announced.

Ryder barely moved. "Doc Meyer," he said.

"Ryder." Doc Meyer checked the monitor, flipped
through Annabeth's chart, then sighed. "How are you
feeling Annabeth?"

"Tired," she answered.

"I need to examine her, Ryder, so you'll have to
move." Doc Meyer put his hands on his hips.

Ryder stood, but didn't let go of Annabeth's hand—
no way anyone would make him let go of her.

Doc Meyer sighed again, but there was a small smile
on his face. "We're going to check on the twins. Heartbeat sounds good."

Ryder realized that was what the static thumping was
and smiled down at Annabeth. She looked so scared it
tore his heart out. He crouched on the floor at her head,
smoothed her hair back and kissed her forehead. "Everything's gonna be okay. You hear me?"

She nodded once, her gaze locking with his. "I hear
you."

A nurse wheeled a cart into the room. He ignored
everything but Annabeth, smoothing her hair, twining
his fingers through hers, smiling at her. He hated feeling helpless.

"There we go." Doc Meyer was pointing at the screen
on the cart. "Looks like we have a boy...yes... A healthy
boy, from the looks of him."

Ryder stared at the screen, smiling at the image that greeted him. His son.

The screen went black, then another baby.

"And a daughter. One of each. She's a tiny thing… but…she looks good, too…" Doc Meyer kept clicking buttons. "I'd say we're pushing twenty-four weeks. Too early to deliver."

Ryder had never felt such excitement and concern all at once. "And Annabeth?"

"Well…" Dr. Meyer looked over her chart again. "Could be pre-eclampsia. Could be diet or stress. Her BP was a little high when she came in, but it's fine now. We'll need to run a few tests to see for sure."

"If it's pre-eclampsia?" Annabeth's voice was soft.

"Bed rest. Here or at home." Doc Meyer looked at the two of them.

"Home, please," Annabeth asked.

"Whatever Doc Meyer says, Princess." He shook his head. "I'm not taking any chances with you."

Doc Meyer cocked an eyebrow. "Let's see what the tests say. We'll need to get some blood. Annabeth, Nurse Garcia will help you to the restroom for a urine sample."

"I'll help," he offered.

"They're not going far, Ryder." Doc Meyer peered at him over the rim of his glasses. "We'll both be in earshot."

He didn't care what Doc Meyer said. He watched the nurse unhook Annabeth from several devices, help her into the wheelchair, then to the bathroom.

"You okay?" Doc Meyer asked Ryder.

Ryder closed his eyes, the enormity of the situation hitting him. "Just tell me what I have to do to keep her safe, Doc. Then I'll be okay."

Chapter 17

Annabeth strolled down the stone patch and over the hill to the dock. She paused, soaking up the heat of the afternoon sun and the pure contentment she felt at the sight that greeted her. Ryder and Cody, side by side in straw cowboy hats and plaid shirts, each holding a fishing pole. Beside them sat two pairs of boots, Ryder's tackle box and the picnic basket she brought to them hours before. She smiled, the sounds of their conversation growing louder the closer she got.

Seeing Ryder with Cody filled her with contentment. She had a family now, people who would always be there for her and Cody. All thanks to her husband. And tonight she would tell Ryder how much she loved him. She'd spent so much time being scared—finding excuses not to tell him the truth even after she *knew* he loved her. But she wasn't afraid anymore. She loved him. She needed him. And she was thankful he was her husband. He should know that.

"Bigger the grasshopper, the bigger the fish," Ryder was saying.

"And they aren't slimy like worms," Cody added, enunciating clearly.

"Never was much for worms," Ryder agreed.

"Except for the ones you'd chase the girls around the playground with?" she asked.

They both looked up at her, wearing almost identical grins. Her heart thumped. She was one lucky woman.

"Well, now, that's an entirely different use. A better use for a worm, if you ask me." Ryder winked at her. "Remember that, Cody."

She rolled her eyes. "Cody, Grandpa Teddy said your show was coming on?"

Cody and Teddy had taken to watching some car-restoration program together. Annabeth had tried to sit through it a few times, but ended up dozing off.

Cody nodded, reeling in his line. "Thanks, Ma." He put his things away, pulled on his boots, gave her a quick hug and ran back to the Lodge.

"He's going to hate moving back to the house." Annabeth watched Cody go. There was room here, to run and play and be a boy.

Ryder packed his things up, glancing up at her. "He'll be fine." Ryder stood, stretching. He held out his hand to her. "Come here."

She hugged him, smiling up at him. "Catch anything?"

"Just you." He kissed her, laughing when an especially hard kick from the twins hit him in the stomach. "They're feisty tonight." He bent, speaking to her stomach. "You two go easy on your mom." He grinned up at her. "Up for going out?"

She nodded. Nervous, but excited, too. "Getting a little stir-crazy. And Doc Meyer said I was fine. Clear for normal activities." She pulled him up. "Are you trying to break our date?"

"No, ma'am." Ryder stared down at her. "A whole night with my wife to myself? Not a chance."

"Renata's here, with pizza. Your dad found some car show marathon—poor Renata. And the bags are in the truck." She took the hand he offered, following him back up the trail to the Lodge. "Still won't tell me where we're going?" She sighed when he shook his head. "Is it far?" The bigger she got, the harder it was to sit still for long periods of time.

"Not far." He opened the back door into the Lodge.

She felt great, reenergized, more than ready to go back to work in a week. And very enthusiastic about a night with her husband. Ryder was still being extra-careful with her, a little too careful with her. But she had high hopes for tonight.

Things had changed since that awful night in the hospital. Most importantly, Ryder loved her. He told her, regularly. And when he didn't say it, he showed it in a way that left no room for doubt.

And, she'd taken the job—then immediately gone on a three-week leave of absence. Ken was all too happy to step in while she was getting the rest Doc Meyer said she needed. Rest and food. Her test results proved she was dehydrated and anemic, and several pounds underweight. Ryder, Cody and Teddy were relentless in their devotion to "fattening her up."

She pressed a kiss to Cody's forehead, thanked Teddy and hugged Renata before Ryder pulled her out the front door and into his truck.

"You in a hurry?" she asked.

"It's getting late. We're losing daylight," he said, as if that explained anything.

"And daylight is necessary for…?" she teased, taking a moment to appreciate her husband's strong profile.

He laughed. "You'll see."

Ryder drove into town, past the elementary school and toward her house. But instead of turning right, he turned left…and stopped in front of the Czinkovic place. The for-sale sign was gone and Ryder's motorcycle was parked out front.

Annabeth stared out the window, frozen.

She was looking at Cody's picture. From the fresh lilac-blue paint with bright white trim and detailed work to the shining stained-glass windows at the top of the gable. The porches, which had drooped sadly, were straight and level. Even the yard had been overhauled, blooming with yellow lantana, tulips and irises waving happily in the spring breeze.

She stepped out of the car, shock and joy leaving her speechless.

In the backyard, in the perfect tree-house tree, was Cody's tree house. It had the winding staircase with a rope bannister and an elevator for Tom—just like his picture. She pressed a hand to her mouth, torn between laughing and sobbing. She couldn't stop the tears that rolled down her cheek, or the joy that washed over her.

Several thumps from her belly and she looked down,

running her hands over her belly. "You two are so lucky. You have the best daddy in the world."

Ryder climbed out of the truck, watching her with a full heart. The look on her face made every early morning and late night working worth it. He smiled as she said something to her stomach, her hands smoothing her yellow shirt into place. She walked to the tree house, her long hair and white skirts blowing in the breeze, as she circled the base of the tree. He followed her, equal parts excitement and anxiety. Trying to give the woman he loved her childhood dream was no small thing.

"You're amazing." Her voice shook, heavy with emotion. "It's too much."

"No, it's not." He brushed the hair from her shoulder.

She stepped forward, wrapping her arms around his waist. The swell of her belly brought out a fierce protectiveness in him. And a sense of peace he'd never felt before. That night, seeing her in that hospital bed, put everything into perspective. Annabeth and Cody were all that mattered—and the twins. No matter what, if he had them life was pretty damn good.

Her voice was muffled against his chest. "Cody is going to be thrilled."

"I hope so. He's gotten pretty attached to Dad." Ryder breathed deep, drawing her scent in. "As much as I'd like to take all the credit, it was a family project. And my brothers had their own opinion on a lot of things. My dad, too." But working toward this, building their family, had brought him closer to his dad than ever before. "Hope we got it right."

"Are you kidding?" She looked up at him. "It's perfect, Ryder."

He grinned. He'd be content to stay just like this, holding her close. But there was more to show her. "We're not done yet. Come on." He let her go, then took her hand in his.

Each room had been completely redone. He'd refinished the floors, repaired the wiring, removed a few walls to open the place up and repainted every square inch. Once that was done, he'd brought over whatever furniture they could salvage from her house. He'd added a few new additions, like the china hutch that displayed her grandmother's china.

"Made sure all the doors are handicap-accessible, too," he murmured, watching the sheer amazement on her lovely face. "For Flo's Sunday dinners. I figure we could rotate between here and the Lodge so Dad's included."

"Ryder…" She walked through the house, opening and closing cabinets and doors. He showed her downstairs, the things he'd pulled from Flo's storage unit, her house and contributions from his family, too. It was truly their home.

He showed her the bed he and John had built for Cody from car parts. "It's safe, no sharp edges, promise." He ran his hand along the steering wheel. "Thought he'd get a kick out of it."

"This is amazing. He will… He will flip." She shook her head.

He led her down the hall to the babies' room, pushing open the door. He'd asked Josie for help and his sister-in-law had delivered. The walls were covered in a gorgeous mural of fairy-tale castles and nursery-rhyme characters.

"A princess." She glanced at one of the details.

He smiled broadly. "Of course."

"So this must be you?" She pointed at the knight on a white horse.

Ryder shook his head. "Dad wanted you to know he made sure we followed the crib instructions. He hovered every second, double-checking our work. I thought Archer was going to pop a gasket."

Annabeth was sniffing when she faced him. "Ryder, how…? When…?"

"Every spare second." He shrugged.

"But…" She shook her head, looking around the nursery. "It's so much work."

"I don't mind working." He grinned. "I think we all enjoyed it."

"It's too much."

"Not for you, Princess."

She shook her head, her gaze traveling slowly over his face. "Since the night you proposed, you've done nothing but take care of me and Cody." She paused. "No, since before that."

He cupped her cheek, staring into her huge hazel eyes. "I've loved you a long time, Annabeth."

Her eyes closed briefly. "I'm sorry." She paused and his heart seemed to stop. "I'm so sorry I haven't shown you the same love and respect you give me, every day." She swallowed, covering his hand with hers. "But I'll spend the next thirty or so years trying to make up for it, I promise." A tear slipped from the corner of her eye. "It scares me how much I love you, Ryder Boone."

His heart thudded against his chest, filling his body with real happiness. He'd wanted that for so long, but never dared to hope. Hope was a dangerous thing.

"But what scares me more is you not knowing that. I

guess I was scared that telling you would change things. That it would scare you…or something. But now I know better. I trust you. I trust us." She paused. "And I'm so glad you're their father." She put his hand on her stomach. "And Cody's father." She stood on tiptoe, twining her arms around his neck. His arms slid around her back. "I packed Option A. You'd mentioned burning it? Or shredding it. Your call. It's not what I want." Her gaze held his. "I know I can make it on my own. But, for the first time in my life, I don't want to. I *need* you." Her voice wavered. "I don't have any way to show you what you mean to me, Ryder…nothing that compares to this." She gestured to the house with one hand, holding on to his with the other.

He rested his forehead against hers, her words filling all the empty spaces in his heart. She needed him. She wanted him. She loved him. He had everything he'd always wanted. "Say it again," he murmured, stooping to kiss her full lips.

"I love you," she whispered, her hands cradling his face as she pressed kisses along his cheek and nose. "I love you."

"I'd say that's a mighty good place to start, Princess."

* * * * *

Trish Milburn is the author of more than fifty novels and novellas, romances set everywhere from quaint small towns in the American West to the bustling city of Seoul, South Korea. When she's not writing or brainstorming new stories, she enjoys reading, listening to K-pop, watching K-dramas, spending probably way too much time on Twitter and, since she lives in Florida, yes, walks on the beach.

Books by Trish Milburn

Harlequin Heartwarming

Jade Valley, Wyoming

The Rancher's Unexpected Twins

Harlequin Western Romance

Blue Falls, Texas

Her Perfect Cowboy
Having the Cowboy's Baby
Marrying the Cowboy
The Doctor's Cowboy
Her Cowboy Groom
The Heart of a Cowboy
Home on the Ranch
A Rancher to Love
The Cowboy Takes a Wife
In the Rancher's Arms

Visit the Author Profile page at Harlequin.com for more titles.

Twins for the Rancher

TRISH MILBURN

Thanks to Beth Pattillo for helping me brainstorm Lauren's character and for being a friend from back when I was taking my first fledgling steps into the world of romance writing.

Chapter 1

The floorboards creaked as Lauren Shayne took her first steps into the building that she'd become the owner of only minutes before. Her hands shook from the enormity of what she'd done. The mortgage on what had been a German restaurant called Otto's years ago wasn't small, but neither was her dream for the place.

A dream that she would have never guessed would take her so far from home.

Despite her initial "this is perfect" reaction to seeing the inside, the fact it was four hours from her home in North Texas gave her significant pause. Taking the leap had required a week of denial, then pondering and number-crunching after every adult member of her family had told her to go for it. She'd finally reasoned she could get the place opened and leave the day-to-day running to a manager who lived in Blue Falls or nearby. If it did well enough for her to expand in the future, then maybe she could finally find a space closer to home.

But she couldn't let her imagination run wild. Not when there was still a lot of work and a ton of luck standing between her and making even one restaurant a success. Loyal watchers of *The Brazos Baker* cooking show, or fans of her cookbooks and magazine alone, weren't going to be enough to keep the place afloat. And she needed to get the bulk of the work done before her TV show resumed production after the current hiatus—that would require her to be back in her kitchen on a regular basis.

She attempted a deep breath, but it was a bit shaky. She hoped she hadn't just gambled her daughters' future security away with a bad business decision.

As her steps echoed in the rafters, where forgotten cloth banners decorated with German coats of arms hung, Lauren saw beyond the dust and detritus to a restaurant filled with people enjoying her grandfather's prize-winning barbecue, and baked goods made with her recipes, while they took in an unbeatable view of Blue Falls Lake.

She smiled as she imagined the look on Papa Ed's face when she finally revealed the finished product to match the images that had been in her head for a couple of years. At times, those images and the support of her family had been the only things that got her through one of the toughest periods of her life.

"Now, that looks like the smile of a woman about to do great things."

Lauren startled at the sound of a guy's voice and grabbed the back of a dust-covered chair at the sight of a tall man standing between her and the front door. He held up his hands, palms out.

"Sorry, I didn't mean to scare you."

"Can I help you?" Miraculously, her voice didn't reveal the runaway beating of her heart.

"Actually, I'm hoping I can help you." He didn't advance any closer, giving Lauren a few moments to take in his appearance, looking for clues to his meaning. Dressed in dark slacks, pressed white shirt and pale blue tie, he didn't come across as a laborer looking for a job. She guessed he stood a bit over six feet, had sandy brown hair and was attractive in that clean-cut "businessman who used to be the high-school quarterback" sort of way.

"Tim Wainwright with Carrington Beef. We provide top-quality beef products to restaurants all over Texas. And it's an educated guess that a barbecue restaurant is going to need a lot of ribs and brisket."

Lauren tilted her head slightly. "How could you possibly know I'd be here or that I planned to open a restaurant? I literally signed the papers fifteen minutes ago."

Tim smiled. "I'm just that good."

Lauren made a sound of disbelief. This guy was full of himself.

Tim motioned, as if waving off his previous words. "It's my job to know when potential new customers come on the scene. I heard from a friend on the local city council about your plans and that you were closing on the property this morning. Took a chance we'd cross paths."

"You must really need the business if you're here now." She indicated their surroundings, covered with enough dust they could probably make dust castles. "As you can see, I'm a long way from opening my doors for business."

"It's never too early to make a good decision."

She lifted an eyebrow. Did he brainstorm these business pickup lines? Her thoughts must have shown on her face because the teasing look on his disappeared. He reached into his pocket and retrieved a business card, which he extended as he walked closer.

"I'd like to sit down with you when it's convenient and discuss what we can offer you. Dinner tonight, perhaps?"

There was something in the way he looked at her that made her wonder if his invitation was just about business. Or did he use his good looks to his professional advantage? That thought did not sit well with her. And with good reason.

"I'm afraid I won't have time tonight." Or any night, she thought as she accepted his card. "But when I'm ready to make those kinds of decisions, I'll know how to reach you."

She thought for a moment he might press for the "hard sell" approach, but thankfully he just nodded.

"The dinner invitation is a standing one. I'm through this area quite often."

She simply nodded and offered a polite smile. No need to reveal that when she wasn't working on *Brazos Baker*–related business, she was doing her best to not suck at being a mom. She'd save that tidbit in reserve in case he attempted to get personal. Nothing like the responsibility of twins in diapers to scare off unwanted advances.

Evidently getting the message that he wasn't going to make any more progress today—professionally or otherwise—Tim gave a nod of his own and headed for the exit. Halfway there, he turned and took a few steps backward as he scanned what would become the dining room.

"Can't wait to see what you do with the place."

After he left, she was hit with just how much work she faced before decisions such as which food vendors to use made any sense. And none of that work was going to move to the "completed" column if she didn't get to it. She rolled up her sleeves and took another step toward her dream.

It was time for Adam Hartley to stop stewing over the potential customer he'd lost and forge ahead. His family had been understanding of the time and funds he'd put in to the branded-beef operation so far, but each day he wondered when that understanding would disappear. Everything his siblings did in addition to their regular ranch duties added to the Rocking Horse Ranch's bottom line. Sure, Sloane's camps for underprivileged kids cost money, but those funds were now coming from the product endorsements her new husband, Jason, had signed after winning the national title in steer wrestling the previous winter.

Adam kept reminding himself that big rewards required big risks. He just hoped his risks ended in the types of rewards he envisioned.

At the sound of the front door opening, followed by fast-approaching footsteps, he looked up from the list of possible customers throughout the Hill Country and into Austin.

"I have great news," Angel said as she darn near slid into the dining room like Tom Cruise in *Risky Business*.

"You sold some photos?" His sister was slowly gaining recognition for her beautiful photos of ranch and rodeo life.

"No, great news for you."

He leaned back in his chair. "I could use some of that."

"I just heard from Justine Ware that the Brazos Baker is opening a restaurant here in town."

"Who?"

"The Brazos Baker, Lauren Shayne." At what must be a confused look on his face, she continued, "She has a cooking show on TV. Mom watches it all the time. She has a magazine, too. Some cookbooks. And now she's planning to open a barbecue restaurant in what used to be Otto's."

No, anywhere but there.

Part of him was excited to have such a high-profile prospective customer, but he'd had his eye on that building for a while. His imagination had seen it as a mercantile filled with Rocking Horse Ranch–branded products—prime steaks from their herd, Ben's hand-tooled saddles and leatherwork, Angel's photographs, his mom's chocolate cake. He'd seen it all so clearly—except for the money to make it possible. The branded-beef operation was supposed to fund those big ideas, but he needed time for it to grow. Time he evidently no longer had.

He had to stop investing so much time and energy in the cart before he could even afford the horse. But maybe, despite the disappointment, this opportunity would help him take a leap forward toward the eventual goal. A goal that would now have to reside somewhere else, though at the moment he couldn't imagine where.

Still, the prospect of supplying not only a restaurant of that size, but also one operated by someone famous felt like Christmas presents for the next decade dropped into his lap.

Angel motioned for him to stand. "You need to go shower and put on clean clothes."

"Um, why?"

"Because when I came through town just now, I saw vehicles at the restaurant. She's probably there right now, just waiting to hear all about awesome locally grown beef."

A shot of adrenaline raced through him. When he started to gather the papers strewn across the table, Angel waved him away.

"I'll take care of this. Go on." As he headed toward the bathroom, Angel called out, "Oh, and tell her Mom loves her show. Maybe that will win you brownie points."

Adam raced through his shower and getting dressed. Before hurtling out the door, however, he decided he should learn a little bit more about this famous cook before showing up to meet her unprepared. He couldn't blow his only shot to make a positive first impression. He opened his laptop, which Angel had deposited in his room, and did a search for the Brazos Baker.

A quick web search brought up her page. He wasn't prepared for the beautiful, smiling face that greeted him. With that long, straight blond hair and those pretty blue eyes, she looked one part model and one part girl-next-door. He wasn't a viewer of cooking shows, but he had to admit the deep-dish apple pie in her hands made his mouth water.

He forced himself to navigate away from her photo

and read about how she got her start—learning from her grandmother, entering 4-H baking competitions, publishing her first cookbook when she was only twenty. Lauren Shayne appeared to be a lot more than just a pretty face.

Nowhere on her site was there any mention of plans for a restaurant, but perhaps that was under wraps. Well, it would be until the Blue Falls gossips got hold of the news, which they probably had ten seconds before she'd even rolled into town. The fact his sister had already found out and blown in like a storm to tell him was proof enough of that.

Not wanting to delay contacting her any longer, he shut down his computer and headed out the door. As he drove toward town, he couldn't keep his imagination from wondering what it would mean to have his family's beef used by a celebrity. Would she mention it on her national television program? The possibilities began to supplant some of the disappointment over her choice of building.

His mind skipped ahead to Rocking Horse Ranch beef appearing on the menus of fancy hotels and the catered events of the increasing number of actors and musicians calling the Austin area home. A flash of brown on the side of the road intruded on his daydream a moment before a deer jumped in front of his truck.

He hit the brakes and tensed less than a breath before the unavoidable *thunk* and jolt as he hit the deer dead-center. His heart was still racing when the hiss of steam rose from his radiator. There were times when Adam thought his family's motto should be One Step Forward, Two Steps Back. Why did that deer decide today was the day he couldn't handle the pressures of life anymore and taken a flying leap in front of a pickup truck? A truck Adam had bought used and finally managed to pay off exactly one week ago, just in time for its tenth birthday. And as a bonus, it appeared his air bags were not operational.

After turning on his hazard flashers, he stepped out onto the pavement to verify the deer that had gotten knocked into the ditch was indeed dead. One look was all the confirmation he needed. Same with the front grille of his truck. With a sigh, he pulled out his phone and dialed Greg Bozeman and his always-busy tow truck.

Half an hour later, instead of introducing himself to Lauren Shayne and singing the praises of his family's locally raised beef, he was at Greg's garage, waiting for the man to tell him how much the tow and repairs were going to cost him.

He considered buying a bag of chips from the wire rack to calm his growling stomach, but he figured that was a buck he should save.

Greg stepped through the doorway between the repair bays and the small office of the garage, which had been in his family for as long as Adam could remember.

"I think your family could keep me in business just replacing radiators and front grilles."

Adam knew Greg was referring to when Adam's brother Ben had accidentally run into Mandy Richardson's car the previous year thanks to a pigeon flying through his truck's window and hitting him in the side of the head. He'd had to repair Mandy's car, but it hadn't turned out so badly in the end. Ben and Mandy were now happily married with an adorable little girl. Adam was pretty sure his encounter wasn't going to turn out with that sort of happily-ever-after ending. The best he could hope for was the lowest possible repair bill Greg could manage.

"Yeah, seems the area wildlife has it in for us."

"At least the deer didn't hit you in the head."

After Greg gave Adam the estimated price and said he needed a couple of days to complete the repairs, he asked if Adam needed a ride anywhere.

"No, thanks. Got a couple things to take care of in town." He'd figure out how to get back to the ranch after that.

Greg waved as he picked up his ringing phone.

Adam started walking toward downtown Blue Falls, thankful the day was overcast so he wouldn't be sweating buckets by the time he reached his destination. Now he needed Lauren Shayne's business more than ever. He'd launched the branded-beef business with his family's blessing, hoping to contribute his part to the diversification that would allow the Rocking Horse Ranch to stay solvent and in the family, something that had been touch-and-go on more than one occasion. But if he didn't land some big accounts soon, he wasn't sure how much longer he could keep seeing money going out without enough coming back in.

Sure, the business was less than a year old, but there wasn't a day that went by when he wasn't conscious of the figures in the operation's balance sheet. None of his siblings, or his parents, had said anything about his shuttering the operation, but he was also aware that his attempt to carve out a distinctive place for himself in the family's business was costing more than Ben's saddle-making or Angel's photography supplies.

By the time he reached the restaurant, he'd managed to adjust his attitude from his earlier annoyance to being the friendly, approachable local businessman he needed to be to meet a potential customer. A small blue hatchback sat alone outside the building. He grinned at the big yellow smiley face sticker on the hatch. It was surrounded by several other stickers—a few flowers, one that said I Brake for Cake, one of a stick figure lying beneath a palm tree and another that read Don't Worry, Be Happy.

Lauren Shayne seemed to be a happy-with-life type of person. He supposed that was easier when your business was a roaring success. Although her car didn't look as if it was driven by one of the rich and famous.

Well, if nothing else, maybe some of her happy vibes would rub off on him and finish vanquishing his frustration and concern.

He took a deep breath, stood tall, fixed his pitch in his mind and walked through the large, wooden double doors. The first thing he saw when he stepped inside was Lauren Shayne standing on the top step of a ten-foot ladder, stretching to reach a banner hanging from one of the large posts supporting the ceiling. His instinct was to steady the ladder, but he was afraid any sudden movement would cause her to fall. Instead, he stood perfectly still until she gave up with a sound of frustration and settled into a safer position on the ladder.

"Would you like some help with that?"

She startled a bit, but not enough to send her careening off her perch, thank goodness.

"Can I help you?" she asked.

He couldn't help but smile. "I thought that's what I was offering." He pointed at the banner.

She stared at him for a moment before descending

the ladder. "That's not necessary. I'll get some help in here at some point."

"I don't mind," he said as he walked slowly toward the ladder, giving her ample time to move away. His mom had taught him and his brothers to never make a woman feel as if she was trapped or threatened. The fact that there was only one vehicle outside and no signs of other people in the building told him that Lauren was here alone. "You almost had it anyway. My just being a little taller should do the trick."

She didn't object again so he climbed the ladder and nabbed the cloth banner bearing some unknown German coat of arms and several years' worth of dust. When his feet hit the wooden floor again, he held up the banner.

"This thing has seen better days."

Lauren made a small sound of amusement. "That it has."

He shifted his gaze to her and momentarily forgot what planet he was on. The picture on Lauren's website didn't do her justice.

"I'd introduce myself, but I'm guessing you already know who I am." She didn't sound snotty or full of herself, more like…

"I suppose you've already had several visitors stop by."

"You suppose correctly."

"Small town. News travels fast."

"Oh, I know. I grew up in a town not much bigger than Blue Falls."

He found himself wanting to ask her about where she grew up, to compare experiences of small-town life, but his visit had a purpose. And that purpose wasn't to keep

Lauren talking so that he could continue to appreciate how pretty she was or how much he liked the sound of her voice, which for some reason reminded him of a field of sunflowers.

Wouldn't his brothers—heck, even his sisters—hurt themselves laughing over the thoughts traipsing through his head right now?

"So, the question remains, what brings you by?"

Right, back to business.

"I'm Adam Hartley, and I wanted to talk to you about locally sourced beef from the Rocking Horse Ranch."

"No mistaking this for anything but the heart of Texas. You're the second beef producer to come see me in the last hour."

Someone had beaten him here? He silently cursed that deer for making him later to arrive than he planned. A sick feeling settled in his stomach.

"May I ask who it was?"

Please don't say Carrington Beef. They'd claimed a number of contracts he'd been in the running for, and if he missed out on being first with this huge opportunity because of hitting a deer, he might have to go to the middle of the ranch so he could scream as loud as he was able.

"Carrington Beef."

Somehow Adam managed not to curse out loud, though the parade of words racing through his head was certainly colorful.

Lauren pulled a business card from her pocket. "A rep named Tim Wainwright."

It was as if Fate said, "You think I can't make your day any worse? Here, hold my beer."

Chapter 2

"Honestly, it's going to be a while before I'm ready for any sort of food products," Lauren said as she shoved the business card back in her pocket. She lifted her gaze to Adam Hartley's in time to see a flash of what looked like frustration on his face before he managed to hide it.

"I understand," he said, back to the friendly, engaging man he'd been since his arrival, as if the moment when he'd clenched his jaw and then finally let out a breath had been nothing more than a figment of her imagination. "I'd appreciate it if I could tell you about our products, however."

His approach was different enough from Tim Wainwright's that she wanted to give him a chance. It was possible that his good looks—dark wavy hair, lean build and a face that was far from difficult to look at—might be a factor in her decision, too. She wasn't interested in getting involved to any extent with anyone—might never be again after what Phil had put her through—but it didn't hurt anything to look.

And while Tim Wainwright had also been attractive, his personality was a little too slick and polished—a bit too much like Phil's, she now realized—for him to appeal to her in that way. Granted, it could all be an act he put on for work, but it didn't really matter. She was so not in the market for a man. The market wasn't even on the same continent.

"If you don't mind talking while I work, go for it."

"Okay," he replied, sounding a bit surprised by her response.

"I'm sorry. I don't mean to be rude. It's just that I have limited time to get a lot done, and I'm running behind." Which hadn't been helped by all the interruptions. Well-meaning ones, but interruptions nonetheless.

"No need to explain. I should have called ahead and made an appointment to meet with you."

"Hard to do when you don't know the number."

"True." He smiled, and wow, did he have a nice smile. He ought to be able to sell beef to half of Texas on that smile alone.

But she also knew better than to trust smiles alone. Phil had an attractive smile, too—until you realized it belonged to a snake.

"The Rocking Horse Ranch has been in my family nearly a century. Everyone who works there is family, and we have a history of producing high-quality beef products—steaks, ground, ribs."

As she listened to Adam's sales pitch, she grabbed one of the tables she aimed to get rid of and started dragging it toward the front wall.

"Here, let me help you with that." Adam lifted the opposite side of the table and together they carried it away from the middle of the large dining room.

Before she could voice an objection to his continuing to help her with manual labor, Adam launched back into his spiel.

"I'm sure you already know that diners are more and more interested in where their food comes from, and with our products you'd be able to tell them it's from a few miles down the road, raised by a family that's been part of Blue Falls for a hundred years."

She had to give him credit—he certainly was passionate about his family's business. Considering her own strong ties to family and the hard work to share her love of food with others, she admired that passion. Still, when it came down to the decision-making, it would have to be based on the price and quality of the beef. Adam Hartley could have all the charm and belief in his products the world had to offer, but it wouldn't matter if she didn't deem his ranch's beef good enough to associate with her own brand.

"Sounds as if you have a fine operation," she said. "If you'll leave your card, I'll call for a sample when I'm closer to making those types of decisions."

After a slight hesitation, he nodded and retrieved a card from his wallet, then handed it over. The ranch brand was like none she'd ever seen before, a little rocking horse like a child might use. She made a mental note to provide rocking horses for the girls when they were old enough.

"Interesting brand."

"With an interesting story behind it," he said as he helped her move another table.

"Well, don't keep me hanging."

"Shortly after my great-grandfather bought the first part of the ranch acreage, he found out my great-grandmother was pregnant with their first child, my grandfather. He used part of a tree he cleared where the house was to be built to make a rocking horse for the baby. And he made the first sign with the name of the ranch using what was left."

"That's sweet."

"Yeah, my mom gets teary every time she tells that story. Oh, by the way, I was informed by my sister to tell you that our mom is a big fan of your show."

"I appreciate that. Are you a fan?" For some reason, she couldn't resist the teasing question.

He placed one of the old chairs next to the growing collection of furniture she needed to get out of the way. "I'm just going to be honest here and say that before today I didn't even know who you were."

She caught the look of concern on his face, as if maybe he'd just shot a giant hole in his chances to land her business. Even seeing that, she couldn't help but laugh.

"I can't say that I'm surprised. I wouldn't peg you as the main demographic."

"If it helps, I do like baked goods. I don't think I've ever said no to pie, cake or cookies."

She pointed at him. "And that's what keeps me in business, the country's collective sweet tooth."

Without direction, Adam rolled an old salad bar toward the rest of the castoffs. "I hope you don't mind me asking, but if you're known for baking—"

"Why a barbecue restaurant?"

"Yeah."

"My grandfather has won more blue ribbons than I can count in barbecue competitions. I want to feature his recipe. He's actually the reason I'm here." She gestured toward their surroundings, glancing up at the high ceiling with the log beams that she imagined gleaming after a good cleaning and polish. "He grew up in Blue Falls."

"I wonder if my parents know him."

"Probably not. He left about fifty years ago."

"Has he moved back?"

She shook her head. Not unless you counted the fact he was camped out at their hotel babysitting while she worked.

"No, and yet he somehow convinced me that this was the place to launch the next phase of my business."

"Blue Falls is a good place to settle."

"I won't be living here, either," she said. "I'll just be here to get this place up and running, then I'll leave it in a manager's hands and go back home."

"Which is where?"

That felt a little too personal to reveal to a man she'd just met.

"Sorry, didn't mean to pry."

Settling for a compromise answer, she said, "North Texas."

Lauren realized when they picked up the next table to move it that it was the last one. "So, have you been helping me haul all this stuff in the hopes I'll award you a contract?"

"No, ma'am. Just being neighborly."

He seemed genuine with that answer, but she wasn't sure she totally bought it. Or maybe she was just extra cautious now, having been so recently burned in a very public way. She wondered if Adam Hartley knew about that. She found herself hoping not, and hated the idea that her recent troubles were what sprang to mind when people saw her now. Maybe if he hadn't known who she was before today, he didn't know all the ugly backstory, either. That would be refreshing.

"Okay, neighbor, I could use a suggestion of who to call to make all this stuff disappear." She pointed toward the pile of furniture they'd moved. It was still serviceable but not at all like what she had in mind for her restaurant.

"Actually, I know someone who would probably love to take if off your hands at no cost. She repurposes things other people don't want anymore."

"Sounds great."

He pulled out his phone and started scrolling through his contacts until he found what he was looking for, then extended the phone to her. She added Ella Bryant's name and number to her own phone before returning his to him.

"Well, I best get out of your hair," he said as he slid the phone back into his pocket.

"Are you kidding? You helped me make up for all the time I lost this morning."

"Glad to help, ma'am."

"Lauren, please."

"It was nice talking with you, Lauren. I look forward to hearing from you about that sample."

As he walked toward the front door, she thought that if she was any other single woman who'd had any other recent past than the one that she'd just experienced over the past eighteen months, she might want a sample all right. A sampling of Adam Hartley.

* * *

Adam hurried across the parking lot of what had until this morning been his dream purchase. Well, he supposed it was still technically a dream, but one that wasn't going to come true. But maybe he could still salvage something positive from the unexpected turn of events. Though he didn't have any sort of commitment of her business, he thought the meeting with Lauren had gone pretty well. He'd even managed not to allow his instant attraction to her show. At least he hoped it hadn't. Now he just needed to get out of sight of the restaurant before she noticed he'd arrived on foot. It wouldn't speak to his professionalism and the success of his company that he didn't even have a running vehicle to drive.

Thinking about his damaged truck brought to mind the fact that he'd almost beaten Tim Wainwright to the punch this time. It was as if the man had spies all over Central Texas, feeding him advance information about potential customers. Judging by the number of accounts Adam had lost to the man, he'd wager Wainwright's commission income was quite a tidy sum. Enough to make him cocky. The times they'd crossed paths, Wainwright acted friendly but it was in that way that said without words that he knew he was always going to win the day. He really hadn't changed that much since his days as quarterback at Jones-Bennett High, one of Blue Falls High's biggest rivals.

Adam's jaw tensed just thinking about the guy's smug look if Carrington Beef convinced Lauren to go with their products. That commission alone would probably send Wainwright on some Caribbean vacation. He likely didn't have a family ranch he was trying to take to the next level, to save for future generations. The idea of Lauren doing business with him stuck in Adam's craw.

Though their initial meeting had gone well, Adam felt as if he needed to do something more to bring Lauren over to his side. But he couldn't be pushy, wouldn't put on a practiced smile and say whatever necessary to garner her business. There had to be a happy medium. He just had to figure out what that was, and quickly.

His stomach let out a growl that would make a grizzly jealous. Thankfully the sound had held off until he was out of earshot of Lauren. Before he texted some member of his family for a ride home, he aimed to settle the ravenous beast. Lunch at the Primrose Café would be a perfect solution. Maybe while he downed the daily special, some tremendous idea for guaranteeing Lauren went with Rocking Horse Ranch beef would occur to him.

At the sound of an approaching vehicle, he moved farther onto the side of the road. When the car slowed and stopped next to him, he looked over and saw Lauren staring back at him. She looked confused, probably because she hadn't passed any disabled vehicles between her building and him.

"Need a ride?"

"I'm good, thanks."

As if to negate his words, a rumble of thunder picked that moment to accompany the overcast skies.

"I wouldn't be very neighborly if I let you get drenched, would I?"

With a sigh, he opened the passenger-side door and slipped inside the car just as the first raindrops fell.

"Thanks."

"No problem. Where to?" Thank goodness she didn't

ask him why he'd been hoofing it down the shoulder of the road.

"Primrose Café, downtown."

"They have good food?"

"Yeah."

"Great. I'll give it a try, too. Was headed out in search of lunch, just hadn't decided where. Though I look a fright."

"No, you don't." Far from it. "And besides, the Primrose isn't fancy. You'll see everyone from tourists to ranchers who have a load of cattle waiting outside."

When they reached the café, the parking lot was pretty full. With her small car, however, she was able to squeeze into a space that would hold only about half of his truck if he split it down the center. Thankfully, the spot was close to the door.

"One of the joys of having a small car," she said. "Along with great gas mileage."

They raced for the front door to the café, which he held open for her.

"Thanks." She offered a brief smile, but it was enough to make his insides feel wobbly. He looked away, trying to convince himself it was just his hunger reasserting itself.

Lauren got the attention of a waitress when they stepped inside. "Who do I see about placing a to-go order?"

"Any of us. But honestly, you'll probably get your food faster if you just eat here. We got a big group take-out order in about two minutes ago, so you'd be behind all those. Different cook working on dine-ins."

Adam looked around the crowded room, not unusual for this time of day, and spotted a two-top over by the wall. He caught Lauren's gaze and pointed toward the table. "You're welcome to join me if you think you can stand me a little longer."

He tried not to take it personally when she hesitated a little too long before nodding.

They'd barely sat down before a woman at the next table said, "Oh, my God. You're the Brazos Baker, aren't you?"

Lauren smiled, similar to the smile she showed on her website. It was different than the more natural ones she wore when not in what could be considered the public spotlight.

"Yes, ma'am."

"I don't believe it." The woman looked at her friends, who suddenly appeared just as excited. "We all love your show."

"I made your pineapple cream cake for my daughter's wedding," one of the other women said. "I had to hide the top tier for her and her husband or it would have been gobbled up, too."

"Well, I'm glad everyone enjoyed it."

The back-and-forth was interrupted by the same waitress who'd greeted them at the entrance. "What can I get for you?"

They hadn't even cracked the menus open, not that Adam ever had to. Other than the daily specials, the menu at the Primrose didn't really change. Still, Lauren hadn't been here before.

"She needs time to look at the menu," he said.

"No, I'm okay. You go ahead. I can decide quickly." She opened up her menu to give it a quick perusal.

"Burger and fries for me," he said, not feeling the daily special of turkey and dressing.

"That actually sounds good," Lauren said. "Give me that, too."

When the waitress hurried away, Lauren pulled out her buzzing phone. "Sorry, I have to respond to this."

"No need to apologize. You're a busy woman."

She flew through answering the text like a teenager who could text faster than she could speak. He took the opportunity to text Angel for a ride home after he ate. When he looked up, Lauren pointed at his phone.

"Looks as if I'm not the only one."

"Arranging the family version of Uber." At the curious expression on her face, he confessed, "I might have run over a deer and crunched the front of my truck on the way into town."

"Oh, no. My sister once completely destroyed her car when she hit, I swear, the biggest buck I've ever seen. He was like a ninety-eight-pointer or something."

He laughed at that mental image. "Bet he had a neck ache before his untimely demise."

One of those genuine smiles appeared on her face, and he swore he'd never seen anything so beautiful.

The waitress had been right. She appeared with their food just as the other staff members behind the counter started bagging up a large number of takeout containers. As their waitress moved on to her next customers, he noticed a couple of the women who'd been chatting with Lauren were now looking at him. They smiled then shifted their gazes away, but he felt odd, as if they'd been sizing him up.

He'd taken one bite of his burger when the group of women started making moves to leave. When they stood, the one who'd originally recognized Lauren drew her attention again.

"I'm so glad to see you doing well and moving on. The way that boy treated you was so wrong. I wanted to hit him upside the head with my purse, and it's not an unsubstantial weapon," she said, lifting what to Adam's eyes looked more like a piece of luggage.

"Uh, thank you." Lauren's answer sounded strangled, as if she suddenly wished she was anywhere but where she sat.

Thankfully, the women didn't stick around any longer, especially since one of the waitresses was already clearing their table so more customers could be seated. But Adam only saw that activity with his peripheral vision because his gaze was fixed on Lauren and how any hint of a smile, of happiness, had just evaporated right before his eyes.

Chapter 3

Lauren had read books where the characters were placed in situations so embarrassing that they wished for a hole to open up and swallow them, but she'd never experienced it herself. Not until now anyway. Even during the trial Phil had forced her into with claims she'd promised him half her business, she hadn't experienced the need to pull herself into a shell to hide like a turtle. Then she'd had her attorney beside her, and she'd been filled instead with righteous anger and a fierce determination to prove that Phil was full of crap and not entitled to one red cent of her money.

The determination had paid off. Only after it was all over did she realize the emotional toll it had taken on her. But as the woman had said, Lauren was moving forward—just not in the way the other woman had assumed. Before Lauren figured out some way to correct her while also not offending Adam, the woman and her friends were already headed for the exit.

Oh, how she wished she hadn't gotten a text from Papa Ed earlier that he and the girls had already eaten and were about to take a nap. She'd intended to order her lunch to go so she could head back to work. She wanted to get a good amount accomplished but also leave plenty of time to play with Bethany and Harper before their bedtime.

Movement across the table brought her back to the present. She couldn't meet Adam's gaze, didn't want to invite any questions about what the other woman had meant. Hoping by some miracle he'd missed it entirely, she latched on to the first nonrelated topic that came to mind.

"So, you said your company only employs family members. How many people is that?"

"We're up to eleven if you don't count the kids, although one's a toddler so she gets a free pass." She smiled at his joke, causing him to do the same. "Some have other jobs, too, but we all pitch in on the ranch whenever and wherever needed. You're welcome to come out and see the operation sometime, if that would help make your decision easier."

"I'll keep that in mind," she said, more out of gratitude that he'd not asked about the woman's comment than any real need to see the beef still on the hoof.

Thankfully, their conversation flowed into even safer territory with him telling her about the various businesses in town that brought in tourists, or that were popular with the locals—or both.

"You're going to have some competition from Keri

Teague. She owns Mehlerhaus Bakery and is considered the best baker in Blue Falls."

"I don't mind a little friendly competition. It's been my experience that there can never be too many desserts available. The number of people with a fondness for sweets is directly proportional to the number of sweets they can get their hands on."

Adam laughed. "You and Keri should get a cut of Dr. Brown's business. He's the local dentist."

She smiled. "That's not a half-bad idea."

Adam's smile lessened a fraction as he glanced beyond her. Before she could turn to investigate why, an older woman stepped up to the table and placed her hand on Adam's shoulder.

"I hear your family's about to get a little bigger again."

"You hear correctly."

Was Adam married? She didn't see a ring on his hand, but that didn't mean anything. She knew ranchers who didn't wear rings so they didn't get caught on machinery and rip off a finger. Of course, he could be a father without a wife. He had mentioned kids on the ranch earlier. Though she barely knew him, she really didn't want to believe he might be married and having a friendly, chatty lunch with her. She was well aware that men and women had business lunches all the time, but the fact that Adam didn't come across as a married man made her hope he wasn't. Not that she wanted to be with him. She just didn't want to be faced with another lying, self-serving man.

Adam made eye contact with Lauren. "My oldest brother, Neil, and his wife just announced they're having their first baby."

"Oh, good for them." She ignored the strange and

unexpected feeling of relief that the child wasn't his. She tried finding a valid reason for her reaction. When she couldn't, she chose to ignore it.

"Yeah, it's so nice seeing all the joyful events your family has been having—weddings, babies." The woman shifted her attention toward Lauren. "I'm sorry. I must have left my manners in the car. I'm Verona Charles. I wanted to welcome you to Blue Falls. Everyone is so excited to have you here, and we can't wait to see what you do with your place."

"Thank you. I appreciate that." She wondered if there was a soul left in the county who didn't know what she was up to. She accepted Verona's hand for a shake. "It's nice to meet you."

"Verona used to be the head of the Blue Falls Tourist Bureau before she retired," Adam said.

"Yeah, but old habits die hard. I still have this urge to greet newcomers and visitors as soon as they cross the city limits."

Lauren caught a shift in Adam's expression—as if he was trying really hard not to smile or maybe even laugh. What was that about?

"Verona, your order's ready," one of the waitresses called out from behind the counter.

"Oh, I better get that. Taking lunch out to everyone at the nursery."

After Verona took her leave, Adam explained her final statement. "Her niece, Elissa, owns Paradise Garden Nursery, a big garden center a short distance outside of town. That's another tourist draw to the area, especially in the spring."

"Ah. So now explain what was so funny."

"You caught that, huh?"

She nodded as she swirled a fry through her pool of ketchup.

"I guess someone should warn you. Verona has appointed herself town matchmaker. If you spend any time here at all, she'll try to pair you up with someone."

A cold ball of dread formed in Lauren's middle. A matchmaker was the absolute last thing she needed in her life right now.

Adam considered himself lucky that his attempt to not laugh at Verona was all Lauren had noticed. If she'd guessed that he'd momentarily been okay with the idea of Verona trying to match up the two of them, that likely would have been the end of any chance he had of winning her business. He had all the evidence he needed in her reactions to what both the unknown woman and Verona had said. He wasn't Sherlock Holmes or anything, but even he was able to deduce she wasn't interested in a romantic relationship. He had to admit he was curious why, but he wasn't about to ask such a personal question of someone he'd met only a little more than an hour ago.

After they'd finished their meals, he asked Lauren if she wanted dessert.

"Better not. I'm so full now that I'm likely to want to take a nap when I get back instead of working."

"Speaking of, you'll want to be careful with that ladder, especially if you're alone. When I first came by earlier, I was afraid you were about to topple off it."

"I'll be careful. A full body cast isn't my idea of a good time."

"That's nobody's idea of a good time."

After they both paid for their meals, he once again held the door open for her. The rain had passed, leaving behind a faint hint of sun trying to burn its way through the clouds.

"You need a ride somewhere else?"

He spotted Angel just pulling into the parking lot. "No, thank you. My ride just showed up."

She glanced across the parking lot. He could tell when she spotted Angel.

"One of the family members who works at Rocking Horse Ranch?"

He nodded. "My sister, Angel. She's mainly a photographer, a darn good one, but she's been known to string fence and muck out stalls."

"My little sister dabbles in photography, too. Nature stuff, mostly. Does Angel specialize?"

"Ranch life and rodeos. She's beginning to gain some recognition, has had some photos in a couple of national magazines."

"That's great. Well, I'll stop talking your ear off and let you get on with your day."

"No problem. Hope to hear from you soon."

She simply nodded and headed toward her car, and he hoped he hadn't come across as too pushy. He didn't think he had, but you never knew how far was too far for other people.

When he realized he'd been watching her a bit too long, he turned away and headed for Angel's vehicle.

"That was her, wasn't it?" Angel asked as soon as he opened the door to her car.

"Yeah."

"Looks as if things must have gone well if you two had lunch together."

"I think our meeting went okay, but lunch was just an accident."

Angel started the engine but didn't pull out of the lot. Instead, she watched as Lauren drove by and gave a quick wave to them.

"How does an accidental lunch happen exactly?"

With a sigh, he recounted the story of his morning, right up until Lauren had given him a ride to the Primrose.

"Well, that's a good sign."

"Not necessarily. She was just being a decent person, preventing me from getting soaked to the bone."

"I'd give you that except she agreed to have lunch with you, too."

"It wasn't her first choice." As Angel finally drove out of the lot onto Main Street, he told her how he and Lauren had come to share a table.

"She could have waited for takeout or gone somewhere else."

"Yeah, but she was hungry then."

"Whatever. I just think you must have made a good impression."

He hoped so, and he tried to tell himself it was only for professional reasons.

"I think she's already in Verona's crosshairs."

"I wonder who Verona has in mind for her," Angel said, not even trying to disguise her teasing tone.

"Well, judging by Lauren's reaction to the idea of a matchmaker, I'm guessing Verona is out of luck on this one."

"Oh, I suppose that does make sense."

"What does that mean?"

"Lauren went through a really ugly and public breakup with her fiancé. And then the bastard took her to court, tried to sue her for a big chunk of her profits."

"Did he help her start her business or something?"

"No. From what I read, he claimed she'd promised him a half stake when they got married. When the engagement got called off, he sued, saying he was still entitled to what he was promised."

"He sounds like an ass." Adam supposed this ex could have been cheated somehow, but his gut told him Lauren wasn't the type of person who would treat someone that way. He based that on the look he'd seen on her face when the woman at the café had mentioned the guy doing Lauren wrong. She'd seemed very adamant in her support of Lauren. What was it with men who couldn't treat women decently?

"That's the general consensus," Angel said.

"Verona ought to know about that and lay off."

"Maybe she thinks the way to get past such a bad breakup is to find someone new and better."

"She might mean well, but she should mind her own business."

"I've wondered sometimes if Verona is lonely. She's never married, and I've never seen her out with anyone."

"Still doesn't give her the right to push people together."

"I think it's more like gentle nudges."

Adam snorted. "I'd hate to receive one of those nudges if I was anywhere near a cliff."

When they reached the ranch, he changed back into work clothes so he could help his brothers replace some rotting timbers on the side of the barn. As he rounded the corner of the barn, he spotted Neil first. His eldest brother was standing back and watching as Ben nailed a board in place.

"Playing supervisor again?" Adam asked.

Neil smiled. "Perk of being the oldest."

"Yeah, you're going to feel old soon when that baby gets here," Ben said. "I speak from experience. There were days in those early months after Cassie was born that I almost had to tape my eyes open to get any work done."

Suddenly, Adam felt more separate from his brothers than he ever had before. Their lives had moved into a different stage, which included marriage and children. They could share experiences, along with their sister, Sloane, to which he had nothing to add. Even Angel had a child, though no husband. In that moment, Adam felt more like an outsider than he had since arriving on this ranch as a child.

"How'd the meeting go?" Neil asked, drawing Adam's attention back to something they did have in common—the ranch and its long-term viability.

"Pretty good. Will be a while before anything can come from it, though."

"Just make sure you kick Wainwright's butt this time," Ben said.

Adam decided not to reveal that Wainwright had beaten him to Lauren's door. He had to believe that one of these days the Rocking Horse operation was going to triumph over Carrington. And he admitted to himself that there was another reason he hoped he would win the contract with Lauren. It would be no hardship to see her on a regular basis. Or would it? He was attracted to her, but he respected that the feeling wasn't mutual. It would have to be enough if they had a business relationship, maybe even became friends.

But as he helped Ben and Neil finish making the repairs to the barn, he couldn't manage to push Lauren from his thoughts. He considered how Neil, Ben and Sloane had all found their other halves when they were least expecting it. And tried not to think about how he sure hadn't expected his reaction to Lauren Shayne.

Lauren walked outside the restaurant with two cold bottles of water in hand to find Ella Bryant and her husband, Austin, loading the last of the tables onto a trailer hooked up to their pickup.

"You two look thirsty," Lauren said as she extended the bottles toward them.

"I feel as if I could drink the lake," Austin said as he hopped down from the trailer.

"Eww," Ella said.

Lauren laughed. "Pretty does not equal potable."

Austin did manage to drink half the contents of his bottle before coming up for air, however.

"I really appreciate all this," Ella said.

"Thank Adam Hartley. He's the one who suggested I call you."

"I'll do that. He's a good guy. All the Hartleys are good people."

"That's reassuring to hear about someone I might do business with in the future."

"I haven't had their beef," Austin said, "but that family is as honest as anyone you'd ever hope to meet."

Now that was more welcome to hear than they could possibly know. Honesty was pretty much at the top of her list of desirable traits these days.

Lauren pointed toward the load of discarded furniture. "I have to admit I'm curious to see what you do with all that."

"I have more ideas and materials now than I have

time to implement. But I guess that's a good problem to have."

"It is indeed."

Ella nodded toward the building. "Do you know what style you're going to put in its place?"

"Honestly, it's going to be like picking the building—I'll know it when I see it. But I want it to be Texas-themed. Part of the building is going to be a store filled with items with that theme, as well."

"You should check out the antiques stores in Poppy. They've always got neat stuff, lots of big items that could be turned into unique tables, large metal Texas stars. And there are a lot of craftsmen and artists in the area who I'm sure would be interested in putting their items in your store if that's the way you want to go with it. We have a local arts-and-crafts trail, so you could surreptitiously check them out in advance if you wanted to."

Now that did sound promising. "Thanks for the tip. I'll do that whenever I get the chance."

"Well, we'll let you get back to work," Austin said. "We look forward to your opening."

"Thanks." She waved goodbye to them, then went back inside to tackle washing all the windows. She'd been putting it off for three days because she hated the task so much. It probably made sense to just wait until all the interior work was done, but she wanted a better idea of how the place would look at different points of the day through actual clean windows. How the sun hit would likely influence how she organized the dining room and the shop.

But the moment she stepped inside, the enormity of the job—not to mention the time she'd have to spend on the ladder Adam had warned her about—hit her, and she just couldn't face the task today. In truth, she didn't feel as if she could face much more than a hot shower, dinner and a face-plant into her bed at the Wildflower Inn.

But mommy duties awaited, and the thought of seeing her smiling babies gave her a boost of energy. At least two wonderful things had come from her relationship with Phil.

She promised herself she'd tackle the windows tomorrow, then grabbed her keys to lock up. As she drove the short distance to the inn, her thoughts wandered through the names and faces she'd met since her arrival in Blue Falls. Everyone seemed nice and she could see why Papa Ed had fond memories of the place. Though she'd been hesitant initially about placing her flagship restaurant here, now she could see that it would fit in perfectly with the community's other offerings.

Thankfully, no one else had mentioned Phil or the trial, so they either didn't know about it or had decided not to bring up the topic. She'd prefer the former but would take either. What she wanted more than anything was to forget Phil even existed and that she'd ever been so blind that she hadn't seen through to his real motive for wanting to marry her. She would never make that kind of mistake again.

For some reason, she wondered if Adam Hartley now knew all the details. After meeting him and Tim Wainwright, she'd done an internet search on both their companies. So it would stand to reason they'd done the same for her. She felt sick to her stomach thinking about Adam sitting in front of his computer reading about the trial. He seemed like a nice guy, but she detested the idea that someone learning about her past might see her as an easy mark.

She shook her head, not wanting to be so cynical. Instead, she'd rather think of Adam as a potential friend. She didn't want him to know about what Phil had done, because it might taint the possibility of a friendship without the accompanying pity she'd seen in the eyes of more than one person she knew. Their hearts were in the right place, but those reactions had only served to make her feel like an even bigger fool.

When she reached the inn, she didn't immediately get out of her car. Instead, she sat in the quiet, looking out across Blue Falls Lake, its surface painted gold by the slant of the setting sun. This area was pretty now, even with winter approaching. She'd bet it was gorgeous in the spring, when all the wildflowers were blooming and carpeting the roadsides throughout the Hill Country.

Hopefully, all the busloads of tourists who visited the area in search of the iconic bluebonnets would fill her restaurant to bursting and keep the cash registers busy. Maybe it was petty or needy of her, but she wanted her first venture since leaving Phil to be so successful he choked on the idea of all the money not going into his pockets. And it would provide undeniable proof that his claim she would be a failure without him was complete garbage.

Not wanting to think about her ex anymore, she made her way inside.

She heard the girls giggling before she even opened the door to her room. When she stepped inside, she smiled at the sight that greeted her. Papa Ed was playing peekaboo with Bethany and Harper, much to their mutual delight.

He straightened from where he was sitting on the edge of the bed next to the girls' travel crib. "Look who's home," he said in that special voice he used with his great-granddaughters.

Lauren didn't point out that nice as it was, the Wild-flower Inn wasn't home. Instead, she headed straight for her little blonde bundles of grins and baby claps. She lifted Bethany from the crib and booped her nose with the tip of her finger.

"Have you been good for Papa Ed today?"

"They were angels, of course," Papa Ed said as he picked up Harper and delivered her into Lauren's other arm.

"I think Papa Ed is fibbing, don't you?" she asked Harper, drawing a slobbery smile.

"Well, you can't fault them for being fussy when they're cutting teeth."

"Yeah, probably a good thing that's something none of us remember doing." Lauren sank onto the chair in the corner of the room so the girls could use her as a jungle gym. "So, what did you all do today?"

"Before the rain, we went for a stroll through the park and played in the sandbox they have down there," he said, referencing the public park at the bottom of the hill below the inn. "We had a picnic and watched ducks on the lake."

"That sounds like quite the exciting day." She dropped kisses on the top of both her babies' heads. "You must be worn out," she said to her grandfather.

"Not at all. We had a nice nap this afternoon. Plus,

reinforcements are on the way. Your mom called and said she was coming down to see the new place."

Lauren laughed a little. "I think it's more likely she's coming to see these two."

"Can't say that I blame her. She's never been away from her grandbabies this long."

"My girls are going to be spoiled so rotten they'll stink all the way to Oklahoma."

"There is no such thing as too much spoiling."

Lauren outright snorted at that comment, making the girls startle then giggle at the strange sound Mommy made.

"I'm pretty sure that's a recent change in opinion. I don't recall it being in place when Violet and I were growing up."

"When someone becomes a great-grandpa, he's allowed to change his mind."

Lauren smiled and shook her head.

"How did your day go?" he asked.

She gave him the rundown as well as what she hoped to get accomplished tomorrow.

"I wish you had some help."

"I will eventually. I just need to be conscious of my expenses right now and do everything I can myself. Plus, Violet will be here soon. She's almost caught up with everything on the to-do list that needs to get done before she can work remotely."

"I'm so glad you two work so well together," Papa Ed said.

"I don't know what I'd do without her, especially over the past year and a half. But don't tell her that or she'll get a big head."

Papa Ed chuckled. "You're probably ready for a shower."

"That I am. And then some food."

He took Harper from her just as there was a knock on the door. Lauren carried Bethany with her as she went to open it. Her mother's face lit up as soon as she saw Bethany. She immediately held out her hands for her granddaughter.

"Gammy's here," her mom said, resulting in some excited bouncing by Bethany.

"Well, I see I've been usurped," Lauren said as she handed over her daughter.

"Someday you'll enjoy being the usurper when they have babies of their own."

"A long, long, long time from now." She was barely used to the idea of having two children of her own. There wasn't enough room in her mind to even contemplate grandchildren someday.

Once the girls were safely ensconced with her mom and grandfather, Lauren grabbed clean clothes and headed for the shower.

After washing away another day of dust and sweat, she was surprised by how much better she felt. She came out of the bathroom to find a note saying for her to join her family in the dining room. When she arrived, she found them talking with Skyler Bradshaw, the owner of the inn.

"Good evening," Skyler said. "I couldn't resist stopping to see these little cuties."

Harper held Skyler's finger as if she'd known her from the day of her birth.

Lauren gently caressed the pair of downy heads. "They do have the ability to stop people in their tracks."

"Is there anything I can do to make your stay more pleasant?"

"No, thank you. Everything has been wonderful."

"Glad to hear it."

After Skyler moved on to chat with other guests, Lauren slipped onto her seat and pulled two jars of baby food from the diaper bag decorated with baby animals.

"Do you want to see the building after dinner?" she asked her mom.

"No, tomorrow's soon enough. Tonight, I just want to spend time with my granddaughters."

Bethany let out an enthusiastic squeal as if to say that was the best idea ever, drawing chuckles from the older couple at the next table.

"Nice set of lungs on that one," the older guy said.

"Let me assure you they are twins in every way," Lauren said as she held a tiny spoon of green beans up to Harper's lips.

After they'd all had a delicious meal, Lauren accompanied her mom back to the room they would share while Papa Ed headed back to his own for a well-deserved rest and, if he could find one, probably a fishing show on TV.

Once back in her room, Lauren opened her computer to check if there were any pressing messages. She grinned at the sight of her mom tickling the girls' bellies, making them laugh.

"They adore you."

"The feeling is mutual." Her mom glanced toward Lauren. "Are we interrupting your work?"

Lauren shook her head. "I've had about enough work for the day. Just checking email and social media."

"If you want to go to sleep—"

"No. It's too early. If I went to sleep now, I'd wake up at two in the morning."

Despite having worked all day, an odd restlessness took hold of her.

"You should go out and do something fun."

"I've already left the girls with Papa Ed all day. I can't just pass them off to you now."

"Why not? You never take time for yourself."

"There's a bit too much on my plate for spur-of-the-moment girls' nights. Besides, I barely know anyone here."

Despite her protestations that she shouldn't just up and leave the girls again after being gone all day, Lauren couldn't concentrate on anything. Maybe it was that she felt confined in such a small space.

Or maybe her mom was right. Since her breakup with Phil and the discovery not long after that she was pregnant with not just one baby, but two, Lauren hadn't taken any real "me" time. She told herself she couldn't afford it, or it wasn't right to leave the girls or expect her family to take care of them while she went off to do something that wasn't work-related. And now she'd added opening a restaurant to the mix, as if she had an unending reserve of both time and energy.

"Why don't you at least go take a walk?" her mom said. "It's supposed to be a lovely, clear night, not too cold yet."

This time Lauren didn't argue against the idea. "I won't be gone long."

"No need to hurry back. These little stinkers and I will be right here discussing all the yummy things their mommy will bake for them when they have more teeth."

The mention of teeth caused Lauren to remember

Adam Hartley's comment about her getting a share of the local dentist's profits. A ball of warmth formed in her chest at the memory of how easy it had been to talk with him, even after the awkward moment with the other woman at the café.

"Lauren?"

"Huh?"

"You had this faraway smile on your face." The unspoken question in her mom's tone sent a jolt through Lauren.

"Just imagining how I'm going to convince the daughters of a baker that they can't have dessert for the main course of every meal."

After a couple minutes of loving on her babies, Lauren left the room for an evening stroll to clear her head and stretch her legs.

Though there was a slight chill in the air, she decided on a walk through town. She felt like meandering along Main Street, since it was quieter and less crowded than during the middle of the day.

As she checked out the window displays of the downtown shops, she made a mental note to do some Christmas shopping soon. It'd be much easier to keep her purchases secret if she shopped when her family was otherwise occupied, especially Violet. Her sister had a habit of trying to find and figure out what her presents were well before Christmas morning. The habit was so annoying that their mother had threatened to stop buying her presents on more than one occasion. Violet would swear she'd reform, but that only lasted about a day at most. Lauren thought Violet perhaps did it mostly to see everyone's reaction.

She promised herself she'd check out the cute outfit

displayed in the window at Yesterwear Boutique, see if A Good Yarn had the lavender-scented candles her mom liked and browse the shelves at the little bookstore. At some point, she'd introduce herself to Keri Teague, the resident baker of Blue Falls, and hope Keri didn't see her as an adversary. But though the bakery still appeared to be open, Lauren didn't feel up to it tonight.

As she eyed a lovely western-themed living room set in the window of a furniture store, the sound of music drew her attention. She followed it to what turned out to be the Blue Falls Music Hall. A man in cowboy attire opened the door for a woman, allowing the sound of a band playing to rush out into the early evening. She found herself walking toward the entrance. After all, if she was going to be a local business owner, she should support the other businesses in town. Maybe it would help pave the way into the fabric of the town, toward acceptance, considering she was an outsider.

She knew how small towns worked. While she had a recognizable name that could bring in additional tourists, some locals might see her as unfair competition. Her goal was to assure everyone she wanted to create a mutually beneficial relationship with the lifelong residents of Blue Falls. She'd only stay a few minutes then return to the inn.

The moment she stepped into the building, Blue Falls didn't seem so small. That or the entire population of the town had crammed inside to drink, dance and listen to music. Picturing all these people streaming into her restaurant brought a smile to her face as she made her way toward the bar. Before she reached it, however, someone asked, "Is that smile for me?" before spinning her onto the dance floor.

Chapter 4

For one horrifying moment, Lauren thought it was Phil who'd grabbed her. Even when she looked up into the face of Tim Wainwright, it still took several moments for her heart to start its descent back to its proper place in her chest from her throat.

"Glad to see you came out to enjoy the nightlife," Tim said.

"Can't say I expected to be accosted as a result."

Tim's eyebrows lifted. "Accosted? I merely meant to claim the first dance before a line formed."

She rolled her eyes. "No need to butter me up. I'm not closer to making a decision about vendors than I was a few days ago."

"Did I say anything about beef?"

She hesitated a moment as he spun her expertly between two couples to avoid a collision that could result in a pile of cowboy hats and boots. Even Tim was dressed in jeans, boots and Stetson tonight. If she wasn't a born-and-bred Texan, she might actually buy that he was a real cowboy.

"No," she finally said.

"I'm off the clock and just wanted to dance with a pretty woman."

She doubted he was ever really off the clock, but what could one dance hurt? It wasn't as if it was a date, or would lead to one.

"Just a bit of friendly advice—perhaps ask for the dance next time rather than assume." Sure, she wanted to make friends here, but his action had rubbed her the wrong way.

He nodded. "Duly noted. I'm sorry."

She simply offered a polite smile in return, not the "It's okay" he possibly expected. Once upon a time she might have uttered it without thinking, but that was before the events of the past year and a half.

"So, how are you liking Blue Falls so far?" he asked.

Thankful to have a neutral topic to discuss, she said, "I really like it. The people are nice, and it has a great feel to the business district. Not to mention it's pretty."

"Glad to hear it."

Lauren began to relax and even allowed Tim to lead her around the dance floor for a second song. Occasionally, she spotted someone she'd met over the course of the past few days. Thank goodness Verona Charles didn't seem to be in attendance. She didn't need the woman getting any ideas about her and Tim. If Tim or Verona headed down that path, Lauren was going to break out her stockpile of stories about poopy diapers and buying teething gel in bulk.

Her breath caught unexpectedly when she spotted Adam Hartley sitting at the bar. Tim spun her around so quickly that she wasn't sure, but she thought Adam had been watching them. And while her gaze had met his only for the briefest of moments, it was long enough for her to get the impression he wasn't pleased.

Most likely it was because he'd seen her dancing with his competitor and feared he'd lost the contract with her. Was he just another guy who'd been nice to her for his own gain? For some reason, the idea of that trait applying to Adam bothered her more than if that was what Tim was doing. Maybe it was because she expected it from Tim from the moment she met him. But she should know better than anybody that it was the ones you didn't expect that posed the biggest threat.

Still, she really hadn't gotten that vibe from Adam, even though she'd been looking for it. That she might have been gravely mistaken again caused her mood to dampen, enough that after the song was finished she excused herself from the dance floor.

"Maybe we can do this again sometime," Tim said as she stepped away.

"It's a small town, so I'm sure we'll see each other here at some point." She saw her noncommittal answer register with him a moment before she turned away and headed for the bar.

She told herself it was to purchase a drink, not to orchestrate a meeting with Adam. But she wasn't very good at lying to herself. The truth was she liked him, and had she not been so recently burned she might be interested in him for reasons beyond friendship. He certainly was attractive, and he'd gotten a seal of approval from the Bryants. But at this stage in her life, she needed to focus on her family, her business and healing herself. Her soul still felt bruised and battered by Phil's betrayal. And she couldn't even think about being with anyone else until that wasn't the case anymore.

Truthfully, with her daughters to consider now, she didn't know if it was possible to trust anyone enough to risk not only her own heart, but also those of her precious babies. They were too young now to realize their father wanted nothing to do with them, so Lauren tried her best to shower them with the love of two parents.

By the time she reached the bar area, she no longer saw Adam. She glanced around but couldn't find him in the crowd, which seemed to have gotten bigger during the time she'd been on the dance floor. Had he left? Maybe that was for the best. No, it was *definitely* for the best. She attributed the unexpected pull toward him as a side effect of being in a new place where she didn't really know anyone, being away from the familiarity and comfort of home, and the frustrating human desire to feel wanted for the right reasons.

A moment after she claimed one of the bar stools, the bartender stepped up in front of her. "What can I get for you?"

She glanced at the menu board above the shelves of liquor bottles. "Just a lemonade."

"Coming right up."

"So, I hear you're going to be my new competition."

Lauren turned to see a pretty woman not more than a few years older than her and quickly deduced her identity. "Keri Teague, right?"

The sense of apprehension tightening Lauren's muscles eased the moment Keri smiled. "In the flesh."

"I hear you are known far and wide as quite the baker."

"Not as far as you, but I do all right."

"Well, as I told someone earlier this week, I don't think there can ever be too many baked goods within close proximity."

Keri laughed. "We're going to get along just fine."

"You don't know how glad I am to hear that."

"Don't tell me that you thought I'd be an ogre. Okay, who's been telling stories about me?"

"Nothing bad," Lauren said. "Adam Hartley just said I might have some friendly competition."

"That's a fair assessment. Good, I won't have to have him arrested."

Lauren felt her eyebrows shoot upward. "Arrested?"

Keri laughed. "Sorry, guess no one told you I'm married to the sheriff and that I get a kick out of teasing people about having him arrest them."

"Uh, no. But I'll be sure to be on my best behavior."

The bartender delivered Lauren's lemonade in a big frosty glass.

"So how do you know Adam?" Keri asked.

"He came by to pitch his family's beef products."

"You going with them?"

"Haven't decided yet. That's a ways down the road."

Keri nodded as if she totally understood, which she probably did since she also ran a food-related business and likely got unsolicited visits from vendors all the time, as well.

"Adam's good people."

"So I keep hearing."

Keri gave her a questioning look, but Lauren pretended not to notice. She didn't know how many of the locals Verona Charles had in league with her on the whole matchmaking thing.

"I saw him a little while ago. Not sure where he got off to." Keri scanned the crowd, and again Lauren pretended not to notice. "Oh, he's out on the dance floor."

He was? Though she was curious as to the identity of his dance partner, Lauren had the presence of mind not to look. Instead, she steered the conversation with Keri in a different direction, asking how long she'd owned the bakery.

For the next few minutes, they shared stories about everything from baking disasters and successes to the inside scoop on various locals. To be honest, with a single conversation and a lot of laughs, Lauren felt more a part of the community. But when she glanced at her phone, she was surprised by how much time had passed.

"I better get going," she said.

"So soon. You barely made use of the dance floor."

"Been a long day. Going to be another one tomorrow."

Keri nodded in understanding. "Well, come by the bakery sometime soon and I'll give you a little treat on the house."

As she thanked Keri and stood to leave, she deliberately didn't check the dance floor or any of the surrounding tables for Adam. One would think after what she'd gone through with Phil, the part of her brain wired to notice attractive men would have been out of order. Evidently not. Thank goodness she had enough sense not to indulge it too far.

As she made her way through the crowd, she felt as if someone was watching her. Though she said she wouldn't, she directed her attention toward the dance floor. Adam was still out there, but he wasn't looking her way. She scanned the sea of faces and didn't see anything out of the ordinary. She shook her head, telling herself not to be so paranoid, and resumed her trek toward the exit.

The moment she stepped outside and the door closed behind her, it was as if someone had turned down a blaring radio to its lowest volume. She could still hear the music inside, but her ears thanked her for the comparative silence of the surrounding night.

It'd gotten chillier since she went inside, so she zipped up her jacket and quickly texted her mom that she was on her way back. She headed across the parking lot, glancing up at the blanket of stars above.

"Well, ain't you a pretty one?"

Her heart leaped immediately to her throat at the sound of the man's voice. Her brain supplied the extra bit of information that he'd had too much to drink and that he wasn't alone. From the look on the other man's face, he was equally inebriated. Neither of them was a small man. Rather, they looked as if they could wrestle a full-size bull to the ground.

Blue Falls seemed so friendly and safe that she hadn't once thought being out after dark by herself would be dangerous, but she supposed there were drunk jerks everywhere. Which was little consolation at the moment. With most of the downtown businesses closed and the noise level inside the music hall, she doubted anyone would even hear her scream.

Her babies' faces flashed through her mind. Thank goodness they were safe with her mother.

"What, you can't speak?" the second guy asked, taking a couple of steps toward her, prompting her to take three backward and hoping she didn't trip over her own feet.

At first she hesitated to take her eyes off the men.

But she knew she couldn't get past them, so her only choice was to get back to the safety of the throng of people inside the building. She shot a quick glance toward the entrance, judging how quickly she could make it. *If* she could make it.

As if her thundering heart had willed it, the door to the hall opened...and out stepped none other than Adam Hartley.

Adam had danced to a few songs with Courtney Heard, a friend from high school, and her cousin, Shannon, who was visiting from El Paso, but as he left the music hall he found his mood hadn't improved to any great extent. He wasn't sure if the sour feeling in his middle was because Lauren had been dancing with someone else, or the fact that the someone else was Tim Wainwright. He'd found himself wondering if Lauren was really averse to dating someone new, or if smooth-talking Tim had already managed to change her mind.

He should have stayed home tonight, but the realization that he was the only adult member of the family who didn't have someone—significant other, child or both—had him itching to get out and do something. Blue Falls nightlife being what it was, he'd had two choices—the Frothy Stein bar or the music hall. Deciding the Stein was the more pathetic of the two, he'd headed for the music hall to see who was playing tonight. The band from Austin was pretty good, and the crowd had helped him shake off the "odd man out" feeling. At least until he'd seen Lauren in Tim's arms on the dance floor. When she'd smiled up at Tim, Adam felt as if a bit too much of his siblings' newfound affinity for happily ever after had rubbed off on him.

When finding his own dance partners hadn't helped, he'd said his good-nights and headed for the exit. But who did he see as soon as he stepped out into the crisp night air? One Lauren Shayne. His momentary "you've got to be kidding me" was immediately replaced by the realization that she was wild-eyed scared. The two hefty guys encroaching on her personal space was obviously the reason why.

Wasting no time, he ate up the distance between them. He'd take on both guys if he had to in order to protect her, even knowing he'd likely be the worse for it after everything was over.

"There you are," he said, swooping in next to Lauren and wrapping his arm around her waist. "Sorry. I got caught up inside."

She stiffened next to him, but must have realized what he was doing because she relaxed slightly the next moment.

"Get your own," one of the guys said, his breath evidence he'd fail a field sobriety test.

"Already did, and you're making her uncomfortable. Why don't you all go inside and ask the bartender for some coffee?" And give Adam time to get Lauren safely away from their meaty claws, not to mention make a call to the sheriff's office to keep these two off the roads tonight.

The two drunks glanced at each other, and it was as if Adam could read their minds.

"Don't even think about it."

Adam didn't know if his warning swayed them or the fact that the door to the music hall opened, spilling out light as well as half a dozen patrons. Whatever the reason, they backed off but cursed as they headed toward the other end of the parking lot. But Adam didn't relinquish his hold on Lauren as he asked her where she was parked.

"I walked here from the Wildflower Inn."

"Then I guess it's my turn to give you a lift."

"Thanks. I'd appreciate that."

He noticed Lauren glance back over her shoulder as he escorted her toward his truck, as if she was afraid the guys would change their minds again and attack them from behind. Once they reached his truck, he opened the passenger door for her.

"Sorry to inconvenience you," she said once she was in the seat and pulling her seat belt across her body.

"It's not a problem. I drive right past the inn on the way home."

"Oh, good."

He hurried around to the driver's side and hit the door locks as soon as he shut his door, giving Lauren an extra layer of protection from her would-be attackers.

"If you don't mind, I'm going to call the sheriff's office first. Those two," he said, pointing toward the men, who now appeared to be arguing, "don't need to be on the road endangering people."

"Good idea."

A sheriff's department vehicle pulled up to the edge of the parking lot before he even got off the phone. Sheriff Simon Teague got out of his cruiser at the same time a department SUV also arrived.

"Is one of those the sheriff?" Lauren asked.

"Yeah, the one already out of his car."

"I met his wife tonight."

"Should we expect the bake-off at the O.K. Corral?"

As he'd hoped, she laughed. "No, Keri's very nice. And despite your teasing me about her competition, she had only nice things to say about you. So do the Bryants. Seems you're 'good people.'"

"Had I given the impression that I wasn't?"

"No. They were completely unsolicited comments."

"It's always good to hear people think well of you, I guess."

He started his truck's engine and left the music hall and the law enforcement activity behind.

"How did you like your first trip to the music hall? I assume it's your first visit anyway."

"It was. Had no intention of going, but I was out for a walk and got drawn in by the music. Nice place, but I think I was just too tired to be in the mood to dance the night away."

She'd seemed to be having a good time with Tim, but he reminded himself that she had practice putting on a friendly face. He'd seen it with the women in the café. At least she hadn't left with Tim. Although her leaving alone had nearly cost her dearly. He squeezed the steering wheel harder, almost wishing the guys had thrown a punch or two at him so he could give it right back. A cold chill went through him just thinking about what might have happened if he hadn't decided to head home when he had.

"I hope you don't let those guys sour your opinion of Blue Falls."

"No. Unfortunately, it doesn't matter how big or small a place is, there are going to be drunken brutes at some point or another."

She was making a valiant effort to not seem too concerned about what had just happened, but he noticed how she had her hands clasped tightly together in her lap. Before he could think better of it, he reached across and gave her arm a reassuring squeeze.

"You're safe now."

He removed his hand after only a moment, not wanting her to fear she'd traded one scary situation for another, and turned in to the inn's lot. He pulled up to the front entrance so she'd only have to walk a few steps to get inside.

"Thank you for the ride. And for helping me out with those guys. I was afraid they were going to jump you."

He grinned. "I'd have made them wish they hadn't."

"You might have gotten in some good licks, but there were two of them and they seemed like the type who'd tackle a *chupacabra* wearing a cactus coat just for the hell of it."

He laughed at that colorful description. "Can't say I've heard that one before."

"It's a Lauren Shayne original. Just now thought of it."

"Somebody ought to draw that and put it on T-shirts. They'd probably sell like beer on the Fourth of July."

"Seriously, though, thank you."

"You're welcome. I doubt you have any more trouble from them, but if you do let me know. We've got enough Hartleys to form a posse."

"I appreciate the offer, but I don't think we have to go full-on Old West." She had her door open in the next breath, then stepped out. "Good night, Adam."

"Good night, Lauren."

He didn't move until he was sure she was safely inside. It wasn't until he was halfway home that he realized he'd been replaying how his name sounded when she said it. And that he'd been imagining her standing much closer to him, looking up into his eyes with the type of interest that had nothing to do with business contracts.

Yep, he was up crazy creek without a paddle.

Chapter 5

As Lauren stepped into the lobby of the inn, she was startled to come face-to-face with Papa Ed. He nodded toward the door, and quite possibly where Adam still was to make sure she got inside safely.

"Who was that?"

"One of the vendors I met earlier in the week. I took a walk through the downtown area, and he gave me a lift back up here."

"That was nice of him." There was no mistaking the tone of her grandfather's voice. It was much more a question than a statement of fact. But she wasn't about to tell him what had happened to precipitate the front-door drop-off.

"Yeah. You were right. People are nice here." With the exception of the two guys who were now hopefully either spending the night in the drunk tank, or were at least in need of a ride of their own because the sheriff had taken their keys away.

Papa Ed gave her one of his looks that said he knew there was more to the story and if he just watched her long enough she'd reveal all. She pretended she didn't notice and instead nodded at the package of little chocolate doughnuts in his hand.

"Munchies?"

He lifted the package and looked at it, then lowered it again as if disappointed in himself. "I know it's not fine eating, but they're a guilty pleasure."

"Plus you already ate all the snacks I brought along."

"It's your fault. If they weren't so good, there'd be plenty left."

She smiled and laughed a little. "And I wouldn't have the career I do."

"True. But at least those little girls give me plenty of ways to stay active and keep the weight at bay."

"Speaking of, I better go relieve Mom. I was gone longer than I anticipated."

"Any particular reason why?"

She'd opened herself back up to the questioning she'd managed to divert him from, dang it. Might as well tell the truth—at least the nonscary part of it.

"I wanted to walk along Main Street when there weren't a lot of people around, and I ended up stopping by the music hall. Thought it was a good idea to start meeting other local business owners. I did meet the owner of the local bakery, Keri Teague, and we talked longer than I planned to be gone."

No need to mention the dancing with Tim or how she'd headed to the bar in order to say hello to Adam, or how the night could have come to a very different end were it not for his fortuitous timing. She barely controlled a shiver down her spine at that train of thought.

"So, your chauffeur back—he the one you said was a little too full of himself, or the one who helped you move the furniture?"

Evidently Violet had spilled the details Lauren had shared with her during one of their phone calls.

"Furniture."

"Hmm, he *is* a nice guy."

Thankfully, Lauren yawned then, and she hadn't even resorted to faking it. Her long day was catching up with her.

"I need to hit the hay. I have an early meeting with an electrician in the morning."

Papa Ed and his processed snack accompanied her down the hall. She gave him a quick peck on the cheek before opening the door to her room. By the quiet that greeted her, she knew the girls were already asleep. Her mom was sitting in bed wearing her pajamas and reading the latest mystery in a series she liked about a baker who solved crimes. Lauren always found it odd that a baker happened upon so many dead bodies.

Lauren eased her way over to the crib and her heart filled at the sight that greeted her. Harper and Bethany were sound asleep with their little hands touching. She couldn't imagine it being possible to love another human more than she loved her babies. She longed to kiss them both, but she didn't want to risk waking them—especially in a hotel room where the other occupants might not be thrilled with the sound of crying infants.

When she turned away from the temptation of snuggling the girls, she said, "Sorry I was gone so long."

"It's no problem, hon. See anything interesting?"

Adam Hartley.

In another life, maybe.

"Some nice shops downtown I'll explore when I have some time." She almost laughed at the idea of having free time before giving her mom the same version of events at the music hall that she'd given Papa Ed.

"Sounds as if Dad might be trying to edge you back into the dating game."

Surprised by her mom's assessment, Lauren looked over at her. "Why would he do that? He knows men aren't high on my favorites list right now."

"He believes people shouldn't go through life alone. He did the same thing to me a couple of years after your father died. It took Dad a long time to realize I wasn't interested in dating again. I had my girls, my teaching career, a life that was satisfying if, admittedly, sometimes a little lonely."

Lauren's heart squeezed. Her mom hadn't ever admitted to that loneliness before.

"But what happened to me wasn't the same thing. Dad didn't choose to leave you." It had been an accident on an icy road, not anyone's fault unless you chose to blame Mother Nature or God.

"I think Dad felt guilty, or maybe just sad, that what your father and I had was cut short while he and Mom were happy all through their long marriage. He was happy and so he wanted everyone around him to be happy, too."

The pain Papa Ed must be going through without Nana Gloria hit Lauren anew. Still, she couldn't imagine her grandfather thinking she'd be the least bit interested in a new relationship, even a casual one. When would she even have time for such a thing?

And yet there was that little flicker of attraction that had led her to the bar in search of Adam Hartley. How did she explain that? Maybe it was possible to still feel physical attraction without wanting anything to come from it. If she was being honest, she didn't know how a woman couldn't be at least somewhat attracted to Adam. Based on her few interactions with him, he was a very pleasing blend of handsome, kind, helpful and dedicated to family and honest work. That was a difficult cocktail to not want to drink in one delicious gulp. Not that she had much opportunity for cocktails these days, either.

"Considering everything, I'm happier than people might expect. Who could complain when they have an awesome job, a great family and two beautiful, healthy baby girls?" And if she sometimes felt lonely while lying alone in her bed, it was a small price to pay for all the other positive things in her life.

"I might seem a hypocrite for saying this, but don't rule out having more when you're ready. Contrary to what Dad may think, I didn't. I just never met anyone else I could imagine spending my life with. I suppose I still could, but I stopped thinking that way quite some time ago. But you're still young."

"With two babies. Most guys aren't into instant family."

"Maybe not, but someone might surprise you."

That would be a surprise indeed. But then she thought about the look on Adam's face when he talked about his family, about his nieces and nephews. Maybe guys who didn't mind being around other people's kids did exist, but it would have to be a special man indeed to make her willing to take a chance again. He might have to be miraculous.

Instead of turning right out of the inn's parking lot, Adam drove back down into the main part of town. There was no sign of either of the guys who'd frightened Lauren in front of the music hall anymore—or law enforcement for that matter. So he headed toward the sheriff's office, intent on making sure those two didn't pose a threat to Lauren or anyone else. Though he'd wanted to teach them a lesson they wouldn't forget, he'd had enough sense to know he was outnumbered. If only his brothers had been with him. He wasn't by nature a violent person, but he'd seen bright red when he'd realized what was happening when he stepped outside the music hall. Thank God he'd left when he had. It didn't escape him that Lauren—or rather his reaction to seeing her with Tim—was what had made him decide to vacate the premises.

As he cruised up to the sheriff's office, he spotted Simon coming out of the building. When he pulled in next to the sheriff, he rolled down his window.

"Please tell me those idiots are sleeping it off in a cell tonight."

Simon crossed his arms. "I'll do you one better. They managed to get themselves arrested. The bigger fella decided it might be fun to take a swing at me. I disavowed him of that notion."

Adam smiled wide. "You just made my night."

"Any reason you're extra interested in them?"

"When I came out of the building, they were about to attack Lauren Shayne."

The look on Simon's face hardened. "I should talk to her."

Adam instinctually shook his head. "They never touched her, just scared the living daylights out of her. But it looked like it was about to go further when I intervened. Honestly, I was probably about to get my ass kicked, but some other people came out before anything happened."

"So I get the impression Miss Shayne doesn't want to be involved any further in this?"

"No." She hadn't actually said that out loud, but he'd somehow managed to read that in her body language. She'd only wanted to leave. "I just wanted to make sure they wouldn't be a problem anymore, for anyone."

It wasn't only about Lauren. His sisters sometimes had a night out at the music hall. Also female friends, tourists and barrel racers in town for the regular rodeos.

"I suspect when they sober up, they'll make bail and go back to Johnsonville and choose to party elsewhere next time around."

"Good."

"So, you already making a move on the pretty baker lady? Got to say from experience that being with a woman that good with desserts is not a bad bonus."

"No, I just happened to be in the right place at the right time to help her out."

"Her knight in shining armor, huh?"

Adam rolled his eyes. "Good night, Simon," he said, then drove away.

As he passed by the inn, he glanced over as if he might catch a glimpse of Lauren. But he doubted after her experience with the drunks that she'd step foot back outside until the sun was well above the horizon.

And when that time came, he needed to be hard at work doing anything but thinking about how he'd been wishing she was dancing with him instead of his biggest rival.

Lauren didn't think she'd ever been so happy to see a sunrise, despite the fact her night had been filled with some of the worst, most interrupted sleep ever. If she wasn't having nightmares about what could have happened outside the music hall if Adam hadn't shown up when he had, she was being awakened—likely along with everyone else in the hotel—by not one but both of the girls crying. It seemed her precious girls were similar in more ways than one, including when they were upset by hunger, wet diapers or the pains of teething. The challenge was trying to get them to stop crying at the same time. Neither seemed to want to be first in that regard. At home it was one thing, but knowing their upset was bothering other people trying to get a good night's sleep frayed Lauren's nerves. Keeping a hotel full of people awake wasn't the best way to win friends and future customers.

When her mom came out of the bathroom, she looked as worn out as Lauren felt.

"Pardon me for saying this," Lauren said, keeping quiet since the girls were actually sleeping peacefully now, "but it doesn't look as if the shower helped much."

Her mom rubbed her hand over her face. "It's been a few years since I've had babies crying their lungs out, and I only had one at a time. You, my dear, are a saint."

She didn't feel like a saint. More like exhausted before the day even started.

"I hate to leave you here with them again today."

Her mom waved off her concern. "I'll let them sleep now, then we'll come down to visit later. Dad and I can lend a hand if you'll let us."

"Normally, I'd say I'm good, but today I may take you up on it." Though it might be nice just to have the quiet and solitude for a few hours. She loved her girls more than life itself, but she'd bet every cent she had that there wasn't a mother alive who didn't want to run away from her children for a little bit every now and then.

Though when she arrived at the restaurant building a few minutes later, she didn't immediately get out of her car. Instead, she fought an uncharacteristic wave of anxiety. What if those guys were inside waiting on her to finish what they'd started? She thought about Adam's business card in her wallet and considered texting him to see if he knew what had happened to the men after they left. But why would he? He'd been going home after he dropped her off, and it wasn't as if the drunks had actually attacked either of them. Thus, no need to have further contact with the sheriff's department.

Taking a deep breath, she told herself that the faster she got in that building and to work, the sooner she and her family could go home. And the thought of letting any other man halt her forward progress sent enough anger through her that it propelled her out of the car and into the blessedly empty building.

She did lock the door behind her this time, but keeping out anyone who could just wander in made sense. Despite her lack of sleep, she managed to get some of the windows cleaned before the electrician arrived. By the time he finished his inspection, however, she was back to wondering what she'd gotten herself into. It was going to take more work to bring things up to code than she'd hoped. The news knocked what little energy she'd mustered right out of her. After the electrician left, she sank onto an old metal bench outside the front door and dropped her head into her hands.

She didn't look up until she heard footsteps approaching. The shot of fear was quickly replaced when she noticed her visitor was Adam. Again, he'd arrived on foot.

"Don't tell me you hit another deer," she said.

"No." He motioned diagonally across the street to the Shop Mart. "Coming back from Austin. I had to stop and get a couple of things for my dad."

She recognized his truck at the edge of the other lot.

"Are you okay?" he asked as he sank onto the identical bench on the opposite side of the front walkway from her. "Excuse me for saying so, but you look as if you didn't sleep last night."

"That's because I didn't, not much anyway."

"Maybe you should take a day off."

She shook her head. "Don't have the time."

"Then how about some help? What do you need?"

"Adam, you've already helped me more than anybody in town." She hadn't consciously realized just how much until she said it out loud. "I'm sure you have your own work to do."

"Not so much that I can't spare a few hours."

"I wouldn't feel right—"

He held up a hand. "You're not going to win this argument, so you might as well put me to work."

She lifted an eyebrow. "And here everyone has been telling me you're a nice guy, but you've got a bossy streak."

He smiled, and she tried to pretend she hadn't felt a flutter in her middle.

Lauren gave up. And if she admitted the truth, she liked having him around. Though he caused her to have unexpected reactions, he was also easy to be around. With each interaction, she was beginning to believe more and more that everyone who said he was a genuinely nice guy was telling the truth. He'd given her no reason to believe otherwise. As long as she didn't allow herself to admire him too much, she'd be okay.

"So, do you do windows?" she asked.

Lauren couldn't believe how much quicker her work progressed with just one extra set of hands. And though she'd still had the same pitiful amount of sleep, having Adam there to talk to made her feel more awake. Granted, that could be the bit of adrenaline still zinging its way through her body after they'd nearly bumped into each other and he'd instinctively placed his hand on her bare arm to steady her. It had been nothing more than a brief touch, and yet she'd swear in a court of law she could still feel his strong, warm fingers against her flesh.

She glanced up to where he stood on the ladder, washing the windows up high. Well, he was supposed to be washing them. It appeared that he was instead writing in the accumulated dust with his finger.

"What are you doing?"

Instead of answering, he shot her a mischievous grin. She pictured a little-boy version of him smiling that same way after some naughty misadventure.

Lauren took a few steps back in order to read what he'd written. *I should get free meals for life for doing this. Including dessert.*

"I don't know. That would depend on how long you're planning on living. What's the longevity like in your family?"

His smile dimmed, and she felt like kicking herself. Life and death wasn't something to joke about, especially when there was the possibility of loss associated with the subject. She ought to know that from experience.

"I'm sorry." She wasn't even sure how to articulate the rest of what she was thinking.

"It's okay. I'm adopted so my parents' genetics don't have any bearing on mine."

"Oh." But what about his birth parents? His grandparents? If he was adopted, did that mean they weren't around anymore? And hadn't been since he was a kid?

Adam proceeded to wash away the humorous words from the window, and it made her inexplicably sad. It was as if the moment a bit of humor strolled into her life, she found a way to erase it.

When he was finished washing the high-up windows, Adam descended the ladder and came over to the front counter, where she was standing sketching out ideas for the placement of customer seating and the gift-shop area. The thoughts that had been eating at her the past few minutes found their way out of her mouth.

"I really am sorry if I brought up bad memories. I should have thought before I spoke."

"It's really okay. It happened a long time ago."

She started to ask what but managed to stop herself. It wasn't any of her business.

"You don't have to be so careful around me," he said. "I won't break."

She looked up at him and realized again just how

much she liked him already. If she hadn't been through what she had with Phil, she wouldn't even question her assessment of Adam. She hated that she now always looked for hidden meaning behind words, selfish intent behind actions.

"My birth parents died in a bridge collapse when I was six. I went to live with my grandmother after that for a year, but then she had a stroke and had to be moved to a care facility."

Without any conscious thought, she placed her hand atop his on the counter. "I'm so sorry." That was a lot of loss to deal with. "I lost my dad when I was five, but I can't imagine losing both parents at once."

"I won't lie and say it wasn't hard, but I got lucky in the end. My parents now are great, and I ended up with brothers and sisters instead of being an only child. They're all adopted, too, so I wasn't alone in that experience, either."

"How many of you are there?"

"Five. Neil, Ben and Sloane are older, and Angel is younger."

"That's amazing that your parents adopted so many kids."

"We tease them that they like to collect strays."

Lauren smiled at that and wondered what life was like when all the Hartleys got together. Just then the door opened, revealing Papa Ed and her mother pushing the double stroller. Lauren realized her hand was still lying atop the masculine warmth of Adam's and she pulled it away, so quickly that it made her appear as if she'd been doing something wrong.

"Hey," she said to the new arrivals, probably sounding way brighter and cheerier than she should.

She didn't miss the curious glances both her mother and Papa Ed leveled at Adam. Before their imaginations ran wild, she gestured toward Adam.

"You're just in time to see what a great job Adam did on washing the windows."

"You hired someone?" her mother asked.

Lauren shook her head. "No, Adam was kind enough to help with the stuff up high."

"This the young man who drove you back last night?" Papa Ed asked.

"Yes. Adam Hartley, this is my grandfather, Ed, and my mom, Jeanie." And now for the part of the introductions that would likely have her seeing the backside of Adam as he suddenly had to be somewhere else. She reminded herself that was okay. "And these two sleeping beauties are my daughters, Harper and Bethany."

Instead of causing a blur as he ran for the exit, Adam crossed the few feet that separated him from the stroller. Lauren held her breath for some reason. When he smiled as he crouched down in front of them, she inexplicably felt like crying happy tears.

"They sure do look as if they don't have a care in the world, don't they?"

Lauren couldn't help the sudden laugh. "Don't let their cherubic faces fool you. They both have an incredible lung capacity, which they put to good use last night."

Adam looked up at her. "That explains why you're so tired."

"You don't know the half of it." There was so much, so very much, behind that simple statement. And to her great surprise, Adam didn't run away. In fact, if she didn't know better she'd swear he'd be perfectly willing to listen to every gory detail. And a bigger surprise than anything was that down deep, a part of her wanted to tell him.

Not trusting herself or the part of her brain that had evidently forgotten the past eighteen months, she shifted her attention to her mom. "Let me show you around."

She forced herself not to look back at Adam again as she led her mom toward the area of the building where the gift shop would eventually be located.

"It certainly has a lovely view," her mom said as she looked out the now-clean windows a couple of minutes later.

"Yeah, that was a big selling point."

Her mom glanced back toward the front of the building, where Lauren could hear Adam talking to Papa Ed but couldn't tell what they were saying. She realized she hadn't warned Adam not to say anything about the two guys outside the music hall. Hopefully, he wouldn't divulge that bit of information she purposely hadn't shared with her family.

"Can't say the view of the other direction is bad, either."

"Mom!" Lauren miraculously kept her voice low enough that she didn't attract the attention of the men.

"What? Am I lying?"

Well, no. Not by a long shot. "He's just being friendly, nothing more."

Her mom gave her one of those "mom" looks that said she was highly suspicious there was something Lauren wasn't telling her.

"Did I say otherwise?"

Damn it. Lauren realized she'd just revealed more than she wanted to admit to herself. She was really attracted to Adam, and not just because he was pleasing to the eye. The part of her that still ached from Phil's betrayal was looking for a balm, and it seemed to want that balm to be named Adam Hartley.

"You don't have to completely turn off your feelings, hon," her mom said. "Use caution, yes, but don't allow yourself to live the rest of your life afraid."

"I barely know him."

"I'm not saying he's the one or if there even is a 'one,' just that I don't want you to let Phil burrow too deeply into your mind. He's not worth it."

She was right about that, but that didn't mean she had any idea how to not let the experience with him color how she responded to people going forward.

Not wanting Adam to realize they were talking about him and perhaps get the wrong idea, she walked back across the building. As they drew close, Harper woke up and her gaze fixed on the tall, handsome man in front of her.

"Well, hello there, cutie," Adam said.

Lauren smiled at the genuine tenderness in his voice. At least it sounded genuine. Surely he wouldn't use fake affection for her children as another way to influence her to do business with him.

Harper smiled and wiggled her feet at the same time she thrust out her arms toward him. Lauren couldn't have been more surprised if her daughter had unhooked herself from the stroller and proceeded to walk across to the windows for a view of the lake.

"Well, will you look at that?" Papa Ed said.

Adam looked confused.

"She's never done anything like that with someone who isn't family," Lauren said. "Neither of them has."

"Do you mind if I hold her? I'll be careful."

"Uh, sure."

Lauren reached down to release the lap belt, but Adam already had it freed and was lifting Harper into his arms. Lauren resisted the urge to stand close in case he dropped his happy bundle. He must have seen the worry on her face because he smiled.

"Don't worry. I have lots of practice. I'm an uncle, remember?"

She had to admit he looked as if he knew what he was doing. He tapped the pad of his finger against the tip of Harper's nose and said, "Boop." Evidently, Harper found that hilarious because she let out a belly laugh before planting her little palm against Adam's nose.

Lauren was pretty sure her ovaries struck up a lively tune and started tap dancing. Not good. Not good at all.

"I think she likes you," Papa Ed said.

As if she didn't like being left out, Bethany woke up and started fussing. Knowing her ovaries couldn't handle seeing both of her babies in Adam's arms, Lauren picked up Bethany and proceeded to do a little dance with her. It had the desired effect of replacing the eminent tears with a precious baby grin.

Adam reached over and booped Bethany's nose the same as he had Harper's and got a similar result.

"Okay, stop trying to become their favorite human," Lauren said. "That's my title."

"Can't help it. They must smell the spoiling uncle on me."

Lauren had the craziest thought that she didn't want him to be their uncle. But she couldn't allow herself to even think he'd be anything more than just a funny guy who made them laugh. There were so many reasons to demand her ovaries knock off the dancing.

But, seriously, how was she supposed to ignore how sexy the man looked holding her daughter and making the babies laugh? That was impossible. Even women who didn't want children would darn near melt at the sight. Women with eyes and any shred of maternal instinct didn't stand a chance.

Adam wasn't quite sure how to interpret the look on Lauren's face. It was almost as if she couldn't believe what she was seeing. Did she think he'd hurt her babies somehow? Was she surprised he actually liked kids? He guessed he should have expected that kind of reaction. After all, he'd witnessed how protective his sisters and sisters-in-law were of their children. And he knew enough guys who didn't want anything to do with kids, especially if they weren't their own.

It hit him that the twins' father must be the ex-fiancé who'd dragged Lauren into court. Did she have to continue to deal with him for their daughters' sake? He couldn't imagine being forced to speak to someone he couldn't stand for the next couple of decades.

"How many nieces and nephews do you have?" Lauren's mother asked.

"Two nieces and one nephew for now, but there's another on the way."

"Big family?"

"Yeah. One big, cobbled-together family."

At Jeanie's look of confusion, Lauren explained, "Adam and his four siblings are all adopted."

"From different families," he added, realizing he hadn't revealed that detail before.

"Well, bless your parents," Jeanie said.

He smiled. "I'm sure there were times when they wondered what they'd gotten themselves into."

"I think all parents wonder that from time to time."

Lauren made an expression of mock affront. "I don't know what you're talking about, Mom. Granted, Violet was a pill, but I was perfect."

Her mom actually snorted at that. "Just like you thought these two were without fault about four this morning."

Adam jostled Harper, causing her to grin and reveal the hint of a tiny tooth about to make its appearance.

"I don't know what these people are talking about," he said to the little girl. "You seem pretty perfect to me."

This time, all three of the other adults were looking at him as if he was a unicorn.

Almost as if they all realized what they were doing at the same time, their expressions changed as they redirected their attention.

"Well, I should probably be heading out," Adam said as he handed over Harper to her grandmother.

"Don't run on our account," Jeanie said. "At least let us treat you to lunch."

"No need, but thank you." Even though he needed to get back to the ranch, he found himself not wanting to leave. Maybe that was why he found himself extending an invitation. "Why don't you all come out to the ranch for dinner while you're here?"

"We wouldn't want to intrude," Lauren replied quickly.

Had he overstepped somehow? Or was she just being polite? One way to find out.

"No imposition. My mom loves having people over. Like I said, she loves your show, so I might even win some 'favorite son' points if I bring you all over for dinner."

Lauren hesitated. It was her grandfather who answered for all of them.

"Well, in that case, we'd be happy to accept." Both Lauren and her mother looked at Ed with surprise, but Lauren was quick to refocus her attention on Adam.

"Thank you. We appreciate it. Hopefully you'll have the same calming effect on Harper and Bethany then." Even though she was nice, he got the feeling she was worried. If she thought a couple of crying babies would bother his family, she was mistaken.

"If I don't, someone will be able to."

As he finally headed for the door a couple of minutes later, he still had the feeling Lauren was on edge. He was honestly surprised she accompanied him outside.

"Thanks again for your help today," she said.

"It was nothing." Despite not being a great fan of washing windows, he'd enjoyed spending time with her. "Listen, I'm sorry if inviting you and your family to dinner made you uncomfortable."

She shook her head. "No, it's okay. That's just a lot of people to invite without asking your mother first."

He laughed. "I could bring home an entire tour bus full of flower peepers and she'd be in hog heaven. We've joked that when we all eventually move out, she's probably going to turn the house into a bed-and-breakfast."

"At least let me bring something. I can bake a cake."

"Where?" He pointed toward the building. "You don't have an operational kitchen yet. Plus, Mom isn't a slouch when it comes to dessert, so no worries there."

Finally, Lauren looked marginally more comfortable with the idea of eating with a family of strangers.

"I promise we don't bite," he said.

She smiled at that, and he found himself wanting to do more to make her smile. "I can't say the same for the girls. Teething makes them want to chew on whatever is handy."

"Then we'll make sure the dog's chew toys aren't within their reach."

He became aware of her mother and grandfather inside, watching them while trying to seem as if they weren't. "Well, see you tomorrow night."

"Okay. And—"

"Don't you dare thank me again."

She made a show of pressing her lips together but he could still see the gratitude in her eyes. Though he didn't need her thanks, it was nicer to see than suspicion.

As he walked across the street to his truck, he tried not to think about other emotions he wouldn't mind seeing in Lauren's eyes.

Chapter 6

Adam walked into the dining room where his mom was busy wrapping Christmas presents. Rolls of colorful paper, tape, tags and scissors were scattered across the surface of the table.

"Any of that for me?"

"No, this is all for the kids. I have to sneak my wrapping in when they aren't here."

He wondered if Lauren was the type of mom to spoil her kids at Christmas, especially their first one.

"I hope you don't mind but I invited some people over for dinner tomorrow night."

"These people have names?"

"Lauren Shayne, her mother, grandfather and twin daughters."

His mom dropped the box containing a toy ranch

set, no doubt for Brent. The stunned expression on her face surprised him.

"Lauren is coming here for dinner?"

"Yeah. I thought it would be okay. If not—"

She waved off what he'd been about to say. "No, it's fine. I just…well, she's famous for her cooking."

"So are you."

"No, I'm not."

"You have no idea how many people we've all told about your chocolate cake. I'm surprised Texas hasn't been invaded by surrounding states yet for a taste."

She made a *pffftt* sound of disbelief. "Nobody would give me a TV show."

"I disagree wholeheartedly with that assumption."

"Be that as it may, I need to figure out what I'm going to cook."

"Mom, seriously, anything will be fine. They're nice, down-to-earth people."

"That right?" There was more to that question than it appeared on the surface. "Did you meet them in town just now?"

"Yes." Better to tell the truth than have her find out some other way. "I was helping Lauren wash some windows she couldn't reach when they came by."

"You seem to be helping Lauren a lot."

"I'm trying to get her business, remember?"

"And yet I've never seen you do manual labor for any other potential customers."

Damn it, she had him there. He'd never felt an attraction toward any of them, and he suspected his mom knew it.

"None of them could give us this kind of exposure."

His mom started cleaning up her wrapping station.

"You go ahead and keep telling yourself it's only business."

"What's that supposed to mean?" He knew full well how her mind worked, especially since her children had started falling in love and getting married. She only had two left unattached, and since they seemed to be going in order of age he was up to the plate.

"You like that girl."

"She's nice." And his heart rate had a habit of speeding up whenever he looked at her, but he wasn't about to say that out loud. Especially since Lauren had already made it known that she wasn't relocating to Blue Falls. And after what she'd gone through with her ex, he suspected she wasn't too hot on dating anyway. Not that it kept him from wondering what it would be like.

"Uh-huh," his mom said, fully aware in that freaky way she had that he was not being totally forthcoming.

He leaned back against the table next to her. "Listen, I'm going to level with you. Yes, I like her. Yes, I think she's pretty and interesting. But you're aware of what her ex-fiancé put her through, right?"

The layer of teasing disappeared from his mom's face. "Yeah, very unfortunate."

"Then don't you think that dating is probably the last thing on her mind right now, especially since she has two babies?"

"I don't know."

He cocked an eyebrow at her. "Yes, you do. I know you're on this kick to see us all married off, and I'm not against the idea with the right person at the right time. But this isn't it."

And that fact made him feel way more disappointed than his and Lauren's short acquaintance should have.

"You never know."

"Mom, please. Just approach this as a new friendship, maybe eventually a working relationship, nothing more. Okay?"

She sighed. "Fine. I wish it was different, but I see your point."

He smiled. "I still think you should make your chocolate cake, though."

She shot him a look that said she knew good and well that he was asking for the cake for his own benefit more than anything else.

"Get out of here or I'll be serving you tapioca pudding."

He made a gagging noise. He hated tapioca. As he turned to leave, she swatted him on the behind with a roll of wrapping paper covered in cartoon reindeer, causing him to laugh.

As he headed outside to haul some hay out to the far side of the pasture, he caught himself whistling a happy tune. And he didn't think it had anything to do with the knowledge that come tomorrow night, he'd be able to dig into his mom's chocolate cake.

Lauren pulled into the ranch's driveway and asked herself for what must have been the thousandth time why she'd agreed to this dinner with the Hartley family. Not only were her feelings toward Adam oddly disconcerting, but she'd also sworn an oath to herself that she'd never mix business and personal relationships again. Not that a business relationship existed yet, and she would classify the personal side of things as budding friendship, nothing more.

Yeah, right. One did not fantasize about the sexy physical attributes of mere friends.

She once again played the refrain in her mind that just because she found him attractive didn't mean she had to act on it. Granted, being around him would be easier without the attraction, but her brain flatly refused to purge the knowledge that Adam Hartley was very pleasing to the eye. Which was only strengthened by the fact that he was friendly, helpful and got along famously with her daughters.

And yet it remained that she'd been on the verge of marrying a man, spending her life with him, only to find out that everything she'd believed about him had been a lie. There was too much at stake now for her to ever allow herself to make that kind of grievous error in judgment again.

Her mom reached across and squeezed Lauren's hand. "You're thinking too much."

Lauren glanced across the car. "How could you possibly know that?"

"I've been your mother for twenty-eight years. This is not a great mystery."

"Annoying."

Her mom laughed. "I'll remind you that you said that in a few years when your daughters are annoyed at you for reading them correctly."

"Seems I know someone else who was irritated by her mother knowing when she was hiding something, too," Papa Ed said from the back seat.

"Oh, hush, Dad," her mom said.

Lauren laughed, thankful for the break in the tension that had been knotted up in her middle. She was overthinking this whole evening anyway. There were just nice people in the world who wanted to be friendly and welcoming. Evidently the Hartleys were among them. There was nothing wrong with being friends with people with whom she might eventually have a business relationship. But that was as far as it could go. It was beyond surprising she was even having to tell herself that.

When they came within sight of the house, she had an immediate sense of welcome. The house was fronted by a long porch, where she could imagine watching the sunset across the pasture that rolled off to the west. On a chilly night like the one ahead promised to be, sitting out here wrapped in a quilt and drinking hot chocolate sounded heavenly. Though it looked completely different, she got the same sense of peace that she did at her own home overlooking the Brazos.

"This place is lovely," her mom said.

Harper piped up with what sounded like a sound of agreement from her car seat in the back.

"The stone and wood does fit in nicely with the surrounding landscape," Lauren said.

After parking, she went to remove Harper from her seat while her mom retrieved Bethany and Papa Ed unfurled himself from the back seat. He stretched and Lauren looked over at him when she heard some of his bones crack.

"Just wait," he said. "One day you'll sound like a bowl of Rice Krispies, too."

A beautiful Australian shepherd came around the back of her car, startling Lauren. She lifted Harper quickly out of reach, not knowing whether the dog would bite.

"She's harmless."

Lauren looked toward the sound of Adam's deep

voice. Was it her imagination or did it sound richer, sexier, today? The sight of him in a checked shirt, jeans and a cowboy hat robbed her of speech. It was as if he got better-looking every time she saw him. More likely, her brain was malfunctioning.

Thankfully, Papa Ed bending down to pet the dog diverted her attention.

"What's her name?" Papa Ed asked.

"Maggie," Adam said, though he continued to look at Lauren for a moment longer before shifting his attention to her grandfather. "She's the official welcoming committee around here. I'm just her assistant."

Harper waved her little chubby arm in Adam's direction, as if she remembered him from their one interaction.

"Hey there, gorgeous," he said to Harper as he waved at her.

Lauren forced herself not to react to the sound of those words on Adam's lips, that for a heart-jolting second she'd imagined him saying them to her.

"Come on in," Adam said, motioning them toward the house.

As they moved that way, Lauren let her mom and grandfather go ahead, and Adam fell into step beside her. His proximity did nothing to help the jittery feeling coursing through her, making her wonder if good sense was a thing of the past.

"Mom is so excited to meet you it's been amusing to watch."

Despite her success, it still seemed so odd to Lauren that people viewed her as a celebrity.

"That's sweet, but I'm just an average person who got lucky."

"From what I hear, you're not giving yourself enough credit."

"Oh, I can cook and I work hard, but the same can be said for a lot of other people."

Adam leaned closer to her. "Maybe just let Mom have her 'meeting a celebrity' moment. The closest she's gotten before is my brother-in-law, Jason, who won the national title in steer wrestling."

She wasn't sure why that struck her as funny, but Lauren laughed. The resulting smile on Adam's face threatened to melt her resolve to not think of him in any sort of romantic light.

As they entered the house to find it filled to the gills with people, Lauren didn't know whether to be overwhelmed or thankful she had more of a buffer between her and Adam.

"Hello, hello," a woman who appeared close to her mother's age said as she crossed the room. "I'm so happy you all could make it."

"Lauren, this is my mom, Diane," Adam said, suddenly at Lauren's side again.

Whether it was because of her buzzing awareness of Adam standing near her or the sheer number of people present, she only retained about a third of the names she heard as he introduced her to his siblings, their spouses, and his nieces, nephew and parents.

"I can't get over how adorable these two are," Diane said as she allowed Harper and Bethany to each grab hold of one of her fingers.

"Thank you. I'm pretty partial to them myself."

Adam's sister Sloane wrapped her arm around her mom's shoulders. "Watch her. She hasn't met a kid she didn't try to spoil absolutely rotten."

Lauren smiled and nodded toward her mom. "She'd have some hefty competition."

"They just don't understand that it's the duty of a grandmother to spoil her grandbabies," Lauren's mom said.

"I know, right?" Diane replied.

"Can I hold the babies?" a pretty young girl asked as she looked up at Diane.

"I don't think so, honey. Go wash your hands. We're about to eat."

The girl—Julia, Angel's daughter, if Lauren was remembering correctly—looked disappointed but did as she was told.

"She was the only child around here for several years," Diane said. "Now that she has cousins and another on the way, she's beside herself."

"I think she's going to take after Mom," Sloane said, "and want to keep them all."

If they hadn't been talking about a child, Lauren would have been tempted to take the twins and run. Maybe all mothers were like that, or maybe her fierce protectiveness of them was at least in part due to what she'd gone through, and that she never wanted them to be hurt in any way. Her rational brain knew they couldn't go through their entire lives without suffering somehow, but it didn't erase her need to prevent it whenever she could.

"Well, dinner is ready, so everyone find a seat," Diane said, directing everyone to the dining room.

Lauren stopped short when she entered the room to find two high chairs set up next to the table.

"I still had the chair I used for Julia, and Mandy

brought over Cassie's since she's sitting in a booster now," Angel said.

"That's very thoughtful," Lauren said. "Thank you."

The Hartleys had brought in an extra fold-up table and an odd assortment of chairs to seat everyone, but not a single soul seemed to mind. Lauren got the impression this wasn't the first time this arrangement had occurred here.

"I'm not a professional like you," Diane said as she was the last to take her seat, "but I hope you enjoy everything."

Lauren looked along the length of the table at the wide variety and sheer amount of food filling bowls and covering platters.

"It looks and smells delicious." The same could be said for the man sitting across from her, though she wasn't about to reveal that fact to everyone.

Instead, she focused on alternating between filling her plate from the dishes being passed around and opening up jars of baby food.

When she attempted to get Bethany to eat some carrots, a new food for her, Bethany let her displeasure show by spitting the orange mess back out and screwing up her face.

"I don't blame you," Adam's brother Ben said to Bethany. "Carrots are gross."

As the conversation and laughter flowed throughout the meal, Lauren gradually relaxed. Even the twins seemed to be having a good time, but that was likely because they had a seemingly endless supply of people to tell them how cute they were and with whom they could play peekaboo.

"There is no better sound than a baby laughing," Diane said.

"I agree," Lauren said as she cleaned the mushy green beans from Harper's chin.

"So when do you think you'll open the restaurant?" Andrew, Adam's dad, asked.

"Unsure. I'd like to be open as early in the New Year as possible so we can work out any kinks before the spring wildflower season starts bringing in tourists."

Of course, it would help if little roadblocks didn't keep popping up. She'd anticipated certain undertakings when it came to cleaning the place and ensuring it was up to code. With Adam's help, some of those smaller tasks during her first few days in Blue Falls had gone quite smoothly. But there'd been other obstacles she hadn't predicted. Like the softball-sized hole she'd found yesterday in one of the restaurant's windows overlooking the lake. Again, her first thought had been of Phil. It felt like a petty type of action she could imagine him taking. But then she'd heard a couple of other businesses in town had experienced the same problem during the overnight hours.

Andrew nodded. "Sounds like a solid plan. If you need any help, you let one of us know." He gestured toward the assembled Hartley clan with his butter knife.

"Thank you. It's kind of you to offer."

Was this family for real? Were they all this nice and helpful, or was she in the midst of a group effort to ensure she chose Rocking Horse Ranch beef for her restaurant? She really hoped it was the former, because she hated to think this many seemingly nice people could deceive her at once.

She listened as Ben told Papa Ed about his saddle-making business, then as Jason detailed the life he'd led on the rodeo circuit before retiring in favor of marriage, fatherhood and training budding steer wrestlers. It seemed a large percentage of the Hartleys had other careers besides working on the ranch.

"How did you all get into the branded-beef business?" she asked.

Adam glanced up from his plate. "Seemed like a good fit for a cattle operation."

Angel bumped her brother's shoulder with her own. "He's being too modest. Adam is our big idea guy."

"Angel," Adam said, obviously wanting her to be quiet, which of course caused Lauren's suspicion antennae to vibrate.

"What, I'm not allowed to brag about my big brother?" Angel shifted her attention to Lauren. "He's always thinking twelve steps ahead of everyone around him. Since we all have such disparate talents, he wants to brand not only the beef, but everything all of us do under the Rocking Horse Ranch name."

Lauren had seen that done successfully by another ranch in Texas, so it made sense on a business level.

"We might have eventually set up shop in the building you bought, but you beat us to the punch," Angel said.

Lauren noticed the tense look on Adam's face, as if he wished he could rewind time to stop his sister from revealing that nugget of information. She searched for some ulterior motive for him getting close to her that was somehow tied to the building he wanted, but wouldn't he want to see her fail instead of doing business with her?

When he met her gaze across the table, she saw a man searching for the right thing to say.

"It was just a thought. It wasn't anywhere near becoming reality."

He was clearly uncomfortable with the subject, which caused her mind to spin with possible reasons why. A quick glance at Angel revealed that she'd shifted her attention to her daughter. No one else seemed to be concerned about the turn of the conversation, which made Lauren wonder if she was once again looking for self-serving purpose where there wasn't any.

Some days she felt as if she needed to start seeing a therapist to work through her erosion of trust—of others and of herself. Because even though she was experiencing it and felt there were valid reasons for its existence, she also was aware enough to know it wasn't healthy or productive.

"Well, who's up for cake?" Diane asked.

Like a classroom filled with eager students who'd just been asked if they wanted an ice-cream party, hands shot up all around the table. Lauren laughed in response.

"Either this family really loves dessert or this is one tremendous cake," she said.

"Both," Adam said, appearing to have shrugged off his discomfort with the earlier topic of conversation.

"It's not Brazos Baker-level baking, but I've never had a complaint," Diane said.

The moment Lauren took her first bite of the rich chocolate cake, she realized just how much Diane had undervalued her baking skills.

"This is delicious," Lauren said. "And I promise you I'm not just saying that to be polite."

Diane beamed. "Oh, my, you've made my day."

"Mom, we've told you a million times that your cake is awesome," Sloane said.

"I know, but—"

Lauren held up a hand. "Please, don't think my opinion matters any more than anyone else's. Like I told Adam, I'm just someone who got lucky."

"And worked hard," her mother said.

"Luck is what happens when preparation meets opportunity."

Lauren couldn't believe her ears. She turned her gaze to Adam, who'd voiced the famous words by the Roman philosopher Seneca. Though she'd never once thought him stupid, the combination of Roman philosophy with hot Texas rancher wasn't something she'd ever imagined witnessing.

"That's literally my favorite quote," she said. "I have it hanging in my office at home."

He smiled a little. "Great minds, I guess."

It felt more as if the universe was attempting to tell her something, but she suspected that was just the traitorous part of her brain trying to find any and all reasons to convince her that it was safe to like this man, to trust him. The problem was she didn't trust that part of her brain.

When the meal was over, Diane flatly refused any help clearing the table or loading the dishwasher. Instead, Lauren and her family were ushered along with the rest of the gathering into the living area. There weren't enough seats for everyone, so the kids and several of the adults plopped down on the floor.

This was the perfect moment for Lauren to say they should be leaving. But before she could form the words, Adam stepped up beside her.

"You can't really see the cattle now, but would you like to see a little bit of the ranch?"

"I don't want to take the girls outside. I'm sure it's gotten chillier now that night's fallen."

"Oh, don't worry," her mom said. "Plenty of hands here to take care of them."

Lauren gave her mom a hard look, but it didn't seem to faze her. Instead, she just took Bethany from Lauren's arms. Harper was busy patting Maggie the shepherd on the head while sitting on Papa Ed's knee.

"Looks as if the babies are in good hands," Adam said.

If she protested now, she risked everyone asking why. And if the thoughts she was having about this man wouldn't go away, they at least needed to stay firmly in her own mind. She couldn't have anyone getting ideas she wasn't willing to act on.

"Okay." Not the most enthusiastic or elegant response, but it seemed to be all she could manage.

She sure hoped no one could tell how fast her heart was beating as Adam opened the door for her. She felt as if she must look like one of those old cartoon characters with her heart visibly beating out of her chest.

Thankfully, the temperature outside had dropped to the point where it cooled her warm cheeks.

"So how did work go today?" he asked as they walked toward the barn.

"Fine right up until the exterminator found evidence of termites." Which had just been the icing on the cake after the rock through the window.

"Bad?"

"Thankfully no, but it's one more thing—along with

having to redo some of the wiring—that I wasn't expecting."

"Starting a business seems to be like that. Just when you think you're going along fine, some obstacle pops up in your path, one you can't just go around."

What obstacles had he faced? Did he count her not making a commitment to buy beef from his ranch one of them?

When they reached the fence next to the barn, he pointed out across the dark rise and fall of the pasture. "Ranching is full of those kinds of things. Storms, drought, whatever Mother Nature decides to throw at you."

"Have you all had a lot of those kinds of problems?" Her suspicious side wondered if this conversation was aimed at generating sympathy.

He shrugged. "No more than pretty much every other rancher. It's just the nature of the business."

She glanced at his profile in the dim light. Even without full illumination, he was a handsome man.

"Is that why you came up with the branding plan Angel was talking about?"

He leaned his forearms against the top of the fence and stared out into the darkness. "I wish she hadn't mentioned that."

"Why?"

"Because they're just ideas at this point, might be all they ever are."

"Now that doesn't sound like you." How odd that she knew that about him after so brief an acquaintance.

He looked over at her. "What makes you say that?"

"You just seem like you're driven. I mean, you were

willing to move furniture just so I'd listen to your sales pitch."

"That's not all it was."

An electric buzzing launched along her nerves. What did he mean by that?

A sudden gust of wind seemed to drop the temperature by several degrees, causing her to shiver.

"Here," Adam said as he pulled off his jacket and wrapped it around her shoulders before she could voice a protest.

The instant warmth that was a product of his body hit her in the same moment as his scent—earthy but clean, as if his shower could never fully wash away the pleasant smell of the outdoors. Without considering how close he still stood, she looked up to thank him. And promptly forgot what she was going to say. Forgot what words even were.

Chapter 7

He couldn't kiss her. No matter how much the need to do exactly that thrummed within him. He knew he should look away, remove his hands from where they held the lapels of the jacket he'd just draped around her shoulders. But he felt frozen in the moment, unwilling to let it thaw quite yet.

"You didn't have to do that," she said, her voice not sounding quite normal.

"I'm fine." When he wondered how she might react if he lowered his lips to hers, it somehow gave him the push he needed to step away. "It'll be warmer inside the barn."

He watched as she glanced toward the house before giving him a quick nod. When he looked away from her toward the barn door, his breath came rushing back into his lungs. It took some effort to remind himself that he shouldn't jeopardize a possible lucrative business relationship by kissing a woman who most likely didn't want to be kissed. If he'd been betrayed like she had been, he doubted he'd want anything to do with a woman for a good long time.

He flicked on the lights as soon as he stepped inside then closed the door behind Lauren to keep out the wind. She started to shrug out of his jacket, so he lightly touched her arm.

"You keep it. I'm really okay."

"I didn't think to bring one. I suppose I should pay more attention to the forecast." No doubt she hadn't had room in her brain for thoughts of the weather because too much had been occupied with nervous anticipation about seeing Adam again.

"Yeah, the weather can be moody this time of year."

Needing some distance between them, she walked over to a dappled gray horse and let him sniff her fingers. She desperately needed something to keep her mind off the words Adam had spoken before he'd wrapped her in his jacket.

That's not all it was.

What had he meant by that? Was she reading too much into a statement that only meant he'd been trying to be nice? Neighborly? She had to find a way to not think everyone had ulterior motives or life was going to be miserable.

Forcing down any hint of the attraction she felt toward him, she turned to face Adam. "So tell me about the plans Angel mentioned."

He leaned against the stall across from her. "Why do you want to know?"

She shrugged. "Curious. You know how they call

people who love politics policy wonks? Well, I'm a bit of a business wonk. I've always been interested in how people find creative ways to make money, especially doing stuff they love. Some kids had lemonade stands. I made little decorated cupcakes when I was a kid and sold them on the playground, on the school bus."

He smiled. "I can just imagine."

"Were you always the same?"

He shook his head and averted his eyes, looking down the length of the barn. "I was a pretty normal kid, both before and after my parents died. But when your livelihood depends on so many factors out of your control, there can be lean years. I saw that not long after Mom and Dad adopted me. One stroke of bad luck you can weather, even if it's hard, but two years in a row brings you to the breaking point. It affected all of us kids, and now we're all determined to make sure we're never that close to losing the ranch again."

His story struck a familiar chord in Lauren's heart, in her memory, and she was thankful he wasn't looking at her or he might see the tears that she quickly blinked away.

"Thing is I don't have a talent like Angel does with photography or Ben does with leather-working. Neil is so much like Dad and following in his footsteps that you'd never know they weren't related by blood. Even Sloane has found a way to increase the ranch's name recognition through philanthropy."

"So the beef operation and the idea for the branded merchandise is your contribution."

He returned his gaze to her. "That's the idea." He pointed toward his temple. "What goes through my head over and over is that it could ensure the ranch not only survives as a family-owned operation, but thrives. There's a new generation now, and I want the ranch to be safe for them as they grow up."

Did he envision that new generation including children of his own? He certainly didn't sound like a guy who would abandon his own children.

But that was totally different to being willing to be a father to children who weren't his. She mentally smacked herself. Could she really imagine him thinking that way when he and his siblings were raised by parents that they'd not been born to?

And why was she even thinking those kinds of thoughts anyway?

"It sounds like a good idea to me," she said.

"Thanks. I just have to be more patient. I get these ideas and wish I could make them a reality overnight."

She laughed a little. "Not how it works." She wandered over to a stack of hay bales and sat down. "People sometimes look at me and think I'm an overnight success, but that couldn't be further from the truth. It's taken years, countless hours of worry and hard work and sleep deprivation to get to this point. And if I'm being honest, I still think I'll make a mistake and lose it all."

Adam crossed to where she was sitting—slowly, as if giving her time to move if she felt crowded—and sat beside her.

"Is that what you're thinking about the restaurant now? If you don't mind me saying, you seem a bit tense and distracted."

Oh, if he only knew what the main reason for that was at this moment.

"Yeah. It's a big investment, and having it so far from

where I live… I guess I'll question the decision until the place is a success."

"It will be."

She glanced over at him, wishing that for a few minutes she was free of any and all concerns about giving in to her attraction. "What makes you so certain?"

"Your determination and the fact you've been a success at every other aspect of your business. That can't just be by chance." He smiled and her heart thumped a bit harder. "I bet even your elementary-school cupcake business was a success."

There was something about Adam that made her want to be open and honest with him, and that scared her. And yet she found herself speaking a truth she didn't share with many people.

"It helped." At his curious expression, she continued. "You said your family went through tough times. Mine did, too, after my dad died. Mom had just been a volunteer aide at my school, but after Dad's accident she went to work full-time at a convenience store. At the same time, she got her teaching degree. My sister and I spent a lot of time at Papa Ed and Nana Gloria's. Nana was the one who taught me how to bake."

"She's gone now?" The tone of Adam's voice was kind, understanding, and she realized there must have been something in the way she said Nana Gloria's name that had revealed the truth.

Lauren nodded. "She passed about a year ago."

"I'm sorry."

"It's honestly why I agreed to visit Blue Falls in the first place. I wanted to do something fun with Papa Ed, and he suggested a trip back to his boyhood home. I had no idea he had something up his sleeve until we were at an empty restaurant building and a real estate agent showed up. I'll admit I was a little worried he was losing it when he suggested I buy the building here."

"But you obviously came around to the idea."

"Nobody was more surprised than I was when I walked inside and it was perfect." She noticed how Adam looked down at the ground between his boots. "I'm sorry it was the place you had your eye on."

"No need to apologize. I mean, it's been sitting there empty for a while."

"Still."

"My mom always says that things turn out how they're supposed to."

"I really like your mom," Lauren said.

"Your family is nice, too. And they obviously think your girls hung the moon."

"You have no idea. If I'm not careful between them and, admittedly, myself, the twins are going to be spoiled rotten to the core." She realized she was probably overcompensating for the fact they were going to grow up without a father in their lives.

"I think it's natural to want to give kids a better life than we had at their age."

She didn't just glance at Adam this time. She openly stared.

"What?" he asked when he noticed.

"You're very perceptive."

"My sisters would disagree with you."

"No, really." She paused, unable to look away from him. It might be dangerous, might be foolish, but she trusted him. "The reason I made those cupcakes and sold them when I was a kid was because I wanted to help my mom pay the bills. I was young but I still saw the worry on her face. I don't want my girls to ever have to experience that. I don't want any of my family to ever have to be concerned about money ever again."

"Sounds as if we're in the same boat."

She had an image of floating along the lake's surface with him in a little boat, much like Rapunzel and Flynn in *Tangled*. She had the same butterfly-wings feeling in her chest now as she'd imagined those two characters felt during that scene.

Logically she knew it was only mere moments, but the time that passed as they stared at each other seemed much longer. When Adam's gaze dropped momentarily to her lips, part of Lauren urged her to lean in and give him permission. But a memory of the last time she'd kissed a man shoved its way to the front of her brain, causing her to look away so quickly it bordered on rude.

"I should be going. Won't be long before I need to get the girls to bed. Hopefully they'll sleep better tonight." She stood and took a few steps away from him.

"If you want a place with more privacy, where you don't have to worry about the girls' crying waking other guests, you should check out the cabins at the Vista Hills Guest Ranch."

"Maybe I will. Thanks."

When he stood, she started to slip out of his jacket again.

"Wait until we get back to the house."

"I won't freeze between here and there."

He smiled. "Neither will I."

As they left the barn, she had to admit she was thankful for the extra layer of protection his jacket provided. The only sounds she heard as they crossed the darker area between the barn and house were the crunch of the gravel under their feet and the call of some night bird she couldn't identify. When they neared the porch, Adam slowed, causing her to do the same, and then she stopped when he did.

He appeared on the verge of asking her something, and her breath caught in her throat—half in anticipation, half in fear. But she saw him change what he'd been about to say as surely as if she'd seen him change hats.

"I hope you all had a nice time tonight."

"Uh, we did. Thank you for inviting us."

"The offer stands to come out and tour the operation when you can actually see something."

She realized it was the first time since her arrival at the ranch that he'd directly addressed their potential working relationship.

"When I get a chance."

He nodded. Again, she thought he had something else to say, but instead he simply escorted her up the front steps.

She was so occupied with wondering what he'd been going to say that she forgot to remove his jacket until she'd already stepped through the front door. Though she was likely imagining things, it felt as if every set of eyes in the room noticed and immediately started assigning deeper meaning to Adam's kind gesture.

Sure, she wasn't entirely sure there wasn't some unspoken meaning, but no one else needed to know that. So she deliberately made eye contact with Adam as she slipped out of the jacket and handed it back to him.

"Thanks." Then before he could respond, she turned toward her mom. "It's gotten quite chilly out there. We need to make sure to wrap up the girls really well."

With so many people present, it was impossible to

make a quick exit. But the flurry of goodbyes did give her time to calm herself a bit before she found herself on the porch with Adam for the final farewell of the night.

"Thanks again for dinner. It was nice to meet everyone and have such a good meal."

"Well, you made my mom's night. Possibly her year."

She imagined him leaning down to kiss her goodnight, found herself wanting that even if it was a peck on the cheek. Which was her cue to leave.

As she drove back toward Blue Falls a few minutes later, she couldn't stop thinking about that moment in the yard when she'd swear he'd been about to say something entirely different to her. She had a feeling that question was much more likely to keep her awake tonight than cranky babies.

Adam was thankful for the late-night storm that had blown through. It gave him an excuse to go ride around the ranch the next day to check on the fencing and the cattle. He needed the time away from his mom's curious gaze. She hadn't questioned him or even made any comments alluding to the time he'd spent outside with Lauren the night before, or the fact Lauren had come back to the house wearing his jacket, but that didn't mean he couldn't see the curiosity, and probably hope, in his mom's eyes.

Despite his determination not to jeopardize the possible contract with her restaurant, he'd almost asked her out. With one question, he could have torpedoed the deal. Maybe even his business if word got out he'd been denied by the famous Brazos Baker in favor of another supplier.

But what if he could land another large account? Would that give him the freedom to ask her out to dinner?

He shook his head as he rode over a rise in the land that gave one of the prettiest panoramic views on the ranch. He reined his horse to a stop and soaked in the sight before him. This was what he was working to protect, ensuring that it stayed in the Hartley family no matter what Mother Nature or the temperamental economy threw at them.

Adam inhaled deeply of the fresh, rain-scented air, always good for clearing his mind. Though Lauren had shared personal details with him the night before, that didn't mean she was interested in him the way he was in her. He reminded himself she had good reason.

And yet there'd been that moment when she'd looked up at him as he'd wrapped his jacket around her shoulders. Had he read it so wrong? Because he would have sworn he saw interest on her part, as well.

Maybe she'd just been startled by his action. But she'd been willing to sit beside him inside the barn and talk about the tough years they'd both experienced as kids. That, however, was something friends would do, not necessarily more than friends.

He rubbed his hand over his face and rode on. But try as he might to think about other things, his thoughts kept coming back to Lauren. What was it about her that drew him so much? Yes, she was beautiful, but she wasn't the only beautiful woman in the world. Not even the only one in Blue Falls. There was more to it, something that pulled at him on a deeper level, though for the life of him he couldn't identify what.

When he saw her again, he had to remember, however, that it wasn't just the potential business deal that should keep him from voicing his feelings. She'd been through a lot, and maybe memories of the past were what caused the nervousness he sometimes sensed she felt around him. Maybe the best thing now was to keep his distance, only occasionally check in with a professional call.

His phone dinged with a text, pulling him from his mental meandering. He slipped the phone from his jacket pocket and a jolt of excitement went through him at the sight of Lauren's name on the display. So much for shoving her from his mind.

He tapped the screen to read the message.

Got any recommendations for a roofer?

Okay, so that wasn't exactly the kind of message he imagined getting from her, but at least it wasn't radio silence. He hadn't scared her off completely.

He texted back a couple of suggestions, then like some sort of lovesick teenager, he stared at his phone until she texted back a simple Thanks. He blew out a breath and headed on toward the southern property boundary.

It was a good thing mind reading wasn't actually a thing because he still hadn't been able to stop thinking about Lauren when he returned to the house late in the afternoon. His brain refused to stop running possible scenarios in which he could preserve the chance to do business with her while also exploring his attraction.

As he left the barn and headed toward the house, he met Arden, Neil's wife, leaving. He remembered then that she'd had a prenatal checkup that morning.

"Hey, how are things going with the little peanut?"

She smiled and placed her hand against her still-flat stomach. "Good. Though I thought your brother was going to pass out he was so nervous. I can't imagine what he'll be like when I actually go in to have the baby."

Adam laughed. "You are the best sister-in-law ever for telling me that. Just don't tell Mandy I said so."

They started to go their separate ways again.

"Adam?"

He turned back toward Arden. "Yeah?"

"Can I ask you something?"

"Sure."

"Is it my imagination or are you interested in Lauren?"

Ah, hell. "She's nice, and I'm hoping we can land her restaurant as a customer."

Arden crossed her arms and gave him an incredulous look he imagined she'd used to great effect with tough interviewees during her years as an international reporter.

"You know that's not what I mean."

He sighed. There was no use lying to someone who'd literally gone to war-torn areas of the globe and gotten the truth out of people who didn't like telling the truth.

"Yes, but I can't do anything about it."

"Why not?"

He retraced his steps and leaned against the side of Arden's car. "Do you know anything about what she's been through?"

"A bit."

He filled in the gaps, and when he was finished, his brother's wife leaned back against the car beside him.

"So you're afraid that she's gun-shy."

He nodded.

She was quiet for a few seconds before speaking again. "It's kind of you to put her feelings first, but she hasn't actually told you she's not interested, has she?"

"No, but I haven't asked, either."

"Then maybe you should."

"I don't want to jeopardize the potential business deal. We need a big win."

"I understand. But I don't want you to miss something that could be way more important."

"How can I tell if she's interested or if I should keep my distance because of what she's been through?"

"Don't come on too strong. One little step at a time. And honestly, she might not be receptive at first. The hurt might be too fresh in her memory. But take it from me, sometimes people don't know what they need until someone shows them."

He knew she was talking about how Neil had initially offered her friendship after she'd come home from being a captive of human traffickers in Africa, and how that friendship had slowly built into something more that neither of them had expected. And now Adam couldn't imagine two people more in love.

He didn't know if anything even remotely similar was in store for him and Lauren. Him and anyone, for that matter. But Arden was right. He wasn't going to find out if he avoided Lauren, if he let his fear of failure keep him from figuring out if their new friendship might eventually grow into something more.

Chapter 8

A cold wind blew off the lake into downtown Blue Falls, making it feel like the perfect weather to do some Christmas shopping. Add in the fact that the restaurant was unbearably noisy at the moment with the roofers doing the needed repairs, and Lauren decided to use the time wisely. Her mom had returned home and to her classroom, but Papa Ed was still on babysitting duty.

Lauren had been so busy lately that she hadn't given the holiday season much thought. But as she strolled down the sidewalk and saw the storefront windows filled with Christmas displays, and as she hummed along with the familiar carols playing on outdoor speakers the length of the Main Street shopping district, she felt the holiday spirit bubble up within her.

At each shop she entered, she was greeted with warmth and enthusiasm. Inevitably people wanted to know when she'd be opening for business, and she would always say the same thing—that she hoped to be open by spring. She still thought she could make that goal if unexpected repairs didn't keep popping up, along with their accompanying price tags. Despite the setbacks, she wasn't about to skimp on Christmas. After everything her family had been through the past couple of years, they all deserved a big, beautiful, happy holiday season.

By the time she reached A Good Yarn, she was toting several bags filled with gifts. The moment she stepped inside the store, she felt as if her first breath inhaled Christmas itself. The delicious scents of cinnamon, clove and nutmeg with a hint of pine filled the air and "Let it Snow" by Dean Martin reminded her of her family's tradition of spending Christmas Eve watching old black-and-white Christmas movies. Everything from classics like *Miracle on 34th Street* to lesser-known films such as *The Shop Around the Corner*, which many people didn't realize was the inspiration for *You've Got Mail.*

"Can I help you?" a pretty woman with curly waves of red hair asked as she emerged from the center aisle.

"It feels so much like Christmas in here I feel as if it might start snowing."

The woman laughed. "Well, that would certainly get the shop on the front page of the paper."

"Lauren, I thought that sounded like you." Mandy Hartley appeared from the back of the store, causing Lauren to remember one of the family facts she'd learned during her dinner with the Hartley family. Mandy was part owner of this store.

Mandy came forward and pulled Lauren into a hug

as if they'd known each other for ages, then turned toward the other woman.

"This is Lauren Shayne."

"Oh, the baker I've heard so much about. Nice to meet you."

"You, too."

"Sorry," Mandy said. "This is Devon Davis, my best friend and the person who started all this." She gestured toward their surroundings.

"Can I stow your shopping bags for you while you look around?" Devon asked.

"Thanks. That would be great. I may have gone a little overboard."

Devon smiled as she accepted the bags. "Feel free to continue to do so."

Lauren smiled, already able to tell she liked Mandy's business partner.

As Devon walked behind the front counter, Mandy asked, "Is there something I can help you find?"

"Do you have lavender-scented candles? My mom loves them."

"Yes, we do." Mandy motioned for Lauren to follow her.

On a large wooden shelving unit along one wall of the store was a display of seemingly every size and scent of candle anyone could ever want.

"Wow."

Mandy smiled. "Yeah, we feature candles from a few different area artisans. Same with a lot of the other products we have."

"I have the oddest desire to take up knitting while enjoying the scent of vanilla candles."

"Well, we can hook you up."

"Hey, I'm going to run to the bakery," Devon called from the front of the store. "Either of you want anything?"

"A hot chocolate sounds nice." Mandy looked at Lauren. "Want one?"

"I don't want to be any trouble."

Mandy waved off Lauren's concern while making a dismissive sound. "Make that two."

"That's taking customer service to a new level," Lauren said as she picked up a large jar containing a lavender candle.

"Small town. And this time of year puts us in a good mood."

"I've got to admit that Blue Falls feels a bit like one of those quintessential small towns in a holiday movie. Everyone is so friendly."

"It has a few stinkers like anywhere else, but overall it's a great place to live and work."

The front door opened, though it was too soon for Devon to be back.

"Look around and if I can help you with anything else, just let me know." Mandy headed toward the front of the store to greet the new arrivals.

The store was so cozy and appealing that Lauren took her time browsing, partly because she didn't want to miss anything and partly because she had a feeling she'd get some good ideas for creating atmosphere for her own gift shop. By the time she wandered back up to the front of the building, she'd put not only the candles for her mom in a basket, but also two large vanilla ones to burn at the restaurant while she was working, some goat milk soaps that smelled heavenly and two little knitted hats for the twins. She also carried a striking painting of a field of wildflowers that she could already envision gracing the entrance to her restaurant.

Even more customers had entered the store, claiming Mandy's attention. It must be just as busy at the bakery because Devon hadn't yet returned. But for once, Lauren wasn't in a hurry. She didn't often allow herself time to just be alone to do whatever she wanted, but the incessant hammering of roofers gave her the perfect excuse. That and the fact Christmas was likely to sneak up on her front steps and pound on the door, demanding to be let in, before she was ready.

Though she didn't knit, she let her gaze drift across the skeins of brightly colored yarn stacked in wooden cubbies along the wall opposite the wall of candles. The woolen rainbow could be seen from outside, which she was certain was by design, aiming to lure inside anyone who'd ever even had a passing thought about knitting.

She glanced past the lovely Christmas display in the window and spotted Adam across the street. He was talking to a man she didn't recognize. Since he was unaware of her gaze upon him, she didn't immediately look away. Instead, she took her first opportunity to simply look at him. Though he wore a tan cowboy hat, she could see the ends of his dark hair curling at the bottom edges. For that unobserved moment, she imagined what it might be like to run her fingers through it. Was the texture soft or coarse? Would he respond in kind, threading his fingers through the length of her hair, as well?

"Like the view?"

Lauren jumped and let loose a little yelp of surprise. So much for being unobserved.

"Was just watching for the hot-chocolate delivery."

"So this has nothing to do with the fact that my brother-in-law is standing across the street?"

"Who?" Seriously, did she just try to pretend she hadn't seen Adam even though she'd been caught staring straight at him. "Oh, Adam. Who is that he's talking to?"

"Adrian Stone, local attorney."

An attorney? A chill ran down her back. Why would he have reason to talk with an attorney? Did this have something to do with the ranch? His plans to open a mercantile?

Or maybe it's a small town and people just know each other.

When she dared a glance at Mandy, Lauren could tell the other woman had picked up on her interest in Adam. But that didn't mean Lauren was going to verify it in any shape or form. And whether Mandy read something on her face or she knew about what had gone down with Phil and decided not to press the point, Mandy didn't pursue the topic of her brother-in-law any further. Instead, she pointed at the basket Lauren held.

"Looks as if you took Devon's advice and found plenty of things to buy."

"It was amazingly easy."

"That's what we like to hear."

Just then Devon returned with a cup carrier and white bag in tow.

"Wow, the bakery is full today," Devon said as she placed her purchases atop the round table surrounded by comfy chairs in the corner opposite the checkout counter. "Seems word has gotten out that Keri is giving away a free cookie—a new flavor—with every beverage purchase."

"Please tell me that's what is in the bag," Mandy said.

"Of course. Do you think I'd refuse free cookies?" Devon pulled out three cookies in paper sleeves and handed one to Mandy and one to Lauren. "Salted caramel sugar cookies."

Lauren's mouth watered and when she took a bite she shut her eyes as the flavors danced across her tongue. At the sounds of appreciation from the other women, she opened her eyes.

"I think I might have chosen to go into business in the wrong community."

"Nonsense," Mandy said. "We need a good barbecue place. I think it's actually against the law for a town in Texas not to have one."

Lauren waited for Mandy to say something about the Rocking Horse Ranch providing the necessary beef for said barbecue, but she didn't. Maybe she was just too busy enjoying what Lauren had to admit was an excellent cookie.

"Tell you what might be interesting, though," Mandy said. "There's a Christmas carnival coming up soon at the elementary school, and one of the booths is going to be a cakewalk. Keri always donates at least one cake. Maybe you could make one, too? We could bill it as 'Battle of the Bakers' and draw a nice crowd."

"I don't think antagonizing the long-established local baker is a good business move."

Mandy and Devon snickered.

"Are you kidding?" Devon said. "Keri will eat it up with a spoon. The people who donate cakes regularly help run the booth, and there is good-natured heckling of each other."

"Plus the money is a big fund-raiser for the local

schools," Mandy added. "This year the funds are going to buy new science textbooks and drums for the band."

"Well, I can't really say no to that, can I?"

"Awesome." Mandy sure did look as if she was happy about Lauren taking part in the carnival.

Lauren was afraid it had less to do with the good of the school and more to do with Adam. If Blue Falls was like most small towns, activities at the schools drew at least half the population.

As Lauren left with her purchases a few minutes later, she had a hard time not fantasizing about Adam winning her cake in the musical-chairs style game and proclaiming it the best thing he'd ever eaten. Thank goodness he no longer stood across the street or she was certain he'd see the truth written on her face.

Lauren had been right about half the town showing up for the Christmas carnival. The gym was so filled with people browsing the craft booths, waiting in line for hot dogs and giant soft pretzels, and playing a wide array of games for prizes that it was a challenge to weave her way through the crowd without dropping or having someone knock the seven-layer spice cake with cream-cheese icing from her hands. Though if it did topple, maybe she could salvage enough to eat herself. Her mouth had watered when she'd pulled it out of the oven that morning.

Baking back in the familiar warmth of her own kitchen had been wonderful, but she'd also found herself anxious to return to Blue Falls at the same time. She knew that had a good bit to do with the fact that she expected to see Adam tonight. It didn't seem to matter how often she told herself the attraction she felt toward him could go no further than daydreams, she continued to think of him way too often.

Evidently she mentioned him too often as well because her sister had picked up on it and felt it necessary to point it out.

"Is there anyone else who lives in Blue Falls?" Violet had asked as they'd cleaned up after the Thanksgiving meal at their mom's house a few days ago.

"What?"

Violet grinned in that playfully wicked way she had. "I should have started a tally chart to see how many times you mentioned Adam Hartley's name."

"You're exaggerating."

"Am I?"

"He's just helped me out a bit. And he has a vested interest."

"Do you really think he's doing all these things to help just so you'll do business with him?"

Her instinct told her no, but how could she be certain? She also suspected if she said no, Violet was going to read way more into his actions than was there.

"It wouldn't be the first time a man has fooled me, would it?"

Violet's gaze darkened. "I can't tell you how many times I've wanted to go find Phil and slap him right off the continent."

"Line forms behind me." Not surprisingly, Phil's child-support payment was missing in action. Of course, so was he.

Thankfully she was in a position to provide whatever her daughters needed. She felt angry on behalf of all the women who weren't as financially stable as she was and still had to deal with deadbeat dads.

Two little boys, each with a handful of game tickets, barreled past Lauren, bringing her back to the present in time to lift her cake up to a safe height. Behind her, Violet squealed and nearly dropped the raspberry strudel she'd made. Her sister had the ability to bake some tasty treats herself when she put her mind to it.

"I feel as if I'm on one of those obstacle-course shows," Violet said.

"Almost there." Ahead she spied the rather elaborately decorated cakewalk area crowned with, no joke, a curved sign that said Battle of the Bakers over the entrance to the cordoned-off, numbered-spaces area for the walkers. She also spotted Mandy, India Parrish, who owned the Yesterwear Boutique, and Keri Teague chatting next to the table already filling up with cakes.

"Hey!" Mandy said and waved when she spotted Lauren. "Glad you made it. I've had probably three dozen people ask me if your cake was here yet." She glanced at Keri. "Inquiries have been neck and neck for you two."

"I'm sure it has nothing to do with the 'Battle of the Bakers' sign," Lauren said.

Mandy smiled. "Remember, it's a good cause."

"Well, here's my contribution to the cause, then." Lauren extended her cake.

"Great, what kind is it?"

"Seven-layer spice with cream-cheese icing."

"Mmm, sounds delicious. Going to be a hard call between this and Keri's gorgeous red velvet cake." Mandy nodded toward what was, indeed, a cake so pretty you wouldn't want to make the first cut.

"Well, I'm only famous adjacent, but here's a raspberry strudel."

"This is my sister, Violet," Lauren said.

Mandy accepted the strudel and extended her hand. "Very nice to meet you."

Lauren made all the introductions as more cakes arrived and attendees made inquiries about when the cakewalk was going to begin.

"In about five minutes," Mandy said. "We have the cakes divided into different rounds."

When the people inquiring left, Mandy turned back toward Lauren and the rest of their little group. "We decided to put your cakes in the last round to build up the suspense." She smiled. "Feel free to take your time showing the twins around the carnival until then."

"Where are those beautiful babies of yours?" Keri asked.

"Our grandfather has them in the stroller out in the lobby. Hard to make it quickly across a crowd this size when everyone wants to admire not one but two babies."

True to her word, Mandy started the cakewalk five minutes later. Lauren got drawn into talking to fans of her show and signing autographs. Even though her cake wasn't up for a prize in the earlier rounds, she convinced several people to go ahead and take part because there were a lot of yummy-looking cakes available. And it was true. Not one of the cakes spread out along the tables looked unappetizing. Even the two store-bought cakes looked good. Granted, she was hungry, but they did look moist and very, very chocolatey, a good combination in her opinion.

It was a good fifteen to twenty minutes before Papa Ed made it to the cakewalk area. Bethany was batting at a yellow helium balloon while Harper examined her little pink terry-cloth bunny as if she'd never seen it before. Some kids had security blankets. Harper had a security bunny.

"There are my girls," Lauren said as she crouched in front of them and played with their little sock-clad toes.

"They've sure been a hit," Papa Ed said, obviously proud to have been able to show them off.

"So has their mom," Violet said. "We may have a cake riot before the night is out."

"Don't be ridiculous." Lauren shook her head. Sure, the people she'd met seemed enthusiastic and she never minded talking to fans, but there was still a part of her that was uncomfortable with being put on any kind of pedestal, even imaginary. She probably always would be. She had to admit that part of her was jealous of Keri, who enjoyed the accolades for her baking and owned a successful business, but who wasn't so exposed. Her relationships and betrayals weren't played out before the public eye.

Though no one had mentioned anything about Phil tonight, had they? Another point in the favor of the residents of Blue Falls.

The music for the cakewalk ended and Mandy called out the winning number. The woman who'd won went immediately to Violet's strudel, which made Violet smile and do a little dance. Lauren couldn't help but laugh at her sister's antics.

"Watch out, sis," Violet called out. "I'm hot on your heels."

As the evening progressed, Lauren saw several more members of the Hartley family. All except the one she hoped to see. Maybe his absence was a sign from the universe, one she should have the good sense to heed. One she shouldn't need in the first place.

Then why did she feel so disheartened?

It was just the season. Christmas was always a tough time of year when you didn't have, or had lost, a significant other. She'd already been through one such holiday season since her breakup with Phil. How quickly she forgot.

"So I hear this is where the action is."

Lauren's pulse jumped at the sound of Adam's voice. It was thrilling and scary at the same time that she could recognize his voice without seeing him. She'd swear it vibrated something within her that she'd feared had been torched to nonexistence by how Phil had treated her.

"It is indeed," Lauren said as she turned to face him.

Mandy called out that the final grouping of cakes was now up for grabs. Several people who'd been lingering around waiting for this moment surged forward onto the numbered spaces.

"Looks as if I'm just in time," Adam said as he held up one red ticket.

"Yes, Keri's red velvet cake looks delicious."

Adam smiled as he stepped onto the last available space. "It's not her cake I intend to win."

There was something new in Adam's eyes tonight, some mixture of determination and… She didn't dare name what else she thought she might see, afraid if she did she'd want it more than she should.

They broke eye contact when the music started.

"I see now why you talk about him so much," Violet said as she came to stand next to Lauren and bumped her shoulder with her own. "He's capital *H-O-T*."

Yes, he was. And she was afraid she wanted him to win her cake more than she had wanted anything in a very long time.

Chapter 9

Adam still wasn't sure his decision to make known his interest in Lauren the person, and not just Lauren the business owner, was the right one. He was making a big gamble, in more ways than one. But his conversation with Arden had stuck with him, making him look at the situation from a different angle. He still wasn't going to push Lauren or give her any reason to doubt him, but he couldn't ignore that he thought about her way more than a passing acquaintance would warrant.

And he trusted Arden. She'd been through a type of hell he'd never wish on anyone, and she'd come back to Blue Falls a broken version of herself. But Neil's friendship and support, based partly on his own experience with trauma, had helped her regain her strength—both physically and mentally—and their friendship had grown into love.

He didn't know if that's what lay ahead for him and Lauren, but he wanted to find out. Arden had suggested he go slowly but to be honest at the same time.

And so he was here feeling admittedly a little silly trying to win her cake. He had to land on the winning number because there was no doubt in his mind that whoever did was going to choose the cake by the famous Brazos Baker.

He glanced over to where she stood with another woman, who looked a good deal like her. Must be her sister, Violet.

The music stopped so suddenly that he nearly bumped into the woman in front of him.

"Number eleven is the lucky winner," Mandy called out.

He looked down and saw that he stood on number seven. Damn. Maybe he should have bribed his sister-in-law to allow him to win.

The kid standing on the winning spot hurried to the table and chose a tray of cupcakes decorated with super-heroes. Unbelievably Adam had another chance. But his excitement dimmed when none other than Tim Wainwright stepped onto the spot vacated by the winner.

Adam's jaw clenched. Tim couldn't win Lauren's cake. The man already had enough going for him, and the memory of seeing him dancing with Lauren raked across Adam's nerves like coarse sandpaper.

"Good luck, everyone," Mandy called out as she started the music again. She looked at Adam, and he could see in her eyes that she was pulling for him. Especially considering one part of his competition.

He made eye contact with Lauren as he walked the circle. She offered a small smile, and he liked to think that maybe she was rooting for him, as well. Of course, it wouldn't matter if the entire gym full of people were on his side, it would all come down to the luck of the draw.

The music seemed to go on forever. When it finally stopped and Mandy identified five as the winner, Adam pressed his lips together to keep from cursing. Wainwright stood on the winning number. And he went right to Lauren's cake.

Feeling like a fool, Adam started to step out of the circle. But before he could, Violet stepped up next to him.

"Give me one of your tickets," she said.

"What?"

"Hurry, before the music starts again."

He did as requested then watched as Violet strode back to where Tim was talking to Lauren, probably trying to convince her that his winning her cake was some sort of sign she should have dinner with him. Adam damn near growled like a bear about to charge. Violet wrapped her arm around her sister's, said something brief and led Lauren toward the circle. Lauren looked startled by her sister's actions, but the disappointed look on Tim's face made Adam's day.

As soon as Lauren stepped onto her spot, Mandy started the music. This time, the round seemed to go quickly, but then Adam spent the entire time watching Lauren up ahead of him while trying to appear as if he wasn't.

When the music stopped yet again and Mandy announced the winning number, Adam glanced down to find he'd finally landed on the right spot. Maybe this was still salvageable. He crossed to the table and spotted Keri's red velvet cake. Though Lauren might be the more famous baker, Keri's talent was a known quantity. He couldn't go wrong with anything she'd made.

"Excellent choice," Keri said from the opposite side of the table as she extended a plastic knife and two forks.

He hadn't seen anyone else offered utensils.

"Which one did you choose?" Violet asked as she once again ushered her older sister where Violet evidently wanted her to go.

He lifted his prize. "Keri's red velvet."

"It looks delicious," Lauren said and smiled at Keri.

"I'm sure Adam can't eat the entire thing," Keri said. "Why don't you help him out?"

Adam suddenly felt as if he'd been sucked into one of Verona Charles's master matchmaking plans. And for once in his life he didn't mind.

"She's right," he said. "But if I take this home, I'll likely not get more than a single slice."

Lauren looked uncertain. "I need to tend to the girls."

"Two little babies don't need three people to take care of them," Violet said. "Papa Ed and I will be fine. We'll check out what else this lovely carnival has to offer."

Adam didn't miss the "you're going to pay for this later" look that Lauren shot her sister. But when she turned toward him, Lauren offered a smile.

"Looks like I get to enjoy some dessert. Been eyeing that cake all night."

Adam nodded toward the bleachers on the top level of the gym. "We can watch all the action from up there."

"Sounds good."

He led the way up the stairs, all the way to the top, where they could lean against the wall. Once they were seated, he handed her a fork then sliced two generous helpings. The moment Lauren took her first bite she closed her eyes and made an "mmm" of appreciation. Adam had to focus his attention on his own slice to keep from thinking about how that sound affected him.

"It's a good thing I'm opening a barbecue restaurant instead of a bakery here," Lauren said. "The two things I've had that Keri made have been to die for."

"I'm sure your cake was delicious, too." As soon as the words left his mouth, he was fully aware of how annoyed he sounded.

"You don't like Tim, do you?"

He shrugged. "Friendly rivalry is all."

Lauren laughed in that way that said she didn't believe him. "I'm not sure friendly is how I'd describe it."

"Would you believe not openly hostile?"

"Yeah, barely."

"I hope that doesn't make you think worse of me."

"No, I understand. He's a bit full of himself. He tried to convince me that since he'd won dessert, we should go out to dinner first."

"I knew it." Adam shoved another bite of cake in his mouth.

"I wasn't going to go. He's not my type."

He looked over at her and decided not to hold in the question that surged to the front of his mind. "What is your type?"

"Honestly, I'm not sure. I thought I knew once, but that didn't turn out so well."

"Sorry. I didn't mean to bring up bad memories."

"No, it's okay. I can't let what happened rule the rest of my life." As soon as she said the words, she looked surprised. As if she hadn't meant to say them out loud or perhaps that she hadn't had the realization before that moment.

It was the closest thing to an opening as he was likely to get.

"If I was to ask you out, would you think I'm no better than Wainwright?"

"I know you're not the same as him, but I don't know if I'm ready for that."

"No pressure but we seem to get along well, and the truth is I really like you. Would it be easier if we started with a coffee?"

Lauren didn't answer. Instead, she cut off another bite of cake with her fork. As she ate it, she looked out over all the activity down on the gym floor. He followed her gaze and spotted her sister pushing the double stroller toward the ladies room.

"Poop happens," Lauren said.

"What?"

She pointed toward the bathroom. "Chances are either they've both gone doody in their diapers or one has and the other one will about the time Violet starts out of the bathroom."

"Oh. For a minute there I thought you were equating a date with me with poop."

"No, of course not."

He took encouragement from how strong her response was, how she seemed horrified he'd thought such a thing.

"Is that a yes, then?"

He noticed the death grip she had on her fork and wondered if she was imagining it was her ex's throat.

"Coffee and Danish at the bakery?" She sounded hesitant, as if she wasn't sure she was doing the right thing.

"Sounds great."

They settled on meeting the next morning before Lauren said she needed to get back to the hotel room and her family.

"I've been up since the crack of dawn, so I'm hitting the wall."

He covered the remainder of the cake and accompanied Lauren back down to the floor.

"Thanks for the cake," she said.

"You're welcome. Still curious what yours tastes like."

"Maybe you'll get the chance to find out sometime." The tentative smile that accompanied her words gave him hope that maybe their coffee date was just the beginning.

Had she just agreed to go on a date with Adam, a man she truly didn't know all that well? By the smile he wore, she'd guess the answer was yes. She knew she should be more concerned, but oddly she wasn't. Like he said, no pressure. Just coffee and a Danish. It wasn't the same level of date seriousness as dinner, and since they were meeting at the bakery she could leave anytime she wanted.

Though would she really want to?

"See you tomorrow morning." Adam looked as if he wanted to hug her goodbye, maybe even plant a kiss on her cheek, but she wasn't ready for that—especially not in the midst of such a large crowd.

A crowd that included her sister, who'd taken one look at Adam and proceeded to push Lauren toward him. It was as if Violet had taken leave of her senses, developed sudden-onset amnesia regarding the past year and a half.

And yet Lauren had enjoyed sharing Adam's cake with him high above the carnival activity.

After Adam disappeared into the crowd that was beginning to thin a little, Lauren couldn't look away like she should have. Adam Hartley looked almost as good walking away as he did facing her.

"See anything interesting?" Violet's voice was full of the kind of teasing that had filled their teenage years.

Instead of answering her sister's question, Lauren turned toward Violet. "What was that?"

"What?" Violet did her best impersonation of innocence.

"You know what. You also know how I feel about getting involved with anyone else."

Then why did you agree to the breakfast date?

"Phil was the king of the asses, but he was only one guy. The best way to stick it to him is to be happy."

"I am happy."

"To a point. But you're young, beautiful and have a lot of love inside you to give."

"I give it every day to my daughters, you, Mom, Papa Ed."

"Not that kind of love. The kind that makes you feel whole and excited to wake up next to someone every morning."

"I had that and look where it got me."

"You didn't really have it, sis, because it didn't go both ways."

"And you think some near stranger with a red velvet cake is the one to change that?"

"Maybe. You two seemed to be having a nice time

up there." Violet pointed toward the top level of the bleacher seating.

Lauren was tired of resisting a truth that she would never have expected to blossom at this point in her life—she really liked Adam, and not in a budding-friendship kind of way.

"Fine, you win."

"What did you win?" Papa Ed asked as he walked up with two tired babies in tow. The bright-eyed twins that had gloried in all the attention paid to them earlier now sported droopy eyelids.

Violet smiled, obviously satisfied with herself. "Lauren just admitted she likes Adam."

"He's a nice young man," Papa Ed said.

"Yeah, he is," Lauren said.

"You don't sound thrilled by that fact."

"It just complicates everything."

"Maybe you just think it does," he said. "No denying you were burned, and badly, but it makes my heart happy to think of you finally moving past it enough to even consider seeing someone else."

Lauren sighed. "It really doesn't make sense though. Even if it could be something, I'm not going to be here in Blue Falls forever. And I don't have it in me to do a long-distance relationship."

"Stop thinking about all the obstacles there could be in the future," Violet said. "Just enjoy the moment. Maybe it doesn't have to be anything other than a bit of fun, which you deserve."

Lauren looked down at her daughters. Harper was already asleep, and Bethany wasn't far behind.

"Don't even think about using these babies as an excuse why you can't go out. Plenty of single moms date."

"I'm aware."

"Now, how do you feel about asking him out?"

"No need."

"Lauren—"

"He already asked me to have coffee in the morning."

For a moment, Violet didn't seem to comprehend. But then her face lit up a moment before she squealed in obvious delight. The noise startled Bethany so much her eyes went wide.

"Sorry," Violet said as she soothed Bethany. "Go to sleep, sweetie."

That was all it took for Bethany's eyes to close. "How do you do that?" Lauren asked her baby-whisperer sister.

"They already know that I'm the cool aunt who will let them get away with all manner of mischief when they're older."

"If your sister doesn't disown you first."

"Aren't they just so precious?"

Lauren looked over to see Verona Charles eyeing the twins.

"Thank you. I think so."

Verona touched Lauren's shoulder in a gesture that said, "Of course you do, and rightly so."

"Verona Charles, I'd like you to meet my sister, Violet, and my grandfather—"

"Ed."

The sound of her grandfather's name spoken by Verona in such utter disbelief caused Lauren to look at the older woman. She appeared as if she might faint.

"Verona, are you okay?" Lauren reached toward the other woman in case she was having a stroke or a heart attack.

Instead of answering Lauren's question, Verona continued to stare at Papa Ed. And when Lauren shifted her gaze to her grandfather, he wore such an expression of sorrow that it was like seeing him the day of Nana Gloria's funeral all over again.

Before Lauren could ask what was going on, Verona took a sudden step back.

"Excuse me."

As she hurried away through the crowd, Lauren shifted her gaze to her grandfather again. "You know Verona?"

He didn't answer immediately, just continued to watch Verona until she disappeared out the door into the gym lobby. "A long time ago."

The look on his face said in no uncertain terms that there was way more to the story, but Lauren feared asking for specifics. Not while Papa Ed wore such a mournful look on his face.

Violet didn't have any such qualms, evidently. "Were you involved?"

Papa Ed finally pulled his gaze away from the door. "Not here. Not now."

Lauren realized he meant he didn't want to talk about it now. She had so many questions, but honestly, she wasn't sure she wanted to know the answers.

As he started walking toward the exit, Lauren and Violet stared after him and then at each other.

"I feel as if I just got dropped into another universe, where Papa Ed has secrets," Violet said.

That summed things up perfectly. Now that she thought about it, maybe an alternate reality also explained why she'd agreed to a date with Adam when Phil's betrayal still burned like a scorpion's sting.

Chapter 10

"You looked like you were having fun last night," Angel said to Adam as he walked into the kitchen the next morning.

"I was." No sense in denying it, even though the cautious voice in his head still worried that he was making a mistake that would torpedo his business.

"So, when you going to ask her out?"

"Already did."

The surprise on his sister's face almost made him laugh.

"When? Where are you taking her? I need details."

"Now. The bakery."

Angel just stared at him as if he was lying. "You're taking a famous baker to a bakery for your first date?"

"Taking it slow."

Angel seemed to think about that for a moment. "You

know, I think you're smarter than I give you credit for. Wise move."

"Well, now that I have my little sister's seal of approval…" he said with no small amount of sarcasm before heading toward the door.

As he drove toward town, a sudden wave of nervousness hit him. Normally, he wasn't prone to being nervous, especially not when going on a date. The fact that he was now told him that this—whatever it was with Lauren—was different. How different, he couldn't say.

When he arrived at the bakery, there was a line nearly out the door. He hadn't thought about all the pairs of eyes belonging to people he knew bearing witness to his date. People who would have questions and who would spread the sighting far and wide.

Oh, who was he kidding? The fact they'd sat in the gym away from everyone else while eating cake the night before likely was already setting the local grapevine on fire. It was just a fact of life in a small town.

Though the place was busy, most of the people were ordering to go. After stopping to talk to three different people in line, Adam finally made it to one of the small tables. He glanced at the time on his phone to find it was ten minutes past when he and Lauren were to meet. Had she heard enough local gossip to make her change her mind? She didn't seem like the type of person to stand him up without at least a text message. Just as he had that thought, she stepped through the front door. He considered it a good sign that she smiled as she approached the table, but as she drew closer he noticed how tired she looked. So much so that he was on the verge of asking if she'd had a bad night with the twins before thinking about how pointing out she looked tired probably wasn't the best way to start their date or get her to agree to a second one.

Instead, he stood to greet her. "Good morning."

"Good morning. Sorry I'm late."

Before he could respond, Karen Harrington, the head of the PTA at the school, came up to them.

"I just wanted to thank you for taking part in the cakewalk last night," she said to Lauren. "We made more on that event than in the twenty-year history of the carnival."

"I'm glad to hear it." Lauren was no doubt sincere, but Adam heard the distraction in her voice.

After Karen headed toward the door, Adam asked, "Would you like to postpone this?" Part of him screamed inside his skull, asking him why he was giving her a chance to walk away and never say yes to a date with him again.

"No." Her answer wasn't particularly convincing, and she seemed to realize it. "Sorry. There's just something going on, family stuff."

"You won't hurt my feelings if you want to reschedule."

She shook her head. "No, it's definitely a 'maple-glazed doughnut' kind of morning."

"One maple-glazed doughnut coming right up. Coffee?"

"Yes, black and strong enough to walk by itself."

When Adam approached the front counter, Keri gave him a knowing grin. As he exchanged money for the order, she glanced to where Lauren sat at a small round table against the wall.

"You two are cute together."

He glanced toward his date, hoping Lauren thought so, too.

When he slipped not one but three maple-glazed doughnuts and a large coffee in front of her, Lauren looked up at him with the least amount of distraction in her expression since she'd arrived.

"You might be my new favorite person."

He smiled, liking the sound of that. "The power of sugar."

"Amen."

Adam sat opposite her and took a bite of his cruller. He watched as Lauren indulged in a huge bite of her first doughnut and dove into her coffee as if it was a life-saving device.

"Want to talk about it?" Adam asked.

Lauren looked up from her coffee. "What?"

"Whatever is bothering you."

She placed her coffee cup back on the table slowly. "That obvious, huh?"

He held up his hand with the tips of his thumb and forefinger close to each other. "A little."

"I'm not entirely sure what it is."

He gave her a curious expression, so she leaned her forearms on the table. "What do you know about Verona Charles?"

Judging by the look on his face, her question wasn't even in the ballpark of what he might have expected.

"She's retired from the tourist bureau. Her niece owns the garden center outside town. And she's the self-appointed matchmaker of Blue Falls." All of which he'd told her before.

"Single?"

"Uh, yeah. Don't think she ever married. Honestly, I've never even seen her out with anyone. Why?"

"We ran into her at the carnival right after you left, and it was obvious she and Papa Ed knew each other. They both looked like they'd received a shock from those paddles they use to restart people's hearts."

"Has he ever mentioned her before?"

"No. In fact, he's always said that he's been gone from Blue Falls so long that he doesn't know anyone from here anymore."

"Did you ask him about it?"

"Yes, not that it did us any good. I've never known him to be so silent on a subject."

"And that has you worried."

"Not really." She sounded as if she wasn't sure of her answer. "Maybe some. It's just so atypical I don't know what to think."

"Gossip being what it is, I'm sure someone knows something if you ask around."

"Don't think I haven't thought about it, but I owe it to Papa Ed to wait until he's ready to share." No matter how hard that might prove to be.

She watched as Adam took a drink of his coffee, as he swallowed. Though he wasn't dressed up, there was no mistaking how handsome he was. Or the fact he was perceptive enough to know something was bothering her. Had Phil ever been that attentive to her moods and feelings? Why had she overlooked the fact he most likely hadn't? Love really did make you blind.

And that made love dangerous.

But there was no reason to worry about that in the current situation. Right? She worried when the answer didn't easily present itself.

"I'm sorry to go on about personal stuff," she said.

"I thought that's what dates were for—to share at least some personal details with each other. Granted, I'm a little rusty."

"At what?" Surely he didn't mean dating, but he hadn't mentioned anything else.

"Honestly, it's been a while since I've been out with anyone."

"I find that hard to believe."

"So either you think I'm a liar or so irresistible that I have dates lined up for miles."

Lauren opened her mouth to respond before she realized she didn't know how. After a moment, Adam laughed.

"It's neither," he said.

"So why haven't you been on a date recently?" Better to talk about his reasons than hers.

He shrugged. "Busy, I guess. Ranches don't run themselves, and I've been putting a lot of time into trying to build the branded-beef business."

She parsed his words, trying to determine if he was aiming to get her to commit to working with him. When she didn't find any pressure directed at her, she was thankful. Because if she decided to go out with him again, there would be no business deal between them. Never again was she mixing business with pleasure.

And pleasure was what she was increasingly thinking of when she was around Adam. Even when she wasn't and simply thought about him. She wondered if his interest in her would disappear if she told him the loss of a contract was the price of going out with her.

Lauren yanked back on her thoughts. She was getting ahead of herself. There was no guarantee that they would see each other again after they shared this one breakfast. Did she even want to?

Yes.

The answer came to her with a speed and certainty that scared her. She really liked him, enjoyed spending time with him. She just hoped she wasn't making another mistake. How was she supposed to know for sure?

"I used to think that all work and no play wasn't the way to live one's life, but I'm not sure anymore."

"Because of your ex-fiancé?"

"Yeah. It's hard to trust after someone betrays you."

"True." He sounded as if he was speaking from experience, and the thought that someone had betrayed him as well caused her anger to heat a few degrees.

"Did someone hurt you?"

He shook his head. "No, but I've seen the effect on some of my brothers and sisters."

Her thoughts went immediately to Angel and the fact that Julia's father didn't seem to be in the picture. But even though she felt herself getting gradually closer to Adam, it wasn't close enough to ask about his sister's situation. Angel's story wasn't her brother's to tell.

"You ever think there are way too many crappy people in the world?"

"More times than I can count. And if you don't mind me saying so, your ex is near the top of that list. He's an idiot for hurting you and his daughters."

The sincerity in Adam's words touched her so deeply that tears sprang to her eyes. "Thank you."

Adam reached across the table and took her hand in his. He gave it a reassuring squeeze. Even though it was gentle, she felt a silent offer of his strength if she needed it. When she met his gaze, she saw the same and it caused a warm, tingly feeling to travel across her skin before sinking down deep into her heart.

The fear she had of trusting a man again made a valiant effort to assert itself, but her growing affection for Adam beat it back.

"You don't have to talk about it, but if you ever want to, I'll listen. I don't know if I can offer anything of value in response, but sometimes it just helps to get it out."

"More experience with your brothers and sisters?"

He nodded. "Really, I think it applies to everyone, even someone who hasn't had it as bad as other people."

Was he saying that compared to his siblings, he'd had an easy past? If so, she couldn't imagine what they'd been through because losing one's entire family at a young age wasn't exactly a "rainbows and puppies" type of childhood.

This time she squeezed his hand. "Don't give your own pain less weight just because others might have more or different traumas to deal with."

His eyes reflected surprise, and then they softened in a way that made her want very much to be taken into his arms. When Adam moved his hand so that he laced his fingers with hers, she wondered if he could read her thoughts.

"I know it's probably hard to trust someone after what your ex did to you, but I like you, Lauren. A lot. And I'd like to take you out on a proper date if you'll let me."

Her heart screamed *Yes!* But her mind, which tended to search constantly for threats to her and her family, for flaws in her own judgment, told her to proceed with caution.

"That sounds nice, but I don't know. I already leave the girls with my sister and grandfather too often."

"We can take the twins with us."

She stared at him, suddenly wondering if he had some sort of angle. "You want to take two teething babies on a date with us?"

"Sure, why not?"

"Um, because they're teething babies, and they tend to cry." Which didn't seem like the most romantic image in her mind.

Though his willingness to include Harper and Bethany certainly was.

"We could go to the Christmas parade and then the ice-sculpture exhibit in Austin. Angel took Julia a couple of times and she loved it."

He was actually serious. She searched for any indication his offer was a joke or some plot to gain something for himself, particularly anything that would benefit his bottom line. But either she was still as blind as she'd been with Phil, or it wasn't there. She didn't think she could adequately express how much she hoped it was the latter.

"Okay." She'd go in with her eyes open this time, but there was no denying that she wanted to spend more time with Adam.

The wide smile that spread across his face filled her heart with something it hadn't felt in a while—hope.

Lauren finished bundling Bethany in her little red outfit that sported dancing reindeer across the front and then gave her a gentle tap on the end of her nose, making her daughter laugh. Spurred by her sister's giggles,

Harper—wearing a similar green outfit with dancing candy canes—joined in.

"They sound as if they're ready for a night on the town," Violet said.

"If only their mom could be as carefree." Lauren placed a hand against her unsettled stomach. "Am I making a mistake dating so soon?"

"It's not that soon."

"Still."

"Has Adam said or done anything suspicious? Remotely Phil-like?"

"No."

"Then why would it be a mistake?"

"Lots of reasons, not the least of which is the fact that my plate is already full. Beyond full."

"You, of all people, should know there's always room for dessert."

Lauren's cheeks heated at the thought of tasting Adam like a decadent dessert.

"I'd bet every dime I have in the bank that you're having naughty thoughts right now," Violet said with mischief in her voice.

"Oh, shut up." Lauren looked around the hotel room as if she might miraculously find an ally. Not even Papa Ed was around. The day after the winter carnival and the awkward interaction with Verona, he'd borrowed Violet's car, claiming he had to go home to take care of some things.

Neither she nor Violet had bought the explanation for his hasty departure, but the look on his face had been enough to keep them from probing for a more believable reason.

And even though she'd spotted Verona across the

street when she'd left the Mehlerhaus Bakery with Adam after their breakfast date, the town's self-professed matchmaker had made herself scarce. Lauren might have chalked it up to the other woman being busy, but Adam had said Verona was never too busy to miss an opportunity to push two people toward each other, especially if they were already pointed in the right direction.

"Have you heard from Papa Ed?"

Violet's expression changed to one of concern. "No. But don't think about that now. Tonight you are to have fun with your babies and that sexy rancher."

"And what exactly are you going to do with your evening?"

"My job. And if I happen to need something to drink and that need takes me to the music hall, where I might find a sexy cowboy of my own, well, who am I to argue with Fate?"

Lauren snorted at her sister then remembered what had happened to her when she'd gone to the music hall alone. She still hadn't told anyone about that incident, but she had to break that silence now.

"Be careful if you go out," she said, then told Violet about her run-in with the two drunk men and how Adam had come to her aid.

"I suddenly like Adam a whole lot more," Violet said when Lauren finished telling her about that night.

"Don't tell Mom or Papa Ed about what happened. I don't want them to worry." Or to read too much into her relationship with Adam before she even knew how serious it might become. She still wasn't sure agreeing to go out with him was wise, but she was finding it more and more difficult to deny what she wanted.

Lauren was so lost in her thoughts that she jumped when someone knocked on the door. Before she could answer it, Violet gripped Lauren's shoulders and all hint of teasing was gone from her expression.

"Try to have a good time. You deserve to be happy, and from what I've seen, spending time with Adam makes you happy."

"I'm just so scared to hope for too much."

"Maybe Adam is your reward for having to go through what you did with Phil."

Lauren liked that idea, and when she opened the door and saw Adam standing there in all his tall, dark-haired, heartwarming-smile glory, she admitted to herself that it would be really easy to fall for him despite how badly she'd been burned before. She hoped with all her heart that Violet was right and Adam Hartley was the universe's way of balancing the scales of Lauren's life, giving her someone who was as good as Phil was bad.

Chapter 11

Adam's heart sped up at the sight of Lauren when she opened the door to her hotel room. It wasn't as if she was dressed appropriately for four-star dining. It had nothing to do with her casual attire, fit for a night out with her babies as companions, but rather there was something new in her eyes. She looked glad to see him instead of afraid he was one step away from betraying her trust. He'd never wanted to prove himself to someone so much in his life, not even his parents when they'd adopted him.

"You look beautiful." He didn't know he'd been about to say those words until they tumbled out of his mouth, but he'd never uttered anything truer.

Lauren's eyes widened a fraction, and she looked flustered by his compliment.

"Uh, thanks." She looked down at the red sweater she

wore as if it had magically transformed into a designer gown, like the kind actresses wore to big award shows.

"You ready to head out?"

She looked up at him and the flustered expression had been replaced by a smile that warmed him all over.

"Your chaperones are ready to blow this joint," Violet said as she rolled the double stroller toward the door. She crouched next to the babies. "I'm trusting you to watch those two and make sure they have tons of fun."

Adam laughed at the sight of Lauren rolling her eyes at her younger sister.

It took a few minutes to get the kids loaded into the car seats they put in the back seat of his mom's SUV. As Lauren secured Bethany, he did the same for Harper and checked to make sure he'd done it right three times. He wasn't going to put Lauren or her twins in any unnecessary danger.

When he and Lauren belted themselves into their seats, Lauren reached across and placed her hand atop his.

"Thank you," she said.

"For what?"

"Taking such care with Harper, for being willing to bring them with us."

"Are you kidding? I get three lovely dates instead of one."

She smiled at that, which caused that warm, tingly feeling all over his body again. The fact he'd never felt anything like it before told him he was falling for her. He didn't know if or how things would work out for them, considering it wasn't a path without obstacles, but he'd take each day and each interaction one at a time in the hope that she would be willing to walk that path with him.

"Plus," he said as he started the engine, "having kids with me gives me a legitimate reason to go down a slide made of ice."

"Oh, well, as long as you don't have an ulterior motive," Lauren said with a laugh.

By the time they reached Austin, the parade route was already filling up with spectators. Adam lucked into a decent parking space and helped Lauren bundle up the girls against the chill.

"It'll probably be easier in this crowd to just carry them," he said as Lauren moved to the back of the SUV to retrieve the stroller.

"They might be small but they get heavy pretty quickly."

"You know what's heavier? Bales of hay." He gave an exaggerated flex of his biceps.

Lauren laughed at his antics. "Remember I warned you."

Making Lauren laugh gave him the best feeling, one he wouldn't mind being a constant companion.

As they searched for a good spot to watch the parade, he carried Harper while Lauren held Bethany. He stepped onto a section of curb vacated by a mom and a wailing youngster who'd obviously gotten in trouble and thus given up his right to watch the parade. Just as Adam ushered Lauren in beside him, a siren announced the beginning of the parade.

"Good timing," Lauren said.

As the siren drew closer, Harper jumped in his arms and let out a cry.

"Now, now," he said as he distracted her by making funny faces.

When Bethany expressed her displeasure at the loud noise, Lauren covered the child's ears.

"Maybe this wasn't such a good idea," Lauren said.

Adam couldn't let her doubts cause her to back out now. Because despite the fact that the noise was indeed bothering the twins, he had no doubt that Lauren's fear of getting involved with someone again was at the root of her sudden hint that they leave. He protected Harper's little ears with his chest and free hand as the police cruiser come closer.

"The siren will be past in a minute." Adam wasn't giving up on this date—or Lauren—that easily. He had the feeling she needed this as much as he wanted it.

Lauren and the girls seemed to relax as the police car gave way to decorated floats, troops of uniformed scouts and bands playing Christmas carols. When he glanced over and saw Lauren smiling as she pointed out to Bethany a person dressed as that snowman from *Frozen*, his heart felt abnormally full. In this moment, he felt as if they were a family and he liked the feeling more than he'd ever expected.

He suspected Lauren's arms were getting tired when she shifted Bethany from one to the other.

"Give her here," he said.

"You already have your arms full."

"This little bit?" He jostled Harper playfully, making her laugh. What was it about baby laughter that made all seem right with the world? He remembered having the same feeling when Julia was a baby, and how his niece's peals of laughter had helped Angel get through those early days of single motherhood with her heart and sanity intact. Did Lauren feel the same?

He scooped Bethany out of Lauren's arms, and the twins seemed to be delighted to be in close proximity again. Lauren stepped closer to him, her arm brushing his, to allow a couple to pass from the street to the sidewalk behind him. When Lauren didn't move away after the man and woman had made their way by, he tried not to grin like the luckiest man in the world. It was early in his and Lauren's relationship, with no guarantee it would progress, but in this moment he felt as if this was one of those big turning points in his life he'd look back on with fondness when he was an old man surrounded by grandchildren. He couldn't help but wonder if Bethany and Harper would be the ones to give him those grandchildren.

With his heart speeding up, he looked over at Lauren and envisioned having even more children with her, of making and growing a family together that would fill in some more empty spaces on the Rocking Horse Ranch.

And in their hearts.

Lauren held on tightly to Bethany as they sped down a slide made of ice descending from an ice castle. Bethany's infectious giggles filled Lauren's heart nearly to bursting. When it came right down to it, the thing she wanted most in the world was to make sure her daughters had a safe and happy childhood. Tonight, Adam was helping her fulfill that wish. Not once had she seen any indication that bringing the twins along on their date annoyed Adam in any way. He really did appear to be having fun with them. When she started to think about how sad it was that their own father wasn't the one giving them these experiences and making them laugh, she forcefully shoved away thoughts of Phil. She didn't want him intruding on this outing.

At the bottom of the slide, she stood and held Bethany close as they watched Adam approach the top of the slide with Harper. The fact she wasn't nervous about Harper's safety told her that Adam had earned her trust—a realization that stunned her.

But it was more than trust she was feeling for Adam, wasn't it?

She doubted all her concerns about trusting too easily had disappeared for good, but tonight they seemed to have at least taken a vacation. And the truth was it felt good to not be so guarded. It felt as if she'd been walking around with all of her muscles tensed, as if prepared for an attack, and now they'd finally relaxed, allowing her to rest and enjoy living in the moment without dwelling on the past or worrying about the future.

"He's really good with your babies."

Lauren looked over to a worker dressed as one of Santa's elves. The woman seemed to have assumed that they were a couple, that Adam was the twins' father.

She found she didn't want to correct the woman's erroneous assumption. For one night she wanted to just pretend she was part of a happy, whole family. And that she was with a man who was honest, kind and loved her daughters—and maybe could love her as well.

Realizing the elf woman was staring at her, Lauren smiled. "Yes, he is," she said, before the other woman smiled and walked away.

With a "whee!" that would be more at home coming from a child, Adam pushed off from the top of the slide with Harper. The wave of laughter coming from

Harper brought tears of happiness to Lauren's eyes. They must have still been there when Adam stood and made eye contact with her.

The joy faded from his face. "Are you okay?"

She nodded.

"But you look like you're about to cry." The concern in his voice just added to the rising well of feeling in her chest.

"Just really happy. Thank you for all this."

Adam took a slow step toward her. Were it not for the fact they each held a baby, she thought he might kiss her. And she might let him.

More than might.

When he lifted his hand to cup her jaw and run a thumb across her cheek that was warm despite their frozen surroundings, she wondered if he was going to kiss her anyway.

"You're welcome." It was a simple response, one she might expect, but the way he was looking at her said so much more.

If she didn't look away, the heat building in her body was going to melt the ice palace and turn this wintry attraction into an indoor whitewater river instead.

After what seemed like hours of staring into Adam's eyes, Lauren became aware that they were standing in the way of other people waiting to descend the slide. Adam's hand dropped away from her face but resettled at the small of her back as they moved on to the next exhibit—a small carousel made of colored ice.

"It's amazing…everything they have in here," Lauren said.

"Yeah, it is."

Something about the tone of Adam's voice drew her

attention back to him. Instead of admiring the crafts-
manship of the ice carvers, he instead was looking at her
as if she was some sort of masterpiece.

Had Phil ever looked at her that way? She knew the
answer before the question fully formed. Looking back
now, she could see how blind she'd been. Granted, Phil
had been good at acting his role as devoted and loving
fiancé, but in the wake of his betrayal it was as if a veil
hiding his true intent had been lifted from her eyes—
one that hid the fact Phil had only cared for himself.

Try as she might, she detected no veil with Adam.
She sent up a silent prayer that she wasn't wrong.

He'd just finished taking some photos of her holding
the girls in a scene of the North Pole made of ice when
another worker dressed as an elf walked up to Adam.

"I can take a picture of all of you together if you'd
like."

When Lauren saw Adam about to decline, she said,
"Thanks. That's nice of you."

Adam's quick look of surprise gave way to a smile
as he handed over her phone and moved to join her and
the girls. He didn't say anything as he took Harper from
her then wrapped his arm around Lauren's shoulders
and pulled her close as if he'd done it a thousand times
before. A lump formed in her throat at the thought that
she wanted this picture-perfect family scene to be real.

"Give me some big smiles," the elf lady said.

Complying wasn't difficult. In fact, Lauren found it
easier to smile in that moment than she had in a long
time.

By the time they left the ice palace and grabbed a
quick dinner at a gourmet burger place, the girls were
tired and getting fussy.

"Sorry," Lauren said as Bethany let out a wail that turned the head of everyone on the sidewalk for a solid block as Lauren and Adam walked back toward his mom's SUV.

"No need to apologize. It's not the first time I've been around a cranky baby. Nothing's going to beat when Julia had colic. I thought her cries might bring down the roof of the house on top of all of us."

Lauren tried to imagine Phil being so understanding and couldn't picture it. Of course, he'd purposely raised doubts about whether the twins were his, even though she'd given him no reason to question her faithfulness.

Neither she nor Adam spoke again until they were on the road heading out the western edge of Austin and the girls had fallen asleep in their car seats. Lauren gazed out her window at the occasional brightly colored Christmas tree in someone's window, or a yard filled with inflatable representations of holiday cheer. She relished the peace and quiet. And thought about how this moment never would have happened with Phil. She couldn't imagine him acting like a child as he headed down a slide made of ice. If she was being honest with herself, she couldn't even picture him holding his daughters. Especially not with undisguised affection the way Adam did.

"You're thinking about him again, aren't you?"

She turned her head to look at Adam. He glanced at her and there was still enough light from their surroundings that she saw the unsure expression on his face. Somehow she knew it wasn't his question he was unsure of, but whether he should have asked it. Oddly, a part of her was glad he had. It showed he paid attention, was concerned about her.

"How could you tell?"

"You get a different look in your eyes—as if your mind has traveled somewhere else—and you go quiet."

"I'm sorry."

Adam took her hand and squeezed. "You keep apologizing for things you don't need to."

"It's just that crying babies and my wandering thoughts probably aren't your idea of a good date."

"Have you heard me complain?"

"Well, no, but—"

"No *buts*. If I minded you bringing the girls, I wouldn't have suggested it. I do, however, wish you could enjoy yourself without thoughts of your ex invading."

"I'm—" She caught herself mid-apology. "It's hard not to see the world through a different lens now."

"I understand."

Maybe he thought he did, but how could he when he didn't know the whole story?

"Did I do something that reminded you of him?"

"No," she said, but then realized that was actually a lie. "I mean, yes, but in a good way."

He glanced at her briefly before returning his attention to the highway. "That's going to require more explanation."

"I was just thinking I couldn't imagine Phil actually having fun at the ice palace."

"Not even for his daughters?"

"Considering he has barely acknowledged their existence and even tried to claim in court they weren't his, no."

"He thought you'd been with someone else?"

The way Adam sounded as he posed the question—as

if he couldn't fathom her cheating in a million years—caused a strange fluttering sensation in her chest.

"More like he was looking for any way he could to punish me."

"For what?"

"For ruining his grand plan to use me as his gravy train."

The look of confusion visible even by viewing only Adam's profile told her he hadn't dug too deeply into the details of the trial.

For the first time, she found herself wanting to share what had happened. When she'd had to reveal everything before, it hadn't been of her choosing. She'd been in a courtroom, forced to stick only to facts with little explanation allowed. Even though she'd won the case, thinking about the ordeal still made her feel raw and exposed.

"You don't have to explain," he said.

But there was something about riding along in the dark and not actually facing him that made it easier for the words to start tumbling out.

"Phil and I were together almost two years. I thought I knew him or I would have never agreed to marry him. But it turned out I didn't really know him at all."

When Adam didn't ask any questions, and instead gave her the freedom to reveal as much or little as she wanted, Lauren took a deep breath and dove into the telling of the most exhausting time of her life.

"I've been trying not to feel like a fool ever since I found out Phil wasn't the person I thought. Some days are harder than others." Like when the fear she'd make the same mistake again reared its head. "I found out he was making promises of business deals for my company without my knowledge. He was signing contracts and taking money when he had no legal right to do so. I didn't want to believe it and couldn't bring myself to confront him—at least not until I was certain. Violet convinced me to hire a private investigator. I still get sick at my stomach thinking about it. I was so afraid of what he'd find or if there was no evidence of wrongdoing Phil would feel betrayed and leave."

"But he did find something," Adam said after a few seconds, making her realize she'd lapsed into silence.

"Yeah. The PI posed as someone wanting to do business with Brazos Baker, and Phil went through with signing a fake contract, claiming he spoke for the company. One, he wasn't an employee. And we weren't married, so even that tie wasn't there. He had his own job as a salesman for a company that sells commercial kitchen supplies. That's how we met—at a trade show for chefs."

She'd once thought if she could go back in time, she'd skip that trade show and thus avoid Phil being a part of her life completely. But then she wouldn't have Bethany and Harper, and despite how frazzled and tired she often felt, she couldn't imagine her life without them now.

"I confronted Phil about it and he tried to wave it off as a misunderstanding. That was until I slapped the evidence from the PI down in front of him. Then he got angry, said I was just trying to find an excuse to get out of the marriage and giving him what he was owed. He was talking nonsense and continued to do so with his attorney. I think the guy actually believed Phil's lies."

"Did he claim he acted on your authority?"

"Yes, and when he couldn't provide proof of that, he claimed that I'd promised him half the company as a wedding present. I'd done no such thing, and he actually shot himself in the foot with that claim because an attorney came forward with evidence that Phil had him draw up a prenuptial agreement." Lauren swallowed the bile rising in her throat. "He intended to get me to agree to it and rob me of half of what I'd worked so hard to build."

Adam reached over and took her hand in his. She latched on to his support before getting to the worst part of the story.

"I sense there's more," he said.

"When I found out I was pregnant, I still felt I should tell him he was going to be a father. A part of me thought it would make him back down, that it would change his entire outlook on things. Instead, he had his attorney blindside me in court, claiming the girls weren't his. He knew they were, and a DNA test proved it. He just wanted to embarrass me, make my viewers question the entire wholesome, family-centered tone of my business. If he couldn't have what he wanted, he didn't intend for me to have it, either."

"Please tell me he's rotting in a prison cell for fraud."

How many times had Lauren fantasized about that very thing?

"No."

"I thought he lost the case."

"He did. It was my choice. It took some convincing of the people he'd conned, the judge, even my own attorney, but everyone finally agreed that it was better he remain free so he could make reparations and do a boatload of community service."

"Why did you let him off so easy?"

"Because his going to jail would have just made bigger headlines, and I wanted all the negative attention to

go away so I could move on and do damage control."
She paused, took a shaky breath. "And because I didn't
want the girls to grow up with the stigma of having a
father in prison."

Adam was quiet for a long moment, one during which
Lauren wondered if he now thought she was the fool
she feared.

"You're a good mother. A great one."

"Thank you," she said, her throat full of rising emotion she couldn't name.

Or was too scared to.

Chapter 12

Adam didn't typically have violent tendencies, even less so than his normally pretty chill brothers. But the more Lauren told him about what Phil had done, the more he wanted to punch the guy into another galaxy. The thought of the jerk walking around free—even if he had lost his job and now had to do court-ordered community service, no doubt working as part of a sanitation crew—just didn't seem right. The fact that Lauren had set aside her own hurt, and probably desire for revenge, in order to protect her daughters said a lot about the kind of person she was—the kind he liked more with each passing minute.

When he pulled in to the parking lot of the Wildflower Inn, he wished the drive back had been longer. He didn't want the night to end, but with two babies to get to bed, there was no chance of it extending further than the next few minutes.

He expected Lauren to get out of the SUV as soon as he parked. Instead, she sat staring out the windshield toward the dark surface of Blue Falls Lake.

"Other than family and attorneys, you're the only person I've told any of that," she said.

Though he wished she hadn't been put through such hell, he felt honored she trusted him enough to share the details with him—especially when he knew trust was a huge obstacle for her.

"For what it's worth, you're one of the strongest women I've ever met. Not a lot of people could have gone through what you did without coming out the other side bitter and angry."

"Oh, trust me there's been plenty of that."

"But it doesn't rule you. It's not what people see when they meet you."

She looked at him and he'd swear he'd never seen anyone so beautiful; she didn't even have to be in full light for it to show.

"What do they see?"

He stared at her, wanting to pull her into his arms and kiss her until they both were forced to surface for oxygen.

"*They* or me?"

Lauren didn't respond at first, instead licking her lips. "You."

He cupped her jaw, loving the feel of her soft skin against his rougher palm. "A woman who is strong, caring, hardworking and so beautiful I sometimes forget how to form words."

She placed her palm against the hand he held to her

cheek and swallowed visibly. "Thank you. I haven't heard anything like that in a long time—and then only from someone who probably didn't mean it."

"Which in itself is a crime."

Lauren lowered her gaze, appearing as if she had no idea how to respond.

Adam started to lean toward her, but one of the girls made a sound in the back, dispersing any romantic thoughts Lauren might have been entertaining.

"I better get them inside. I don't want them getting too cold."

The interior of the SUV might have been cooling now that the engine and thus the heater weren't running, but Adam hadn't noticed. His blood had heated at Lauren's nearness, at the fact she hadn't pulled away, even more so when he'd thought they might finally share a kiss.

The speed with which she opened her door and slipped out caused him to wonder if it had less to do with getting the babies inside and a lot more with the fact he'd spooked her. What he'd said about her being strong was true, but he had to wonder if Phil's actions had done more damage than Lauren realized.

With a sigh, he got out as well, aiming to retrieve Harper from her seat behind his. When they reached Lauren's room with the babies still half-asleep a few minutes later, he handed Harper off to Violet. He noticed Lauren's sister glancing between them, no doubt curious how the date went. He'd likely encounter similar curiosity when he arrived home. The thought made him halfway want to get a room here at the inn tonight.

Of course, that thought made him think of how he might use that room.

When Lauren turned to say good-night, he wondered if she could see his thoughts. Especially when he considered she wore a smile that was shyer than he knew her to be.

"Thanks for tonight," she said. "I had a nice time. And though they can't say it yet, the girls did, too."

He nodded. "Me, too." The moment grew awkward. "Well, good night."

"Good night."

During his walk back to the parking lot, an odd emptiness accompanied him. A feeling of being incomplete. He walked a few feet past his mom's SUV to the grassy crest of the hill that led down to the lakeside park. He shivered against a sudden brisk wind off the lake that eliminated what little of his earlier warmth still lingered.

"Adam?"

At first he thought he'd imagined Lauren's voice, but then he heard footsteps behind him. He turned to find her standing a short distance away.

"Is everything okay?" he asked.

She appeared to be about to say something, but in the next moment she erased the few feet between them, placed her hands on his shoulders and lifted onto her toes. As her lips touched his, Adam wrapped his arms around her and pulled her even closer.

And the incomplete feeling went completely away.

Lauren let go of the last bit of resistance holding her back and fell completely into the kiss. When Adam's arms came around her, pulling her closer, she didn't think she'd ever loved the feel of anything more.

Though the air around them was cold enough she'd

seen her breath on the walk out here, she was fairly certain flames were licking at her body. Were it not for her sister and daughters inside, she would lead Adam back to the room and see where things went. It'd been so long since she'd been held by a man, since she'd felt any passion.

Truth was she'd never felt a hunger like what was gnawing at her now. She wanted Adam, all of him, more than she could adequately describe. That should scare her, would have only minutes ago, but in this moment it didn't. Because crossing this line had been her move. He'd given her that. And now he was showing her just how much he had been holding back. Because there was no way the hunger she felt from him had just been born when she captured his lips with hers.

She had no idea how much time had elapsed when their lips finally left each other. Were it not for Adam's hands against her back, Lauren would have been pretty certain she would have stumbled and perhaps toppled right over. The feeling in her head was similar to the dizzy feeling she got when on a boat.

"I'm sorry," Adam said, sounding breathless. "Too much?"

Not enough. Not nearly enough.

"Don't apologize. I seem to remember I started that."

A slow, sexy grin transformed Adam from apologist to a man she was having an extraordinarily hard time not shoving into the back seat of his mom's SUV and steaming up the windows so much that someone was bound to call the cops.

That mental image caused her to laugh, which wiped the grin from Adam's face.

"My turn to apologize," she said as she motioned toward her head. "Inappropriate thoughts."

The grin raced back to his mouth. "That right?"

"And no, I'm not sharing them."

Adam tugged her closer, and there was no mistaking just what kind of effect their hot make-out session had on him. Honestly, she was surprised there wasn't visible steam coming off her own body.

Lauren thought about how she'd run out on Violet without an explanation, not that she didn't think her sister had already come up with something juicy. "I should get back inside."

"Can't say I like that idea."

She smiled up at Adam and hoped with all her might that he was the good guy he seemed. "I should be scared out of my mind right now, but I'm not."

Adam ran the tips of his fingers softly along the edge of her face. "Does that mean you'll go out with me again?"

"Yes. And maybe I can arrange a babysitter next time." She hated to keep depending on her family to look after the girls so much, but if she didn't get some alone time with Adam she was afraid she might combust. Maybe she could hire a babysitter and give them all a free night.

"As cute as the girls are, I like the sound of that."

Though she didn't want to, she made herself take a step backward and then another. "I'll let you know, okay?"

Another step and the only part of them that was still touching was their hands, but then Adam pulled her quickly back into his arms and kissed her again—a deep, thorough kiss that left her wondering if she had enough energy left to walk back to the room.

"I better let you go before I act on some of my own inappropriate thoughts," he said, but then gave her another mind-spinning kiss before breaking all contact and stepping toward the SUV. "I'll wait until you get inside."

Inside the SUV? Yes, please.

But no, he meant the inn. Somehow she remembered how walking worked, so she turned and headed for the light of the lobby. She didn't allow herself to look back at Adam or she might walk right back to him. Possibly run. Her entire body was shaking as she entered the light and warmth of the lobby. A quick glance toward the check-in desk revealed that the young woman there appeared to be hiding a smile. Had she seen Lauren and Adam getting hot and heavy in the parking lot?

Good grief, she had to be careful. Everyone had a cell phone, and the last thing she needed was a video of her and Adam all over each other in a dark parking lot hitting the internet. It would shoot all her work to put the coverage of the trial and questions about her morality firmly behind her and out of the minds of her viewers.

She walked on legs that felt like overcooked noodles down the hallway toward her room. When she reached it, she didn't immediately enter. Instead, she leaned against the wall and tried to get her breathing under control. To slow her heart rate. To formulate some sort of response to the questions she knew waited for her on the other side of the door.

She caught movement out of the corner of her eye, and her heart jumped into her throat. When she turned toward the end of the corridor, she fully expected to see

Phil staring at her. She'd swear she saw him. Anger propelled her down the hallway. When she reached him, she was going to fire at him with both barrels with everything she'd imagined saying to him that she hadn't been able to in that courtroom. Punish him for intruding on this moment when she was basking in the glow of having kissed Adam.

But when she reached the end of the hallway and looked in both directions, there was no one in sight. And there was nowhere he could have hidden that quickly. She'd imagined him. Was this the universe's way of warning her she was making a mistake again?

No, Adam was a good guy. He'd proven that over and over, hadn't he?

With a sigh, she turned and walked back to her room. She took a deep breath and pulled the key card out of her pocket. But before she could slip it into the slot, the exit door at the end of the hall opened and she jerked toward the sound. But it still wasn't Phil. Instead, Papa Ed stepped inside. Had he arrived back while she was gone to Austin? If so, why had he just been outside? Surely he hadn't driven back this late.

What worried her more than his driving several hours alone after dark was how he appeared to be carrying a heavy but invisible burden on his shoulders.

"Papa Ed?"

He looked up as he neared her, seeming startled to find her out in the corridor.

"Did you just get back?"

He gave a quick nod, looking as if he wanted nothing more than to slip inside his room and fall asleep. But he halted midway to reaching for his door and turned toward her.

"Is Violet awake?"

"Yeah."

"I'd like to talk to you both."

Something cold and foreboding settled in the pit of her stomach. "Is Mom okay?"

"She's fine, honey. And before you ask, I'm okay, too. I just have something I need to talk to you about."

Despite what he said, it had to be something serious if he wasn't willing to wait until morning. Before she allowed her mind to jump to all kinds of horrible conclusions, she slipped her key in the door and eased inside so as not to wake up the girls.

Violet jumped up from where she sat at the small desk working on the computer with an excited look on her face, all those questions Lauren had imagined shining in her sister's eyes—until she saw Papa Ed behind her.

"What's wrong?"

Lauren gave a little shake of her head as she checked the girls and saw they were fast asleep. She also noticed that Violet had gotten a miniature lighted Christmas tree from somewhere and placed it on top of the small fridge. It'd be enough to make Lauren smile if she wasn't so concerned about Papa Ed. She had the awful feeling that after the most wonderful night she'd had in ages, a bomb was about to be dropped on her life yet again.

Suddenly exhausted, she sank onto the side of her bed. She watched as Papa Ed walked over to where his great-granddaughters were sleeping. He smiled as he looked down at them.

"They really are the most beautiful little girls," he said.

"Papa Ed, tell us what's going on. You're freaking me out," Violet said.

Lauren couldn't have more perfectly voiced her feelings as her grandfather sat on Violet's bed. She noticed him fidgeting with the fabric of his pants, as if nervous. It wasn't a state in which she'd very often seen him. Just as she was about to ask him again what was wrong, he took a deep breath and began to speak.

"I know you have been curious about that incident with Verona Charles at the carnival," he said. "The simple answer is that we used to know each other a long time ago."

"And the 'not simple' answer?" Lauren prompted. "Was she an old girlfriend?" It was hard to imagine him with anyone other than Nana Gloria, but she knew they'd had lives before they'd gotten married.

He nodded. "We were pretty serious." He paused, as if the weight of the past was crushing him. "I loved her."

Lauren glanced at Violet, whose eyes had widened at that revelation, before she returned her attention to Papa Ed. "What happened?"

"I had dated your grandmother before Verona and I got together, and...well, your mother was the result."

It was as if Lauren's brain encountered a thick bank of fog, preventing it from processing her grandfather's meaning. But then Violet gasped, jerking Lauren out of the fog as if she'd been lassoed and yanked out by a speeding horse.

"Explain." It was the only word she could get past her lips, though she was beginning to form a picture in her mind.

"It was a different time then, so I did the right thing and married your grandmother."

"You didn't love Nana?" Violet said, sounding one part sad and one part angry.

"Of course I did," Papa Ed responded with so much feeling that Lauren believed him. Plus, there was no way he could have feigned the obvious love for Nana Gloria all those years. "I cared for her before, but we had a fight about something stupid and inconsequential, and broke up. I started dating Verona and fell hard for her, but there was no way I was going to leave Gloria to raise our child alone. So we got married and moved away from Blue Falls."

"To get away from Verona?" Lauren asked.

"And to protect Gloria's reputation."

"But you still loved Verona?" Violet asked as she got up to pace the room.

Lauren didn't know how her sister found the energy to stand. She sure didn't have enough herself.

"Yes, but I never talked to her again." He hesitated, looking as if his mind had been transported to another time. "I didn't have the courage to face her, so I just left her a note telling her I had to go." He shook his head. "I handled it so wrong, but I was a scared kid who'd just found out he was going to be a father."

He sighed and shook his head slowly.

"Distance and time changed things," he said. "Gloria and I grew closer, and I would not trade all the years I had with her for anything. I loved her with all my heart." His voice broke on the last word.

Lauren reached over and took his hand in hers. "We know you did. That much was obvious."

"Is Verona the reason you wanted Lauren to come here, to open her restaurant in Blue Falls?" Violet was still pacing, in danger of wearing a visible path in the carpet.

Papa Ed shook his head. "No. I had no idea she was

still here, or that she'd even recognize me if we did happen to cross paths. I just... I guess a part of me was homesick for my boyhood home after Gloria passed. I wanted to see it one more time. But when I happened across the empty restaurant for sale, it felt like some sort of sign. I can't really explain other than to say I thought..." He stopped and didn't appear as if he was going to go on.

It hit Lauren what he'd been about to say.

"You felt as if Nana was telling you something."

He nodded. "I know that sounds crazy, that I was just looking for a connection to her that wasn't there."

"I don't think it's crazy," Lauren said.

"You don't?" Violet looked at her sister as if she thought everyone in the room was off their rocker except for her and the sleeping babies.

"I think there are lots of things that none of us will ever fully understand. Whether Nana wanted us to come to Blue Falls, I have no idea. But I think the fact that Papa Ed ran into someone he used to love, someone who never got married, isn't pure coincidence."

"She never got married?" Papa Ed sounded shocked and as if maybe the news had broken his heart all over again.

"That's what I heard." She had to say something to banish the sadness she saw in his eyes. "But from all accounts she had a successful career and is now known far and wide as the town's unofficial matchmaker."

Lauren wondered if Verona spent so much time arranging happily-ever-afters for other people because she'd never gotten her own. The thought was incredibly sad, and there was just too damn much sadness in the world. Especially for good people.

"Maybe Nana wants you to have a second chance."

Papa Ed's forehead crinkled in confusion.

"With Verona," Lauren said to clarify.

He shook his head. "Oh, no, I can't do that to her."

"Who? Nana or Verona?"

"I loved your grandmother."

Lauren squeezed his hand. "We know that. But you don't have to live the rest of your life alone to prove that to anyone, not even yourself."

"You're talking silliness," he said. "Besides, you saw how she reacted when she saw me. I doubt she ever wants to clap eyes on me again."

"You won't know until you ask."

"Lauren—"

It had been a long time since she'd shushed her little sister, but Lauren did it now. Violet looked shocked but thankfully kept quiet.

"I don't know." Papa Ed looked down at where Lauren's hand sat atop his.

"Listen, if nothing else maybe you can reconnect and set things right."

"It seems a little late for that."

"I'm speaking not as your granddaughter now, but as a woman. I saw the look on Verona's face. I don't really know her, but that look told me that she hasn't forgotten." Probably hadn't forgiven. "I think you have to try. If it doesn't work, then at least you tried. If you can be friends, even better. And if you can rekindle a spark, well, I want to see you happy. I've always worried about Mom being alone since Dad died, and I know you've been sad since Nana passed." Not to mention how she'd felt since the truth about Phil had come to light, though it wasn't the same thing. "It feels like time for our family to have something positive happen in the romantic realm, you know?"

"My money's on you," Papa Ed said as he looked up at her.

Lauren glanced at Violet, who shrugged. "I might have mentioned to Mom you were out on a date tonight."

"He seems like a fine young man, and the fact he took the girls with you speaks highly of him."

Papa Ed was likely using the turn in the conversation to avoid talking about Verona anymore, but Lauren had said her piece and any further action was up to him.

Time for her own honesty.

"He is. At least he seems to be."

Papa Ed sandwiched her hand between his. "We can never be one-hundred-percent certain about a person. We just have to go on our best judgment and faith."

"My belief in both of those is pretty shaky right now."

"But not shaky enough to prevent you from going back outside to grab a good-night kiss?" Violet asked, her natural teasing seeming to edge out her upset over Papa Ed's revelation.

"Did you leave the girls alone to spy on me?"

Violet smiled. "No, but you just confirmed my suspicion."

"We're not talking about me."

"Yeah, we are."

Lauren started to object before realizing she was just too tired.

Papa Ed stood. "I'll go and let you all get some rest. I feel as if I could sleep twelve hours myself."

Lauren accompanied him to the door. "Will you at least think about what I said?"

He placed his hand on her shoulder. "If you promise to give that young man a real chance. You deserve to be happy the same as the rest of us."

She nodded because she didn't know how else to respond. And the truth was those minutes in the parking lot had her thinking that she'd allowed herself to feel more for Adam than she'd even realized. If she was alone, she might very well close her eyes, touch her lips and relive every delicious moment of his kisses, the heart-pumping feel of his hands running over her. How much better would it feel if there was nothing between them?

Before her face lit up like a bright red railroad-crossing sign, she opened the door and kissed Papa Ed on the cheek. When she closed the door behind him, she halfway dreaded turning to face her sister. But the rest of her wanted to hop on her bed and tell Violet everything, to squeal like a teenage girl who'd just gone on a date with her dream guy.

Could Adam be that—a dream come true? Because the last man in her life had turned out to be a nightmare.

When she retraced her steps into the room, she found Violet sitting against the headboard of her bed.

"I honestly don't know what to even feel right now," Violet said.

"Papa Ed's not getting any younger. If there's the possibility that he could find love again, wouldn't you want him to?"

Violet shrugged. "I guess. But what if Verona hurts him instead? I don't want to have to go off on an old lady."

"I think Papa Ed can handle things himself." Not that she wouldn't be there for him if he needed it, but something was telling her that everything would be okay with him. Maybe Nana Gloria was speaking to her, too. She smiled at that thought.

"So, that smile have to do with what happened in the parking lot? Speaking of, tell me exactly what did happen in the parking lot."

Lauren sat on the edge of her bed and flopped backward to stare at the ceiling. "Tell me I'm not being a fool."

"Well, I can't do that until you tell me what happened."

"I walked straight up to Adam and kissed him. Really kissed him."

"And did he kiss you back?"

"Yes."

"Peck? Smooch? French? I need details, woman."

Lauren lifted her feet. "Are there still soles on my shoes? Because it felt as if they might have melted off."

Violet squealed, causing one of the twins to make a startled sound in her sleep.

Lauren sat up straight and pointed at her sister. "If you wake them up, I'm going to leave you here with them and go sleep at the restaurant."

An evil grin spread across Violet's face. "Are you sure that's where you'd go? Or maybe you wouldn't be alone there."

Lauren's cheeks heated at the thought, at the way her skin tingled as if she could already feel Adam's hands there.

"My initial question remains."

"Are you a fool?" Violet scooted to the edge of her bed to face Lauren. "No. You'd be a fool if you let what happened with Phil keep you from finding happiness with someone else."

"But there are—"

Violet held up her hand. "I'm going to stop you right there. I understand why you do it—I probably would as well in your situation—but you need to stop overthinking everything. There is no way to know with total certainty that someone will never hurt you."

Lauren let out her breath and dropped her face into her hands for a few seconds before facing her sister again. "I really like him, but I'm scared. And it's not just me I have to consider now."

"The man just took your babies on a date with you."

"True."

"Go slowly if you want to, but just go."

Lauren bit her bottom lip and realized she could still taste Adam there. "Okay."

It took an amazing amount of willpower not to go immediately. Go toward what she hoped was the beginning of something great.

Chapter 13

Adam smiled as he looked at the photo Lauren had just texted him. She was in the midst of cleaning out the flowerbeds around the restaurant building, thus hot, sweaty and dirty, with her hair escaping from the edges of the bandanna on her head.

Sure you still want to go out with this?

He typed a response.

More than ever.

She responded with several laughing emojis, but he was telling the truth. Since the night she'd walked out of the inn to kiss him two weeks before, they'd seen each other every day. And never missed an opportunity to kiss. Just the night before, she and her sister had come out to the ranch for dinner with the twins. He'd stolen Lauren away for a few minutes and taken her to the barn, where they had some time alone. Their kisses had gotten so hot and heavy that he'd had to force himself to step away. He wanted more, but he didn't know if she was ready to make herself that vulnerable, especially when he still saw doubt in her eyes sometimes. He counted himself lucky she'd gone as far as she had considering all he knew about Phil and how wrong he'd treated her. He hoped Phil was gone from her life for good, but he worried. The more he learned about the guy, the more he wondered if he'd really accept his humiliation without some sort of attempt at payback.

Phil had better not do anything that even approached hurting Lauren again. Or the twins. Adam had grown to love those little girls. It was impossible not to. And to say his mom had fallen for them too was the biggest of understatements. He knew without her saying a word that she was already envisioning them being her grandchildren someday.

Of course, that was putting the romantic cart way, way before the horse.

"That has to be the goofiest grin I've ever seen on your face, and that's saying something," Angel said as she plopped down on the opposite side of the dining room table, where he was sitting with his computer and a pile of paperwork he'd been working on before Lauren's text came in.

He placed his phone display down on the table. "Anyone ever tell you that you're a pest?"

"Repeatedly. It's the curse of being the baby of the family."

He scrolled down on his screen, making a notation about a new appointment he'd made a few minutes earlier to meet with a hotel owner in San Antonio. In order to increase the likelihood of making the branded-beef business profitable, he was expanding his area of exploration. He still hoped to be able to be Lauren's supplier, but lately business was the furthest thing from his mind when he was with her.

"So it seems things are going well with Lauren," Angel said.

"So far, so good."

Angel laughed.

He looked up from the computer screen. "What?"

"You've fallen for her."

He didn't deny it. He doubted there was any use.

"Have you told her?"

Adam shook his head. "I don't want to scare her away."

"You don't think she feels the same?"

He sat back in his chair with his hands laced behind his head. "I think she cares, but I could just be a rebound relationship."

He hated the very thought of that being true because he fell for Lauren more each time they were together. Maybe he'd been falling since the first moment he'd met her and feared she'd topple off that rickety ladder.

"Not a chance."

Adam focused on his sister. "What makes you say that?"

"I'm a woman. I can tell when another woman more than just cares for a man. There's a difference between just wanting to get, shall we say, carnal with a guy and loving him."

"Okay, this conversation just got weird." Though the

possibility that Lauren might be falling for him, too, sent a thrill through him he'd never experienced before.

Angel smiled. "I'm happy for you."

"Don't jinx it."

The fact that he worried something was going to make Lauren change her mind kept dogging him over the next few days. When he was out meeting with clients, ironing out details with the meat packager, even when he was with Lauren. It didn't matter if they were sharing pizza at Gia's, helping his parents set up their enormous Christmas tree, or enjoying lingering kisses before they went their separate ways for the night, he couldn't shake the feeling that their time together was ticking down.

He told himself he was being paranoid, that he was just thinking that way because he wasn't sure how invested Lauren was in their relationship. Sure, she seemed to enjoy their time together. Really enjoy it when they were in each other's arms. But she hadn't even hinted she wanted more, and he was concerned if he pushed for it he'd lose her altogether. And she'd come to mean too much to him for her to not be in his life anymore.

He was getting ready to meet her for dinner at the Wildflower Inn when she texted that she'd moved to a cabin at the Vista Hills Guest Ranch and to meet her there and they'd figure out what to do for the evening.

She and Violet had talked about making the move as the twins got crankier with their teething, so maybe Lauren had finally decided to exchange the convenience of being in town for the privacy of being in a cabin, where the girls crying in the middle of the night wouldn't bother any other guests.

He waved at Ryan Teague as he passed him on the drive into the Teagues' guest ranch half an hour later. The family had done what he and his siblings hoped to—diversified their ranch's income to ensure its future survival.

When he reached the cabin Lauren had indicated, he noticed that only her car was parked next to it. Violet's and Ed's weren't anywhere in sight. The idea of actually being alone with Lauren sent a rush of heat through him.

As he walked up to the front door, he noticed the miniature Christmas tree that had been in their hotel room now sat on a table in the front window. He supposed he should start thinking about a Christmas present for Lauren. And something for the twins.

He raised his hand to knock on the door, but Lauren opened it before he could. She greeted him with a smile he had the sudden need to see every day for the rest of his life. Best not to say that out loud and risk freaking her out.

"You look beautiful," he said instead as he glanced at the bright blue dress that made her eyes look even bluer.

"Thanks." She ran her hand down the side of the dress, looking as if she was nervous.

That's when he noticed the candles and place settings on the dining table. *Two* place settings. His heart rate sped up. Then the delicious smells coming from the kitchen hit him and his stomach growled in response.

Lauren chuckled. "I hope that means you're hungry."

"You cooked?" Maybe that was why she'd moved to the cabin, so she'd have a kitchen again. Perhaps she had to do some cooking for her magazine pieces, or she was trying out new recipes for the restaurant.

"Yeah, I hope you don't mind that instead of going out."

Or maybe this was exactly what it looked like, a romantic dinner for two.

"Based on the smell, I doubt any place could beat it." Adam stepped inside and shut the door against the December chill. He took Lauren's hand and gently pulled her close. "But I'd be happy eating gas-station food if it was with you."

He lowered his mouth to hers and indulged in a kiss that stoked the flames that had been smoldering within him since that night in the Wildflower Inn parking lot.

A ding from the kitchen caused Lauren to startle, thus ending the kiss.

"Sorry, I have to get that," she said before hurrying off toward the small kitchen area.

He watched as she bent to pull what looked and smelled like barbecued chicken from the oven.

"I know it's not beef, but this is one of my favorite dishes."

"I live on a cattle ranch. I can have beef anytime I want it."

A flash of something that almost looked like a wince crossed her face before she turned back to moving the casserole dish from the oven to the spot reserved for it on the table.

"Everything okay?"

"Yeah, fine."

But as they ate and talked about other things, he could tell something was still weighing on her mind. "Out with it," he said as he took her hand in his and ran his thumb across her knuckles.

"Nothing, just more annoyances at the restaurant this week. A variety of little things, but combined with the new roof and the unexpected wiring issues, I just sometimes wonder if I bit off more than I can chew."

"Nope. You're going to make this a big success, no doubt about it."

She stared at him as if looking for something more, then glanced down at where their hands were joined. "I need to tell you something."

Her tone concerned him, but the fact she'd made this delicious dinner just for the two of them indicated she wasn't going to toss him out of her life, right?

"Okay."

She looked up and it seemed she had a conflicting mix of determination and sorrow in her expression.

"I know you've been hoping to get a deal with the restaurant for your ranch's beef, but I promised myself that I would never again mix business with personal relationships. The last time I let the two coexist, it nearly destroyed my life."

Maybe he was wrong and she was about to dump him.

"I've loved all this time we've been spending together," she said. "I care about you, a lot, but if we continue to see each other, you have to know that I won't be able to use the Rocking Horse's beef."

He didn't realize until that moment how much he'd grown convinced that the deal was as good as signed, and a shot of anger went through him, as if he'd been strung along. But when he took a breath and considered everything she'd shared with him about what Phil had done, he had to admit he understood where she was coming from. A wave of concern about the viability of the branded-beef operation hit him, but he did his best to hide it. He'd figure out some way to make it profitable. He had to have faith something would present itself. The business had taken hits before and he always found some way to scrape by. But in that moment, the woman sitting across the table meant so much more to him than selling beef. He was pretty damn sure he loved her.

"If you think I'd walk away from you because of losing business, you're wrong." He lifted her hand and planted a soft kiss on her fingers without breaking eye contact.

She blinked eyes that looked brighter on the heels of his words. "How would you feel about skipping dessert?"

It took a moment for it to register what she meant. When it did, his entire body seemed to vibrate in anticipation. Instead of answering, he stood without releasing her hand and urged her to her feet. He pulled her close and caressed her cheek.

"Are you sure?"

"I won't lie and say I'm not nervous, but I've been fantasizing about this for a while."

He grinned. "That right?"

She ran her hand slowly up his chest. "Yes."

He glanced toward the clock on the mantel above the fireplace. "How long do we have?"

"All night."

Those flames within him exploded into a wildfire as he wrapped his arms around Lauren and captured her mouth with his.

Lauren's nervousness about taking the next, huge step with Adam got shoved way into the background as he kissed her as if he was a hero in some great love story. She'd swear she heard a swell of romantic music wrap around them as she gave in to her desire. She kissed Adam back with the full force of all the feelings she'd been holding back for fear he'd crush her even more than Phil had.

Adam's hands on her bare arms made her want to rid them both of anything standing between more skin-on-skin contact. When had she ever felt so much potent desire? Ever?

She had loved Phil once, but she was certain the very idea of sex with him had never felt like what was consuming her now.

Not willing to wait any longer, she clasped Adam's hand and led him toward the bedroom. Once they were standing next to the bed, she slowly started to unbutton his shirt. He let her. His watching her without saying a word or making a move was the sexiest thing she'd ever experienced.

When she shoved his shirt from his arms and he simply let it drop to the floor, she had difficulty catching her breath. Unable to stop herself, she let her fingertips travel lightly over his exposed chest. His sharp intake of breath sent a thrill of power and excitement through her.

In the next moment he lowered his lips to hers again, and it seemed his hands were everywhere. So many places it was hard to focus. All her senses jumped from the taste of his lips and the feel of his tongue dueling with hers to the length of his body pressed against her to the slide of the zipper along the back of her dress.

Lauren wasn't a novice in the bedroom, but she'd never experienced anything like being undressed by Adam. He took his time even though she suspected there was a part of him that just wanted to rip off every stitch of their clothing and get to business. Or maybe that was just her.

Instead, he paused and ran his fingertips across the swell of her breasts, kissed the curve of her shoulder, let his breath linger next to her ear, making her tingle from her scalp to the tips of her toes.

Needing to feel more of him, she ran her hands up his arms then pressed her lips against his chest. Feeling more daring than she ever had before, she ran her tongue along his warm flesh as her fingers began the work of freeing him from his jeans. The sharp intake of his breath was like a fresh supply of fuel to her desire.

Adam stepped out of his jeans and grabbed her at the back of her thighs, lifting her so that her legs were on either side of his hips as he crossed the rest of the distance to the bed. The strength it took for him to lower her slowly to the bed caused her pulse to accelerate.

"You're so beautiful," he said as he ran his fingertips along the edge of her face. The way he said those simple words made it apparent he believed what he said but that her physical attributes were not the only things that attracted him.

She wanted to tell him how handsome she thought he was, how being near him made her feel more alive than she ever had, but before she could speak he lowered his mouth to hers and she was lost.

What little was left of their clothing was tossed aside, leaving absolutely nothing between them. When Adam took care of the protection without her even having to ask, she fell for him even more. Not that she hated the idea of more children, especially with the right man, but at this stage she had all she could handle without losing her mind.

All of which she could tackle later. Now she wanted to focus on nothing but the man in her arms. And the feeling seemed to be mutual, judging by the way Adam was making every inch of her come alive beneath his touch.

The moment she'd been literally dreaming about arrived and she answered the question in his eyes with a smile. Everything else in her life disappeared as they made love. It wasn't just sex. And he wasn't only making love to her. It was the most beautiful give-and-take, like a ride on the world's most sensual roller coaster. When she felt herself approaching climax, she dug her fingers into Adam's strong shoulders, deriving even more pleasure from the feel of his muscles moving beneath his warm, taut skin.

She closed her eyes and pressed her head back into her pillow as she climaxed, followed in the next breath by Adam.

Her mind was still spinning when Adam curled around her body and pulled a quilt over them.

"Well, I don't need anything else for Christmas," he said.

She playfully swatted against his shoulder, causing him to laugh. Although she could safely echo his words and mean every one. So many things were flying through her mind, but she found herself drifting. Wasn't it the man who usually fell asleep approximately five seconds after finishing? Of course, between the various aspects of work and caring for two teething babies, sleep was a rare commodity. So feeling more relaxed than she had in ages, she snuggled close to Adam's warmth, smiling as he wrapped his wonderful arms around her, and allowed herself to drift toward blissful sleep.

In the days following his night with Lauren, Adam alternated between whistling and grinning like a fool.

At least that's how he felt. He'd never had a more wonderful night in his life, and the days since hadn't been half-bad either. He'd helped Lauren at the restaurant, and they were making decent progress despite minor annoyances continuing to crop up or how many times they got distracted by kissing and, well, other things.

Even business for the branded-beef operation was looking up. He'd signed a deal with a small restaurant in Fredericksburg, agreed to provide the steaks for a large society wedding in Austin, and was moments away from inking another contract to provide a variety of beef products for a newer winery bed-and-breakfast about an hour away from Blue Falls.

Jamie Barrett looked up before signing her portion of the agreement. "I know our customers are going to love your products."

"I appreciate your business."

"It's so exciting to think we'll have the same supplier as the Brazos Baker's new restaurant."

What? Where had she heard that?

"Maybe you can convince her to come out and do a demonstration for our guests sometime. And I'd love for her shop to carry some of our wine." The way she said it implied she knew that he and Lauren were dating and that he'd use his influence to give his customers special access.

Before he could correct her assumption, she signed her name on the contract with an excited flourish. Damn it. He'd have to tell Lauren about this and hope she didn't assume he'd used her the same way Phil had.

He could tell Jamie she was mistaken, but would that do more harm than good now? Though he'd not even mentioned Lauren, would Jamie feel misled into a business deal that wouldn't provide all the benefits she'd hoped? What if she decided to sue? Of course, she didn't have a case, but neither had Phil when he'd taken Lauren to court. Lauren had won but her business had taken a hit—the kind of hit his wouldn't survive. He'd just explain the situation to Lauren and ask her how she'd prefer he handle it. Maybe she'd even like the idea of working with the winery, despite how the connection had come about.

When he left a few minutes later, he sat in his truck staring at his phone. He didn't want to have this conversation with Lauren over the phone. He needed her to see his eyes when he told her, hear his voice in person. But that wouldn't be able to happen until later that night at the earliest. He had three more appointments, one of them all the way in Seguin, east of San Antonio. He'd been happy that his widening the area he was canvassing had yielded some results, but now he wondered if somehow word had gotten out that if someone did business with him they'd have an in with the famous Brazos Baker.

A sick pit formed in his stomach, not only at the potential mistake on everyone else's part, but also that his recent successes might have nothing to do with his hard work, or the quality of the Rocking Horse's beef.

Movement outside drew his attention and he looked up from where he'd been staring at his phone. Jamie gave him a big smile and a wave before she got into her car. Realizing he was going to be late to his next appointment if he didn't leave, he started the truck's engine and pulled out onto the road. But the sick, tight ball in his stomach didn't ease, not even when no one mentioned Lauren at his next meeting. Instead, it grew larger, and he remembered the feeling he'd had that something was going to derail his relationship with her.

Telling himself that he was simply blowing a misunderstanding out of proportion and promising himself he'd address it with Lauren as soon as he got back to Blue Falls, he drove toward his last appointment in Seguin even though he wanted nothing more than to race back home to Lauren. But he needed to keep building his business, to succeed on his own so that no one, not even Lauren, could say he'd only succeeded because of his association with her. To prove to her that he didn't need or want part of her company. He only wanted her.

Chapter 14

Lauren paused outside of the Blue Falls Tourist Bureau and Chamber of Commerce's combined office when she got a text. She smiled when she saw it was from Adam. Just the thought of him made her happier than she'd ever been. The time they spent together was the most awesome reward for her allowing herself to believe she might find love again, and with someone who wouldn't betray her.

Can I see you when I get back to town later?

Of course the answer was yes, no matter how tired she was at the end of a long day. She typed her response.

Yes. What time will you be back?

In two or three hours. Last meeting got delayed.

Okay, heading into the business holiday mixer.

Have a good time.

She'd have a better time with him, but she needed to push those sexy thoughts aside so that no one could read them on her face like a headline in two-hundred-point bold type. When she stepped inside, she spotted her sister. Papa Ed was on babysitting duty tonight along with Verona, who had finally warmed up to him after they'd had several long talks about the past and the intervening years over coffee and pastries.

"From the grin on your face, you must have just talked to a certain hunky cowboy," Violet said.

"Possibly."

Lauren glanced around the room filled with people who owned businesses in Blue Falls and the surrounding Hill Country. This was a social event for the holidays, but she was hoping to make more connections now that the time to actually start planning for the restaurant's opening was near. Earlier that day, she'd met with some food vendors, and a couple of days before, she and Adam had driven the arts-and-crafts trail so she could meet local artisans. She came away with plans to carry some of their items in her gift shop.

Though he didn't say anything, she suspected that Adam wished there was a way for them to be together and still have the Rocking Horse's beef served in her restaurant. Honestly, she'd been thinking about caving. After all, Adam was nothing like Phil. And what were the odds that two men in a row would use her success to advance their own? Could she mix business with pleasure again?

She and Violet began to mingle as they snacked on a variety of yummy hors d'oeuvres. It wasn't until Lauren bit into a crab-stuffed mushroom that she realized how hungry she was, that she'd barely eaten all day with how packed her schedule had been. Between meeting with vendors and overseeing the polishing of the floor, not to mention doing some editing on her next cookbook, lunch had come and gone with her only managing to down a leftover mini pork slider from the night before.

A pretty redhead wearing a wide smile approached Lauren just as she swallowed the last bite of mushroom. The other woman extended her hand.

"Lauren Shayne, it's so nice to meet you," she said. "Jamie Barrett. I own a winery and bed-and-breakfast about a half hour on the other side of Poppy."

Lauren shook the other woman's hand. "Nice to meet you, too."

"I'm sure you hear this a lot, but I'm a big fan. I was just telling Adam that this afternoon when we finalized our deal to serve Rocking Horse beef. I figure if it's good enough for the Brazos Baker, it's a 'can't lose' business decision on my part."

The appetizers she'd eaten threatened to come back up. Surely this woman wasn't saying what it sounded like, that Adam was telling potential customers that she'd agreed to serve Rocking Horse Ranch beef in her restaurant. That couldn't be right. He'd chosen her over business. Hadn't he? She had to know the truth, but the moment she opened her mouth to ask for clarification, Violet was suddenly at her elbow.

"I'm sorry to interrupt, but do you mind if I borrow my sister for a minute?" Violet asked Jamie.

"Not at all. The night's young. Maybe we can chat about your gift shop carrying a selection of our wine later."

Violet made a noncommittal sound and practically dragged Lauren out to the building's lobby.

"I know what you're thinking, and I don't want you to jump to conclusions," Violet said before Lauren could object to her sister's behavior.

"What else could it mean?" Her stomach started to churn. "Oh, my God, I've been a complete fool yet again."

"No, you haven't."

"You don't know that." Lauren pointed toward the gathering in the other part of the building. "Because it sounded a whole lot like Adam told that woman that we would be serving Rocking Horse beef at the restaurant when we're not."

"It could just be a misunderstanding."

"How? How could there be a misunderstanding if the topic doesn't even come up? And if it did, why didn't he correct her?"

"I don't know, but perhaps that's something you should ask him."

Lauren forced herself to take a deep breath, to try not to jump to the most-dreaded conclusion. After all, she'd even given Phil the benefit of the doubt until she'd had irrevocable proof that he'd betrayed her, used her. The mere thought that Adam might have done the same, knowing how much it had hurt her the last time, made her heart ache terribly.

"Adam isn't like Phil," Violet said.

"You don't know that for sure."

"I'd bet every cent I have that I'm right. You're letting your old fears shove aside how great these past weeks have been for you. I haven't seen you this happy in a very long time." Violet made a dismissive motion with her hand. "No, I take that back. I've never seen you this happy. Adam is a good guy, and he's good for you. He deserves a chance to explain, if he's even aware of what's going on."

Lauren wanted to believe her sister, to believe in Adam's faithfulness, but she couldn't silence the doubts barraging her mind. If he had betrayed her, she was done with men. She would follow in her mother's footsteps and raise her daughters alone, live the rest of her life surrounded only by the family she already had and be content with that.

But as she thought about life without Adam in it, tears welled in her eyes.

"Let's go back inside and mingle some more," Violet said. "I was just talking to Ryan Teague and I love the idea of carrying his carved wooden angels in the shop."

Lauren shook her head. "I can't. You go ahead, but I'm going back to the restaurant."

"You've already put in, what, twelve hours today?"

"I aim to talk to Adam about this tonight, and I'd rather do it somewhere other than the cabin." If this ended up being the end of her and Adam, she didn't want to have the rest of her family witness the demise of yet another of her relationships.

Violet grabbed Lauren's hands. "Please just give him a chance to explain, and try to listen without having already judged him guilty."

Lauren nodded. "I will."

Because she would love nothing more than for Jamie

Barrett to have made the entire thing up, though that didn't seem likely, either.

"Want me to go with you? I can stay until he gets there."

"No. I'd rather have some time to think and calm down by myself."

"Okay, but I'm only a call or text away. The beauty of small towns—I can be there in a handful of minutes."

Lauren bit her lip as she accepted a hug from Violet before heading out to her car and driving back to the restaurant. Every conversation, every interaction she'd ever had with Adam, replayed in her head. She hoped the fact that she couldn't think of anything that made him look guilty was a good sign, but she remembered she hadn't suspected Phil, either.

Unbidden, reasons why Adam might betray her in the same way bubbled up from the darkest part of her mind. He wanted to increase his own business, which he'd admitted had been hard, by association with someone more successful. He was upset that she had refused to do business with him. Did he think that if it got out that she would be serving Rocking Horse beef, she'd have to reverse her decision? Heck, even the building she'd bought had once been part of his big plan for the Rocking Horse's future.

But he'd told her he understood why she couldn't buy his products and have a romantic relationship with him at the same time. And she'd believed him. Had he done so knowing he could benefit from their relationship in another way?

She pulled into the parking lot outside the restaurant but didn't immediately get out of her car. She felt as if any strength or energy she'd once possessed had been siphoned out of her the moment Jamie Barrett had introduced herself. But sitting here in the dark wasn't going to accomplish anything. If she was going to stay here and wait for Adam's return, she could at least get some more work done. There were dishes to order and menus to plan and a sign to design. Violet had worked on a lot of those things earlier, but it was still Lauren's job to finalize every aspect of her business.

She drew a shaky breath, almost as if her lungs had forgotten how to work in concert, and headed inside. Suddenly, she got the feeling someone was watching her—the same as that night at the inn. A chill ran down her spine as she remembered the two drunk guys outside the music hall. Did they blame her for their arrest? Had they come back and found her even more alone this time? She hurried toward the building since it was closer than her car.

As soon as she stepped through the door and her foot made a splashing sound, the creeped-out feeling gave way to a hard thud of her heart against her chest.

Oh, no. No, no, no!

She flicked on the overhead lights to reveal the awful truth. As far as she could see in each direction, the floor stood under what looked like an indoor lake.

When Adam returned to Blue Falls and texted Lauren, she didn't respond with where he could find her. He noticed several people standing around talking outside the tourist bureau office, so he parked and went in search of her. Maybe she'd gotten to chatting with other business owners and hadn't heard her phone.

"Hey, Adam," Keri Teague said when she spotted him. "You missed the festivities."

"I'm looking for Lauren. She said she was here earlier."

A concerned expression erased Keri's smile. "She left pretty early in the evening. Then Violet left soon thereafter, rather quickly."

There was no way they could have found out about the misunderstanding with Jamie Barrett, was there? Did Lauren just have a sixth sense for betrayal now and had somehow detected it without him saying a word?

A couple of the other people standing outside moved to leave, and what he saw made his heart stop. Jamie Barrett stood talking with India Parrish, owner of Yesterwear Boutique. Without saying goodbye to Keri, he strode straight toward the other woman.

"Excuse me," he said, butting in to the conversation between Jamie and India, then staring straight at Jamie. "Can I speak with you?"

He knew he sounded abrupt, but this was partly— no, there was no *partly* about it. This was *entirely* his fault, but he had to know if what he was assuming was indeed true.

India, likely detecting his mood, moved away after saying it was nice to chat with Jamie.

"Is something wrong?" Jamie looked so genuinely concerned that he did his best to calm down.

"Did you talk to Lauren here tonight?"

Jamie smiled. "Oh, yes. Such a lovely person. I might have gushed a bit about being a fan."

He bit his bottom lip before asking his next question. "Did you mention our business deal?"

Now she appeared confused. "Yes. Why?"

He took a fortifying breath, knowing what he was about to say might lead to the invalidation of his contract with her and quite possibly send a ripple of bad publicity out about Rocking Horse Ranch. Might even sound the death knell for the branded-beef business. He'd deal with that if the time came. Making things right with Lauren was more important.

"I allowed you to believe that Lauren's restaurant would be serving our beef products, but it won't be. We decided to keep our personal and professional relationships separate. I'm sorry about the misunderstanding, and I'll understand if you want to cancel our contract."

"Oh, my God," Jamie said with a gasp. "Please tell me I didn't mess up things between you."

Adam hadn't expected that reaction and it took him a few seconds to form an appropriate reply. "I don't know. I'm sure it'll be okay."

He sure hoped so.

"I'm so sorry."

"It's not your fault. It's mine. If you'll excuse me…"

He had to find Lauren. Before driving all the way out to the Vista Hills Guest Ranch, he headed toward the restaurant. Chances were better than average that she was there, considering how much time she spent working toward her goal of being open before the spring wildflowers started blooming.

When he pulled into the parking lot, he noticed not only Lauren's vehicle, but also Violet's. And the front door was standing wide open. He'd much rather talk to Lauren by herself, but he couldn't put off the conversation even if Violet was within earshot.

He heard the slosh of water as he approached the entrance before it registered why. He stopped at the threshold and just stared at the water covering every inch of the floor. Lauren looked up at him from where she stood in the middle of it with her sister.

"What happened?"

"I need to know you didn't do this," Lauren said, looking as if she were on the verge of breaking down. "And don't lie."

Shocked by the question and the heat of the anger toward him, he just stared at her for a long moment. "Of course not. Why would I do this?"

"Revenge."

A wave of his own anger rose up so fast that it nearly choked Adam. Yes, he'd made a mistake not correcting Jamie's assumption immediately, but how could Lauren think he'd do this kind of damage to her restaurant? It made no sense, and he didn't deserve her anger—at least not for that. Especially when he'd been nothing but supportive despite the fact she refused to do business with his family's ranch.

Before he could vent his anger, Violet stepped forward. "She's upset. Someone came in and deliberately flooded the place by turning on every faucet, the water heater and just about every water valve in the building, not to mention stopping up the sinks and toilets."

"Phil," he growled. Who else would have this much obvious hate for Lauren?

"That's my thought." Violet looked over her shoulder toward Lauren. "But she's upset and doubting—"

"Because of Jamie Barrett."

Violet looked startled for a moment before nodding. "I'll wait outside while you two talk."

Despite how frustrated and mad he was, Adam wanted to hug Violet. She seemed to believe in him despite everything that potentially put him in the same horrible light as Lauren's ex-fiancé. She gave his upper arm a quick squeeze of support before heading outside.

He cringed at the sound his feet made moving through the water, and he shivered. December was far from the best month for something like this to happen, if there was such a thing. Thank goodness they weren't somewhere like Montana.

"You should get out of the water before you catch a chill." He might be upset by her attack, but he still cared about her.

"I doubt I could get any colder."

He didn't think she was talking entirely about the water and the winter air.

"I stopped by the tourist bureau and I saw Jamie Barrett—"

"Did you use me, Adam?"

"No." The answer came out fast and sharp, with the same kind of edge as her accusatory questions. "I didn't even know she had any idea we knew each other until she mentioned it right as she was signing the contract." He stepped toward her and brought his hands up to touch her, but she moved away as if she never wanted to touch him again. "I swear to you on my life that I would never treat you the way Phil did."

He told her every single detail of the meeting, including how he'd been so surprised by the turn in the conversation that he'd made the mistake of not immediately correcting Jamie's erroneous assumption. She listened but the way she held herself stiff, arms wrapped around herself, made him wonder if his words were getting through.

"It's what I wanted to talk to you about when I texted you earlier, but I wanted to tell you in person."

He couldn't tell if she believed him, and he grudgingly admitted that from her point of view it could be seen as a convenient explanation.

"It doesn't matter now," she said.

"What do you mean?"

She gestured toward the standing water. "It's the final straw, a sign that this wasn't meant to be."

Adam feared she was talking about more than the restaurant.

"You're insured, right?"

"Yes, but I'm just tired." And she sounded it. Below the anger and perceived betrayal, she sounded completely spent. "I put so much into this place even though it was crazy to start a business so far from where I live. There were all the unexpected expenses. I need to just stick to what I know and chalk this up to another of my huge life mistakes."

He got the feeling she was lumping her relationship with him into that mistake. Still, he wanted to pull her close, make her believe that she could get through this and have success on the other side. But instinct told him that she wouldn't be receptive to any of that. And a part of him was ticked off that she was pushing him away, using this setback as an excuse to put her walls back up. But he clamped down on that part that wanted to scream at her to stop feeling sorry for herself and see the truth.

"You need a hot shower and a good night's sleep. Tomorrow is soon enough to deal with this."

"I can't leave yet. I'm waiting for the sheriff."

His heart thumped, but then he realized why Simon Teague would be called. If it was obvious someone had sabotaged the restaurant, this was a crime scene.

The arrival of another vehicle outside, followed by

a second, proved to be Simon and one of his deputies, Conner Murphy, who'd just gotten free of another call on the far side of the county. Over the next hour, the two questioned Lauren, Violet and Adam. He'd had to account for his whereabouts from the time Lauren left the restaurant until she'd returned to find the flooding. Even though Adam hadn't had anything to do with the damage, he found himself squirming and forcing himself to keep a lid on his frustration when Lauren wouldn't even look at him.

By the time all statements were taken and what felt like thousands of photos snapped of the damage and the identified sources, it was getting late and Lauren looked as if she might fall over from exhaustion. To be honest, he was beginning to feel the same. He wanted nothing more than for Lauren to realize she'd been wrong to suspect him so he could curl up with her, comfort her and sleep until noon the next day. But the fact that she couldn't meet his eyes told him she wouldn't welcome the company. He just needed to give her time to rest and come to grips with the shock of what had happened. Hopefully, then she'd be able to forgive him for his mistake and believe he'd never deliberately betray her.

As they all walked outside, Lauren paused next to her car as if feeling she needed to say something, but either didn't know what or didn't have the energy.

"You look completely exhausted," he said. "I don't think you should drive right now."

"She won't," Violet said as she approached them.

Violet may very well believe he was innocent in the vandalism, but she was wearing enough protective-sister vibes that he took a step away from Lauren.

"I'll call you tomorrow," he said to Lauren.

After Violet got into the driver's seat and started the car, Lauren turned halfway toward him but still didn't look him in the eye.

"Please don't." She took a shaky breath. "I can't do this."

His heart sank. "Do what?"

"I can't be with someone I can't trust."

"I didn't do this. You know that."

She motioned between the two of them. "This was a mistake."

Damn it, he was getting angry again. "You're using your past as an excuse to run away. That's not fair, to either of us."

"Life's not fair."

Her complete belief in her words, that life had once again put someone in her path who'd betrayed her, hollowed him out as he watched her get into the car and close the door. As he watched the Shayne sisters drive away into the night, the night seemed to cry out that it was for the last time.

Chapter 15

Adam listened to the laughter of his family in the living room as they opened up a round of Christmas gag gifts. He'd somehow made it through the big holiday meal and the opening of his gifts before he vacated the room. There were few times in his life he'd felt less like celebrating.

He sat on the side of his bed turning the small, gift-wrapped box in his hands over and over. He'd looked forward to giving the silver charm bracelet to Lauren, imagined her smiling as she examined the tiny spatula, mixing bowl, whisk and cookbook. He should have returned it for a refund by now because it was obvious they were over. He didn't know it was possible for a person to feel this empty.

She'd been gone for a week without a word. Even his anger couldn't cover up his heartache anymore.

Someone knocked on his bedroom door and he shoved the box into a drawer in his dresser.

"Yeah."

Angel opened the door then came to sit beside him on the bed. "Missing Lauren, huh?"

He nodded. No sense in pretending otherwise.

"Have you talked to her?"

"No." Some of his anger tried to reassert itself when he thought about how his voice mails and texts had been met with telling silence.

"You're not giving up, are you?"

"She doesn't want anything to do with me, and I don't want to be with someone who looks at me and only sees the ways I might betray her."

"Maybe she just needs time to get over the shock of what happened."

He shook his head. "She's not coming back to Blue Falls."

"Then you need to make sure she has a reason to come back."

He sighed. "Such as?"

"Well, you could start by telling her you love her, for one."

He didn't even bother asking Angel how she knew that when he'd just admitted the truth to himself in the days since Lauren had left town.

"Pretty sure she wouldn't believe me." And did he even want to admit the truth to a woman who'd so easily dumped him?

"Won't know until you try. And remember what we told Ben when he was trying to win Mandy—women love big, romantic gestures."

He was lying in bed later that night thinking about

what his sister had said. A big, romantic gesture. Was he willing to try one more time to save what he and Lauren had? Could he think of something that would fit that "big, romantic gesture" description? He fell asleep still turning the idea over and over in his head, but it wasn't until he woke up the next morning that the perfect plan came to him. At least he hoped it was perfect. But he couldn't do it alone.

"Where are you headed?" Angel asked when he was walking out the front door with his truck keys a while later.

"Operation Big, Romantic Gesture."

Angel pumped her fist. "Yes!"

Adam laughed for the first time in more than a week.

Lauren tested the lemon cake she'd just baked and found it lacking. She shoved it across the counter in frustration.

"What's wrong?" Violet asked as she entered their kitchen.

"I've lost my ability to bake anything remotely edible."

Violet came over and took a bite. "Are you kidding? This is delicious."

"You're just saying that." Her entire family had been noticeably careful around her since their return home.

"When have I ever given you false praise?"

Admittedly that wasn't her sister's style.

"Okay, enough," Violet said. "You're finding fault with your baking because you're not willing to admit you screwed up with Adam."

Lauren wanted to defend herself but it was difficult to find the words. Maybe because she knew Violet was right. Even before she'd found out that Phil was behind the flooding, the rock through the window and even the creepy feelings of being watched, she'd realized she'd been wrong to doubt Adam.

Lauren stared out the window at the Brazos River. "I've let too much time pass. He'll never be able to forgive me."

"Think maybe you're underestimating him again?"

Was she? "How do I fix this?"

"I suggest groveling. And, oh, I don't know, telling him the truth."

Violet's suggestions were a good start, but she needed something more, something bigger.

It wasn't until she was walking beside the river later and spotted her neighbor's cattle that the answer came to her. She smiled then hurried back to the house.

Violet and the twins startled when Lauren came rushing back in.

"What in the world is chasing you?"

"A plan to win back Adam."

"Which is?"

"Cows."

Violet looked at the girls. "Your mom has gone crazy."

Yeah, crazy in love.

Lauren watched the world flash by outside the passenger-side window of Violet's car. It'd been almost three weeks since she'd been in Blue Falls, and her stomach was in knots as they got closer. What if she'd totally ruined her chances with Adam? What if the fact she was asking for his forgiveness only after the investigation cleared him made him believe she'd never trust him? She'd been missing Adam terribly. But after she'd run away from him after basically accusing him of being just like Phil and then not communicating with him, she couldn't imagine that he'd welcome the sight of her. She had to change his mind.

At least Papa Ed's romantic prospects were looking up. He and Verona were taking it slowly, but they talked every day and had discovered the spark that had once burned between them was still there. Older, wiser, but still there.

Violet pulled over at a gas station at the edge of Blue Falls. "Gotta pee."

"We're literally a mile from the restaurant." Where her grand plan had to be put into motion.

"When you've got to go, you've got to go."

Violet thankfully didn't take long. When they reached the restaurant, Lauren felt a wave of exhaustion similar to the night she'd left here. The thought of all the work she faced could overwhelm her if she let it. But right now that took a back seat to winning back the man she loved.

"Ready to go in?" Violet asked.

She nodded.

"We should probably see how things look before we take that in." Violet pointed over her shoulder toward Lauren's gift to Adam.

"Agreed." She didn't want to lug it inside only to find the water removal and mold remediation hadn't worked.

Violet walked in ahead of Lauren then quickly stepped to the side.

"Surprise!"

Lauren jumped at the sound of so many voices calling out at once. At first her mind couldn't comprehend what she was seeing, but then she started to recognize individual faces. Her mother and Papa Ed holding the twins. Verona smiling as she gripped Papa Ed's arm. Several of the town's other business owners. Even Jamie Barrett. And the entirety of the Hartley family stood smiling at Lauren.

Her heart leaped when she spotted Adam standing right in the middle.

They all stood on a brand-new floor. The tables and chairs she'd ordered were set up, ready for diners. Art hung on the walls. The corner devoted to the gift shop was prepped to receive merchandise.

"I don't understand," she said, her words having to push their way past the lump in her throat.

"Adam organized the community to fix what Phil tried to destroy," Violet said.

Lauren couldn't hold back the tears anymore. "I can't believe what you all did here."

"We weren't going to let your dream die," Papa Ed said. "Adam is one determined young man."

"Thank you." The words felt so weak, so unable to convey the depth of her gratitude. Nowhere near powerful enough to let this man know how much he meant to her. She hoped the work he'd put into resurrecting her restaurant meant he could forgive her, that this wasn't just a grand apology for the misunderstanding with Jamie Barrett.

The crowd moved then, some coming forward to greet her and say how excited they were about the restaurant's future opening and others moving toward a wide assortment of food. She eventually made her way through all the well-wishers to Adam. She faced him with her heart threatening to beat so fast she couldn't distinguish between one beat and the next.

"I can't believe you did this," she said.

"I had a lot of help."

"It looks beautiful. I don't know how I'll ever be able to thank you."

"If you'll give us another chance, that's enough."

She bit her lip to keep it from trembling before responding. "I was thinking on the way here how you'd never be able to forgive me. I'm sorry for how I doubted you, how I ran away and broke off all contact."

Adam stepped forward and placed his palms gently against her shoulders. "Part of me understood."

"But part didn't."

"It hurt that you could believe I'd do anything to harm you, but I've let that go."

"Why?" He had every right to be upset.

"Because I'm hopelessly in love with you."

Her lip trembled. "I love you, too."

Adam's eyes widened as if he hadn't expected his feelings to be reciprocated. "Can I kiss you?"

"I wish you would."

His lips had barely touched hers when she heard applause. Adam's mouth curved into a smile for just a moment before he pulled her close and sealed his declaration with a kiss that erased any last vestiges of doubt that might have been hanging around in her mind, waiting to pounce.

Over the next hour or so, she enjoyed spending time with the people that she now knew were the very best kind of friends. When everyone finally left, leaving her and Adam alone, he escorted her out to the stone patio that would be used for outdoor dining come spring.

"I have something I want to give you," he said as he produced a small box wrapped in red foil.

"You've already given me the best gift possible." And she didn't just mean the repairs to the restaurant.

"This was your Christmas present I wasn't able to give you."

She accepted the box and opened it. When she saw the silver charm bracelet, she ran her fingertip over the adorable charms. "It's perfect."

"I'm glad you like it."

"I have a present for you, too."

"Another kiss, I hope."

She didn't argue with that assumption and kissed him, trying to make up for the time they'd been apart.

"While very enjoyable," she said when they finally parted, "that wasn't what I was going to say. You weren't the only one who had plans of trying to get back together today."

"Well, now I'm really curious."

She nodded toward the gift she'd had Violet and her mom hide out here.

"What is it?"

"Uncover it and find out."

He lifted the blanket to reveal a sign she'd had made—Brazos Baker Gift Shop, Featuring the Rocking Horse Ranch Collection.

"And when Brazos Baker Barbecue opens in the spring, we're going to be serving Rocking Horse Ranch beef."

He stared down at her as if he didn't trust what he'd seen or heard. "What happened to not mixing business with personal relationships?"

"I thought I needed that policy in place to protect me from making another stupid mistake." She lifted her hand to his face and smiled. "I don't need it anymore because letting myself love you was the best decision I've ever made."

"You're not scared?"

"Not one bit." She waited for the inner fear she'd carried around for so long to make a liar of her, but it didn't appear. She was pretty sure it no longer existed.

"Does this mean you might move to Blue Falls?"

She let her hands slide down the front of his shirt. "You might be able to convince me."

Adam pulled her close to his delicious, strong warmth and set about convincing. She'd already made her decision that Blue Falls would be her new home, but maybe she'd let him think she needed convincing for a little bit longer.

"You've already decided, haven't you?" he asked.

"Yes. But that doesn't mean we have to stop this."

He grinned. "You're right, it doesn't."

And his lips returned to hers.

* * * * *